Punishment
A Love Story

Eve Tushnet

Clickworks Press
Baltimore, MD

First publication: Clickworks Press, 2019
Release: ELT-ETSA1-INT-E.M-1.0
Sign up for updates, deals, and exclusive sneak peeks at
clickworkspress.com/join.

Ebook ISBN: 978-1-943383-51-1
Paperback ISBN: 978-1-943383-52-8
Hardcover ISBN: 978-1-943383-53-5

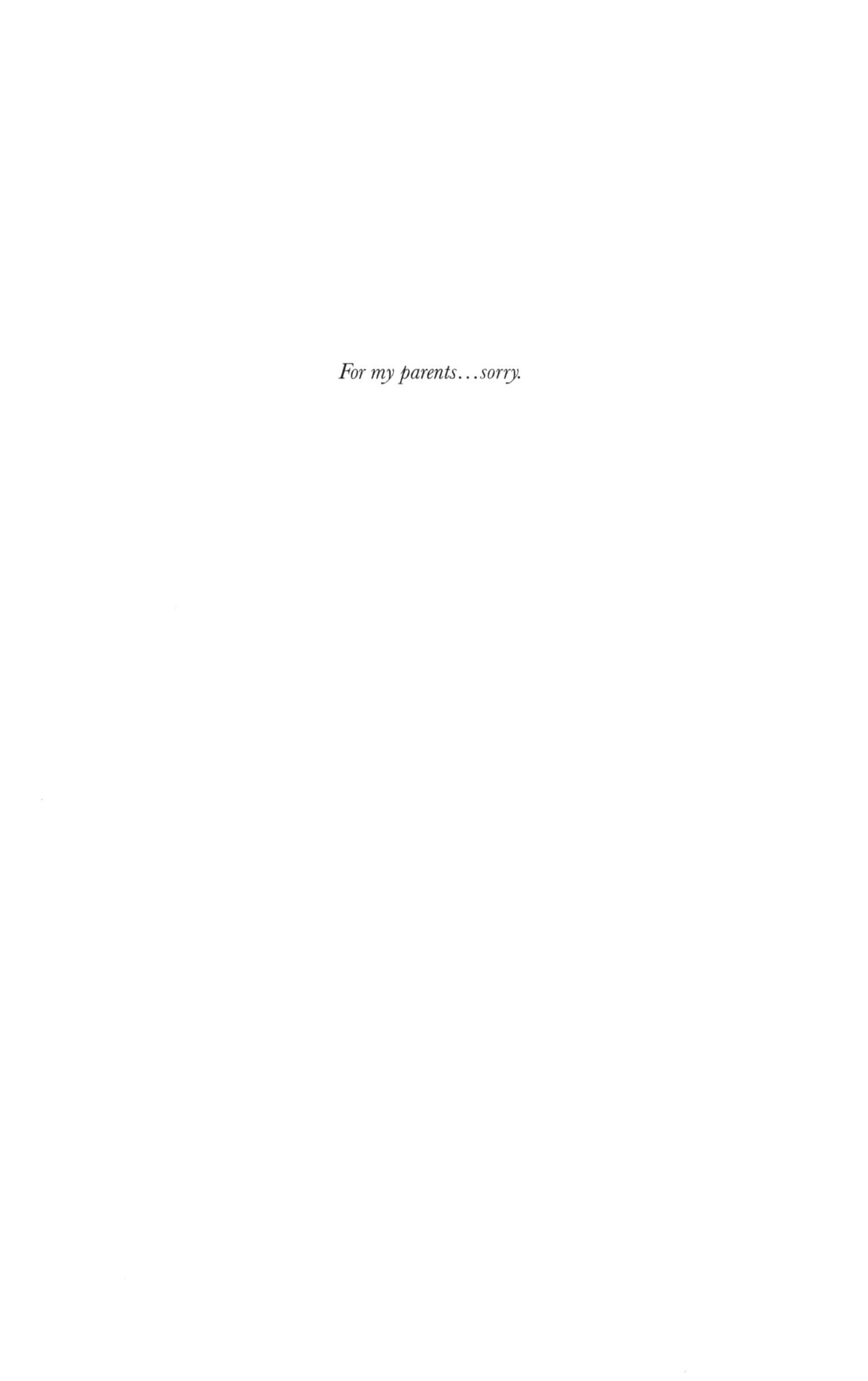

For my parents…sorry.

Contents

Pull Yourself Together

1	Halfway Home	3
2	Cavity Searches	15
3	Strange Bedfellows	33
4	Love Slaves of the Horror Hand	55
5	Community Supervision	65
6	Semi–In Touch	85
7	I'll Never Petition to Expunge You From the Record of My Heart	99
8	Jean Grey Died on the Moon	107

Don't Say No

9	He Drank Up All the Water, He Ate Up All the Soap. He Tried to Eat the Bathtub But It Wouldn't Go Down His Throat!	123
10	You Should Be Grateful	137
11	Wig-Wam Bam	163
12	Memorial Spectacular	183

Prisoners of Upper Northwest

13	Rope Work	189
14	Beauty's Predicament	221
15	The Shield of Achilles	239
16	Misrepresentations	251
17	Now and at the Hour	259
18	If You Want a Friend in Washington	271
19	The Soul Searchers	303

Pull Yourself Together

Chapter 1
Halfway Home

March 2016
Washington, D.C.

Desiree Schulman stepped down from the bus a few blocks from the Anacostia metro, into the arms of the late March night. The bus door closed and suddenly she was alone with the quiet. Natural shadows and open space: no buzzing yellow lights or shivering white lights flecked with black, no announcements, no rules posted, no walls, no yelling and no tense silence. Not the isolation of solitary and not the unbearable intimacy of a four-bunk cell. For the first time in four years she felt open sky and privacy. Neither chaos nor order, but peace.

Engines roared behind her and four werewolves came howling down the street, rearing up on the back wheels of their motorbikes.

They were young kids, late teens or maybe early twenties, with not just Halloween wolf heads but also tufty gray fur on gauntlets up their arms. And furry gloves with thick black plastic claws, curling around the bike handles like acrylic nails. The roaring bikes had green and golden flame decals along the sides.

The werewolves were howling at the moon—no, they were

howling at Des. Just a quick friendly howl of male mammals to a female mammal; they howled and then they were gone.

She had jumped when they roared onto the scene—she was keyed-up, all edgy energy, she hadn't slept in days, and so she couldn't control it, she jumped at everything. But when they disappeared, she eased up. "Welcome home," she said to herself, grinning. Catcalled by werewolves: the ultimate multiculturalism.

And then, sighing a little, "Welcome halfway home." She settled the clear plastic bag with her belongings over her shoulder and headed down the dark street.

The open darkness was disorienting, and she kept darting glances around as if she was trying to find the wall. She was glad that this area was low-lying, all the streets rising from where she stood. It made her feel a little less like she was about to fly off the face of the earth. When she crossed a street the cars seemed to come too fast and stop too close. After four years in federal prison in West Virginia she wasn't used to where things were supposed to be in a city.

This world used to belong to her. It was hard to believe.

Soft night noises. Burrs from a sweetgum tree scattered along the sidewalk. A weeping willow with long curved branches, little white blossoms clustering along the branches' ends, like a cornrowed head with beads along the braids. Sirens in the distance, shouting, the drifting smells of fried food and marijuana, the scrape of a faraway gate and the clash of its latch swinging shut, footsteps behind her like hard rain. And before she'd even noticed how she'd tensed up— somebody slamming into her from behind.

"Get out the way, bitch! This ain't a standing area!"

Des spun and choked. Her vision seemed to crack and she couldn't orient herself in the dark street. She stumbled and her heart was hammering, and the plastic bag fell and split open as she braced for violence, her body taut and terrorized and anticipating its suffering.

But in a fraction of a second her instincts rearranged themselves. She heard that hometown accent, that D.C. accent that sounds best in a moan or a purr. A way of talking made for flirtation and lament, complaint and self-defense, for all the ways human nature asserts itself but doesn't expect you to listen to or respect: a foot jammed against a closing door. *This ain't a standin urr-ea.* Des, still gasping, her heart still racing, turned with a grin all the way across her face.

"Sorry," she offered. She bent to pick up her things; the smaller bag from the Walgreens in Union Station hadn't burst, so she could stuff her extra release clothing and the scraps of plastic in beside the freshly-purchased toiletries.

The girl who had slammed into her was short and stocky, with a cheeky round imp-face. In camo pants and a faded black t-shirt, cornrows snaking down her neck. A summer anger, intense and already passing. She was cute and muscular, looked like she could twist your arm. *Twist my arm.*

"I'm gonna miss my curfew!" the girl yelled, not really at Des. She pounded her fist against her thigh and ran further up the street.

"Oh shit, me too," Des said, also not to anyone in particular. She walked in the way the girl had gone—just walking, not running, but faster, making an effort.

There were storefronts along this quick stretch of sidewalk: Creation Laundry; Early Bird Liquors; a uniform store called Pull Yourself Together, next to The Last Shall Be First Secondhand Clothing; a takeout window offering Neighborly Chicken and Check Cashing. A wheatpasted poster on a streetlamp said, U.S. OUT OF ANACOSTIA. A police car rolled by slow. Des tried not to notice if she was nervous. Then more houses.

Des reached the house she was looking for: three stories of weathered white clapboard, and a porch swing next to a giant fake hibiscus plant in a giant fake Grecian urn. There were daffodils and crocuses in the yard, and somebody's bikini-cut red and yellow striped underwear. A sign shaped like a house said, in purple hand-painted lettering,

LOVE'S LABORS LOFT

Your Almost Home.

Des went up the steps and rang the bell. The door opened—and there was the girl who had slammed into her on the street.

The girl looked at her like she was the answer to prayer. "Miss Imani! This her, this the lady. *Tell her*," and this, directed at Des, in tones of deep menace, "I bumped into you. That's why I was late for curfew."

A woman appeared behind the girl. She was tall and wiry, ebony, dressed in lavender scrubs, with thick multicolored braids looping around her head. She seemed wry and somehow futuristic—those hair-loops, maybe, or the silver stud just above her upper lip, with a green jewel that looked like it might shoot lasers. She had the cagey, intelligent look of someone used to sizing up situations and people, and then making decisions about them. There was something unexpected about her, something not quite uniform; but it wasn't something Des was inclined to trust.

"*You* bumped into *her?*," this woman said, with meaning.

The impfaced girl made another D.C. noise: a low coo of disappointment and reproach. "*Miss Imani*," she said. "I don't think I owe this person an amends. I was coming down the street minding my business. She was just standing there staring with her face out, looking for Elvis!"

"You aren't very late, anyway," Miss Imani said. She held out her hand to Des. "I'm Imani Rollins."

"Desiree Schulman," she said, shifting her small bundle of

personal effects so she could shake hands. The impfaced girl moaned somewhere in the background.

Imani Rollins's hand felt confident and trained. Des was pretty sure her own hand felt clammy.

"Welcome," Miss Imani said. And then, turning to the impfaced girl, "I'm going to take our new guest into the office. Ms. Schulman, please follow me. And please meet Ranae Goins," and here Miss Imani couldn't help but grin a little, "your mentor."

"Ray Ray," the girl clarified. Des wondered if she should hold out her hand, but Miss Imani was already walking down the hall so Des figured it was best to follow.

Down the short front hallway and through the dining room, through a door framed in Christmas lights. A tiny cottage with rose bushes was painted on the white porcelain doorknob.

Miss Imani's office was narrow and crowded with papers. There was only one chair, so Des stood while Miss Imani explained the seven forms she'd have to fill out: standard intake, client service agreement, release of information form so she could tell everybody Des's business, house rules, grievance procedure form, job readiness form, wellness form.

Oh good, Des thought, *I've been wondering if I'm well.*

Des tried to read as little of each form as possible before signing. There was a line on the intake form that just said "Current problems: ______________" and she considered and rejected answering with an infinity sign, or her full legal name. Then she squinted and saw the tiny writing underneath the line: THIS PORTION TO BE FILLED OUT BY INTAKE ADMINISTRATOR.

She hesitated for a long time, trying to think of some alternative, before sighing and putting her parents as her emergency contacts.

The form asked, "Describe your relationship to your emergency contact person." Des misunderstood the question and wrote, *Fraught,* before realizing and crossing it out to write, *Parents*.

The wellness assessment asked how long she had spent in a "controlled environment" and Des said, "Uh… I had a really good childhood?"

Miss Imani explained that the form meant how long she'd been in prison. Apparently people thought prison was controlled.

It also asked, "What are your strengths? ___________________" and Des looked for the tiny print, but they expected her to fill that part out herself.

Miss Imani read the rules to her out loud and so Des had to pay attention. It felt worse than she'd expected—she'd loved the luxury of distraction, there on the Anacostia sidewalk where she'd been "looking for Elvis." Now she had to hand over the keys to her attention again. The rules hinted at hidden stories: "I will not remove, tamper with, or disable the toilet seat. I will not use any of the furnishings of the halfway house, including the doorknobs, for sexual pleasure."

She had to put her initials beside each rule as Imani Rollins read it out. After every fifth rule Imani read, "Failure to adhere to any of these rules may result in a violation of your conditions of release, which would cause you to return to prison." Des respected the way she made her voice sound just as urgent the tenth time as the first.

"That's all of it," Imani said at last. "Initials here and then you're done."

Des said, "Yes—okay." She still wasn't sure if "Yes, ma'am" was what was appropriate here.

"Done" turned out to be an optimistic interpretation. They still had to do fingerprinting, and a urine test in the locked bathroom attached to the office, and then an unusually polite search of her belongings, clothes, and person. Then she dressed again and Miss Imani led her out to the kitchen to get to know her new life.

Ranae, or Ray Ray, was waiting for them in the kitchen. She gave Miss Imani an anxious, ingratiating smile. "Was I for real late," she said.

Des said, "She, uh, I really was just kind of standing in the middle of the sidewalk. Ma'am."

"I can use the time on the kitchen clock when I choose to," Miss Imani said in amusement, and pointed at the clock on the microwave. "By the kitchen clock you got in right at ten p.m."

Imani Rollins took her on a tour of the downstairs of the halfway house. It looked about a million times nicer than Des had expected. It was clean, for one thing—there were chore charts on the refrigerator, next to the glow-in-the-dark green Mr. Yuk magnet from the poison control center and the Safeway ad for win-a-free-Cuisinart and a heart-shaped promotional magnet from the makers of Suboxone. There was a coffeemaker labeled COMMUNITY, which, Imani explained, whoever had kitchen duty was responsible for filling each evening. On top of one cabinet there perched a huge stuffed red lobster in a pot, its claws spilling out to brush the sides of the wooden cabinet. There was a small white security camera, like an egg dipped in ink, just at the upper right-hand corner of the back door.

The knobs of all the kitchen cabinets matched the doorknob to Miss Imani's office: white porcelain, painted with bright little cottages. Painted ivy twined from the cottages along the knobs to the cabinets themselves. By the front door there was an umbrella bucket and a coatrack and an American flag. In the front hallway there was a family photograph.

"This is all of us," Imani said when she saw Des looking at it. "My parents," two grim pioneers with their hard-won family, "then us oldest to youngest."

Her finger moved along the line of children (the oldest was at that time only a teenager, in a red track suit with high natural hair), not quite touching the glass front of the photo. "Reginald, Hope, Imani, Nzinga, Cinque, Fidel, Industrialization."

Des looked at her.

"My parents," and the dark red amusement that seemed to ripple through her voice pulsed stronger, "moved left over the course of the '70s."

Desiree nodded and smiled and thought, *They can name their next child "Complicity."*

The past four years had trained her in these silent conversational contributions. She looked and maybe nodded and whatever thing she'd thought of remained behind her eyes to bring her pleasure instead of humiliation. Learning to shut up seemed like it should have made her modest, but in fact there was something sour in this private savoring of unspoken cleverness.

Imani continued, "They don't approve of my work here. I'm part of the 'treatment-industrial complex.' I tell them they live in the Gaithersburg-industrial complex."

Desiree was well-acquainted with both familial disapproval and familial leftism. Her paternal grandmother had been called to testify before the House Un-American Activities Committee (of New Jersey), and had denounced them for "turning the Bill of Rights into a *shmatte*." And then Des's paternal grandfather hadn't spoken to his wife for a week, until at last, disconsolately picking at the breakfast fish, he'd exclaimed, "You're waving around the U.S. Constitution now? What's the Soviet constitution—chopped liver?"

This was the closest encounter anyone in her family had ever had with the business end of the criminal-justice system. Until quite recently.

Next to the photograph of Imani Rollins's family there was an oval mirror, its frame decorated with cake-frosting roses in white plaster. Des glanced at it—she couldn't stop herself—but even in the shadowed hallway and the dust-streaked glass, she could see how bad she looked. Hollow-eyed and lumpy, eyes worn out, like a sick person. She looked like she'd been dragged up out of a grave.

Ray Ray spoke up helpfully: "By the way, Miss Imani, them wolfmans is back."

"Yes, so I heard. Keep in mind that it wouldn't be a good idea for you to talk to them, given your release conditions."

"Yes, ma'am," Ray Ray said, which gave Des the answer to one question, at least.

Imani showed Des the dining room, where the chairs were grouped in two clusters at the corners of the table so that no one would have to sit with her back to a door. The dining table had a plastic tablecloth over a real tablecloth. Then the parlor—which really was a parlor, with a piano covered in doilies, a plaster bust of what looked like Marian Anderson but was maybe one of Imani's less-Communist forebears, and a stiff-cushioned fainting couch with a back like a breaking wave. Everything in the parlor was done in lilting shades of rose and gold. The heavy rose velvet curtains had gold tasseled cords. Just above and to the right of the fainting couch a laminated poster gave the signs of and treatment for narcotics overdose.

Coming out of the parlor they reached the front hall again, and a small round table at the base of the staircase. On the table a circle of burnt-down tea lights, flanked by two black plaster angels, surrounded a thick scrapbook bulging with photos. The embroidered front cover read, in rainbow colors, *The Homegoers*.

A white paper scroll taped to the side of the staircase, above the little altar, read, "'The goal of this place is to make sure people miss you when you die.' —Diamond Dawkins, LLL Graduate November 2011."

"All right," Imani said, "I have to go to work now. You'll be sharing a room with your mentor—Ranae, if you could show our new guest up to her room." She slipped out and left them alone.

The room just off the third floor landing was small and intimidatingly neat, with two twin beds. The wall beside one bed was decorated with many, many colorful drawings of the same black woman: dancing, sitting on a stoop smoking a blunt, looking over her shoulder with a fingertip pressed delicately to her lips, as a mermaid swimming amid seashells, flying. Always posed so you could see both the breasts and the butt. The detailing on the scales of the mermaid's ass—Des had never bothered to wonder whether a mermaid would have a booty—was especially impressive.

Ray Ray sat cross-legged on her bed, and then toppled over dramatically. She reached a romantic arm across to one of the pictures, a pencil sketch, and tapped it with her knuckles. "This my wifey," she said, and rolled over to look hard at Des.

"Not bad," Des said, emptying the Walgreens bag onto her bed. And *not* bad, either: huge soft doe eyes, eyebrows lifted, full lips making a heart, everything soft and feminine and just slightly concerned about you. This was a face that would ask you where you were last night.

Ray Ray nodded. She tried to look tough but it fell apart; she grinned as her knuckles stroked the edge of the sketch. "Bae got a body like Wild World," she boasted. "You ride that ride you take your *life* in your hands! They say my girl reckless—I say she reck more than most!"

She sighed, her face shifting from pride to reverie, and tapped the picture again. "This *my* pleasure," she said, with all the soft sincerity of a real butch in love.

And then her mouth turned down and a furrow went between her brows as she said, "And she difficult as fuck, too. I don't listen to nobody who say pleasure is just fun and games."

"What's her name?"

"Ty'heaven," Ray Ray said tenderly. "She the prettiest piece a bait I ever knew."

Des put her few possessions in the empty bottom drawer of the bureau. She messed with the pillows on her bed and wished she had her eyemask.

Ray Ray rolled onto her stomach, sprawled with her arms and legs hanging over the sides of the bed and the side of her face mashed against the top blanket, and said, "Say your name again?"

"Desiree."

"Pretty," Ray Ray conceded. "I knew a Desiree one time who said it like that. I thought it was Des-a-ree at first."

And Des remembered a conversation from her first year in prison. A woman named Emeraldcity, in her early fifties but incarcerated since she was twenty-two, offering a theory of etymology: "I'm 'bout to be a parolee. All these words that end in *eeee*," she shook her head, "always mean something's gonna get done *to* you. It's like a root word. Like how J-U-D means the law, judge, judicial, adjudicated, E-E means things being done to a person. Evacuee, refugee, amputee. Employee."

"Desiree," Des had said. And when the other woman had looked at her she'd explained, "It isn't *spelled* the way it *sounds*."

That had been one of the only things she said that year; and it had confirmed her decision to talk as little as possible, since everybody made fun of her for it. "Desireeeee!" they'd call after her, and exaggerate a TV white girl accent to say, "It isn't spelled the way it sounds." Or, "*Actually*," which she hadn't even said, "it isn't spelled *quite* the way it sounds." Sometimes it seemed like prison was basically the seventh grade in whatever school district covered Hell.

She hadn't said much to Ray Ray or Imani Rollins. But she felt looser than she'd expected. Maybe it was just the hometown accents again. The scent of spring in the trees, and the go-go music—they loosened tongues, lifted hearts.

Chapter 2
Cavity Searches

On her first full day after prison Des woke up with a start. She lay in the bed curled on her side. Her heart pounded. The sheets were soft and the blankets thick above her; her hair felt clean. She could smell her sweat mingled with the smell of laundry detergent and cheap soap. Golden sunlight poured into the room from two big windows, and a chilly, rain-scented breeze stirred the air; she was alone, and her heart hurt, because this was a dream.

Then memory started to silt back in. She sat up. Scratched herself, which she didn't think she would bother to do in a dream. She turned over onto all fours and stretched like a cat, her ass in the air and her knuckles pressed against the headboard, in the hopes that a theatrical gesture would make the scene feel more real. She stood up and walked over to the open windows. A strip of masking tape along the top frame of the right one said, in thick black printing, DON'T OPEN ME OR I WILL JAM. Under that in thin red cursive it said, *Sorry*.

Des sniffed the clean air and listened to the shouts and

jackhammering outside—far away. She spent a minute or so flicking the lights on and off, chuckling, and then gathered some clothes. She was going to choose her own clothes—from a sharply limited selection, but still. Then she would go down to the bathroom alone and pee in privacy, and take a *bath*, her second bath in two days (and also her second bath in four years), and use women's fucking deodorant, and *floss*, which she hadn't done before she went to prison but she was sure as hell going to start now, and she would do all of this behind a door she'd locked herself, to keep other people out.

That was her first real disappointment. Last night, during her first bath in four years, it had seemed like the bathroom door lock worked just fine. But now, with the small slot-shaped bathroom window open, the wind made the door rattle in a way that made it obvious that it was barely on the latch. Des stood there naked and messing with it, and it kept half-opening, until she pounded her fist on the edge of the sink and yelled, "*Fuck!* Can't they give us some fucking privacy here?"

Somebody knocked on the door—which also almost opened it—and said, in a low hungover-sounding voice, "Are you almost done in there? I gotta get to work."

"Ten minutes!"

"I gotta get to work. Stand behind the curtain and let me get my shit."

So Des, cursing, went and stood behind the shower curtain. And then realized that the door had locked, somehow, so she had to go and open it and then go back. A tall Asian girl with a thick curtain of hair falling over her face, wearing a light blue men's shirt and probably underpants and nothing else, padded in and grabbed some toiletries off of one of the shelves. She turned to go.

"Hey."

"Oh, sorry," the girl said. Her voice still had a growl in it, but a sincere, well-meaning growl. "I'm Fang."

"My name is Des, but that isn't what I was going to ask you. I wanted to know how to make the door lock."

"Oh. Sure. It locks if you don't want it to."

With that she turned and went out. The door clicked shut behind her, and Des stood in the bathtub and moaned, "Well fuuuuuuuuck."

She tried to take a long hot bath, but her conscience bothered her, now that she knew she'd already cheated one housemate out of that pleasure. She toweled off after ten minutes and tried to enjoy being a good person as much as she would have enjoyed an hour-long bath.

After she brushed and spat toothpaste into the toilet (and flossed; it hurt) she assessed her new surroundings. The bathroom was small and shockingly, poignantly clean. The walls were painted a soft periwinkle. Everyone had a shelf for toiletries, and on two of the shelves there were little abstract sculptures made of seashells.

On the wall between the sink and the shower-bath there was a painting, in crisp black outline, of a little girl with Afro puffs blowing out a dandelion clock. Underneath, in cursive script inside a ribbon, it said, "Counting Days. Levanna Newsome, LLL Graduate May 2008."

In the shower the grout was eggshell-white, without a hint of schmutz. On the tiled wall there were four black plastic hooks in a row, the kind that stick when you press them into place. On three of the hooks hung bath objects: an orange puff; a sort of soft complex green dodecahedron; and a rock, of all the things. These dangled from loops of different lengths, just like modern art. They were mismatched and yet seemed designed and ordered by some whimsical, benevolent intelligence.

The shower head was a huge heavy thing like a steel sunflower, on a thick silver neck. Des guessed the women here must be pretty low-drama since they probably wouldn't be allowed to keep the shower head if somebody had been beaten to death with it.

With that thought, she was ready to put her bathroom inspection aside. She liked it—she liked this place—but it wasn't as if anything would change if she didn't.

There were three main tasks for her that day and none of them were going to be pleasant. She got a cup of community coffee and sat out on the porch swing, took a breath, and called her old employers.

"*Agony and Irony*, how may I direct your call?"

"Hey, does Jon Joylegs still work here? If not, can you get me editorial?" And then, just in case, "If you don't have editorial anymore can you get me marketing?"

But Joylegs picked up. A light, considering voice; a voice with a well-trimmed beard, you couldn't help but feel.

"Hey, it's Desiree Schulman," she said. Her voice sounded rougher than she'd like. It was the kind of voice where you can't tell if the person is unreliable because they're broke or broke because they're unreliable. She didn't sound like she expected the call to go well.

"You're back! Congratulations! We've been waiting for you ever since your earliest projected release date."

"Oh, I shouldn't've told you guys that date. Uh, sorry. You know me, I don't know what you expected."

"We expect only the best for you," he said warmly.

"So, I need a favor."

"If it's money I'd need to go to the ATM. I can't cut you a check yet."

The morning sunlight was making her nose and cheeks very hot. "It isn't money. It's my job description. I talked to my—the officer that's supervising my release," which was not a thing she enjoyed saying to an editor ten years younger than her, "and she said 'Contributing Editor' isn't on the approved list for rehabilitative employment in my program."

"Whoa, really?"

"Yeah, she says it has to be a job that somebody knows what it is."

Long pause. "Whoa. I don't know if we have any."

Des scratched at the arm of the porch swing. "Yeah, she suggested I could ask if you had something open in custodial. Or if you can get the name of the cleaning service at your building and, I don't know, put in a good word for me."

"Oh! Sure, you want to do a service job! That makes so much sense. Do you know *Custodian of Souls*, by Jabez Pruitt?"

"No. Do you know 'Janitor of Lunacy,' by Nico?"

"We can mail you the Pruitt. I loved it, you'll love it. You can review it for us, it's all about finding purpose in life through menial labor. Are you back living with your parents?"

"No, uh—"

"Oh, that's too bad, that would have been an added element of humility."

Des noticed a small white clay figurine of a thatch-roofed house, attached to the frame of the porch swing with black wire. She thought of the little cottages painted on the kitchen knobs. *If I were reviewing this halfway house*, she thought, *I don't know if I'd find all the home imagery poignant or a little too on-the-nose.*

She gave Joylegs the address of Love's Labors Loft, and he promised to list her on the masthead as a janitor, and then it was time to go to the Community Supervision field office, where she was urine-tested again and subjected to paperwork that was similar to last night's but less personal, and they checked her for tattoos, of which she was surprisingly bare. They gave her "re-entry support": a Metro card with $1.75 already on it.

That's one fare! she thought, with familiar dull outrage. But all she said was, "Thank you, ma'am."

Then to her parents'. The bus ride took about an hour and twenty minutes, with one transfer. Not really too bad. She didn't have any books yet, so she looked out the window at the bare branches and the scattering of blossoms, and listened in on the unlucky people riding the bus.

"Did he find a job yet?", maternal, concerned rather than gossipy.

"He peed for one on Monday. That Marriott job."

And across the aisle, complaining into her cell phone: "I say you bring somet'ing when you come people house. I said it's African tradition. West African tradition! So I tell him, you bring somet'ing. Next time he come he bring laundry!"

And a man, an older man, musing: "She's dangerous. That's *why* they elected her the mayor."

His companion, an older woman: "What do you mean by 'dangerous'?"

"Well I don't have anything against Caucasians. But you go down there to her office. You know where her office at? And ninety percent of the people there, that's what they are. That's all."

Desiree was the only white person on that bus for a while, but the District had changed so much that others joined her before they even got into Northwest.

The bus rolled west. Past an Ethiopian restaurant where questions and answers from the citizenship exam scrolled past on a streaming light display; past a church whose sign said, OUR HEAVENLY FATHER'S ARMS WILL ONE DAY CATCH HIS CHILDREN.

And then the bus transfer and a sudden wind that sent a shower of white blossoms across the windshield of the bus, rolling down

Sixteenth Street past all the churches. The short walk up the hill to home.

There was the big plantation-style house at the corner where they'd shot off fireworks half the Saturday nights of Des's childhood. She had always thought they were gunshots, and it was only when she grew up and heard a real shot that the disappointing realization came. There were the Georgian brick houses behind delicate dogwoods, still in bud. And the Japanese maples outside the Spanish-style house where the blue dove-shaped sign in the front yard still said what it had said since 1980: WAR IS NOT THE ANSWER. (The sign that said FREE SOVIET JEWRY had been retired.) Porches without porch swings, lawns without lawn furniture or children's toys, small round security-corporation signs stuck in every lawn. A sign for Bernie Sanders.

The house next door, where the little old ladies used to live, had a rainbow flag over the door now—unless that was still the little old ladies, and Des's gaydar didn't work on the postmenopausal. Then the old dying pine tree with its ragged empty needle-skirt, the wizened dogwoods, and the droopy greenish hydrangeas, which had been flourishing little pink and orange azalea bushes before Des's parents decided to class the place up. And a sign, which was new, saying, SOLITARY CONFINEMENT IS MEAN.

The back bumper of the car in front of the house was covered in stickers. That was new too. PEACE IS THE BOMB. HELP ALL HOBOS FIRST.

PFLAG, Mothers of the Incarcerated, Families Against Mandatory Minimums, PROUD MOM OF A LESBIAN INMATE. SOMEBODY IN FEDERAL PRISON LOVES ME.

And a Harvard sticker on the back windshield, commemorating Des's sister's alma mater. They'd never bothered to do that before, but Des guessed they had to balance things out.

A slim white cat with what looked like burnt patches of dirty orange on its back slipped away down an alley, past the huge yucca plant at the house where the orthodontist couple lived—the yucca leaves had fine white threads like dental floss, it was a theme—and hurried away under the canopy of cherry trees and mulberry and pear. All the trees Des had stolen fruit from, like Augustine at the supermarket, in her misspent youth.

She didn't let herself look at the sign as she walked up the crumbling concrete steps and tried the doorknob. She hadn't been able to have the keys to this house on her person when she surrendered herself.

The doorknob didn't turn, but a cat began to yell inside the house and Des's mother's face appeared at the little window next to the door.

Anna Pokorny opened the door. For a sharp, silent moment they looked at each other. They looked a lot alike—strong jawline, but with a lumpiness around the face that made them look patient; brown eyes made smaller by their glasses. Anna wore her thick brown hair cut to just about an inch above her shoulders, an eighty-dollar haircut so simple it was indistinguishable from her daughter's prison stylings. She wore a raveling dark red sweater and slacks, and socks with sandals: the kind of thing you wear when you're only going to see family. Des had dressed up as best she could, in her nicer jeans, with leggings underneath so you couldn't see her underwear, and a floral print blouse that pulled too tight across her breasts and belly. Her assumption that she'd lost weight in prison had proven, that morning, to be optimistic.

Anna's smile was strenuous and hopeful. Her daughter's was crooked and ironic. Des knew irony was bad manners on such an occasion but she couldn't figure out what to do with her face. Then Anna moved to hug her but missed, since she was bending down to talk to the cat.

They collided, and awkwardly disengaged. Des stood up and hugged her mom, which went on much longer than either one of them was used to or prepared for, and then Des squatted and made eye contact with the cat, a lithe unfriendly tabby. He was crouching behind her mother's legs with his tail fluffed out and his ears back.

"He may not recognize you," her mother said. "He's not good with strangers. Not that you're a stranger, he just needs to get used to you again."

Des made cooing noises and held her hands out. "How are you and Dad?" she asked, looking at the cat.

"Oh, fine. Dad's in Brussels. We're sorry we couldn't come and pick you up."

"That's okay. I had to go directly to the place I'm staying, anyway."

"How is that place? Is it safe? —What happened to your arm?"

Des laughed a little and tugged her sleeve down so the deep narrow scar wouldn't show. "You did that," she told the cat.

"Oh," her mother said, in deep relief.

"I've had that for years. I was trying to brush his fangs. You'd think he might recognize the scar he gave me—I guess there's a reason Homer didn't have Odysseus come home to his faithful cat."

"*Is* it safe?"

"Oh yeah, that whole area is completely transformed. They have art galleries and a hydroponic… thing. Our part is pretty, leafy, woodsy—there's a sort of park next door that has a lot of purple and white clover, Queen Anne's lace, things like cattails, big flat-leaved tropical plants. Very shady."

Her mother frowned. "That sounds like an abandoned lot. Are you living next door to a vacant lot? Are there snakes?"

"I haven't seen any snakes," Desiree said carefully.

Her mother sighed. "The people you're living with—?"

She was too liberal to finish the question.

"I've only met a couple of them. My roommate seems fine."

"And it's all women? Nonviolent offenses—of course, so many things are defined as violent nowadays, but—"

"I'm not sure—it isn't considered polite to ask. It can't be all nonviolent offenders or I wouldn't be able to be there."

She knew her mother deserved more. Some kind of answer, some endearing little detail.

"The door on the bathroom doesn't work," she offered. "One of the other girls says it only works when you don't want it to."

And that was definitely the wrong endearing detail to pick. Her mother radiated concern. "Is it *safe?*"

And then Des looked up and they caught one another's eyes, and Anna said, almost laughing, "I'm your mother. I'm a mom. I have to ask."

Des laughed, and they made a tacit agreement to treat this insistent question, is it *safe?*, as if it made her mother ridiculous. A little ridiculous, even in her own eyes.

"The bathroom seems safe," Des said. "There are these cute little sculptures made of seashells that are totally the kind of thing somebody would steal, if there were people there who stole stuff. But they're still there. So I think it's fine."

"I wish you didn't know what kind of seashell sculptures people like to steal," her mother said sadly.

"Can I, um, do you have like a grocery bag or something that I could borrow?"

"Of course!" Anna said, and went out to the kitchen to do some grateful burrowing and fussing in the cabinets. She came up with two options: a big glittery blue and purple bag with a kind of lacquer coating, which said YOU'RE THE STAR OF YOUR BAR

MITZVAH!, and a cloth bag from Whole Foods which said, GIRLS DON'T LIKE BOYS, GIRLS LIKE EGGS AND HONEY. Des took both of them and went down into the basement. The cat padded suspiciously behind her; her mother stood at the top of the staircase and watched.

As Desiree headed down the staircase to the basement she realized why the lawn sign and the bumper stickers had bothered her. They meant that something in her mother hadn't survived Des's sentence.

Des had never wanted to take away even a scrap of her mother's dignity; not even the simple dignity of an unadorned bumper.

In the unfinished basement she stood on the buckled concrete floor, marked by waves of water damage, and looked at the boxes from her old apartment. It was impossible to know where to start, since she'd been very drunk when she'd packed them—and, she remembered, she'd intentionally mislabeled them, in the hope that this would keep her mom from finding her porn. So when she ripped open the box that said PERSONAL she found pretty much only toiletries, which she scooped into the bar mitzvah bag, and clothes. She held the clothes to her face and smelled them before tossing them in the bag as well. They didn't smell great—they smelled like they'd been kept in a cardboard box in a flooded basement with an angry cat—but they were soft and familiar. Under the other smells a faint scent of detergent still clung to them.

The box that said CLOTHES had mostly utensils, for whatever reason. Des found her novelty Pizza Hut glass from 1982: E.T. reaching out a spindly gray finger and saying, "Be Good." With a fine high sense of irony she shoved it into the bar mitzvah bag.

Under the utensils there were fifth-generation xeroxes of *J.D.s*, and her collar and handcuffs and various things you could be hit with. She left all of those where they were for now except for the wide-backed wooden hairbrush, which she figured she could try using on her hair. The hairbrush also offered the plausible deniability that a flogger or even a ping-pong paddle might not. *I mean nobody has a good reason to own one ping-pong paddle*, she figured. Her kinkier books: the political ones from the '90s and the technical manuals from the '00s, plus the Meese Report and *Discipline and Punish* with the good parts dog-eared.

Pages torn from books. In her early to late twenties Des went through a phase where she aggressively disrespected books. She handled them now, with their soft ragged edges: the opening pages of "Such, Such Were the Joys" where he's beaten for bed-wetting (*God, you were a philistine*, she thought, *that's his greatest essay*); the first of various bodice-ripping scenes from *Sweet Savage Love*; some disturbing Moomin material about the Groke. That scene from Genet where they're all spitting on the one prisoner.

Her heart made itself unpleasantly known. *It's okay*, she told herself with a voiceless ghostly laugh, *it's all prisoners*. No COs in this scene. The inequality which had aroused her was caused only by desire, untouched by surveillance or injustice. That was how you knew Genet was writing about miracles.

Either that, or she'd always been misreading that passage. *You could check the context, if you hadn't ripped the scene out of the book like a total asshole.*

Her hands were shaking as she put the pages back. She was gripped by an emotion so unexpected, so intense, and so involved with the landscape of her mind rather than her real surroundings, that she confused it for lust before she recognized it as fear.

She breathed. The basement smelled like a soiled and avoided place, but a place she knew as home. She had been happy here—she could still make out the places on the uneven, stained gray floor where she'd spray-painted a wolf's head during her wolf phase, a pentagram during her witch phase. The clothesline was still up, unused for decades. When she'd lost her left roller skate she'd put the right one on and used that clothesline to haul herself at high speed across the bumpy basement. This excess of ingenuity ended when one end of the clothesline came loose and she concussed herself. She pictured herself lying there, stunned, the wheels of her one skate still spinning; and she laughed and felt calmer. She set the Genet pages aside and delved deeper into the box where she'd hidden her sex life.

Where she found the first-aid kit, wrapped in a light long-sleeved shirt for summertime bruises.

When Des and Lucinda first got together Lucinda had been so careful. She'd said she was always very respectful: "I will treat your bottom like an end in itself."

But then Des started pushing for what she really wanted. She was pretty sure Lucinda had liked it, back then, when Des's idea of seduction had been goading. *I will let you go too far with me.*

In her online profile Des had said her limits were, "Nothing requiring medical care and don't mark my face," this standard tough-chick line. You could hear Philip Marlowe trotting that one out right before the cops beat him up. And eventually Lucinda had learned that just like Marlowe, Des didn't mean it. Her left wrist still ached in damp weather. She still laughed when she remembered trying to get the ER nurse's number after she cracked her ribs: "You asking me if I come here often?"

Every problem in your life is a fractal for all the problems in your life.

"I'm going to do what I want," Lucinda had muttered in her ear, holding her by the hair. "You look so good in black and blue."

It was only afterward that Lucinda had thought about what she was doing. Lucinda thought about things, while Des poured shots and yanked down her underwear so she could grin at her bruises in the mirror. And thinking about what she was doing had scared Lucinda, which, Des figured, was a good reason not to think about it.

Lucinda arguing, "We're just using the symbols of domination. There's no actual subjugation happening; this is play."

And Des, rolling her eyes: "Why did you learn the alphabet if you don't want to say the words?"

Des had been the enforcer, the Phyllis Schlafly of kink, lecturing Lucinda about how to put her in her place. Lucinda wanted their sex life to be epistemological: an intimacy, a harmony, a mutual understanding that was the highest form of knowledge. Sadomasochism, the queen of the sciences. Whereas Des just wanted to be taught a good hard lesson. In retrospect it wasn't too surprising that things had ended badly for them.

Oh God, there it was in the first-aid kit, their sex CD. This was from when things were already starting to slope sideways and they'd been trying to reconcile via increasingly ill-advised sexual displays. They role-played, the things people come up with, shoplifter and security guard, prisoner and cruel lady warden; everything old will be new again someday. Then they fought over who was insufficiently interested in searching whose anus.

Des had done a sort of aerobics routine, in nothing but leg warmers and lace fingerless gloves, to Erasure's "A Little Respect." Lucinda taught her as much as she could remember from her high-school Tantric Breathing class. (She'd gone to school in California; they also had an elective in Deep, Morbid Poetry, but her notes from that class improved the relationship even less.) They tried to fuck to music, hence the sex mix, but Des got too distracted and it turned out not to help their sex life when one partner would rather listen to "Territorial Pissings" and sink into nostalgia for the damaged, uncommunicative sex of the Riot Grrrl era.

They played Greek myths. Lucinda had her chance to open

Pandora's box. And might have at that time still believed that hope was stuck somewhere inside, even though all she ever found in there was a Cheeto.

Des tossed the sex mix aside. There was no point in trying to salvage that, probably.

Underneath the first-aid kit she found a Ziploc bag with a clumpy brown substance in it.

"The fuck?" Des muttered. She held the bag and ran her fingers over the lumps. She glanced up at the stairs, but her mom wasn't there anymore. She looked at the bag for a long time, not thinking about anything, just watching herself and wondering what the right thing to do would be, and what she was going to do instead. Then she opened the bag and sniffed it, and when nothing happened, she scraped at the brown stuff with her fingernail and tasted it.

"Oh my God," she said. Brown sugar. In a Ziploc bag because— because she'd spilled a drink on the box it came in, she remembered, and then also there had been cockroaches.

She set it aside to throw away and checked to make sure she'd gone through all her boxes. There were other boxes here as well— her father's magazine box, for example, with its stacks of late-'80s issues of *Marxist History*, *Marxism Today*, *Postmarxism*, *Between Marxisms*, and *Tikkun*. Des flipped through these; she picked up the December 1989 *Tikkun* and it fell open with surprising ease to the personal essay by a lesbian held in the women's prison at Chowchilla.

The title was, "Buber Behind Bars" (Des wondered if the next issue would have "Buber Behind Bars II: Bigger Buber"), and at first glance it appeared to be an essay on the difficulties of maintaining I–Thou relations with one's fellow creatures in the I–It environment of prison. Des thought she should probably read it, and had no intention of doing so.

She was surprised that her father had apparently read it with enough attention to crease the pages. He had never shown much interest in Buber or Frankl or any of those Jews for Meaning. Marxist theory, of course; Marxist praxis sometimes; Jewish ritual when necessary; Jewish religion, perhaps behind some furtive closed door of the heart, maybe in the place where he did his suffering; but Jewish theory, Judaism domesticated and intelligible and useful, Judaism for people and not for "the people" or for our people or for G-d, why bother?

And then she noticed that the essay's pull-quote said, "In what you call 'the free world' I learned that a lover can pierce your clit. But only in prison did I learn how a lover can pierce your soul."

In the middle of this meditation on Martin Buber there was a vivid, two-page description of the physical side of prison love, and it was these pages which were stiff with re-reading. Des, with a quick embarrassed grin, understood now why her father had read this essay more often and with more attention than Vaclav Havel's thoughts on "Renewing the Democratic Conscience" in the same issue. It turned out that the way to get her father to read a reflection on abandoning objectification and encountering another person's mysterious reality was to start it off with, "Dear *Penthouse* Forum, I never thought it would happen to me...."

Every problem in your life is a fractal of the problems of everybody you love.

Fine, okay, she thought, and threw the magazine into her shopping bag. She went back upstairs, put the bags on the kitchen island and threw the Ziploc bag into the trash can—and Anna Pokorny said, in a voice a little too bright and casual, "Oh, what was that?"

Des straightened up and looked at her. "Brown sugar," she said, just as casual; performatively normal. "I had to bag it up because I spilled something on the box and the cardboard started to soak through."

"Oh, of course," Anna said.

Des was trying to figure out why she felt like she had done something wrong. "Do you want to make sure?" she asked, and fished in the garbage until she found the little bag.

"Oh, no," Anna said quickly, and her voice was sadder. That hadn't been the right thing either, apparently. "I trust you."

They both stood still for a moment, Des holding the Ziploc bag and trying not to ask, *Why would you ever do that?*

She took a breath. "Okay so, they did this thing with us, when they were preparing us for release. Where we're supposed to, uh, ask ourselves in every decision we make, 'What is the most humble thing to do?' And that's usually, apparently, the right thing, instead of whatever we might think is right. So—would you *mind* tasting this? It really is just brown sugar."

Anna wanted to say, *This isn't necessary*; but she took the bag. She took a pinch of the brown crumbly stuff and tasted.

Only then did Desiree realize that making your mom eat from the trash was not a normal person's definition of humility.

Chapter 3
Strange Bedfellows

"I'm pretty sure this bagelry used to be a Salvation Army," Desiree muttered as she waited for the woman checking the reservation list to tell her where to go.

"No, no," the hostess said. "It's a fascinating story! This building was *burnt* out in 1968, during the riots after the Reverend Doctor Martin Luther King, Jr. was shot—excuse me, assassinated. This whole area was an open-air drug market during the worst of Washington's years as a killing field in the crack epidemic. And now we've reclaimed this lost urban space to sell bagels!"

"Oh my God, no, this was Aces High," Des remembered. "This place was the greatest—they'd serve an infant. Serving the underage from legal last call through daybreak. We went here after prom to buy pot, I think."

"Oh," the hostess said. "That isn't in the history of the building we've been given. Can I take you to your party?"

I don't know, Des thought, *do you have a time machine?*

But she followed the hostess into the back room, where the local sadomasochistic community was holding its monthly brunch.

Des scanned the tables. About fifteen people, and she didn't know as many of them as she'd expected. A lot of the old faces were gone.

Like Lucinda. The ski-jump nose and angle-cut blonde bob, the big deep-set wounded eyes, the exhausting integrity and the everpresent hideous therapy chihuachshund, all nowhere to be found—Des put her shoulders down and smiled and sighed in a semiconvincing performance of relief.

At the far end of one table, by an empty seat, she spotted someone she knew. She was heading over to him when he glanced over to the doorway—and, for the first time in four years, somebody's whole face lit up when he saw her.

"*Desiree!*" Trash cried, setting his cocktail down so hard it splashed. "Come here right now! Is it really you, or is this fantasy? My *gosh*."

Desiree slipped onto the chair next to him. "Hi Trash," she said wryly.

"Somebody get this woman a drink! No, here, have mine," he said, pushing it toward her.

"No, actually I—it's fine," she laughed. "Have your drink. It's fine. How have you been?"

"Delightful! I can't figure out how to hug you in these chairs. Let me free my *body*." As Trash stood halfway up, then bent down to wrap her in an awkward, sincere embrace, Des was overwhelmed with a kind of miserable happiness. She had forgotten what he was like: every other word in italics, everything swollen with a vivacious glee. He could make "Welcome *back!*" seem like the very wickedest dish.

Trash was not tall, about five-five, with a lopsided cheekbony face, one eyebrow perpetually higher than the other. He had a wide comic mouth and unruly brunet curls, and in general looked like he'd been drawn in crayon. His best feature, which was obscured now that he was sitting down again, was his prominent and much-coveted ass. He was almost thirty, but he looked barely out of high school—and talked like a veteran queen.

"So how are things with you these days?" Des asked. "Are you skating yet? I don't know what season it is for you."

"No, not yet," he sighed. "Another month before show season. At the moment I'm just a barista. Orange caramel macchiatos. It's very fucking special. Here—let me grab you a menu."

Des looked at the menu just long enough to camouflage the fact that she already knew she couldn't afford anything.

"What's good here," Trash said, "bagels are good here. They do a maple bacon bourbon bagel burger, I like that. And you've got to try the Manis-chew-itz cocktails. They're very sticky." He licked his fingers evocatively.

"Manis-schev-itz," Des said, in horror.

"Oh, is it Hebrew? I didn't know you speak Hebrew! What a beautiful language," he said, "all the *chhhuhhh, chhuhh*—it must be very healthy. Ohhhh, it's not Hebrew, I can tell by your face—is it the other one? Jewish? No, your face just got worse, it's not called 'Jewish,' is it. I have butterfingers of the *brain*."

He flapped his fingers by the side of his head and added, "I'm mostly a decorative object, as you know."

"There's no reason you should know.... So do you like the barista life? Better than waiting tables?"

"No, there's much more washing of things. I don't thing-wash, as a rule, but now I am a Scrubbing Bubble on the champagne glass of life. But, you know, it's essentially the same job. Workin' and flirtin'. I'm grateful," which Desiree suddenly realized was something she'd only ever heard people say about low-status jobs, "but I'll be glad to get back on the ice."

There was a pause, and Trash looked her over; then he just said, "I should introduce you around."

"Yeah, I don't know anybody here."

"Well, Washington—people come and go," he said. And, raising his voice: "Everybody! This is Desiree. —Oh, I'm sorry, is it okay if I use your name?"

Des laughed. "What, are you worried you'll ruin my reputation? Go for it."

"Desiree is back with us at last! She's a critic of the arts, a graduate of Yale University—"

"Okay, that's enough," she said.

"A warm welcome," he ordered. Then he went around the table and introduced everyone. There were various familiar social types—the programmer who had an Instagram where he posed with a bullwhip; the other programmer, who had a fancy rat on a leash in his purse; the polyamorous world travelers in a "vee" with the husband, the wife, and the intern, who'd written off their sex swing on their taxes under "office supplies." The creepy Christian couple with a theology of spanking. The Ren Fest throuple in matching poet shirts, where the women both called the man "milord."

Des wished that just once her community would take inspiration from the inequalities of less-cliched eras. Maybe a sub chick could deck herself out as Liza Minnelli and call her dom "mein Herr"? Or get the man in a toga with a costume thunderbolt, and the woman swanned out like Bjork. Or "delinquent schoolgirl rocker and '70s record exec."

Des recognized only one person, a woman who called herself Mistress Mariah. Des was surprised to see her there, since she was really only a domme to pay for her ceramics degree.

She looked just like she had four years ago. Five foot nine and dark-skinned, canny eyes and a smile always twitching at her mouth. She always wore flowing feminine clothes to set off her wiry, muscular body—today it was a knee-length white dress with cap sleeves, so when she crossed her legs you could see those hardworking thighs. Mistress Mariah observed these brunches like a grimly-amused Grace Jones. Grace Jones, playing a lady spy pretending to be a hippie, always ten seconds away from either fulfilling your fantasies or cutting your throat with a jeweled fingernail. Or both, some people have a complicated inner life.

Now she just nodded, with a little smile and a somehow covert laugh, like a cough. As if by showing up Des had passed some secret test.

Next to her was a tiny white girl. Her blond hair had been cropped so short and unevenly that it stuck up in tufts around her skull. She was wearing a long-sleeved cardigan in a thick dark green fabric, with gappy stitches—it looked sewn by hand, and not well. She had huge blue eyes, a short nose with big nostrils, and blond eyebrows.

"This is Toya," Trash said.

"I'm a trainee with a self-improvement group," Toya said, getting the words out quick before somebody could tell her to stop. "The Morningstar Center. We give you a life you can boast about! We—"

Trash, who had clearly heard this before, cut her off with, "Toya, this is Desiree."

"Oh," the girl said, and she made her eyes even bigger. Her pallid, chapped rosebud lips made an actual "O" as she nodded hard. "I know you! They told me—you're the one who used drugs and went to prison."

"Yes," Desiree said. "I am that one American."

But—*In every decision you make, you must ask: What is the most humble thing to do?* And so she took a breath and said, "Actually, I sort of destroyed a historic tree while trespassing on federal property, and I resisted arrest. Uh, and I had an outstanding warrant. So it wasn't just drugs."

"Oh, I'm so sorry!" the girl said. "I didn't mean to insult you—they only told me about the drugs—I didn't know you had committed so many crimes. Please, accept my apologies."

Once again Des felt that she had somehow not quite managed to achieve humility.

"That's fine," she said. "No harm done."

"And *last*," Trash said firmly, "here is Lizzie. I will introduce you two. Everyone, you may resume your conversations." (Everybody but Toya already had.)

When Toya had turned her attention back toward her plate, Trash said, "Sorry about that. She is... different? We call her the Little Shorn Lamb. Try not to mind it."

"I'm good."

"Lizzie also works in media! She's a—well, I'll let her decide how much she wants to disclose. She is one of my *favorites*."

Lizzie was in her late twenties, and intimidatingly blonde. She had perfectly symmetrical features and perfect makeup; she was thin, almost bony, and she leaned forward when she talked so you could look down her sleeveless white blouse.

"Lizzie," she said, extending to Desiree a regal hand. She didn't say more. There was an awkward pause.

"Okay, we're being mysterious," Trash said. "If you won't talk I guess I have to do my news."

He took a quick breath and looked apprehensive, or embarrassed. "I got my HIV results back," he said. "Which are negative, don't worry. So that's... good."

"You sound not so sure," Des said.

"Well, I'd just spent so much time psyching myself up in case it came out the other way. Just given my general... living up to my name. Like, the last guy I hooked up with gave me his business card afterward, which would be flattering except that he's a psych nurse. So I'm *terribly* grateful. But I knew that it was my responsibility to be grateful no matter how the test came out."

Des's face felt hot and her heart beat faster. Suddenly prison was much too close. "Who told you you'd have to be grateful for having a disease?" she asked.

He cocked his head at her.

"It isn't something people told me I had to do," he said lightly. "But you know the drill: 'Thank you, sir, may I please have another?' You have to be thankful for everything—don't you?—even the difficult things. Like you're in a 24/7 D/s relationship with... life, really."

Des and Lizzie both looked at him. Lizzie held the swirly straw of her margarita between her perfect lips, took a long eloquent drag, and released it. "Has he always been like this?" she asked Des.

Trash went on, undeterred: "I've spent the past three months talking myself through this. Like, 'You can be grateful that you know,' which is just no help at all, or, 'Well, John Curry had HIV, and this is probably your only chance to have something in common with John Curry.'"

Lizzie asked, kindly, "Is that a figure skater?"

"Oh yes, sorry. He was the Olympic *champion* in—I don't know why I say these things."

"Whenever Trash says a dude's name and it's somebody that nobody's heard of, it's a figure skater," Lizzie said.

"Yeah, I remember. Hey—though—I, I can't help but notice that some familiar faces are gone. Brandon. Lucinda."

Trash looked at Des with a sort of embarrassed pity. "Lucinda isn't around anymore, usually," he said.

"Sure. Of course," Des said, nodding. Feeling that humiliation when you realize you've lowered your expectations, but not far enough. "Does anybody know where––"

But they were already shaking their heads.

"And Brandon is out of our *lives*, okay?" Lizzie said, making a big X with her arms. Des noticed that her unchipped nail polish matched her scarlet lipstick. Leaning toward Des, she said, "I hope you weren't a Brandonite."

Trash laughed. "She was the opposite of a Brandonite. She was Kryptonite to Brandonites."

"Tell me you dumped him," Des said. "I want the details."

"A, I did dump him and he flung a poodle at me, but B, honestly, he's not that bad. We're still semi–in touch."

"He's your evil ex!" Des laughed. "You don't stay in touch with your evil ex!"

"That's completely wrong," Trash said. "*Everybody* stays in touch with their evil ex. That's the one ex you do stay in touch with."

Lizzie, trying for a stern forthright tone, said, "He punched you. He punched you, and almost got you fired because you didn't uphold a 'family image.'"

"Holy shit," Des said. "He punched you? Fuck him, what scum."

"First of all," Trash said. "I was not ever going to get fired from an ice show because my boyfriend hit me. That wasn't a thing that would happen. They were possibly going to fire me because I *lied* to them and they thought I was involved in, I don't know, drugs or gangs or something, I don't know how people get black eyes."

"You do, actually, know that," Lizzie said.

"And you're still *semi*–in touch with him? God, he's worthless."

"Second of all, everybody hits me, you know that."

"But nonconsensually," Lizzie put in. "He hit you without your consent."

"I consented! Retroactively. I forgave him. That's basically retroactive consent, I think."

"That's not even remotely a thing," Lizzie said.

"And *third* of all, he was not in his usual state of mind. He was hangry."

Lizzie and Des both looked at him.

"It's a new word," Trash explained, "that I think people came up with while you were—away. It means when you get angry because you're hungry. So, 'hangry.'"

"None of that explains what you think it explains," Des said.

"He apologized after he'd had a Slim Jim. Anyway, I've broken up with him, I've done what I'm supposed to do, all is well."

"How's the *poodle* though," Lizzie said pointedly.

"Fifi is fine! Fifi is always fine. They always land on their feet. — Or no, that's cats, but my point is, Fifi is scrappy. She was a fighting dog in Les Ballets Trockadero de West Texas."

Des looked around the table at all the strangers of her community, eating Nutella bagels and BBQ pork bagels and "po' bagels" stuffed with shrimp. It was hard to come home only to find that home had somehow managed to move away.

The next week was a blur of supervised-release requirements. Jon Joylegs hadn't been able to negotiate a job for Des on the cleaning staff at their office, but he did manage to find a few people in the marketing department who could use a housecleaner. He also commissioned her to review the Newseum, but she gave up on it after she'd spent two hours just typing and deleting the words "the 9/11 Gallery Presented by Comcast" over and over. It had cost her twenty-four ninety-five plus tax to get into the museum; she'd tried to get a press pass but the woman at the desk said, "They told us you were a janitor."

Every morning, the shock moment where you think this must be a dream came later and later. After six days she made it all the way out to the porch with her community coffee before she had to acclimate to the unintelligible reality of her conditional freedom.

She got used to taking a shit in a paradise of privacy. Crapping in the daylight, with the sun spilling through the high narrow window, utterly unwatched. She attended Work and Hygiene classes. She learned job-readiness skills, such as how to wear shoulder pads, and took notes on the physiological symptoms of addiction, which included "chaos."

Des got to know the neighborhood. The blocks right by the Anacostia metro were a haven of focused, dedicated black middle-class purpose: a high school, a huge Baptist church, all those organizations like the National Black Campground and Waterpark Association, the Association of African-American Arborists, the National Council of Negro Gymnasts. Each one a marker on some overlooked avenue of American racism.

Behind these nonprofits there were commercial streets, and behind the commerce there was a hilly neighborhood of two- and three-story houses with surrounding yards. Trees, vines, and wildflowers were everywhere—it was as lush and green as the neighborhood where Des had grown up, although there was a lot more trash lodged in the vines and bushes. Every street seemed to be made of alternating patches of order and rampant green neglect. Around the metro she saw other white people all the time, but once you got a few streets back they disappeared.

The women of Love's Labors Loft went out together to see Fang play bass guitar with her band, Train Your Replacements, on Clean and Sober Night at the Crystal Stair. It was Ray Ray and Des, and a tall dark-skinned girl from the Caribbean named Douceline, and Caretta, a backwoodsy freckled light-skinned girl who was so eager and yappy that Des found it impossible not to look down on her. Ray Ray didn't even try: "She a bamma," she confided in Des as they headed down U Street toward the club, "in case you couldn't tell."

"I can tell."

"You even know what that is, a bamma?"

Des laughed, and Ray Ray laughed too. "I know what it is! I grew up here, okay? I know, occasionally, what things are."

"Mean she ain't got no style, ain't got no sense."

"I know." And then, straining towards humility: "Thank you for telling me *a thing I know*."

Imani Rollins didn't come—she didn't mix work and pleasure—and neither did the seventh housemate, Stephanie, a half-bedridden older woman who spoke exclusively in Bible quotes.

The Crystal Stair had huge windows but they couldn't see inside—the windows were steamed up. People had scrawled messages in the steam:

A LIE IS A WISH YOUR HEART MAKES.

FILM THE POLICE.

GOD WILL TURN IT AROUND.

And—an ephemeral tribute, a relic of Des's childhood—COOL "DISCO" DAN.

In the transparent loops of handwriting Des could see thin curving strips of dancers, moving bodies, as if the music were whittling the dancers and casting their discarded scraps and shavings to the floor.

Then they got inside and it was like being inside a thundercloud made of knockoff cologne. They hovered inside the doorway gawking; Des kept twitching and glancing back over her shoulder. Edging toward the walls, bumping into the steamed-up glass window and nearly jumping out of her skin, thinking she saw something terrible out of the corner of her eye but unable to catch it when she turned to look. Even when nobody was touching her she felt like someone was touching her.

"It be a rack of white girls in here," Ray Ray said. "No offense."

But then she pulled herself together. She straightened her faded black t-shirt and turned to Des with a cheeky grin and said, "Learn from my hustle."

Des tried to laugh; tried to focus on her mentor. Ray Ray strode to the center of the dance floor.

Most of the people seemed to be trying to get somewhere else. They didn't so much dance as plunge rhythmically through the thin places in the crowd. Ray Ray had more dramatic ideas. She began to work every joint in her body, all akimbo, like a doll attacking its owner. She dropped her torso toward the floor and bounced her ass up and down. Her feet turned out, then turned in, then began to hop stiffly across the floor. Somebody in the lighting booth must have seen her, because suddenly she was dancing in an orange spotlight: backlit, the orange shifting through red and then to white, a glittering play of light and shadow across her round cheeks, sweat gleaming in her hair. She threw her hands up and then dropped her right hand to her forehead, her whole body falling backward as if in a faint—she was ready for the Spirit.

Until then Des had just been watching, but when Ray Ray straightened up from her ecstasy she pantomimed lassoing Des and whipping her around the dance floor. Des had wanted to get away from the crowd but instead Ray Ray pulled her into it, as if against her will. She did her best to portray a reluctant, bucking donkey under Ray Ray's command.

"I'm gonna come up behind you and rub up on you," Ray Ray shouted. "Is that okay?"

They had talked about this in group, how you should always announce yourself before you came up behind somebody. You never know who might be a trauma survivor. Or in their case, you did know.

"I'd prefer it if you didn't!" Des said in a discreet yell.

"I'd prefer to. I'm just telling you beforehand. It won't take but a minute."

"Do what you gotta do," Des said, and bent over.

"'Preciate it," Ray Ray said, or maybe, "Preach!"

Ray Ray gave just a few gentlemanly thrusts at the air, with her hands on Des's hips, not even making contact with Des's ass. She was performing to be seen by other people—hotter, less recently-imprisoned women.

But she did bend forward, after the third or fourth thrust, and Des could feel the body heat on her hips and shoulders and the back of her neck. She was tense, she couldn't see anything, on the verge of panic, only kept in place because she was taking some of Ray Ray's weight now. And Ray Ray said, right up against her ear, sweet and low, "Easy, girl. You good. I got'chu."

Des liked to think of herself as someone who didn't need or yearn for praise from the women who fucked her, and anyway this whole situation was too unfamiliar and too public for her to give way. But something inside her let go. Some knot she hadn't noticed went slack, and she felt safe. It was humiliating to be so grateful for it.

Ray Ray pulled back, Des stood up and extricated herself from the dance, and Ray Ray shrugged and slipped away into the crowd.

Even the shrug was musical. Des, heading toward the entrance to get her back against a wall, marveled at the way Ray Ray could make not only herself but everybody around her feel at home—there was no threat in her loping gangster walk, nothing in her sexy sidelong grin but a good time.

Des slipped outside the club and took a deep breath. The street gleamed—all the new cupcake stores and restaurants with slender menus. White people pushed around her wrapped in bright sharp laughter as she tried to get her bearings. Des remembered when this street had been burnt out. Chewed-up men sprawling on the crumbling stoops, and huge broad green tropical leaves growing up through the floorboards. There had been fewer people then, and she hadn't been afraid of any of them. Little high-school Desiree had headed out to the clubs in a Boy Scout shirt unbuttoned practically to her navel, past the skullfaced men who were too out of it to catcall her. She had barely even smoked pot but she'd thought she shared some secret with those men, the crack-smokers. At the time she had been wrong; she was a little less wrong now.

She lurked outside the club, trying to look like she was just about to light up a cigarette, until Fang's band finished playing and the others came out. Ray Ray had two girls, who'd been straight when they started their night, hanging all over her. They cooed and fluttered and petted at her cornrows. She was gleaming with sweat and success.

"Now you see how I do," she crowed to Desiree as they were coming back to the metro. Douceline was limping and swinging her stiletto heels from one hand. Fang was lugging her guitar. Caretta was cursing herself for talking to a guy who said he already had a girlfriend, but she could be his side piece. Caretta had gotten his number and it had felt like a triumph at the time, but now she was thinking real triumphs didn't come that easy.

Des was feeling shitty because everybody else had managed to be inside that pent-up space, that clamor of shadows and bodies, to support Fang. She kept waiting for them to make fun of her for leaving, so she could feel put-upon and indignant; instead she had to be grateful, which made it worse.

Ray Ray said, "You know, I realized something. Your name got 'Ray' in it too. So you can be L'il Ray Ray."

Desiree pointed out, "I am ten years older than you. And half a foot taller."

"L'il is a state of mind."

So that helped.

Afterward, when they got home in time for ten o'clock curfew, Des was eating Nutella out of the jar while Ray Ray and Douceline fought over the remote. Ray Ray wanted to watch "COPS" and laugh at poor white people; Douceline wanted to watch "Girls" and laugh at rich white people.

Ray Ray started flipping through channels at random. "If you want to see imaginary made-up white chicks taking they clothes off there is one hundred channels available to you!" she argued. "You can see that anytime. You can see that on the street! I bet L'il Ray Ray here would take her shirt off for you if you asked nice!"

"I'm not made-up," Des noted, and swiped a dollop of Nutella off the plastic cover that protected the tablecloth. She was watching Douceline's expression for any hint of openness to lesbianism, even if it was only for the sake of argument.

Then Ray Ray flipped the channel again and Des said, "Wait— stop there. I know that girl."

Because there, on a cable access channel, was Lizzie from the sadomasochists' brunch. She looked just the same: sun-kissed, heavily eyeshadowed, cleavagey. She had a crimson velvet choker on, with a silver eagle pendant in the middle.

"Hello and *welcome* to Strange Bedfellows!" she gushed, flashing her big straight white teeth and fully shimmying at the camera to give a glimpse of her big straight white boobs. "On the right, I'm Lizzie Pearl."

"And I'm David Lav," her companion said. He was a tall, skinny guy with dark curls and a prominent Adam's apple. He was sitting in a complex draped position, legs crossed and arms folded over his legs. They were on a bare-bones set, with a couple houseplants and a cheesy graffiti-style drawing of the White House and the Washington Monument on a movable wall behind them.

With a sudden awkward shuffle Lizzie's co-host undraped himself, went briefly akimbo, and said, his cheeks reddening, "Sorry! 'On the left, I'm David Lav.' Sorry, I always forget."

He was sweaty on the forehead, and the high ridges of his cheeks were red. Lizzie, who looked like she had a personal air-conditioning system installed behind her ribcage, said kindly, "You're doing fine."

"Well," he said, recovering himself, "Lizzie will start us off with the Trump news."

"Yes, I have to do the Trump news because way long ago," as she waved a long golden arm at the past, "like after Christmas, I said there was no way Trump would win a single primary. But now this guy's dorsal-fin toupee is cutting through the blood-flecked waters of the Republican Party—"

"And I'm sorry for you," David said, recovering himself, "except that I couldn't be happier. It couldn't happen to a nicer party."

"It couldn't happen to a nicer *country!* Anyway this week Mr. Trump got two more endorsements. Wayne James Rideaway, leader of the movement Help Our Own Hobos First, threw his support to the Donald at an emotional press conference in which he said, 'Donald Trump is the future of the American worker.' And Hoss Hayes, the Californian evangelical-cartoon mogul, offered a surprising endorsement of Trump as, I quote, 'not under the influence of Satan.'"

"That *is* surprising."

"I remember those cartoons, you know, the Hayes tracts," Lizzie mused. "I used to get them instead of tips when I waitressed. And the guidance counselor would hand them out if you looked like you might be taking birth control. Like if your acne cleared up too quick, boom, here's a pamphlet about how the Vatican has its own money."

Ray Ray, grabbing for the remote, said, "This shit jiah boring. Turn back to the naked white girl."

"I'll do your chores tomorrow if you let me watch," Des said absently; Ray Ray gave up and wandered off.

"What will you do for me though," Douceline said.

"I have some food in the fridge—you can take something. One thing. There's ice cream in the freezer."

"No, I ate that already. That chocolate swirl? I ate that."

Desiree, turning away from the TV, glared at her. "The fuck, though? That was mine."

"Sorry," Douceline said. You could hear the shrug.

A lot of bad emotions collapsed together in Des's stomach: fear of what would happen if she defended her turf, dread of what would happen from now on if she didn't, horror that she was having to think about this shit again when she was supposed to be free, colossal lesbian disappointment that women were such fucking bitches for no reason. It felt like outrage, only unpleasant.

She was starting to push her chair back when Douceline said, "This doesn't have to be a thing. Sometimes people take things and you don't have to fight about it. Control your anger. Breathe in."

Des, having breathed in, snapped, "Don't take my fucking ice cream."

"I won't take it again, even if you back down. This is what they're trying to teach us here: how to handle a second chance."

Des glared. She was trying to work out why what Douceline had said was wrong.

"You just told me I could have it, anyway." The lakelike placidity of Douceline's voice never wavered.

"Motherfuck. *Fine*. Good luck with your rehabilitation to society, that's all."

And on the television David Lav said, "But Lizzie, I want to pin you down on this."

"I bet you do," his co-host purred, and leaned in again to the camera and winked.

"Uh—yeah, I mean," he stammered, "no, but—about politics—I mean—"

"You want me to tell you, 'Why Trump?'," she said.

"*Yes*," he said in obvious relief. And then, laughing, "It is fascinating to watch a political party flirt with suicide right before our eyes. —Are you okay, L.P.?"

Lizzie, who seemed off her game for the first time in the show, gave a quick rallying laugh and said, "I'm always okay. But I can't help you here. I don't get it! I don't get it, people. This man is the betrayal of everything the Republican Party and the conservative movement stand for."

"I don't know how you can say that when he's well on his way to winning the nomination. He is the Republican Party."

"But he's a chaos monster!" She threw her hands in the air in disgust, and shuddered with her breasts. "He goes against everything we need from our government: rules, predictability, stability, normal bedtimes! Mitt Romney is probably drinking a glass of *milk*, right now. Because it does a body good! Meanwhile Donald Trump is screaming at a hooker."

"He's gonna sue us now," her co-host said. "He'll say he wasn't screaming, that's his normal speaking voice."

Lizzie said, "Yeah, him and my mom's second husband. Look, in my experience most of life is just—chaos—like anywhere you turn there could be, out of nowhere, an orgy or—or *suicide*, right in front of you, and all of my politics is about creating a place where everybody is wearing correct clothing and nothing is awful and out of place. And you can feel like maybe there are rules here, and parents."

Douceline padded out of the dining room. Possibly to root through Des's food in the fridge; possibly feeling that educating Des on the realities of reentry was enough of a reward.

And Des sat at the dining-room table, where the chairs all stood facing the doors, wondering if Lizzie was being a hot mess on purpose. Was this what people tuned in for? To see her rip open her blouse and flash her pert, creamy childhood damage?

On the screen David Lav said, with something like rue in his sad, judgmental voice: "That chaos is what I feel when I look at the trading floor at the New York Stock Exchange. Or a gun show, or a cop convention. Like it's something obscene."

Lizzie didn't even hesitate. "When was the last time you were on the trading floor of the New York Stock Exchange? Like really, when was the last time you were there?"

"Well—these are things we see on television—"

"Or a *gun show*, or a cop convention? This is the Left, people! This is the problem—all your ideas are just based on *ideas* about things! You're never actually there. Remember when you told me it was bad to teach kids literacy?"

"I didn't say it was wrong of you to do it. I said it was the government's responsibility."

"Well, I'm sorry," she said, with real tenderness. "I remember it differently, what you said, but I'm a hot mess" (Des laughed out loud: *She said it!*) "and I just make things up in my head sometimes, because I don't pay attention."

Des's eyes widened. Behind the self-parody there was, maybe, some mutant, sexy form of humility.

"But the point is," Lizzie said, "you were never there and yet you think you're better than the people who are."

"I don't think I'm better than you," David Lav said, and he was just as sincere; it was the weirdest thing Des had ever seen on television, two humans trying to love each other on a talk show.

When she went to bed Desiree kept thinking about that show. It seemed cruel to expose those two in their extended adolescence, David Lav who had so much self-absorbed anxiety that he couldn't even sit in a chair right and Lizzie, hot for teacher, wielding her sexuality like an oversized comedy mallet. Some force had convinced those two to go on television; it seemed like a bad sign for the country.

And there she was, watching it with all the rest. Something about Lizzie got to her. Lizzie with her calculated, sincere hints about her awful childhood. Blowsy Lizzie who gave you all the opposition research she'd already done on herself.

Maybe it was honest, in a way—more honest than Des had been, back when she'd worked in "media" too. She'd thought she was getting away with it; after all, she worked from home. People treated her as if she were competent and her opinions were based in reality, instead of broadcasting live from the snake house in her head.

Then she'd had to call her editor from the D.C. Jail, right after they let her get her things and go home, and all Jon Joylegs had said was, "Whoa, I guess Andrea wins. She's the one who had 'jail' in the pool this week."

"...The pool?"

Shaking uncontrollably from alcohol withdrawal. Seeing tall sketchy dudes ducking behind corners, just at the edges of her vision. (She'd eventually realized, with great relief, that these were hallucinations.)

"Yeah, the pool where we guess why you'll miss your deadline. I've had 'grandmother's funeral' for most of this year and I've won three times."

Of course one drawback to Lizzie's persona was that if you're a hot mess for money, you have a strong incentive not to get your shit together. Even honesty can be a rationalization.

And with that uncomforting thought Des fell asleep.

Chapter 4
Love Slaves of the Horror Hand

That May was cold and rainy in D.C. The days lengthened, the sun like a woman pulling her hem up a quarter-inch at a time, to madden you. One morning Des came outside with her community coffee and all the cherry blossoms had fallen, carpeting close around the trunks as if the trees had flung them down in disgust. The tulip poplars bloomed and filled the chilly air with their consoling scent. Two weeks of rain. The longest unbroken chain of rainy days in… but Des wandered off before Caretta finished reading the sentence off her Twitter.

After the rain the temperature rose. The magnolias bloomed, and glowing purple chicory flourished in all the abandoned places. One slender sunflower dominated a neighbor's yard. The white roses outside Love's Labors Loft had a rich smell, but the red roses outside the Moorish Science Temple had no smell at all.

Desiree learned her many assigned routines. She wasn't yet allowed to clear trash from the yard, the sidewalks, and the vacant lot next door. (It was in fact a vacant lot and not a very small meadow.)

This was a duty assigned only to trustworthy women who had lived sober in the halfway house for at least four months. The reason was that the trash could be triggering. Crumpled plastic half-pints of vodka, classic green-and-white-striped Newport packs, Miller High Life cans with their nostalgic rancid morning-after smell. So she had to keep vacuuming the stairs—the very worst chore, which everybody cursed through as they plucked fluff from the threadbare carpeting and apologized for ramming the back of the vacuum into the walls.

She went to her housecleaning gigs, hauling the vacuum cleaner she'd borrowed from her parents. Grappling with and dropping all the cleaning products she'd bought with money she also borrowed from her parents. (She had given them the receipts; they tried to reassure her by not looking at them, but they kept them in case they wanted to look at them later.) She observed other housecleaners and bought a smock with pockets, and stopped dropping bleach canisters everywhere. She remembered Trash saying he was grateful for his job and strove to be like that; and then felt pretty pleased with herself, since nothing could express more humility than imitating Trash of all people.

One woman said, "I hope you understand that we can't pay the rate you initially told us. It's been a difficult year for us, as I'm sure you can appreciate."

Des, who needed the work to meet her release conditions, said that it was fine. She fantasized about revenge while she cleaned the bathroom. She thought the traditional Hollywood revenge in these circumstances was to stick the person's toothbrush up her ass, but that seemed like it would be more uncomfortable for her than anything else. So she tried instead to take a certain self-righteous pleasure in scrubbing that woman's tile with especial thoroughness. She noted that she was managing to scrub an asshole's floor with pleasure, and, her pleasure peaking, chalked it up to her newfound gratitude and humility.

She scrubbed on hands and knees; people say the maid services only make you do it that way to reinforce class boundaries, but there's no other way to get things reliably clean.

Love's Labor's Loft held regular, mandatory group counseling. The women sat in a circle and described what they perceived to be significant events, past or present. Sometimes the sessions seemed like a list of all the things a child could be hit with: fly swatter, kitchen spoon, toy fire truck, dead snake, broken porch railing, extension cord; kitten. A Richard Scarry picture dictionary in which all the definitions just read, "A is for **attitude**. Don't give me that **attitude**, Lowly Worm."

Sometimes—not with the kitten—the women laughed about it, sided with their long-suffering moms. (Or, much more rarely, with their father or their mom's boyfriend.) Then Des would worry that they were glancing over at her, and noticing that she wasn't laughing along. She'd already had to admit, "My parents never hit me or anything like that," and although she had been embarrassed the other women had acted like she was bragging about it.

It wasn't that Des's parents had been models of modern childrearing. They had not breast-fed or co-slept, or explained themselves. They were not believers in attachment parenting or in teaching children empathy. Because they lacked any theory of parenting, they were free from any self-righteousness about their own parental fitness. Their parenting was instinctive, crammed into the gaps in the day, and best described as "unintentional." They corrected and even scolded, but didn't explain the basis of their ethics; explaining morality was too much like expressing emotions.

And so Des learned by trial and error what was whiny, rude, or generally intolerable. Her own most shameful memories involved parental forgiveness—their quiet reaching for her hand, their encouraging her to do the smart version of whatever stupid thing she'd tried to do, their tactful silence when she corrected her behavior so strenuously that her guilty conscience was practically fluorescent.

Nobody ever called this thing her parents were doing "forgiveness." It was a household where people talked about justice but not mercy, equality but not humility. So most of the family's emotional life took place in covert operations.

None of this was something she could talk about in group. She had neither the desire nor the ability to assess her parents' forgiveness, to agree or disagree with their decisions, or to laugh about it. And she couldn't understand why her reticence, which she was pretty sure was modesty and a desire to protect her parents' privacy, should feel so much like noncompliance.

Still, it was hard to imagine the other women understanding what she was talking about. Imani Rollins was the exception. Imani, with her stable personal life and her good works, probably nurtured her own guilty conscience. But Des was convinced that even if she could understand this one aspect of Des's personality, Miss Imani, nestled deep in the gentlest part of the Treatment-Industrial Complex, would not get Des as a person. By contrast Ray Ray might not get any specific thing about Des, but Des was certain that in some unexpected and maybe unwanted way, Ray Ray got her.

So she tried to sit the way Ray Ray was sitting, leaning forward with her hands clasped between her spread legs. It was a position that made her feel ruggedly, wholesomely lesbian: a posture that raised the consciousness.

In this posture Des was listening to Ray Ray talk about Halloween. Ray Ray had hit puberty early and hard. It had been awful: big boobs at age seven, catcalls and child molesters, but the thing she had hated most about it was Halloween. All the other kids in her class would go around with their plastic pumpkins and adults would hand out compliments and fun-size Twix. And then when Ray Ray showed up they'd frown and say, "Aren't you a little old for this?"

"So I hid behind the bushes and beat they ass up and stole the candy," she said, and that impish grin danced across her face. Des was surprised and heartened to see that the other women were grinning too—even Imani—at this long-ago delinquent triumph. She wondered what it would have been like to get beat up by seven-year-old Ray Ray. That was the role she would've played in this story; she had never been beaten up in her childhood, and she wondered if she would have been able to take it with gusto.

"You should've just gone later," Caretta said. "That's the rules of trick or treat. Teenagers can come as long as they come at the end, when everybody trying to get rid of they candy. You ain't even need to be in costume."

Des thought this was a little bit belated, and not to the point; but Ray Ray said, "I didn't know that. Do you think I could go now?"

Caretta allowed that now might be too late.

Des wanted to come up with some plausible, explanatory trauma. She felt confused and bereft when she sorted through her memories and came up with nothing that would stand up against the others' stories. The only thing she could think of—the only moment when, looking back, she should have known where she was heading—was the Freddy Krueger hand.

The Freddy hand belonged to Gabrielle, a light-skinned black girl who lived two streets north in a hillside home much larger and more lavish than Des's. Gabrielle went to private school, so Des wasn't sure how they'd met, but they were the same age and for about two years Gabrielle was Des's best friend on the days when her school friends were busy.

Most of the games Des and Gabrielle played didn't require the Freddy hand. There was the one where Des was an oppressed dishwashing robot—it was only years later that she'd realized this had been a very convenient game for Gabrielle, since Des could be oppressed into doing her chores for her. The dishwashing robot always wore an apron, and Des was convinced that it came from a cartoon, although years of half-drunk Googling "dishwashing robot prison planet '80s cartoon" had only turned up some distressing Transformers pornography. Gabrielle's role was to order her around and to host parties where she told an imaginary crowd of human aristocrats, "You see, they don't feel things the way we do," and demonstrate by slapping Des on the arm or thigh.

They also played nuclear fallout. In this game the crawlspace under Gabrielle's mother's refinished porch, which had been the prison for disobedient robots, became a refuge for mutants. Des was always a mutant. She had to persuade Gabrielle not to kill her, using only the mutant language of gurgling grunts.

In retrospect Des noticed how many of their games involved her trying to convince Gabrielle that she had human, or robot, dignity. She always wanted to fail at this task. If Gabrielle gave in and agreed that she deserved civil rights, the game got much more boring.

Once at a party she'd said, as if discovering the fact for the first time, "You know, it's odd how many of my childhood games were about trying to prove to somebody that I was human." And the other woman, who was half-Jewish like Des but on the more respectable maternal side, had nodded and replied, "Ah yes, the Holocaust."

And Des had stared at her, off-guard and appalled. *This is the closest thing I have to a winsome quirk*, she'd thought in baffled outrage, *and all it says to you is trauma?*

She and Gabrielle had also played She-Ra vs. Catra. Des was

always Catra. She-Ra always vanquished Catra, and as Gabrielle stood over Des's prone body—sometimes tied up with jump rope or lightly whipped with switches broken off from convenient trees—she would conclude the game by stating the moral, with deliciously syrupy smugness.

"In today's story we learned that Catra has the magical powers of a cat, but she doesn't have the greatest power of all," she would say. "And that's... the power of *love*."

And lilac blossoms from the switch fluttered down onto Des's unprotected calves.

This pattern also never changed: Des was the villainess. If they played things with no obvious villain, like Punky Brewster or house, then Des could be a servant or a robot, or a thief.

Des usually picked the game and assigned roles. She didn't bother with the details, unless she had an idea—a particularly humiliating dance that the robot could be made to perform, for example. Otherwise the specifics of her punishment were left to Gabrielle: "I'm going to walk ahead of you and fart, and you have to walk behind me and smell my farts." Then Gabrielle would prance through the alleys with her ass stuck out, waggling it and blowing raspberries to indicate that Des should wrinkle up her face and sniff exaggeratedly and look sad.

Des wouldn't have come up with this farting thing on her own, and didn't think it fit the aesthetic of the robot prison planet, but she maintained a secret pride that even as a child she was able to recognize that submitting to stupid or displeasing orders was part of the point of being an oppressed robot. Desiree didn't believe in "topping from the bottom."

All of Des's games with Gabrielle had an element of self-exposure. These weren't games she played with her school friends. But the games with the Freddy hand were different.

Gabrielle had actually seen *A Nightmare on Elm Street*; Des wasn't allowed to watch R-rated movies, and at that stage in her life her crimes were confined to hiding food she didn't want to eat and stealing books from her sister. When they brought out the horror hand Gabrielle's voice would get spooky and she would begin to talk about "the world of dreams—the ecstasy and the nightmare."

A dreamlike atmosphere always did hang over the games with the hand. For some reason in Des's memory these particular games were only played in the burning depth of summer: on July and August days when heat hung in a silvery haze and the streets melted underfoot. Gabrielle would make her run to Georgia Avenue to buy a Slurpee or a lollipop ring for them to share—Gabrielle would wear the plastic ring, which pinched the underside of her finger, and they'd take turns sucking on the giant purple jewel—and then when she was sweat-soaked and panting Gabrielle would say, "I want to go and get Freddy."

Or, with even more menace and promise: "Freddy's ready."

And when she rose up out of her basement wearing the hand, a tall thin wavering shadow with wrong fingers, Des had to hold completely still. She had to freeze, in some contorted attitude—part of the game was for Des to horse around while she was waiting for Gabrielle to come up the stairs. Hanging off the furniture or rolling around on the floor. Hunching witchlike around the living room with great stomping steps, caught with her leg raised. *Hold still.*

Gabrielle would walk toward her, very slowly. And the horror hand would find some bare expanse of flesh and trace—just draw a thin line along her skin. Time stood still.

There were times when the horror hand moved up below her t-shirt, or pulled it up to her shoulders; there were times when the hand slid over her underwear, or inside it, between her legs. But these incidents only emphasized the real tension of the game: Des's helpless stillness, her rapt attention as she shuddered and wanted to beg just to *know* what the horror hand would do.

The pretense of the game was that neither of them had any responsibility. The hand chose. They pretended that neither of them had any control when, if you had to be literal about it, either of them could have stopped it at any time.

During the other games Des was always conscious of her status with Gabrielle. She was always trying to win approval and stay popular with this girl, even though on some level she must have looked down on Gabrielle since she never even attempted to play with her if her school friends were available. But during the games with the Freddy hand she was aware of nothing but the hand: its scraping gray plastic claws, its fake leather glove, its ruts and seams and its progress across her skin. Gabrielle's rough dream-voice commanding her not to move or giving her relief from her position. They could play like this for hours: mouths open, almost silent, drugged.

At some point Gabrielle had moved away, probably—Des's memory was hazy but she hadn't run into Gabrielle in the alleys anymore, so that seemed like the most likely explanation. And Des hadn't thought about Gabrielle or the Freddy hand. At least, she didn't remember thinking about it. When she was fourteen she started secretly dating an older girl. She would stand, kissing open-mouthed, her hands on the girl's round breasts. When she was sixteen she got drunk for the first time. Later there were other drugs, mostly cocaine. (And pot, but she didn't count pot because it was boring; the only good thing about pot was showing off how well she could suck a bong.) It was only when she was trying to describe what was so rapturous about these experiences that she remembered the Freddy hand.

So in group counseling at her halfway house she found herself saying, "I, uh, in elementary school there was this girl who had like a Freddy Krueger hand, I mean a toy hand, not a real hand on her body, and when she would touch me with it, I would sort of let go of myself, I had to do whatever she said. It was as if time stood still."

"You felt as though you were not in your own body," Imani said.

"Or—not in my own mind. I was really intensely in my body."

"Where would she touch you?" Ray Ray asked.

Imani frowned at her, but Des's hand drifted involuntarily along her thigh.

"On your bathing suit area?" Ray Ray said, just like a worksheet.

"Okay, I'm not five," Desiree said. "And no. Or—yes, sometimes, but that really wasn't the point...."

She wasn't sure how to explain what the point had been.

"Dissociation," Imani said, carefully and softly, "is a common coping strategy for people who are experiencing sexual trauma."

"It was the greatest feeling in the world."

Ray Ray, with undisguised contempt: "It shows."

"Ranae," Imani said. "Everyone is allowed to self-define. And to reach self-understanding in her own time frame."

"You been telling us all these things to do to reach self-awareness. Like set an alarm each day, take a multivitamin. Concentrate our attention on a plant. I'm telling you there ain't no multivitamin that can fix *that*."

Des said, "I don't think I'm explaining it well."

Chapter 5
Community Supervision

Des went to brunch again—late, because she'd had to meet with her Community Supervision Officer. While they were going over her Yelp reviews from the people who'd hired her for housecleaning, the smeared windows of the community supervision office turned black and the thunder cracked.

So Des walked from the Metro in the pouring rain—the first real summer thunderstorm—and she squelched into the back room of the retro pancakery with her white blouse soaked so that everybody could see that she needed a professional bra fitting, her hair coming down witchily all over her face. Toya, the Little Shorn Lamb, wearing another unflattering green cardigan or maybe the same one, turned to her and made that "O" with her mouth and asked, "Oh, is it raining?"

Desiree gave her an extremely prison look—the look of someone throttling inside—and managed not to say anything. Even when it turned out that the Lamb's chair was positioned so Des had to squeeze past her in order to get to the bathroom and wring herself out, Des just growled, "Excuse me," instead of the fifty things she believed she really, *finally* deserved to say.

Very few people wanted to talk to her, but she made a point of asking everybody about Lucinda before resorting to the seat next to Trash. Everyone claimed they didn't know what Lucinda was doing these days. On her way back from the bathroom Des had to push past the Little Shorn Lamb again; a wave of body odor rolled toward her, the smell of days-old clothing worn in summer. She allowed herself to visibly recoil. Every now and then, she reflected, the kink community would remind you that there's such a thing as being *too* accepting.

Trash was squirmy and buoyant. "I have met a new *man*," he confided. "I have to tell you, he is intense. I have these blisters? Like all along the bottom part of my ass, they're *huge*, they're shiny. Puffy and shiny, very '80s. I haven't had anything like that before."

"Oh, that's nothing," Lizzie Pearl said. "Those are fine, they go down on their own. Don't pop them."

"No, I know, I'm not worried. He's just utterly dominant. The last time I saw him he was like, 'You look like shit, why can't you learn to dress yourself?', and as punishment for not looking nice he made me change my Grindr profile so it was totally honest."

"Oh my God," Lizzie said.

"*Incredibly* humiliating. And straight up, a *priest* messaged me to be like, 'I'm not a play by the rules kind of guy, but you sound like a mess, do you want to come over to my place and go to confession?' I had no idea what to say to that so we ended up getting in a conversation about whether or not he was a Habsburg."

"A who?"

"A Habsburg, they're Catholics with these jaws," and he demonstrated an underbite. "I was like, 'I couldn't help noticing your jawline, just be aware that you might have hemophilia.' I try to be helpful to people."

"I think he'd know if he had hemophilia," Des said, giving up on the menu.

Lizzie said, "Gotta say, though, I'm not into the guys who think domination is just about insulting you. Or anything to do with talking. What I go for is a man who can dominate me without running his *mouth* all the time," and she made a yap-yap-yap gesture with her hand. "I don't do negging."

"Oh, I love negging," Trash said. "It's great for my self-esteem."

They looked at him.

"Fine," Des said, "I'll bite. How is negging good for your self-esteem?"

"It takes my mind off of other people. If I'm all tangled up in thinking about my own inadequacies—I'm not saying that's *great*, it's a distraction from higher things, and I really do try to think more about work, and my choreography—but at least I'm not sitting around judging other people. So I feel a lot less guilt."

Seeing their skepticism, he elaborated: "Like yesterday I was super angry at this guy I work with, because he ditched his *opening* shift and our manager called me, like literally called me on the phone with his *voice*, at three in the morning to make me come in and cover. And all day I was angry, like if you asked me if the Summer Splurge Fruit Blast was good I'd say, 'Oh, it's delightful, unlike Jaquan—and it's available at this location, *unlike Jaquan*.' But today I didn't think about that at all. I spent most of today learning about skin care. Did you know that you can make a mask for your skin with avocado and broccoli?"

"I try to eat food, for the most part," Lizzie said, "and wash myself with things that aren't food."

"Oh, of course, you're a conservative," he said.

Des snickered. "Yeah, capitalism really narrows the boundaries of which things can be used for what," she said. "You need a specialized product for everything. No ingenuity."

"In Communist countries people eat fried tarantulas, I'm just saying," Lizzie said. "That's ingenuity. It's also *gross*. Crunch crunch."

She spidered her hands out and flexed the fingers, to show them.

"Euchhh!" Trash shuddered. And then asked himself, "Would I eat a tarantula? I might. I think somebody would have to make me do it. I'm very cowardly if I'm not being ordered around. Like I've lost all my triple jumps, now that I have to be my own coach."

"I had to eat a spider once," the Little Shorn Lamb butted in.

The three of them looked at her.

After a long moment, she looked away.

Desiree's Community Supervision Officer was a caring, bald, tattooed white woman who had kicked heroin eight years ago and now had a wife and kids. She held power over every aspect of Des's life. She made Des write out what she ate every day, and assigned her to eat more bananas: "You need potassium."

"Can I look up other things that have potassium in them and—"

"I would be more comfortable with bananas."

The theme of the Community Supervision field office's décor was "resentment." There were the cheery posters (BRING A FRIEND IF YOU'VE STILL GOT ONE!) and the diagrams showing you how to stand in a line. There was the ashtray superglued to the stained wall of the elevator, with a handmade sign taped above it: IF YOU GOING TO SPIT, SPIT IN THE SPITTOON, with an arrow pointing down. DO NOT SPIT ON THE ELEVATOR BUTTONS. But the buttons were sticky anyway and Des quickly learned to always bring a pen to push them.

The windows were streaky with some unidentifiable industrial waste, and the air conditioning was broken, which her CSO complained about a lot. Des just nodded. She wondered if fanning herself with her work readiness assessment would look like some kind of commentary. Don't complain and don't comment; you don't want to get a reputation for noncompliance.

They did a standard reentry exercise in which Des had to describe her crimes.

"Our purpose here," the CSO said, "is to restore your identity. The criminal justice system needs to reduce you to a set of circumstances, they need to make you a type. An abstraction: This person is a drug addict, this person is a violent offender. People think they know what kind of person you are, because of your status as an offender. We're going to show that you're not a *kind* of person. You're just a person."

"Okay."

"So," lifting her knuckly hands up, fingers flexed, as if she was lifting the whole weight of Des's criminal identity so Des could slither out from under it, "tell me about the night you were arrested."

"You mean, the second time? I was really drunk and I'd done a bunch of drugs, mostly coke, and I ended up on federal parkland, and I got arrested for trespassing and possession and resisting arrest. And, uh, damaging government property, because I tried to climb what turned out to be a tree that people really care about. Like, a tree that has a Facebook page. And then when they put me into the database or whatever, they found out that I'd done the whole failure to appear thing."

"Okay, now we're going to take that description and expand it, a little at a time. Can you give me more detail?"

"Uh, I can give you more detail for the first part. After that it gets hazy."

"Well, let's start with the first part. Tell me some small, humanizing details—anything that surprised you, anything you remember that makes this experience more than just an entry on a rap sheet."

"Okay. I was over at my ex's place, I was showing her how to float grain alcohol over the top of a drink and set it on fire, in exchange for her calling her dealer because mine had kind of run an intervention on me the last time I saw him. She was really nice to me; that's a surprising detail."

"Anything else?"

"Well...."

Des suddenly remembered how she'd said, "You're my mixer." Fondly, sadly.

So Lucinda had said—because God forbid Lucinda should let a compliment pass without rubbing her own cleverness all over it—"You mean I'm completely unnecessary to anything you actually care about?"

Des had pouted, "I meant that you make my life more aesthetically pleasing, but okay."

Lucinda didn't yell, because yelling wasn't classy, even though Des would have found it less annoying. Yelling at each other when you're drunk could be a real bonding experience for a couple, she felt. Lucinda had been telling her she was going too far, which had made her worried that Lucinda knew somehow about her previous arrest, the one she still hadn't been sentenced for. The one she hadn't told anybody about. So she'd countered, "Maybe I haven't gone far enough!"

None of that seemed likely to impress her CSO or help her case.

But it brought back a few other scraps of memory. "When I poured out the whiskey for her I said, 'Synchronize scotches!' I thought that was clever."

"And then?"

"And then I was in the park."

"And she was with you."

"No, by that point, no."

"Can you describe what happened in the park in more detail?"

Des laughed. "You know more than I do, man. I don't remember any of it, I was blackout like Pepco."

"...You don't remember—is there video of the arrest? Or witnesses?"

"Don't think so."

The CSO crossed her muscled arms, in her poorly-fitted white blouse. The buttons gaped over her breasts. "So you just accepted the police account here? You have no idea whether you did any of this—are you sure those were your drugs?"

"'Sure' in what sense?"

The CSO was looking increasingly dismayed. "But if you don't remember any of this, and there's no video, no witnesses, why did you believe the police when they said you resisted arrest?"

Des shook her head, uncomprehending. "I don't know, it just seemed like the kind of thing I would do."

Her CSO sighed for a very long time. "...Okay. If you don't remember the events of the arrest, let's try this a different way. We can look at the earlier events. Can you describe going over to your ex's place, and what you did there, but instead of just telling me that one thing happened and then another thing happened, try to use linking words. Like, 'This happened *because* that happened.' Or, 'I wanted to do this, *so* I did that.'"

"But I don't know if anything like that applies here."

The CSO took a deep breath and Des wondered if the buttons would pop. She knew she should feel remorse for thinking about her Community Supervision Officer's bra and not about the task that was supposed to help her reintegrate into society, but instead of remorse she just felt scared. She didn't want to make her CSO angry, but she couldn't seem to make herself do or say the right things.

"I don't know what I wanted or why I was doing things," she said. She made sure it sounded serious; her voice cracked. "I don't always do things because of other things. It's a fallacy, isn't it?, to think that we always do things because of the things that came before? That's post hoc ergo propter hoc."

"I didn't go to Yale," her CSO said, and Jesus, was that in her file?, "but I would've thought that anybody smart enough to say that shit would be smart enough to know *not* to say it."

And Desiree failed to stop herself from answering, "Yeah, but those are two different kinds of smart. And I'm the other kind."

"Well—in better news, I see you got a five-star Yelp rating this week."

Des nodded. She didn't see any reason to admit that her five-star reviewer was the guy who'd greeted her at the door visibly erect, in a loosely-knotted silk robe and nothing else. He'd stayed clothed while she was vacuuming, but when she put her hair up and started scrubbing his kitchen floor, he let the robe fall open. She was just grateful he'd used a handkerchief; she hadn't been looking forward to washing sperm out of her hair in someone else's kitchen sink.

Everyone has issues, she figured. *Hygiene is rich in sexual symbolism,* as they'd taught her at Yale—in Contemporary White Male Literature or Abnormal Psych, she couldn't remember which.

Jon Joylegs had sent Des *Custodian of Souls,* and she cracked it open as the 90 bus trundled toward her cleaning assignment in Mount Pleasant. The author, Jabez Pruitt, was raised by a bookish family in a Chicago suburb. He grew up around goats and chickens, "made his way" to Harvard and thence to Skadden Arps. Des was reluctantly impressed by the firm and more-reluctantly impressed that Pruitt didn't explain its prestige. In his late twenties he'd had "nothing so gauche as a nervous breakdown. But I found that I simply *could not go to work.*"

He tried psychoanalysis, cognitive behavioral therapy, Cymbalta and Fluoxetine and various other things that sounded like Captain Kirk's romantic conquests. But at last he'd tried "something truly radical": He'd asked his father to get him a job mopping floors at Dad's friend's dental practice. He spent a year as a janitor, "in the greatest finals club of all: the finals club of Humility."

At the front of the bus there was a sudden commotion. A skinny woman in a short red dress had stumbled coming up the steps onto the bus, and was now yelling at the passengers: "Fuck all y'all D.C. niggas! I'm from New York, bitch! You ain't know shit! I'm a hot New York bitch and a bad motherfucker!"

As a custodian I learned the true satisfaction of bringing order to a chaotic world. From the water swirling under my mop I learned what in Taoism is called "wu wei," and in medieval Italy was known as "sprezzatura": the natural, spontaneous harmony of action which produces peace in the outer world and in the soul. In what we call "manual labor" I found an escape from the American obsession with work. I discovered, in a clean floor, serenity.

"This clankety-ass old bus, how y'all D.C. motherfuckers stand this bus? Fuck this bus! In New York—"

A young man said, "Ma'am, there are children on this bus!"

The woman snapped, "You think I ain't see that there's children on this bus? I'm from New York and I know how to handle *my* business!"

The bus driver held the bus at a green light and said something Des couldn't hear. She tried to focus on her reading.

I learned that those we overlook, people in the lowest positions in society, often lead lives of the greatest peace.

"Driver bitch, don't you tell me to lower my voice! You just a bus driver, you ain't shit! I'll snatch that wig off your head! I'm from

Schenectady, New York—"

And Des looked up then, as the whole bus burst out laughing.

"What makes him so different is that he's a *conceptual* dom," Trash confided, dunking a french fry in his daiquiri. "So he does all the standard stuff, he has this one exceptional paddle that you can add all kinds of terrifying attachments to, spikes and electro-things, it's like a Mr. Potato Head of pain. That's nice. But the other day he had me dress up as a clown and reenact one of my worst memories."

"Was that *sexy?*" Lizzie asked. This time the sadomasochists' brunch was at a place selling high-end half-smokes. You could buy *Hamilton*-themed shot glasses, and four-ounce jars of mumbo sauce for $15.99.

"That was more for the correction of my character," Trash said. "It was difficult to think of anything—you know I've had such a sheltered life—so I ended up in clown makeup, in my underwear and a curly wig and big floppy shoes and a pompom stuck up my ass, reenacting my father's funeral. The red nose that you honk, you know the thing I mean?, it got all stuffed up with snot because I was crying so hard.

"It really put things in perspective," he said. "I was so grateful that when it happened in real life, when I was seven, I was allowed much more dignity and protection. Even though I behaved with so little thoughtfulness toward others, and didn't deserve their kindness. I've been so lucky in my life."

"This seems like a weirdly Hallmark thing to get out of your kinky sex life," Lizzie commented. "It's like if I saw a Hummel figurine in bondage gear. I don't think I want this stuff to be wholesome."

"How are things going with *your* friend?" Des asked Lizzie.

"My who now?"

"That guy you do the show with—you two seemed to have a little—"

"Oh my God, no—no no no!" Lizzie laughed in horror and added, "I don't date the well-meaning."

Des looked around the half-smoke shop. Along with the mumbo sauce they were selling pots of marionberry jam: The label read, "Don't get JAMMED up! Marionberry, black, earthy and sweet." There were matryoshka dolls with all the mayors of the city. The biggest doll was Barry, huge and smiling on the outside. (It should've been Walter Washington, but there's only one Mayor-for-Life.) One doll had been taken apart for display, so you could see the increasingly-diminutive versions of Washington, Kelly, Williams, Fenty, Gray, Bowser. And then Barry again, still smiling, hidden deep inside.

And inside the little Barry, in the secret heart of the District, a tiny toy crack pipe. Des laughed a little when she saw it, but she felt somehow exposed and judged. *It's not as if we've ever had complete home rule*, she thought, for no obvious reason.

June exposed some of the new divisions in the neighborhood. You could tell which businesses had come in with gentrification because they all had the rainbow flag out. There were two ice-cream shops right next to each other on Howard Road. The one with the rainbow flag had just opened and sold D.C.-themed flavors, Foggy Bottom (coffee-marshmallow) and Rock Creek Park (pawpaw-walnut with cherry swirl) and Thanks Obama (chocolate chocolate-chunk). The one without the rainbow flag was established in 1977 and sold chocolate, vanilla, and strawberry. Des made up for the fact that she never patronized the old one by never patronizing the new one.

At Love's Labors the summer meant everybody sat out on the porch. Afternoons with shirtless young men, their jeans pulled down below their butt cheeks, sidling and strolling in a haze of marijuana. Evenings with fireflies and police sirens, and old ladies working in their gardens. (Des said they should go over and offer to help, but she was relieved when Ray Ray laughed and said, "Them old ladies don't want help. You think you can plant they geraniums better than they can?") Silver mornings with community coffee and the tidal shrieking of insects.

"That's a mourning dove," Fang said.

"A who?" Des was surprised; Fang basically never talked except to tell them her band's new name (currently, Anansi Reagan) and invite them to gigs.

"That thing that just went, *a woo, whoooo. Whooo*," Fang cooed. They were both coated in a thin sheen of sweat. "That's a mourning dove. They're pretty much like, if you were a pigeon's mom, a mourning dove is what you'd always be comparing your kid to. Why can't you be like the mourning dove, you look fat in those feathers, your cousin the mourning dove is going to a *real* college. That kind of thing."

"Do you know pretty much all birds now?" Des asked. Fang was working at a wild bird rescue in suburban Maryland.

"I mostly work with birds of prey. They think those are the most therapeutic."

"Are they... pleasant?"

"The vultures are nice!" Fang scraped her thick black hair out of her eyes. Des had never heard her languid, husky voice so animated. "The vultures are pretty much like toddlers. They're friendly and fun once you earn their trust. And they puke on you and smell like a corpse, which is kind of like some toddlers."

And then, meditatively, "Owls are little bitches. I wouldn't even lend an owl five dollars, they'd just bite you. Fuck an owl, pretty much, people only like owls because of *Harry Potter*."

Ray Ray came out onto the porch holding a smoothie. "It's hot!" she said. "If it's this hot at nine in the morning I be running down the street Butterball naked by noon."

"I can talk to Miss Imani about the window again if you want," Des offered.

"It's okay," Ray Ray said. "I know you like it hot as shit. Might as well just keep it open."

She plopped down onto the porch swing and shoved Fang over. Fang, who was less fond of Ray Ray's bullshit than Des, glowered and pointedly gulped the last of her coffee and went back inside.

"Fine," Ray Ray said, "she don't wanna hear my news, she don't have to."

The mourning dove called again.

"What news? Also that's a mourning dove."

"A who?" But Ray Ray was not in an ornithological mood. "Ty'heaven got let out. My wifey coming back."

"Oh, that's great! Is she coming here? Do you want me to keep it secret?"

"If you asking should you tell my P.O.," Ray Ray said, looking at Desiree hard.

She lifted her hands. "I wouldn't do that."

Ray Ray grunted. "I wish she'd tell me where she staying at. She loyal but she haphazard. A lot of what she say is suspect."

Des wondered if she should ask about that, but instead she just stared out at the street and went, "Mmm," and sipped her coffee. She wasn't sure if she was being callous or tactful. Life after prison seemed full of these unsettling double meanings, like the optical illusion with the old woman who's also a duck. For the first time she was conscious of her own mixed motives.

And her own comforting half-truths. Like the thing she'd told her CSO, about how she didn't have reasons for things, she lived post hoc but not propter hoc. That was only sort of true. It was possible that things had gotten so far out of hand for her, the night she climbed the Sycamore of 1812, because she had a bench warrant.

She hadn't even—it was bitterly unfair that you couldn't complain about this—failed to appear in court. Or at least, she hadn't failed to appear at the courthouse. She had turned up at the Superior Court of the District of Columbia in sandals and two pairs of slush-soaked socks, because it was January and she was not leading the kind of life where you remember to buy boots before it snows. Melting ice glinted amid the dandruff in her hair.

She had forgotten to bring the letter with the information about where to go and what to do, so she tried reading the listing of courtrooms to see if anything sounded familiar. After much pointless wandering she asked a security guard where she should go and he told her, and she went there, but it was the wrong courtroom or the wrong time, and she sat there in the back for a while but nobody told her what was happening, and then she had to go and throw up.

As she stumbled out of the stall in the ladies' room a woman who'd been chatting into her cell phone about her jury service looked at her and said kindly, "You better tell them about that in voir dire, honey. They'll let you go home."

Des felt little confidence in this woman's ability to accurately assess evidence.

She stood there in front of the mirrors. Turned the tap and there were cockroaches coming out of the water faucet, just for a second. By the time she'd shaken her hands violently in shock they were gone.

That's not nice, she had thought, *to displace your personal problems onto some God's-honest water faucet.* She felt sorry for it. This poor stained object. There was rust crinkling around its lip, a little dried blood, just where you'd kiss if you were perhaps a lady water faucet with questionable taste in spouts.

As she was heading out the courthouse's front doors, numb and blank and freezing, a white guy called down joyfully from the top of the escalator: "It's good, man, the test came back good!"

In a New York accent, calling and waving, "The test is good, it's not your baby!"

Desiree did not drive, so she did not get pulled over. (And only in revisiting this awful scene, from the grateful safety of the Love's Labors porch, did she realize that if she'd passed the D.C. drivers' exam way back in 1994 she might be a murderer by now.) She did not jaywalk because she never went anywhere. Court was not the only place she was failing to appear back in 2011. Slowly fading from her own life like that girl in the painting in *The Witches*. When she'd been busted the first time trying to buy coke she had still been living with Lucinda, but they almost immediately split up and got separate apartments. Desiree, continuing to act exactly like a specific kind of person, did not leave a forwarding address.

And so she did not get caught until more than a year later, when bored Park Police headlights spotted something in the woods that was too big to be a raccoon and too sleazy to be a deer.

Ray Ray was staring out into space, taking her own hike down the sketchier stretches of Memory Lane. Then she sucked disconsolately on her smoothie and muttered, in an unconvincing voice, "At least when she was locked up I knew where the fuck she was."

Toya Tannen, the Little Shorn Lamb with her hair starting to grow out from its uneven crop, was sitting in the back row of one of the classrooms on the first floor of the Morningstar Center. She was listening raptly as the man who called himself Max Lord led his smoking-cessation workshop.

Toya'd received special permission to attend. Trina Lawton, the co-founder of Morningstar and Max Lord's second-in-command (her title was "Certified Women's Life Specialist"), had asked, "Toya, have you ever even smoked?" and Toya had admitted, "Not... physically?"

But she couldn't bear the thought of missing a single session of Max Lord's classes. He had changed her life.

Now he was standing at the front of the classroom, jutting forward over a lectern. He usually held on to things while he taught, to take weight off his bad leg. Seeing him leaning there filled Toya with compassion.

Max Lord was not an attractive man to look at; there were no photographs of him on Morningstar's website, though there were several head shots of Trina. But photographs would have been little use. They wouldn't prepare anyone for the Max Lord experience.

He was quick to laugh, and his laugh had a covert satisfaction. Sometimes it made you feel like he was laughing at you, and you desperately wanted to prove to him that you weren't laughable, you were cool. Sometimes it made you feel like he was letting you in on the joke: that you understood him, and in understanding him, understood your own life. His eyes prowled the women he taught, lingering on their bodies in ways they found flattering and then meeting their eyes so that they caught their breath.

Everything Max Lord said seemed to Toya symbolic. Just the other day he had asked, "When you use the last paper towel on the roll, why wouldn't you put another roll on the dowel?" And she had mused on this koan for an hour, and wrote down in her gratitude journal, *Learned what a dowel is*. She'd had to ask one of the other Morningstar women if it was only used for paper towels, so now some of them called her Towel Dowel. She was glad that Trina hadn't been around. She thought Trina might have come up with plans for her and that dowel.

The answer to Max Lord's question, she'd decided, was probably lack of mindfulness.

Now he was gripping the edge of the lectern and asking, in his deep resonant Hollywood voice, "Why do people smoke? They smoke because it comforts them to give control of their lives to an inanimate object. The cigarette makes life predictable. When I smoke the cigarette, I am calm. When I am not calm, I smoke the cigarette. They no longer need to rely on *people*—they no longer need to learn to trust men. To trust themselves. Smoking gives the thrill and pain which always accompany growth" (Toya wrote this down verbatim, her pen skidding and scrawling because she couldn't take her eyes off of him) "but instead of connecting to another person, you're just holding a pathetic little object as it dwindles... in your fingers... down to ash."

Then he laughed. And Toya was so grateful not to be a cigarette butt.

Max Lord's great theme was that true empowerment came as the result of unconditional trust in another person. He explained that women nowadays were damaged. They weren't able to trust, because they had been hurt so many times by men: "Your boyfriends, your daddies, your pastors." Max Lord said that he, too, had been damaged—though he did not give specifics—and so he had made it his mission to surround himself with damaged women and teach them, guide them, help them grow.

During Toya's intake interview he had asked her, "Who hurt you?"

She said, "My father—broke my collarbone. But only once, and it's okay now. Does that count?"

Max Lord smiled, slowly. "What a beautiful and vulnerable answer. Please take off your shirt so I can see where it happened."

Toya tried to come up with some reason not to do it. But he held her gaze. And suddenly she was smiling, just a small smile, and she took her t-shirt off and he nodded, and a kind of padlock in her chest seemed to release.

"Lovely. *Thank* you. Who are your close friends?" he had asked.

She had shivered, wondering, in her bra. "I think maybe my shift supervisor? Is it a 'close' friend if they know where you grew up?"

"Sometimes," he said, and his smile quirked up on one end to reassure her. (Toya had no idea, even now, where Max Lord came from. She had a vague idea that he had spent time in California, maybe in Silicon Valley or L.A., but she had not yet earned the right to such personal information.)

"Unhook your bra," he'd murmured. "...Good."

When the smoking-cessation class ended Toya closed her Morningstar notebook and clipped the Morningstar pen to the front cover. She waited in her seat as all the regular workshop attendees filed out. Trina caught her by the arm as she slipped out of the classroom and turned her to face Max Lord; she had been staring at him for the past hour and yet it was intimidating to be turned toward him by Trina.

"She needs a haircut," Trina said, with humor edging her words.

"After dinner," Max Lord said.

Dinner was the usual assortment of very large things. Two baguettes' worth of garlic bread; a meatloaf the size of a watermelon; a watermelon. A few months ago Toya had been in a grocery store, trying to encourage the cheesemonger to try a class with Morningstar, and she'd seen something labeled, "Personal Watermelon." It was the size of a bowling ball—a small bowling ball. Toya had felt a rush of warmth as she thought, *I will never have to eat a personal watermelon. The rest of my life will be family-size.*

After dinner she followed Max Lord into the bathroom, took the bucket out of the cupboard under the sink, and knelt before him with her head bowed. She flinched when the razor buzzed into life.

At first Max was silent as he ran the razor carelessly over her head, letting it bump and skip around. But then he asked, "What would I have to do to make you hit me?"

She jerked her head up and the razor cut her. "What?" she asked.

"Hold still. Come on," teasing, "what would I have to do to make you hit me?"

"Oh, I could *never!*" she breathed.

"That's right," he said. "Right now, you can't. But as you grow in confidence, through the techniques we're teaching you and the trust you place in me, you'll reach a place where you're able to hit me. You'll just choose not to."

And Max Lord laid a hand on the back of her neck.

"You're special, Toya," he said. And she waited for the punchline, the kind of thing the boys at school would have said: *Yeah, like Special Ed!* or just, Special stupid. But it didn't come.

The last and only honor Toya had received was when her high school class voted her Most Likely to Marry a Cousin. She'd been so relieved; one of the yearbook girls had told her it would be Most Likely to Sell Her Body for Funyuns.

She wore Max Lord's hand like a royal diadem.

Chapter 6
Semi-In Touch

Javier Navarro's phone buzzed, and the submissive guy standing against the wall with his shorts around his ankles jumped at the sound.

"Hold still," Javier said sharply, although neither the sub nor the phone obeyed his command, the sub wriggling his shoulders and the phone skittering away across his faux-marble coffee table.

He grabbed the phone and saw that it was a photo from Trash: He was smiling, squinting at the camera, and pointing to two bulging black garbage bags at his feet. He texted then to say, "2 blocks away from u!"

"My other sub is coming over," Javier said. "When he comes to the door, you'll be leaving. So," gentling his voice, starting the transition to aftercare, "why don't you get dressed and come here."

He noticed that he was grinning, and he was distracted as he checked over and praised the guy he'd just paddled. He often found himself smiling when he knew Trash was imminent. Trash was far from his most sexually-appealing regular sub, so it wasn't that; he wasn't sure what it was.

Javier Navarro enjoyed being a dom, and felt he brought a certain flair to it. He demanded that his subs reimagine the world such that any object or situation could become a participant in their degradation. He'd select some random item, a hula hoop or kitchen tongs or a clothes hamper, and tell them to come up with a punishment involving this item. "I feel like I'm in a game show run by supervillains!" one guy had groaned. Javier found that making them come up with the ideas themselves got inside their heads more; made their eventual sexual release more intense and earned. Plus the absurdity was a humiliation for them.

He ordered his subs to pretend they were a table, which was pretty standard; or a wall, which was good for making them look on helplessly as you fucked somebody else; or two ferrets fighting over a corncob. "Is the corncob my dick?" one guy had asked, and had gotten his mouth scrubbed with soap for language. After which he'd protested, spitting and wincing, that nobody cared if ferrets cursed, which Javier had to admit was a fair point.

Last week he'd made Trash turn into a cupcake.

"Oh, like a choreography exercise!" Trash had exclaimed, shedding his clothes. And after a moment's thought he'd sunk into a deep plié and arched his arms elegantly over his head. It was surprisingly realistic. Then he'd started wiggling his fingers like he was trying to shake something off of them.

"What are those?" Javier asked, pointing.

Trash, helpfully: "The sprinkles."

Javier suppressed a giggle as he commanded, "Give an account of yourself, cupcake!"

Trash stared at him, visibly baffled and just as visibly aroused. "Uh—I'm a chocolate cupcake, I think," he said, "with thick, creamy frosting. I'm, what do people want cupcakes to be? Is it 'moist'? How horrible."

But then Trash reconsidered and said, "Wait, no, 'give an account of yourself' means say what you do wrong, doesn't it? Ask to be put in your place. So I'm sorry, sir, please punish me, I am insufficiently moist."

"You like being put in your place, don't you?" Javier said. It was an honest question, even though it didn't sound like one. Trash was Javier's weirdest sub, and Javier would resort to any means—including deceit and unkindness—to figure out what on earth he was thinking, and how to please him.

"Yes, sir," Trash had said. "Thank you for making me admit it."

Now Trash knocked on his door and Javier opened it wide, letting in a rush of tropical air from the hallway, to make sure Trash could watch him give the other sub a hug and a quick squeeze of the shoulder. Trash stood back from them a little, with his head slightly bowed, and an expression on his face that made it clear he knew this wasn't a sight he was meant to enjoy. He swallowed hard and lowered his head further when Javier shut the door. He shivered a little; it was sweltering outside, and Javier kept his home artificially breezy.

"You walked from Petworth?" Javier asked, not as sternly as he'd meant to. Trash was grimy and sweaty, wearing clothes Javier had given him: a thin, now badly-soiled white t-shirt, pink shorts, and an orange vest that said COMMUNITY SERVICE across the back. His curls were dark and sweat-soaked, and there were streaks of filth on his arms and legs and face.

"Yes, sir. The bags are in the garbage and recycling out back."

Javier took his seat and waved Trash over. He had a huge, ridiculous chair he'd bought at one of those gentrification shops on U Street. It had tiger-print cushions, a huge curving back like a hood that came up above his head, and armrests made to look like tusks, with jeweled rims. He would only play with subs who were willing to consider this thing magnificent.

And then, too, before he'd bought the chair he'd sometimes felt like he could tell what his sex partners were imagining, and he hadn't liked it.

Javier was a realtor, and owned his Dupont Circle row house. On the night he got his acceptance letter to UCLA he drove with his mother out to Playa del Rey and roasted *elotes* over a fire fueled by financial aid paperwork and the letter from the guidance counselor that said he should consider "the custodial arts."

But that wasn't what the guys he'd met on Grindr and Craigslist saw. He thought that they saw what they wanted: the dom as brute. (He tried not to think that they saw what they wanted, a brown thug.) In response they let themselves become dehumanized too. They played at being helpless and without will or heart. The brute and the victim.

Javier's weird demands, and the trappings like the ridiculous chair, added something unnecessary and human to what had too often felt like an exchange of shame.

Javier gazed at Trash and tried to decide what he wanted to do. He kept trying to play with Trash but it was too much like the play of children, serious and poetic. Javier tried to be what he thought Trash might enjoy but Trash kept enjoying it in unanticipated and unsettling ways.

There was the time he ran out of insults—while Trash was blowing him he'd said Trash was a whore, filthy and perverted, only good for sex and not much good at that, and then he'd lost his train of thought and sputtered out, "You've got a weird nose!" and out of all the people in the world only Trash wouldn't laugh at him for that.

And then he'd found himself saying, as Trash swallowed and gently released him, "And you don't deserve to be loved."

Trash had stared up at him in abjection, nodding and fighting back tears. Javier felt like a complete heel. *Why do I say these things?* he'd wondered. *When will I learn to find that line between a strict dom and a drama queen?*

But then Trash's brow had wrinkled, and he'd laughed and said, "Hard truths! Oh, that's what I need. That's what makes me so thankful to be here."

Javier had shaken his head. "You place a lot of trust in me, you know," he said.

Trash had grinned up at him and said, "I get off on trusting people."

Now Javier ordered Trash to wash his hands and get him a club soda on the rocks. Trash did a kind of curtsy as he presented the drink. He kept his back straight, and there was a classical elegance in his movements. The golden light of early evening slanted over his body, gleaming and lingering on the beads of cooling sweat. Even the dirt smeared on Trash's body seemed somehow captivating, in the honey light.

Then Javier wrinkled his nose as Trash's scent hit him. He really did smell like the boys' locker room at Garbage Dump Senior High.

"How did you like your assignment?" he asked.

"Thank you so much," Trash said, with a certain restraint. He'd straightened up and was standing in front of the tusk chair with his shoulders thrown back and his hands clasped at the base of his spine. Gazing straight ahead, not allowing himself to look down at his dom.

"It was so good for me!" he said. "Very humiliating to be... shown, to my own neighborhood, as someone who has to pick up trash on the street because he broke the law. They'll think very differently of me now."

"Did anybody ask you what you'd done?"

"Not in so many words," he said, smiling. He was more eager now. "But several people said hello. They seemed… nervous? Like it was embarrassing to be around me. I hoped some kind of explanation would put them at their ease. So I just said I'd been court-ordered to do street cleaning, and if they seemed like they wanted to know more, or if they asked what had happened, I said it was for public indecency."

Javier laughed. "Not bad."

"I thought that was a good mix of humiliating for me, but not the kind of thing that would make the neighbors afraid. I said I'd learned my lesson."

He hesitated, and then said, "It was especially good for me because I've tried to be a good neighbor. I went with the cat lady to look for that kitten that turned out to be a rat. And when that girl was stabbed I brought her a Ho-Ho to eat while we were waiting for the ambulance. So it was good to let people know the other side of me. The cat lady said she'd pray for me, which was very kind."

He knelt then, with unwonted awkwardness, and looked up pleadingly at Javier.

Javier took his time, sipping his soda and clinking the ice against the glistening side of the glass, before he said, "Something you want to say?"

"Yes, sir."

Another good long pause, to keep him in his place. Then Javier said, "You can speak freely."

Trash gave a quick smile, then ducked his head and said, "Thank you, sir. The only thing is, with the vest. I know it's part of the scene you were setting and the role you were putting me in, but—a friend of mine just came back from the prison system and—I don't know, what is the word, not 'racist,' but what's the thing where you pretend to be something you're not, because really you're just a privileged white person? Or I mean I am, not you, sir."

Javier considered this. "'Appropriative'?" he suggested.

"*Yes*, thank you."

Javier studied Trash's face: Trash was sincere, afraid that he was being impertinent, but also smiling a little. A sunny, propitiating smile, badly wanting to please. Other subs looked at Javier like he was a test-your-strength machine; suffering him would tell them something about themselves. Trash looked at him with sheer misplaced awe. It was a little too confusing to be a turn-on.

"I'll take it into consideration," he said, and Trash beamed in relief and admiration.

And then Javier said, "Were you jealous when you came in? Your face told a story."

Trash's smile vanished; he looked tired and miserable. "I'm sorry, sir. I'm grateful that others get to experience your discipline."

"You didn't look grateful."

And then, when Trash simply bowed his head and apologized again, Javier asked, "Did something happen?" He tried to make it sound casual, even a bit cruel, an intrusion into Trash's privacy rather than an expression of concern. He thought that might be the best way of getting an honest answer.

Trash took it like a slap. "I—it's been a long day, sir. I saw my ex this morning," he said.

"The one you let punch you in the face," Javier said, and immediately regretted it.

"Yes, sir. I'm sorry, sir."

Javier sighed. "*You're* not the one who needs to apologize for that. What happened?"

Trash lowered his head and said, "He came to my work and wanted to talk about us getting back together, and I said no *again* and also that I was working and if he wanted to be in the line he had to order something. So he ordered a tall non-fat latte with half foam. He's always had sophisticated tastes. When I used to cook for him he taught me that everything is better with beef blood and demerara sugar."

Javier shuddered. *That explains the cheesecake on my birthday*, he thought.

"The problem is that I couldn't figure out how much foam is 'half foam.' I tried, but it didn't give customer satisfaction. So then he told everybody in the line about what I like in bed. Or not bed, but you know. I—started crying, actually, and got written up for causing drama."

"Everyone cries in retail," Javier offered.

"I thought I'd get fired, but my shift manager says they can't fire me just for being a lousy lay, even though I thought that might reflect poorly on my work ethic."

"You're not a lousy lay."

Trash observed, with a hint of rebuke, "You use a lot of positive reinforcement in your domination."

Javier glared at him. *What the fuck, don't get mad at me for refusing to insult you*, he thought. But didn't say, so Trash might have a point about him.

"Make yourself useful," he said, "pick up this room and put everything away. You know where it goes."

Trash gave him a wide smile and complied. "This is why you always have me come last," he said.

Javier lifted an eyebrow. He hadn't noticed it, but he did always want to see Trash at the end of a long day. His cheerful competence as a housekeeper was soothing.

Trash picked up a green sheaf of sawtoothed leaves covered in fine hairs, and yelped in pain. "Are these *plants?*"

"Stinging nettles."

"Where do they go?"

Javier allowed himself a quick cackle. "Those can go in the seat of your underpants. Enjoy!"

"Oh no," Trash said, grimacing and shaking his reddening hand. "These must be very environmental. After all, plants are the environment. —Oh, this hurts *much* more than I thought it would."

Javier said, "Hand me that cane. You can bend over the other armchair. Shorts down, underwear up."

Trash gasped a little. "With the *thistles?*"

Javier grinned. "You can take it," he said, already hard just thinking about it, although Trash didn't seem to register the compliment.

He let Trash feel the width and weight of the cane resting against his ass. Trash shuddered hard, all the way down his body, and Javier's heart raced. He kicked Trash's feet apart a little further so he had to adjust his elbows on the armchair. He paused, and Trash quietly asked to be hit. Javier lifted the cane.

Javier had pulled him by the ear and hit him with a belt; insulted him and slapped him in the face with a wet sock; made him sing "I'm a Little Teapot" while dressed only in a hula skirt. He'd subjected Trash to condescension and exhaustion, incomprehensible demands and accurate personal criticism, and Trash had responded to it all without complaint, with an unchanging eager gratitude which Javier found utterly opaque. How do you know who a person is if you never hit his limits? The only things Trash had ever objected to were the appropriative use of "community service," and aftercare.

(Trash's perspective on aftercare: "If I want to be reassured and *coddled* I can just get therapy. Or I can't really, I'm sure my insurance doesn't cover it, but my point is, I'll do what you tell me as long as you don't expect me to feel good about myself when it's over.")

"What actually happened with you and Brandon?" Javier asked;

and let the cane slice through the air.

Trash gasped, much harder and more desperately than before, and gave a quick cry of pain. He pressed his forehead against the heels of his hands and stifled a sob. Javier was aroused: not so much by Trash's pain but by his willingness, how after the first cut he lowered his torso and spread his legs more to make himself easier to hit. How intensely he responded to Javier's every action. But there was also some concern, under the arousal, since Trash rarely cried so quickly.

"He held me to a very high standard," Trash said, sniffling. He waited, but Javier didn't hit him again, so he kept talking. "He was detail-oriented. For example, if I was chopping garlic, all the pieces had to be different thicknesses and sizes. The same thing with vegetables or chicken. So they'd cook unevenly, and there would be variety in the textures and flavors."

"*What*," Javier said, almost laughing in horror. "Okay, your ex is a monster."

He gave Trash another blow with the cane, not as hard as the first one. Trash took a few tearful breaths to recover and said, "He taught me a lot of self-improvement techniques. Like there's a thing called CBT, but it isn't what you think it is, it's a thing where you replace wrong ideas in your head with good ones. So if I was getting really down on myself and all, 'I screw up everything!', he'd teach me to think, 'No, I mostly just screw up relationships and things that require intelligence. I make a great beef cheesecake.'"

Cane again. Trash whimpered. His knees and thighs were trembling from stress.

"Go on," Javier said softly. Fighting the urge to stroke himself. Worrying that he was going to end up with a fetish for horrifying food if this conversation continued.

"He also used—visualization," Trash said, punctuating it with small gasps. His back heaved and his fingers dug into the upholstery of the armchair as he struggled for control. Javier wished Trash were talking about him instead of Brandon.

Javier struck him again, just above his thighs, where he knew it would hurt. Trash slumped forward against the armchair and sobbed.

Between deep unsteady breaths, Trash explained, "I had to picture, whenever I said something stupid, that it was like I had vomited all over myself. Use all five senses, the smell of the stupidness-vomit and the taste of it in my mouth and how disgusted other people must feel to be around me, how embarrassing it is to be publicly covered in your own vomit. It was supposed to help me think before I speak, but instead I just got used to being disgusting."

"*God*," Javier said. And he had no idea what else to say. He realized, too late, that he shouldn't have started a conversation about feelings when he was this turned on. Then he was lifting Trash and turning him so they faced each other, setting him down hard on the arm of the chair, and his hands were going everywhere with sudden helpless confused urgency.

Trash pulled back to look at him. Wrinkling his brow, he asked, "Wait, is that—sexy?"

"No!"

But that made Trash wince and nod and duck his head in humiliation, which was the last thing Javier wanted. Javier cursed himself silently as he tried to clear his head. Figure out how to fix things. None of this had been on his agenda for the scene.

"Look—I'm sorry," he tried. "It's sexy. Uh, I guess. Don't cry. I like it when you say... odd things."

Trash laughed shakily. "Yes, all my friends find my lack of intelligence amusing," he said. "I've never been sure what to think about that."

Javier touched his face then. Trash flinched, and then made himself relax. That trusting smile. Javier was startled by what it felt like to touch Trash tenderly. It *was* sexy, definitely, although that didn't seem to be the point of it. He noticed how strong Trash looked, how much he had taken that day and how visibly he was holding himself together. Trash's face was a deep red and he was gasping for breath. It should have been ugly; it wasn't.

Trash waved his hand toward the floor and slid down a little, brushed his hand against Javier's zipper, silently asking, *Should I get on my knees and get down to business?*

"Don't move," Javier said.

Trash, looking confused and a bit worried, strained his neck up to give Javier a few unexpectedly gentle kisses in a line along his jaw. Javier almost couldn't bear it. He wanted to press his mouth hard onto Trash's; he didn't want to stop what was happening.

Trash's arms came up and his hands clasped Javier's neck and shoulder. Javier always forgot, until they were together, how Trash could do anything elegantly—trained, but never seeming merely professional.

Then Trash dropped his arms and glanced at him in fear and said, "I'm sorry. You said don't move."

"You can move your arms," Javier said helplessly. Kissed him hard. "I just—"

He was grinding against Trash's thigh, he was going to completely lose it and come right there. He was trying to put his face everywhere at once against Trash's face and neck. Trash was trying to balance on the arm of the chair in a way that wouldn't hurt his caned and nettle-stung ass so much, but Javier's urgency kept knocking him off balance so he'd wince and gasp.

Javier panted, losing himself: "I just need you—"

And Trash, arching up against him, stroking his back,

bewildered: "I'm right here."

When they kissed Javier could feel Trash's ribs under his hands, his stomach trembling, his filthy t-shirt pulled up almost to his armpits. He broke away and there was that unnecessarily awestruck look, Trash gazing up at him, smiling. Javier came in his jeans.

When he'd pulled himself together a little Trash was still looking at him like that.

"Ugh, I've made your face such a mess," Trash said. "Let me up, and I'll go get a washcloth."

Panting: "Say 'please.'"

Trash laughed—a wrung-out laugh, relieved and almost harsh in its sudden brightness. "Please, sir," he said, "let me clean my *snot* off your *face*."

Maybe this is his problem: that he's addicted to forgiveness, Javier thought. *And I do not want to get addicted to being forgiven.*

Javier was pretty sure he was a good person—he'd never doubted this—but when Trash looked at him the way a good person might be looked at, he felt baffled and guilty. Trash would gaze up at him, like something out of a romance novel; and, just like in a romance novel whose author can't create believable conflict, he would feel that they were miscommunicating.

Chapter 7
I'll Never Petition to Expunge You From the Record of My Heart

June melted into July. The neighborhood's July Fourth fireworks started the last night of June, and went on for about a week after Independence Day; they all got to make fun of Caretta for hitting the floor whenever anything went bang. The Fourth itself was steamy and sticky. Des asked if Imani was going down to the Mall to see the fireworks and Miss Imani said, "I'll just stick around the neighborhood. And you should too. If you go down to the Mall you'll miss curfew."

Gosh, thanks for the reminder, Des thought. And then scolded herself for thinking it resentfully, when she should have been grateful for the help.

But the night of the Fourth Des walked through the neighborhood in a phalanx of criminal women, just like she'd said she would in the zines she made in high school. There were booms and crackles all around them, from every side. On the corners crouching men taught their little daughters to set off sparklers. Dangerous light arced right above their heads; it showered down, all white and red, close enough to touch. Men swept up the smoky fluff the fireworks left behind. The moon drifted behind haze, smoke hung along the streets, and the soft wet summer breeze moved along the skin like a lover's hand.

At the new apartment buildings huddled around the Metro people were standing on the roofs to look out over the Anacostia at the official show, but down in the streets, there were fireworks everywhere. Washington had one celebration and D.C. enjoyed her own. The city shimmered with explosions.

Ray Ray seemed to know everybody. She introduced them to a kid from that local gang who dressed like werewolves, in his leather jacket with fur at the elbows and the shoulders: her "play brother" Donatello. He complained, "Don't be calling me out my name, Ray Ray."

"I'm calling you *into* your name," she retorted. "You was born Donatello, you gon' die Donatello."

He was still insisting that she should call him D-Money when she told him if she spent another thirty seconds with him she'd violate her parole. Des made a mental note to remember this line for when she needed to duck out of dull conversations.

Fang's band, the Jon Bon Joni, played a gig July 5. They were a country outfit now, country-rap, with songs called "They Sent the Fire Trucks Again" and "Last Night I Lost the Right to Judge." Ray Ray had drawn their posters. She put them all in crop tops and Daisy Dukes, which Fang said would get them sued for false advertising when they showed up in work shirts and jeans. But in return Fang wrote a song for her, dedicated to Ty'heaven: "Is It Still Criminal Association If I See You in My Dreams?"

Because this, it turned out, was why Ty'heaven had been so tight-lipped about her location and activities. She wasn't cheating on Ray Ray, except with Uncle Sam. She had said, "I know you gonna do what you do, but I am not gonna violate my parole. If you want to fuck around, find a bitch without a felony record, because when this is over I want us to be together for real."

Ray Ray had recounted this in group, all soft and misty. She insisted that she would stay faithful if Ty'heaven did.

"And even if she don't," she confessed; Des had almost forgotten what those old-school, gallant butch girls were like, their stoic helplessness.

In their room that night she'd admitted to Des that they had texted each other, just enough times to work out that they could meet "accidentally" at Fang's shows. Texting was also prohibited by their release conditions, but so far the CSOs hadn't checked their phones.

"So I won't be totally cut off from that pussy," Ray Ray noted, her voice like a song.

Meanwhile Des was writing less and cleaning more. And trying not to think about that. She didn't want an identity as a housecleaner, but she also and more fervently didn't want an identity as somebody who didn't want to be a housecleaner.

Cleaning took up a lot more of Des's time than she'd expected. She got terrible Yelp reviews: *Arrived late, left streaks. Said layer of cat hair on curtains "serves a purpose" which is only true if you are a cat. Did not resolve fridge odor. One and a half stars.*

Not detail orientated, which made Des smugly, helplessly self-righteous.

When I asked her why the bathroom wall has a dent in it now she just said she has PTSD. I don't want to be offensive but I think she punched my wall.

Seems to think she deserves better, which is not a quality I want in a maid.

Does not accept Bitcoin, to which Des silently retorted that she didn't accept a lot of things in this life. Which, she had to admit, was maybe part of her problem.

Everything in my house looks like a felon touched it. Two and a half stars. Which Des did not think was as cute or clever as the woman who'd written it evidently did. But she had to be grateful, since it was one of her highest ratings.

It turned out that getting yelled at in prison laundries and playing mistress-and-maid with Lucinda had not prepared her for professional housecleaning as well as she'd anticipated. So she found herself spending a lot of her time watching YouTube videos about how to scrub floors, and joining Facebook groups.

Up until then, going on Facebook had felt like crashing a party where half the people were showing off their socially-beneficial children and adorable careers, and the other half were yelling about Bernie Sanders. Now she discovered the true purpose of Facebook: learning how to polish different kinds of doorknobs.

There was a group dedicated to Common Myths About Tile. There was a group where every Friday you were supposed to post a "crap shot"—mop heads in glamorous close-up, their blackened ropes held together with clumps of horror; buckets of bilge; your best shot of your family's filth. One time Desiree ended up by mistake at a page which rated kitchen tables in pornos. ("Charmingly vintage for such a kinky scene—check out the aluminum edge trim between Natasha Getchuoff's thighs!") But she also found an online course with something called "Clorox University," where she earned the right to list herself as a certified detergents professional. Her ratings began to climb toward "average."

At Work and Hygiene she suffered through the didactic jokes that the tall black pastor leading their group threw out to them with a toothy smile: "How did the man eat the airplane?"

They all shifted on their folding chairs and wouldn't look at him, so he gave them the answer: "One bite at a time, y'all. One bite at a time."

Afterward Des was telling her housemates about this and said, "The thing I want to know, though, is not how did the man eat the airplane. It's fuckin' *why* did the man eat the airplane?"

Fang shrugged. "Had to get rid of it somehow."

So Des asked Trash. She and Trash and Lizzie were walking back to the bus stop from yet another sadomasochists' brunch where nobody seemed to know anything about where Lucinda had gone, and Trash was chattering about his conceptual dom.

"He holds me to a *very* high standard," he said contentedly. "But he seems to care a lot about my emotional life. I don't get it, but I guess it is his kink?"

Des, depressed, was in no mood for Trash's misadventures in masochism. "How did the man eat the airplane?" she asked. She told the joke and gave the punchline, and then said, "But the thing I don't understand is, *why* did the man eat the airplane?"

And Lizzie, fanning herself with a pink Heritage Foundation fan with the logo TAKE BACK THE NIGHT and a pistol silhouette, shrugged her bare golden shoulders and said, "Well, somebody's got to."

At the bus stop a woman asked them for money. Des gave an uncomfortable smile; Lizzie made her lips very sad and shook her head. Trash dug into his jeans pocket and pulled out a fat fistful of bills, and handed the whole roll over.

The woman—white, with sun-baked skin—took the money in both hands, nodded intently, and said, "I can't take this."

"Of course you can," Trash said. He pressed his hands over hers, over the money. She nodded again, then shook her head.

Des and Lizzie started to shuffle past her, but Trash said, "I love your layers."

He touched his own shoulders lightly to show what he meant. Des looked at the woman more closely and saw that she had a pink washcloth draped over her head, under her panama hat, and what had looked like a purple shirt with gray sleeves was actually two t-shirts. The lower shirt was a deep purple. The woman had put her arms into the sleeves of the gray shirt but her head wasn't in the head hole. Instead she'd pulled the hem of the t-shirt up over her head and behind her neck, so it draped tightly around her shoulders.

"Turn around?" Trash said, and she did. The head hole of the gray t-shirt sat right between her shoulder blades, like a porthole onto a purple sea. She was also wearing a man's watch, thick silvery metal, like a futuristic handcuff. It slid around on her slender arm.

"Delightful," Trash said, nodding. The woman thanked him and blessed him, and headed off.

"That was nice of you," Lizzie said dubiously.

"Oh, it's just customer service," he said. "Plus she did have a *look*, you know—very Little Edie."

"I meant the money."

"Oh!" Trash shrugged. "That's all from something I wasn't expecting to be paid for."

In answer to their curious looks, he said, "I tried out to be a dancer at the Come and See. I did a Nijinsky-inspired routine, 'L'Après-Midi d'un Thong.' They were like, 'Yeah no, you're supposed to be a go-go boy, not a ballerina,' but I got to keep my tips! I think there's a fifty in there, no joke. It's a fifty that's been in my underwear, but still."

And he added, "In the words of St. Augustine, 'Easy come, easy go.'"

"I've always wondered," Desiree said, "how you occasionally know things."

Trash laughed. "Yes, I'm terrible at thing-knowing. In my defense, I was mostly homeschooled so I could focus on my skating. So I'm very," and he moved his hand in an up-and-down path, as if sketching out a mountain range. "But like... just last week I learned that there are different kinds of Muslims! Did you guys know that? Ooh, I can tell that you did. There are at least three kinds. But their names all start with *S*. I think that's so beautiful."

On the bus he rode further with her than Lizzie did. And when she was silent and staring out the window, he said, "This is maybe a dumb question, but I read a thing the other day about how people who, uh, the ex-offender community, don't always have a grasp on modern technology. So, have you tried Facebook-stalking her?"

Desiree had been perfectly capable of using Facebook before she went to prison but afterward for some reason hadn't even thought about using it to find Lucinda. So she spent almost an hour sitting at the dining-room table scrolling through the profiles of friends of friends. She put "Strange Bedfellows" on in the background. On the TV David Lav said, awkwardly, "You look lovely today."

"Oh thank you!" Lizzie trilled. "You always compliment me when I dress modestly. I'm just saying, *mmmmmmmmaybe* men respect women more when we cover up."

"I don't just compliment women I respect! I mean, uh—"

"A sleeveless turtleneck, I love this top. I can turn like this, and like this, and I can even lean way far forward—you like that, Mr. and Mrs. America?, *mhmm*—and you can't see my girls. 2016 is the year of modesty for me. Because I watched a bunch of our shows from 2014, and whoa nelly, I am bustin' out like springtime! In the one that went viral, for like half the show you can see my whole sideboob," and she turned her profile to the camera and swept her hand down the side of her turtleneck, to help the audience remember. "That's the show that got us on CNN that one time, I'm just saying. Keepin' it real."

"Fight for 15," David said firmly.

"Yes, sorry folks, our topic today: the minimum wage. I'll never have to worry about raising the minimum wage, because they'll never build a robot that can shimmy like this."

And then Des found her. She'd shortened her first name to Luce and changed her last name to Waller. She had a wife and a child, and a job at a restaurant instead of a think tank. But there was no mistaking those huge, well-meaning eyes.

The sense of accomplishment Des felt in that moment was the last one she'd get for a very long time.

Chapter 8
Jean Grey Died on the Moon

It was so hot that the chicory blossoms had shriveled up; it was so humid that a rainbow crossed the sky even though there had been no rain. On the D.C. side of Chevy Chase the nannies sweated under their kerchiefs as they pushed their strollers.

By afternoon the neighborhood was quiet. The lawnmowers came in the morning. There were no sirens; people called the police here to report fireworks, or a "suspicious person" (usually a workman). The lawn signs in former seasons had supported Carol Schwartz and David Catania, and were now all for Hillary. There were rumors that a Georgian brick house just off Chevy Chase Circle had been bought by a meth dealer, but in general the people in this neighborhood had to drive to Maryland to buy their drugs. The biggest sensation on the neighborhood Facebook group was the sighting a few months back—complete with blurry phone photos— of a legitimate, unmistakable coyote.

The Morningstar Center for Personal Restoration (For Women Only) didn't stand out on its street. It was a white colonial-style home, three stories, with an impeccable broad front lawn and a front stoop where nobody ever sat. The fence around the backyard was very high and the security system was rigorous, but these things weren't unusual in that neighborhood. The fence even had a cover of morning glories, as if it was primarily a trellis.

The top floor of the Center was an unfinished attic. It was badly-heated in winter and badly-cooled in summer, and mostly used for work and punishment. The second floor was all bedrooms: dormitory-style rooms for the women who'd earned some privileges, and the master bedroom for the cofounders, Max Lord and Trina Lawton. The ground floor was used for classes: assertiveness, anger management, job readiness, budgeting, personal grooming, appealing to men, and other life skills. The basement was unfinished and full of spiders, and it flooded in big thunderstorms and snowmelts. It held the washer and dryer, the boiler, a locked bathroom and a bucket, and six decades-old, mildewed sleeping bags for the women who hadn't earned their way to the second floor.

In the backyard there was a thing like a small greenhouse, which everyone called the Training Parlor for reasons that had been lost to time. The house-facing wall of the Training Parlor was all glass, so anyone who looked out of the windows could see Toya Tannen there, facing away from them, standing with her legs spread and her hands clasped on her shorn blond head.

She stared straight ahead. She was dressed in clothes she'd made herself: a badly-seamed blouse with a high uneven collar and sweat stains at the armpits; a thick green wool cardigan that bagged past her waist; a wool skirt in a sort of mud-green color that hung to her ankles. She hadn't made her socks, but she had made her underpants, which were stained gray wool. She didn't wear a bra.

She could feel sweat trickling and pricking the back of her neck, oozing down from her scalp. Sweat ran down her ribs and down the crack of her ass, and she could feel it on her inner thighs and calves. Now and then sweat stung her eyes and she had to blink and grimace until it stopped, or just teach herself again to endure it. The greenhouse glass trapped her under the eye of the sun.

She was almost crying. Her arms were trembling; she'd been holding them out, with the elbows crooked so she could lace her fingers on top of her head, for about three hours. Shuffling her hands on her throbbing head, adjusting her arms, hoping nobody was watching, never giving herself more than a few seconds of relief. Enduring all the familiar sensations: first cramping, then numbness in her pinky finger or her foot, then the feeling that her arms were full of needles. The little burning shiver that went all the way to her left wrist if she took a deep breath. She had cried earlier and even, for no reason she could understand, let her mouth hang open until she drooled. She hoped that when they came to get her they would think it was just sweat or snot.

Toya had met Max Lord four years ago. She had been twenty years old, living in Hyattsville and working the night shift at a CVS in Fairfax. She was standing on the platform at Metro Center at nine o'clock in the evening when the next-train board started to mix itself up. The schedule moved back five minutes; then trains started to disappear. People on the platform, piled deep, started to mutter and curse. A weary black woman's voice announced, "Attention, passengers traveling on or connecting to the Blue, Orange, and Silver Line trains. We are currently experiencing delays in both directions due to scheduled track maintenance, unscheduled track maintenance, police activity, and fire. Please allow additional time to your travel plans. Thank you for riding Metro."

The train schedule went VIENNA – 22 and then VIENNA – 50 and then, inexplicably, GEORGET – 21, and then it went black.

Toya had already been reprimanded twice for being late. When it hit her that she would probably lose her job, she burst into tears.

There were other people crying on the platform or shouting, and an animal was having some sort of breakdown, so she thought it would be safe to just squeeze past people, sink down and sit on the floor with her back against a pillar and weep.

But then a slender blonde girl with thick, pointy-arched black eyebrows sat down next to her and turned to her with a small smile that was somehow the warmest and tenderest expression Toya had ever seen. The girl asked, "Is there any way I can help?" That was Trina: Toya's introduction to Morningstar's program for the reparenting of untaught young women.

When Trina found her, Toya had been living on her own for two years. She didn't know how to choose a cell phone plan or sign up for health insurance. She had never done her taxes, she had never spent the night with someone (unless you counted the hospital staff the night her father broke her collarbone, when she was sixteen), she had never Googled. She didn't know that there was a difference between dish soap and hand soap. She had failed to make dishes such as "bowl of spaghetti" and "beans." (She had failed to make beans four times, with three different kinds of beans. Twice, with beans from cans.) She had failed to host Taco Tuesday for herself. She had not had a friend since fourth grade. When she heard what Morningstar was all about, no power in the world could have kept her from spending her last paycheck on their introductory course.

Morningstar had their own binders and pens, with their logo of one big star glowing beside a smaller inferior star; these were included when you paid for a class. Nobody had ever given Toya swag before. It felt amazingly adult, like something out of a movie, to go to the special folding table and pick up the binder and pen meant just for her. She had always fantasized about taking notes: about diligence, recognized and rewarded. She took down, with her special pen in her special notebook, what Max Lord was saying in his first lesson: "You can learn to control your own life. No longer will you feel pity for those who have hurt you. No longer will you feel longing for those who don't deserve it. No longer will you feel affection for people and habits which are useless to you. Confidence and certainty will replace anxiety and fear."

He hadn't emphasized that last sentence, but Toya underlined it.

After class all the Morningstar women hugged her, and shared with her those glowing smiles. They were lit by something deep within.

After her sixth class, Max Lord took her aside and said that he saw something special in her. He said that if she continued in the program, she could come and stay in the house. Toya, who'd had no idea how she would pay her rent, felt as though she'd swung blindly through life and somehow struck a piñata filled with hope.

Max Lord was a tall man with bad posture. (He and Trina both slumped. The women they trained all held their shoulders back and kept their spines straight. They were generous in that way: They made others better than themselves.) He was blond and balding, and he walked with a limp.

"This is my didactic limp," he would tell them. "All great teachers have a limp."

He taught that women were weak and wounded, but he could understand them, because he was weak and wounded too. "Men intimidate you," he said in his rich deep movie-star voice, which sounded so unnerving coming from a flat-faced man with snaggle teeth, "but with me you can feel safe."

He didn't pick a favorite in every class. But every now and then he would offer a place in the house to a special pupil.

Life in the house was very different from what Toya had imagined. There was still a lot of hugging—the women hugged each other after they gave criticism, and sometimes before punishment. Max or Trina could call you at any time, point you at somebody and tell you to hug her. If you were called to hug or be hugged while you were in the shower you didn't hesitate; Morningstar was a family, and when your family needs positive reinforcement, you don't stop to put on pants. They ate as a family, passing bowls of pasta and baskets of bread, touching one another's hands or shoulders to ask for the salt. Although women who behaved childishly had to sit at the kiddie table.

Toya worked about eight hours a day painting miniature fantasy gaming figures (she specialized in rare paladins) and she was grateful that Max fit in some therapy for her in her free time. He sent her out on tasks: get a paying job by knocking on doors in Congress Heights; make a friend at Wheaton Plaza. When she failed these tests he motivated her.

Eventually he had decided that she needed to bring in new clients for Morningstar. She had tried various meetups but the only group that had invited her to their next event was the sadomasochists. She described them to Max Lord and he laughed. "Sure, why not," he said. "They sound weird and desperate, so maybe you'll finally have some success."

But she hadn't. She had tried to make conversation, which was a skill Morningstar emphasized. She had tried to flirt with the one she found most attractive: She had worn a low-cut top under her cardigan, and shared an edgy, intimate memory about eating a spider. But nobody had asked her why she ate the spider, so she lost the chance to tell them more about her life-skills group.

"Oh, is there an email list?" Mistress Mariah had asked, and when Toya had eagerly said that there could be one, she'd nodded and said, "Don't put me on your email list."

Her legs were cramping. She tried to let her mind drift. It

confused her, the way Max and Trina described the task they had given her differently: Max said standing like this in the heat was meant to help her dissociate from her petty thoughts and problems. Trina just said it was punishment.

Toya worried that Trina didn't like her, because she wasn't able to put a tampon in. Trina had tried to teach her several times—she made Toya demonstrate for each new woman in the house how she couldn't get it to go in and stay in. Trina would sometimes try to find out what exactly she *could* fit in her vagina: "Do you think she can get a peanut up there? I mean an unshelled peanut. There we go. Good girl! What about a zucchini, we've always got to be looking for ways to use up our CSA. What about the handle of the toilet brush? Toya, those things are a hell of a lot bigger than a tampon!"

The other women would get into it: "Trina, give her your softball bat. Let's see if she can—"

But Trina said, "No, that thing is a souvenir. I'm not letting Toya shove that into her giant cave vagina. Who knows what she's got in there? She's got a Vag of Holding. She's got a mongoose up there! She's got that Malaysia Airlines plane up her cooch!"

And then, inevitably, "There we go, she's bawling. What's the prize for making her cry in under five minutes?"

(This was a rhetorical question. There were games where the goal was to make Toya cry, but there wasn't ever any prize; the thing was its own reward.)

"You know, Toya," Max Lord would say later, "you are self-centered. People just want to have fun and you make it all about your emotions. Crying all the time is a pretty obvious sign of immaturity. What do I tell you?"

"'Tears are the poop of the eyes,'" Toya recited.

"Now do you want to be a little poopy eye-baby?"

"No...."

"Do you need to wear a diaper on your face to catch your eye-poop?"

"No!"

"Maybe you do. ...Even right now you can't control it. You're leaking."

Outside the Training Parlor the sun was descending in burning gold and purple. Dragonflies cut in black arcs across the flaming sky. Anyone looking into the Parlor would have seen Toya, green-black and motionless against the glass. There is so much beauty in the surfaces of things.

When she was in middle school there had been a used bookstore whose owner never made her buy anything. He sold comic books as well as regular books, and when he got floppies that were too beat-up to resell, he'd let her have them for free. So in the early 2000s she'd become engrossed in the Dark Phoenix Saga. She'd memorized it; she imagined destroying worlds, eating stars, total freedom. She wept when Jean Grey sacrificed herself.

In later years retroactive continuity had its way with the Dark Phoenix Saga. There is no final death in Marvel comics, so Jean Grey lived again. She had to go out and live through endless arcs and crossovers, unresting, unsacrificed. Jean Grey's rerun resurrections became a joke. But in Toya's mind her first death was still the real one.

And in the hardest times—when she lay in the hospital trying to figure out what would happen if she told the nurses how her collarbone had been broken, or now, as she stood dizzy and shaking in the heat—Toya would think, *Maybe that happened to me too.*

Maybe she had died long ago, and none of this was real. Maybe there was a true and heroic self out there, mourned and beloved, instead of this despised enduring shadow.

Her cracked lips moved. She panted, and she repeated the

closest thing she had to a prayer: *Jean Grey died on the moon.*

The door of the Training Parlor opened behind her.

Toya didn't move until the woman behind her said, "You can put your arms down." Then she turned, she bent one leg—her skin glittering with sweat—and fainted.

The Morningstar woman let her fall.

Don't Say No

Chapter 9
He Drank Up All the Water, He Ate Up All the Soap. He Tried to Eat the Bathtub But It Wouldn't Go Down His Throat!

"Donna died!"

"How'd she die?"

"Oh she died like this," Ray Ray said, jutting her hip out and doing what Desiree thought of as the "walk like an Egyptian" pose.

"Oh she died like this," Desiree echoed her, with her hip thrust out and wrists and elbows working.

Des and Ray Ray had been out on the porch, Des with her community coffee and Ray Ray with her smoothie. Des was stroking the ivy that twined up along the porch railing, and comparing it to the plastic hibiscus in its urn. She was surprised at how soft the ivy was, and how resolutely, satisfyingly the hibiscus boinged back into place when she tugged on the blossoms and let them go.

They had complained companionably about whoever was leaving dishes in the drying rack without washing them, and established that whatever their manifest defects of character, both of them knew how to wash a fucking dinner plate, at least. Then Des had asked Ray Ray how her rehabilitative job was going, cutting grass for the National Park Service.

And Ray Ray burst up out of her chair, screaming, "Shut up about my fucking job, bitch!" She spun away from Desiree so she'd slam her fist into the solid wooden door instead of into Des's face.

Des sat there with her heart pounding and didn't say anything at all. And when Ray Ray had said, "Fuck! I'm *sorry*, I wasn't gonna hit you," Desiree said, "I'm sorry."

She had no idea how or even why she was reacting so calmly: a complete disconnect between the terrified heartbeat and the careful, peacemaking face. "It's none of my business," she said.

"You dam' right it ain't."

And then Ray Ray had sighed for a long time, and said, "I'll bring it up in group. You'll hear all the fuck about it then."

"You don't have to," Des said.

"Nigga, don't tell me what I don't have to do!"

And there'd been a pause, and Ray Ray had done this thing where she said, "Shit!", but it sounded like a laugh, shaking her head back and forth. "Don't tell Miss Imani I called you 'the N-word,'" making the quotation marks with her voice.

And Desiree said, again without any understanding of why she was saying this, "I've been meaning to ask you. When you were little, like on the playground, do you remember a thing like, 'Miss Sue, Miss Sue, Miss Sue from Alabama'?"

"...Nah, I ain't."

"Miss Lucy? 'Miss Lucy had a steamboat, the steamboat had a bell—ding, ding!'" Desiree yanked down on a phantom bellrope.

It turned out that, whether due to generational or neighborhood differences, Ray Ray didn't know any of the playground rhymes Des had grown up with: "Down by the banks of the Hanky Panky," "I don't want to go to Mexico no more-more-more," the ABC one that sometimes ended with "We got the power!" and the Black Power salute but sometimes ended, "Now you got the chicken power!" The only one they both knew was, "Donna died."

So they'd gone in together and herded all the others out onto the porch. Everyone except Miss Imani: Fang, Douceline, Caretta, and the new girl who'd taken Stephanie's place when Stephanie got a room in Days of Dice and Roses Urban Senior Center. The new girl's name was Zita. She was light-skinned and she had a heart-shaped face and she was barely twenty-one. Ray Ray and Des took seriously their task of handing on their traditions to the youth.

"Donna living," Ray Ray called.

And Des obliged: "Where's she living?"

Both of them together sang, "Oh she's living in a place called—Tennessee! She wears short-short dresses up above her knee!"

They did the whole chant and ended, in unison, "She never went to college, she never went to school! But I found out she was a educated fool." (Except that Des said "an," which wasn't how she'd learned it.)

And then they looked at one another warily. Each of them felt that she was being somehow covertly mocked.

But the others wanted to learn. To learn the new playground chants, and teach the ones they knew, and figure out which songs they all held in common. So the morning that had almost started with a beatdown turned into all six of them standing out on the porch in a line, yowling, "Stop! In the Name of Love," and doing all the hand signs.

"I think you're being unfair," Trash said. "I don't mean to be critical, but there's a pattern where you tend to dislike all my boyfriends. It's nice, in a way, since it's not like I'm going to be bringing them home to my mom, but in a way it's also not nice."

"Oh my God," Lizzie said. "I have disliked exactly two of your boyfriends: the one who *punched* you, have we forgotten this?, and the one who literally told you you don't deserve to be loved."

"Nobody deserves to be loved," he said.

"What happened to Hot Cop?" Lizzie asked. "I liked him. Or I liked his profile pic."

"Oh no, Hot Cop was a donut too far for me," Trash said. "I woke up one morning on his porch with my hands zip-tied behind my back. I was like, 'Ooh, I feel like we have political differences, probably.'"

Lizzie rattled the menu. "It says here the macaroni and cheese comes with *dog-foraged* truffles. Do you think it's literally a dog, like, 'woof-woof'? I feel like dogs are patriotic and macaroni and cheese is patriotic, but putting them too close together may be a mistake."

Trash, uncharacteristically, pursued his own agenda rather than being distracted by others' concerns. "Anyway, Javier is selfless," he said. "You know how everybody likes their own smell, you can sit around and sniff your farts and things? Well, he likes the smell of *other people's* sweat and farts and old socks. He told me to do a full workout in the same clothes for a week and then give him the clothes, and last time when I went over there he had my socks on his pillow. He cares about me."

"He cares about your socks, at least," Lizzie said. "Why are you defending him, when he treats you like *goo?*"

"Ooh, speaking of other people's smells," Des said; the Little Shorn Lamb had just come in.

"Somebody needs to talk to her about that," Lizzie said, in a voice that made it clear she was designating this as somebody else's problem.

"Why are you looking at me," Des said.

"Trash can't do it because he's male and it's tacky. I can't do it because I don't want to."

"What am I going to tell her? 'Women in federal prison smell better than you'?"

"Oh, that's good," Trash said, "you can empathize with her because you've also been in a situation where your personal grooming was very... difficult, for whatever reason. Maybe she's allergic to deodorant, and you can share some tips and tricks from your time away. I read this thing about how women make hair dye and mascara in prison."

"I did not use any tips or tricks to make my own deodorant. We bought from the commissary. Two-ninety for a mini and all they ever had was Right Guard. In a *women's* institution. I was musky as fuck," Des reminisced.

"Ooh, oddly sexy," Lizzie said. "I'd be into that if it was Old Spice, I think."

"My point is that we tried. If she isn't even trying then nothing I can say will make a difference."

"I think she likes us, is the problem," Trash said. "Which makes her our responsibility. She likes you, specifically."

"Ugh, what did I do to deserve this?"

Des spent half that Sunday's brunch trying to come up with the humblest possible way of telling Toya that she smelled. Eventually she decided this was an impossible task. She also didn't want to do it; but this, she decided, shouldn't worry her. She had to put her humility first.

The next day was Lucinda's day off. She had agreed to meet up with Des for lunch at Off the Record. Lucinda got a free thing because she was industry; this turned out to be a pickle platter. Pickled grapes, pickled plums, pickled eggs, pickled horseradish, pickled regular radish, pickled watermelon rind, and something identified only as "wild pickle," which appeared to be flowers. It tasted about how you would imagine pickled flowers to taste. Des had to admit that the pickled grapes were great but by the end of the platter her mouth was turning inside-out from sourness. She felt that they were eating a metaphor for their late relationship.

Lucinda looked different. Her face was carved down, her arms muscled; her breasts seemed bigger and saggier. She seemed to have more moral heft. She'd kept her short haircut but instead of looking angular and troubled—the artsy haircut of someone who was tapering her meds—it looked momlike. She looked like one of those hetero married moms who look like butch lesbians.

From Lucinda's expression when they greeted each other Des must have looked different too, but not in a good way.

"So," Des said, "cooking. The life of a chef."

"I'm not a chef," Lucinda said immediately. "I'm a line cook."

"How do you like it?"

"I *love* it. I'm the worst cook in my kitchen—it's amazing. I've never been the worst person at my job before."

Des, who was pretty sick of being the worst housecleaner in the DMV, made what she hoped was an encouraging noise. She pushed her fork around to hide things under the watermelon rind.

"You know how I hated working at the Institute for White Papers," Lucinda said, although Des hadn't known. "I was so good at it, and everyone always asked me to write more—I'd mention that I grabbed a Slurpee the other night and they'd say I should do an analysis on whether late-night impulse buying offsets the social stratification of gentrifying neighborhoods. There was no way I could stay clean and sober in that job."

"How did you pick what you wanted to switch to?"

"I took a course," Lucinda said, and there it was: the evangelical entreaty in her eyes. The hopeful desire for Des to *understand* and agree and conform. Des swallowed a pickled grape whole and nearly choked.

When she'd recovered, Lucinda explained, "I took a meditation course at a place called the Center for Silence in the Public Interest. This was maybe a year after I'd met Midori, and we were talking about marriage, having a baby. I was restless; I wasn't sure I liked what was happening to my life. Objectively I could see that things were much better than when I was with you, but it was hard to imagine that I would still be me if I gave up all my bullshit. But then in the silence I let go of my opinions—which were my job, you know, this was a real sacrifice—and I let go of this idea that I had a self that I should care about. I gave up my brand. And when I came home that night I locked my Twitter and sent in my resignation and went out to find a restaurant that needed somebody in a hurry."

"And now you're the worst person at your job," Des said, "and happy."

She poked at what she was feeling and was gratified to find that she wasn't insulted. She mostly just felt tired.

"Yeah—it means I'm always learning. I feel like my whole *being* is a muscle, and every day it can work harder."

"I know I owe you amends," Des said, "if there's ever anything I can do for you."

Lucinda reached for the bread then, and Des noticed for the first time that her hands and forearms were striped with burns. Suddenly she shivered. For the first time since prison she felt it: She was shaken and claimed by sexual desire, that feeling like a fist that yearns. It had been so good to be under Lucinda's hands when they were smooth; her heart raced as she imagined being touched by them as they were now.

"It wasn't just you," Lucinda said. "We were chatterers and dilettantes. We made the world worse."

"I think it's more that we were drug addicts," Des said, which once she'd said it didn't seem like a great defense.

"Half the guys I work with now are drug addicts," Lucinda retorted. "But they're not assholes. Or—they are assholes, okay. But they're not assholes for the public good. They don't think it's their civic duty to be an asshole, to shit their opinions all over everything. And when they look down at their work they see something other than their own faces."

"I liked seeing your face in your research," Des said. "I liked seeing the world through your preoccupations. It was poetic."

Lucinda was eating something called "shaved buffalo" now. She set it on top of her ragged bread. Blood soaked into the butter. The burns on her forearms looked like she'd been lashed by a tiny dominatrix. She sucked butter off the meaty part of her thumb.

That night Des was in the kitchen, shivering from the air conditioning, drinking orange soda out of the Pizza Hut E.T. glass and making pasta with garlic and peanut butter. Fang was eating at the kitchen counter and filming herself on her phone; her vocational rehab class required the ex-offenders to play videos of their table manners in class so they could receive feedback on how they fed.

Ray Ray and Caretta had been pointing out where she should aim the camera: "You got some bits of turkey there. Show 'em your turkey on the floor." Now they were talking about how Des always ate healthily, and it must cost a lot. It was a way of sounding like they admired her while actually judging her.

Zita was rinsing her own dishes and putting them in the dish rack. Des reached for a plate and, pulling it out, realized that it was still covered in sticky bits of food.

It was you! she thought, just like a murder mystery, and she turned toward Zita. A triumphant outrage filled her: She had accomplished something by detecting the culprit, *and* she now had the moral high ground.

So she wasn't sure why, when she spoke, her voice was light and ditzy. "Oh, it's not completely clean," she said, holding up the plate.

"It don't always get clean," Zita explained. "I don't know why. I think these plates is no good."

Des, still sounding fluff-brained, wafted out, "Oh, you have to scrub them."

She demonstrated. One good strong scrub. The plate was now clean.

Zita said, "Huh, I never seen that before. I'll try that next time."

Desiree turned away so Zita wouldn't see her look of abject bafflement. Ray Ray was laughing and maybe about to start some shit, when all at once they heard gunshots from the street out front.

The shots were loud and somehow penetrating, like a physical blow to the chest, and they echoed through the kitchen. Caretta shrieked. She and Fang and Ray Ray all jumped out of their chairs; Fang and Ray Ray crouched down behind the kitchen counter and Caretta pressed herself full-length against the floor.

A bullet broke the front window and buried itself in the piano. Its strings hummed.

Outside they could hear shouting and the howls of the wolfmen.

"Oh, shit! Oh shit!" Caretta yelled. "That time it was bullets! Y'all always be telling me it ain't bullets but this time it was! Oh Jesus!"

Nobody else said anything.

Sirens; flashing red and blue lights across the fainting couch and the bookshelves and the piano, all the pale rose and gold upholstery of the parlor. "Dem boys," Ray Ray said unnecessarily.

Miss Imani came out of her first-floor office.

Des, still not knowing why she was doing things, padded over to the window with the bullet hole and looked out. She could hear shouting but she couldn't see any people.

Then three figures ran downhill along the street, black capes streaming out behind their narrow forms. One had long black hair and that streamed as well.

Well, I'm definitely not going to tell my mother about this, Desiree thought.

Ray Ray came up alongside her and peered out the window, standing so she couldn't be seen from outside. Caretta was already on her phone, telling them what Twitter was saying: This was a vendetta between a black gang who dressed like werewolves, and a Latino gang who dressed like vampires. "I don't want to be in a war!" she wailed.

"It's not a war," Des said with some scorn.

"It's kind of a war," Ray Ray said. "It's not a peace."

"I'm just glad all of you are safe," Miss Imani said.

"Whoever was 'posed to clean this floor didn't do it," Caretta observed, fussing with her clothing. "I just swept the floor for you with my face."

Desiree muttered, "I was going to do it tonight. I still have plenty of time, it's a *weekly* chore."

"I got a corn chip stuck in my eyelashes."

"I didn't realize your face was gonna be on the floor before I had a chance to clean it. I don't feel like I could have predicted that."

Caretta extracted the corn chip, strode into the parlor, and regally held it out to Des. "Here. You can get started now."

"It took you longer to walk over here and hand that to me than it would to just throw it away," Des said.

Douceline, leaning down from the second floor over the banister, called out, "Let me announce to you all that I just went in the bathroom up here, and somebody has spattered blood all over the toilet seat, and smeared it on the wall, and left it somehow on the ceiling. That girl with the dandelion looks like she got caught in *The Purge.* So let's not pretend that the werewolves are the only antisocial elements in this neighborhood. I don't know how some women manage to be antisocial with their—"

Miss Imani played a loud chord on the piano. Desiree muttered, "Just *some* women?"

Des and Ray Ray came down to the parlor early for group counseling, and they settled down—Des on a high-backed armchair that turned out to be stiffer and more confining than she'd expected, so she kept squirming and leaning sideways over the arm; Ray Ray sprawling on the fainting couch. Everyone always wanted the fainting couch, and Des had been trying to decide if she was going to be selfless about it when Ray Ray had plunked herself down and rolled over onto her belly to claim her place.

They tried reading, but both of them found that their attention kept wandering.

"What you got there?" Ray Ray asked.

Des held up the copy of *Tikkun* she'd taken from her parents' basement. "Magazine," she said.

Ray Ray made an eloquent face. "I can see that, yo," she said. "I'll trade you."

Des shrugged and handed the magazine over. She'd been trying to read an article about "the politics of meaning" but it was three pages without a single concrete noun. "We ourselves must meet the spiritual demand of our hopes," like an apparatchik at prayer. The author left the impression that G-d had not fulfilled the production quotas.

Ray Ray had been reading a novel titled *Kingpin Bitch.* The front cover looked like a '90s sex thriller, but with Sharon Stone replaced by Gabrielle Union. Des flipped through the book and noted that Ray Ray had underlined and dog-eared the pages. Then her eyes widened as she began to read.

It was the most bizarrely-structured book Desiree could recall. The author, one "Slim Red," moved freely between how-to discussions of hustles and scams, girl-on-girl porn, and inspirational mottos. A highly emotional flashback in which a drive-by shooting took the life of the main character's girlfriend was followed by a sex scene involving words like "slurping"; Ray Ray had dog-eared that page, as well as a page with detailed instructions on tax fraud. But on the tax-fraud page what she'd underlined was, "Don't just hustle for the paper. Hustle for your woman and get that blessing."

"This a religious magazine?" Ray Ray asked, from the fainting couch.

"It's Jewish," Des said, turning her voice up at the end to indicate the coexistence of faith and doubt. And then, more securely, "I'm Jewish."

"I never took you for a religious person," Ray Ray said, with a certain respect. Des couldn't help but feel insulted.

This feeling of insult perhaps explained Des's unwonted self-assertion during group therapy. Miss Imani explained that in this session, the women would explore how to avoid "criminal thinking and antisocial behavior."

Des asked, with some truculence, "Why are we assuming that being criminal is always antisocial?"

Imani looked at her. "What service to the community do you suppose you might perform by doing crimes?"

Caretta had gone to prison for killing her stepfather, but Des didn't feel that she could bring up other people's histories.

"Tell me how you're going to demonstrate humility by sniffing drugs or shooting up," Imani continued.

"There's something honest about shooting up," Des argued. "Like at that point you can't pretend you're not who you are."

Ray Ray snorted.

"Nobody here agrees with you on that," Imani pointed out. "But I will say that if you'd like to share some self-knowledge about how other people's antisocial behavior and criminal thinking affected your life, we can do that too. I'm not trying to place all the blame just on you."

"I wasn't trying to avoid *blame*," Des sulked. What she'd been trying to avoid was self-knowledge.

The others seemed to enjoy group sessions. They liked getting the chance to talk through their problems and resolve the past. They described their dreams, while the other women picked at their nails or fiddled with their braids; they theorized and opined on the subject of their own souls. Only Des never had anything to say.

Today she retreated into her usual silence, as the other women took Miss Imani's suggestion and shared their memories of abuse and betrayal. Des remembered her childhood as a tapestry of golden afternoons and stupid cruelty—but all the cruelty was her own, not other people's. She had only good memories and shame.

She had thought that dwelling on her own failures was the humble thing to do, but they had an over-sweet, caramel taste in her mind, and she realized she was indulging in self-pity. Feeling sorry for herself because she lacked a history of powerlessness. She herself was responsible for all her memories.

I've had a good life, she thought. Trying to haul herself from self-laceration into gratitude. She smiled as she remembered: the letter she'd received at summer camp, in an envelope her friend Quantiya had adorned with a colored-pencil drawing of Jimi Hendrix smoking a fat blunt. Playing crack ho with her school friends, hiding under the battered metal slide on the playground so they could suck rock candy and hug each other. (They weren't too clear on what either prostitution or drug abuse entailed.) Tasting a perfect Long Island iced tea—burnished and shimmering, when Lucinda made them they didn't taste like alcohol at all, they were just cola with secret plans—and feeling the long bad night ahead start to smoke in her veins. Singing "The Old Main Drag" at the top of her lungs in the hallways of Lucinda's apartment building; proving she could run in high heels.

A good life. But a bad sign, she realized, that all those happy memories were about drinking or drugs, or the image of drinking and drugs. The image of a life she ended up living all the way down.

These are memories of friendship, she argued to herself, and that was true. But it was as if all her friendships and her love affairs had a secret third member: as if she stood on one side of a marble statue, and her friend stood on the other, and they both kissed the cold perfect cheek and called that love.

Miss Imani wanted her to contribute.

"She never want to," Ray Ray pointed out. "You can make her try, but she don't got anything useful to say."

"Ranae."

"I ain't mean it in a bad way! Maybe she don't have nothing. Sometimes I wonder what's the point of talking about how people hurt you. It don't really explain nothing. People hurt everybody, but we the only ones in this room."

Imani nodded, like she'd heard this before. "We're here to have epiphanies. A dramatic realization about our past, that has the power to change our future."

Ray Ray grinned then, that grin like liquor: "I got one. Is it okay if I just say this? I always been like this. If it be a fight, a woman, a crime or whatever: When the gun's in my hand, I don't say no."

She shrugged. What else was there to say?

Chapter 10
You Should Be Grateful

July melted into August. The city lay within a sweaty fist that would clench slowly around it until the summer storm would come and huge white feathers of rain would sweep through the air and scour the place. Then the next day the city would lie balmy in relief, on furlough, as the relaxed upcurling fingers of the hand began to close again.

Des sweated out her cleaning gigs in the apartments of elderly people who couldn't afford to fix their air-conditioning. Crawling all over king-size mattresses to bleach their urine stains, as the old people muttered grimly, hoping she would soak up some of their shame. Then staggering under the huge mattress, disappearing under its saggy bulk, as she struggled to turn it. Its owner saying, "Hey! Hey, girl, you be careful how you turning that thing. You almost knocked my mama's photograph down."

Old people's apartments were harder because the old people were usually still in them; but also easier, because Des felt sorry for them and so she didn't judge the streaks of shit in the shower or the empty liquor bottles hidden behind the dresser, in back of the TV, beneath a wide-skirted doll intended to hide the toilet paper. Des felt that she was doing research for some as-yet-unspecified writing project: color schemes of the 1970s, the burnt-orange afghan on the faded avocado couch; racial differences in where people hide their antidepressants. She had never before considered how much "social observation" journalism relied on self-righteousness.

Her nightmares changed. From nightmares about drinking she shifted to nightmares where she kept planning to drink, hiding bottles, but never managed to take that first gulp. Hiding bottles in rattling, shaking trains where everybody in the cabins had killed somebody; hiding bottles in rickety shacks in small towns where everybody was a secret vampire. (What was strange was how she always knew, the whole time, what awful secret the other people were hiding. It never occurred to her to wonder what they knew about her.) She'd wake up sweating on top of her bedsheets and identify the genre: Agatha Christie, Stephen King. The Angela Carter nightmare was a good one. She lived inside a Venus flytrap and somehow she also was the flytrap, her throat stretched and gaping red, and she also was its prey. She woke up feeling disgusted and aroused, and wary of plants.

All these prison dreams. There was the flytrap one, and the humiliatingly on-the-nose one where she was a moth trapped in a glass bottle. *Why am I always an insect?* she'd thought when she woke up, and as if in answer, the very next night she'd been a spider mummied up in its own web.

There was the noir one where she was running from the woman she'd framed (why and how did the barred shadows of venetian blinds follow her when she was leaping from rooftop to rooftop?) and the pornographic one where she was a teenage boy waiting to be birched for low marks. Waiting in the drifting, hazy August heat, in the stark institutional corridors, standing facing the tiled wall yellowed from generations of caught schoolboys' breath. The door to the Headmaster's study opened and Des the delinquent boy gasped, his heart pounding; but only the Headmaster's thick-veined hand crawled out, to turn on the hallway lights against the growing dusk. Miserably Des lowered his head and tried to compose himself and prepare again for his well-earned punishment. With a wretched breathy laugh he thought, *The waiting is really starting to get to me*; and Des the middle-aged woman, on the verge of waking, tried to tell him that it was designed to.

Early August marked a small milestone: At Work and Hygiene Des took a sincere note. A dark-skinned man, who had served fifteen years for shoplifting somewhere down South, said in a deep slow voice, "I'm just trying to figure out how to have self-respect without ego." She wrote that down on the back of a receipt for a urine test and stuck it in Jabez Pruitt's *Custodian of Souls*.

Then they played bingo on cards printed with "ex-offender excuses," and the shoplifting guy won a $5 CVS gift card.

Des completed her various worksheets for Work and Hygiene: the one where she had to circle which expectations were unrealistic, the one where she had to check off which characteristics of institutionalization she displayed. This structured self-confrontation turned out to be much less awful than the limitless kind she'd experienced in prison, the inescapable hours running your mind over what your future might hold and what you'd fucked up in your past. Questionnaires and worksheets had rules and limits. They were safe, sane, and... well, not consensual, but what is?

When they handed out the worksheets she held the paper to her face and sniffed it, but times had changed, life had moved on, and there was no acrid, rainlike scent of blue ditto ink, the most nostalgic smell in the world.

*   *   *

At the first sadomasochists' brunch of August Trash was uncharacteristically gloomy, since he'd broken up with the "conceptual dom" who'd made him dress up like a clown.

It started because Trash was trying to find a new place to live. "It's gotten to the point where every time I hear gunfire I think, 'Oh thank God, my rent won't go up this month,'" he said. The "conceptual dom" ordered Trash to list him as a reference when he applied to rooming houses.

"Which is—in this housing market that's a lot to ask," Trash said, "but I try not to have boundaries. So that was all right. But then he said, 'Let me tell you who to vote for,' and at that point I knew I had to say no. He said it didn't matter, it was purely symbolic since D.C. always goes big for the Democrats, but I was like, 'If symbols don't matter then why did you make me dress up like a clown?'"

Lizzie admitted, "I still don't really get why he did that myself."

After brunch Des headed over to the Community Supervision field office. As she got off the bus an old man caught her eye and said, with a covert grin, "Hiya, cute white girl."

Desiree looked him in the eye and said, "Good Lord, you have low standards. Love yourself."

The fat young dude hanging out on the bus bench behind him burst out laughing at that. He and Des grinned at each other and in a deep rumbling voice he said, "Careful, sweetness."

And as they tipped laughing mistrustful neighborly smiles at one another she felt a lot better about being an ex-offender under community supervision. This feeling lasted right up until she learned that she had new release requirements.

Des's Community Supervision Officer sounded as annoyed by the new rules as Des was: "So every day I'll need you to email me a list of your accomplishments, with one item highlighted as your

'Achievement of the Day.'"

"Like here's a list of toilets I scrubbed, this toilet was my favorite?"

Des had brought her "Be Good" glass from Love's Labors and filled it with water from the women's room sink, in advance of her drug test. The water tasted yellow and sort of woolly.

Her CSO switched to a voice of professional and distancing apology: "This is policy."

Des didn't say anything.

"I also wonder if you've considered wearing a uniform."

Des drank warm, woolly water. Her back ached, and she shifted in her seat—this wasn't a good idea, they'd told her in reentry prep that if you shift around you look shifty, but the combination of manual labor and a soft mattress was brutal.

Her CSO prompted her: "What are some of the advantages of wearing a uniform in your work?"

"It would make it easier to tell who I am. In case I have clients who get confused and think I might be their wife, or their kid. So far I haven't had clients like that though."

"Clarity about your role," the CSO said, nodding. Des noted with disappointment that she'd gotten a better-fitting blouse: no more distracting gaps between the buttons. "That's one benefit. What are some others?"

Des sipped, and pulled at the front of her own blouse with her other hand. The office was still not air-conditioned, and the windows didn't work. A fan was thumping in the corner, but it was pointing at the CSO, not at her. She glared around the yellowed office, with its scuff marks and dirty corners, and thought that she should offer to give the whole place a professional cleaning. Wearing clothes she chose for herself, because that was a thing you were supposed to be able to do once you were out of prison.

But then she sighed angrily. *In every decision you make, you must ask: What is the most humble thing to do?*

"One advantage of wearing a uniform," she said carefully, "is that I don't want to do it at all, and so doing it would display humility. Uh, if you can display humility. I mean if it stays humility once you've displayed it. And if something can be humble if you're only doing it to satisfy your supervised-release requirements, which also seems super sketchy to me."

"What I'm hearing is that meeting your requirements is important to you," the CSO said. "If you were considering colors, would you prefer orange and teal, or navy and peach?"

"Is that *legal?*"

"I'm on your side here," the CSO said, fanning herself with Des's file. "I can't be on your side if you won't be on it yourself."

"And I am on your side," Des said, "which is my side. Which is the orange and teal side, apparently. Could I have another glass of water?"

"Ah, you're so much like my daughter," the CSO said fondly. "Always trying to delay with another glass of water or a story before bed. Come on, let's go to the toilets."

"Yeah, when they said women always go to the bathroom together I don't think this is what they meant," Des muttered. But she got up; as her black polyester pants pulled away from the seat she felt sweat cooling at her crotch and ass.

"Think of it from my perspective," the CSO suggested. "I have to do this ten times a day. I spend more time in the bathroom than a pregnant woman with a fetish for grout."

When Des had pulled her pants and underwear down, held her blouse up with her hand and made a 180-degree turn in front of her CSO, and when she'd sat down on the toilet and managed to get a stream of pee going, the officer said, "So what do you think about when you're not doing anything?"

"Sorry?"

"When you aren't focusing on anything. Or when you are focusing, what distracts you?"

This was obviously some kind of diagnostic. Des wondered if the protocols said it had to be administered while she was pissing. She considered several possible answers: arguing in her head about whether Willow and Tara should've paid Buffy rent in season six; carefully framing answers to her parents' eternal hopeful question, "What are you working on these days?"; keeping the running tally of times Fang had washed her long-ass hair and forgotten to clear the fucking shower drain. She decided to go for something that might make her sound creative and unusual.

"I have a sort of story I tell myself," she said, yanking on the one-ply toilet paper and rolling it into a ball in her hand. She'd read somewhere that butches were folders—an efficient number of sheets of toilet paper, neatly folded—and femmes were environmentally-unsound wadders. "I'm a swimmer, I have a tortured relationship with another swimmer because of some awful stuff I said about her in the press, but eventually she becomes my coach and we go to the Olympics, where I win bronze."

"Only bronze?"

Des wrote her ID number on the label of the sample cup and flushed. "Like, I can't swim. Olympic bronze seems pretty great for somebody who can't personally swim."

"People often develop maladaptive daydreaming in prison," her CSO said with sympathy. "Especially if they spend a lot of time in solitary."

Des, buttoning up and adjusting her clothes, pointed out, "I've been doing this since I was in middle school, though."

Her CSO nodded. "Well, that too."

They walked out into the hallway; the CSO held the door for Des, which was unexpected and made her feel obscurely guilty. So she offered, "I think about, I don't know, the smell of the chlorine. The different shades of turquoise and the way the light plays on the water. What it's like to give interviews about how you placed last, right after you get out of the water and you're still gasping so your voice is all high and breathy. How different people would react to me, like, I'm on the cover of the *Advocate*, if that's still around. My comeback."

They were almost at the elevators. The CSO was looking at her the way authority figures always looked at Des now if they weren't just exasperated.

"Bronze, though," she said, with something like sorrow.

"I was grateful to win Olympic bronze," Des said mulishly. "I didn't feel like I had lost."

She was waiting for the bus, munching a banana and idly trying to figure out why she should be grateful for her backache. This was a game she'd started playing in prison: You Should Be Grateful. The only rule was that you had to figure out some reason you owed (the universe? Des hadn't bothered to ask whom) gratitude for whatever you were currently miserable about. So, for example, you should be grateful for insomnia, since at least it isn't nightmares. That one could work the other way around as well. You should be grateful for the C.O.s' contempt, because it's all stuff you would say in your own head anyway and now you don't have to—you can outsource your self-loathing. You should be grateful for fear; it burns calories.

She knuckled the muscles alongside the base of her spine and wondered if it was cheating to try to relieve the pain while she was still trying to be grateful for it. She was sitting on a low brick wall outside somebody's house. The owner had embedded rough upward-thrusting triangular rocks into the top of the wall, probably to keep people from sitting on it while they waited for the bus.

It was late morning, after a group session with the women who didn't work until later in the day and also Ray Ray, who had called in sick. They'd been sharing work woes. Caretta wanted to know if it was normal for your supervisor to tell you to roll your skirt up at the waistband so the hem hit your thighs. "He said all the females in the upward mobility program got to have higher hems," she said.

Miss Imani said she'd make a few calls.

Fang told them that somebody had broken into the wild bird shelter and stolen a great horned owl.

"Who steals a helpless owl?" she asked. "Like I know you're always telling us, 'To compare is to despair,' but I have to say, I stole a lot of shit but never a living being. You have to be an animal to steal an animal."

Then Ray Ray was explaining why she'd called in sick. Ray Ray worked cutting grass for the National Park Service. She'd started off on a bad foot, since all the other workers had at least associate's degrees in landscape arts if not master's degrees in applied environmental philosophy. Ray Ray could run a mower as well as any of them, but that made it worse, not better.

She'd been making headway, though, proving herself. Last month she'd overheard two of the other women chatting about her in the bathroom: about how exposure to "Park Service culture" was training her in civic virtue.

"Upkeep in a *park* brings uplift to the *heart*," one of them said contentedly.

"We do more with less," the other replied—this was a refrain in the era of budget cuts and deferred maintenance. Ray Ray wasn't thrilled to be the "less," but at least people weren't locking their lockers at her anymore.

The thing was, a week ago nobody had been able to find a work order. Ray Ray, acting solely for the benefit of America's parks, and with (she thought) understandable pride in the reputation of her team and outrage at the incompetence of others, had kicked up a huge fuss because the forms hadn't been faxed over.

"I used the term, 'Y'all fool-ass fools,'" she admitted.

All of this went over big with her coworkers. Ray Ray had been a hero. There was only one problem: The very next afternoon she'd found the work order in her locker, under the motivational letter about how laziness by Park Service employees spreads Zika.

For days Ray Ray smoldered with guilt and fear. She rolled up the forms and hid them under her pant leg, and then under her pillow, where they gave her nightmares. She was sick with misery.

At last she resorted to asking the women of Love's Labors for advice. (She hadn't asked Des, because who would?) She'd pointed out that her boss had backed her up to the federal office, and would lose face if Ray Ray admitted fault on their end. The women had laughed at her—she recounted this with indignation, and Des professed silently that she would not have laughed—and told her to make it look like the work order had vanished by accident. Douceline suggested she leave the forms on the floor near the bathroom, where somebody would be sure to find them; Caretta, more excitable, said she should burn them and eat the ashes.

What she had done instead was to slide the forms into the locker of one of the other lawnmowers. This way, she thought, the forms would be found, the grass would get cut and mosquitoes evicted much faster than if new forms had to be requested, and nobody would have any idea how the order could have wound up there so nobody would get in trouble.

"Lord have mercy," Caretta said. "That is not what we told you to do!"

"You told me to eat that joint!" Ray Ray protested.

Douceline shook her head. "And you somehow managed to find a solution even worse than that one."

So now the other lawnmower had been fired—not actually for losing the work order but for "her attitude" when she was scolded after turning it in.

"If I say I did it," Ray Ray said, "it won't even necessarily be that she gets her job back. If she do, she'll hate me. And if she do hate me it won't even matter because I'll be fired from a job I need to stay out of prison."

Having laid out the situation she asked, "What should I do?"

Imani's voice was gentle. Against the background of Ray Ray's anguish it was either consoling or obscene, depending on how you chose to take it: "What do *you* think you should do?"

Ray Ray just stared, miserable, with her lips pressed tight together. And Des suddenly recognized the situation. It was the worst moment: the moment when you realize that you are choosing. As soon as you realize you are about to make a choice you know which one you have to make. The only way to get away with things was to hide them from yourself, skid into them, run off the cliff before you looked down. *When the gun's in my hand, I don't say no.*

Des had gone through life avoiding unbearable pain by living always in the "already": Don't look down at your hand until the gun is already there. (Not a gun in her case, but pretty much anything else.) In the end that had not turned out to be a permanent solution to the problem of self-knowledge.

And so, waiting at the bus stop, she asked herself: If she were Ray Ray, would she have hidden the file? She actually thought, probably not. It was a specific kind of dishonesty she would find very hard to conceal from herself, and also she thought maybe she would've realized that it wouldn't work. But having hidden the file, would she come clean? That was a harder question.

It was possible to choose wrongdoing. But it felt so, so awful. That was one of the parts of adulthood nobody warned you about— the way doing the wrong thing on purpose would start to make you feel wretched instead of gleeful. Des had managed it in the past only by being convinced of her own helplessness.

The bus pulled in, a welcome distraction. On the bus she stared out the window and noticed how bad her eyes had gotten. It made the city surreal, edged with a comic-book menace: A yellow banner near Eastern Market read, APES FOR RENT. Down by Gallaudet, a storefront promised SELFHOOD, WINGS AND MORE! A bus passed by them going the other way, and in the ad along its side, a lush toothy smile was adorned with a cartoon speech bubble reading, "I LOVE D.C." DEATH SAYS.

She'd been able to work out the first two for herself—apartments; seafood, which was especially disappointing since Des would finally be in the market for some selfhood if it came with wings. But the cartoon killer smile she couldn't understand at all.

She was able to read a church sign, on a church next to a library: ANY BOOK CAN CHANGE YOUR MIND BUT ONLY THE BIBLE CAN CHANGE YOUR HEART, which struck her as a bit passive-aggressive. The bus passed a new apartment building, with a drag queen's huge face all silver lipstick on the sign: WELCOME TO THE G SPOT, A LGBT-FRIENDLY LIVING EXPERIENCE IN THE HEART OF WASHINGTON. On the next corner somebody was being evicted. A couch, a dresser drawer spilling clothes, the neighbors serenely plundering. A kitchen playset in pink and purple, which an old man rocked back and forth as if checking its structural soundness.

At her transfer stop she glanced at the electronic display that usually said when the next bus was coming. Instead it just said, "Due to police activity," with a comma. She watched it but it didn't change.

"It's been saying that for days," said a Hispanic woman with her groceries on her head.

Des felt that if any entity should not be allowed to become a metaphor for her life, it was the D.C. Metro system.

She was on her way to have visitation with her cat, and to be reassuring at her parents. They were both in the country at the same time so it was an opportunity not to be missed. Her mother was an internationally-recognized poet, whose latest collection explored her experience of visiting her daughter in prison, through the metaphor of a series of donuts with inexplicable and disgusting fillings. A donut filled with bolts and screws, in a poem turning on "screw" as prison slang for a CO; a donut filled with used condoms, which Des thought was unfair, as she neither smuggled drugs nor risked pregnancy; a donut filled with hope, which made you hungrier the more you ate it.

Des's father was a legal theorist. He had just gotten back from Athens, where they'd given him an award for his work on need-based property rights. He was renowned in his profession, in part because he was so good at deploying concepts like "need," the parsing and limiting of which could fill several subsidiary theorists' careers. He'd received a medal from the Theoretical Workers' Party of the Republic of Georgia, *The Gramscian* had him as No. 36 on their list of "Eighty Marxists Under Eighty," and *Prolix* magazine had named him a "Deep Thinker—Second Class."

No one in her family knowingly broke laws. They did not illegally download music. They did not serve the underage. (Words like "underage" rarely entered their personal lives.) They were temperate, thoughtful people who put ideas first, other people second, and themselves wherever they might fit. Out of her entire extended family, unto the third and fourth generation, Des was the only criminal.

This family background might help explain an unsettling disconnect she'd always sensed between justice and punishment. And in fact Desiree's fair, careful parents had not once in her life punished her. This was not because they were indulgent or distracted; they had no adjective or ideology that would explain a lack of punishment. It was just that Des had never needed it.

She misbehaved constantly, but when she was caught she didn't even need scolding. All they had to do was say, "That was the wrong thing to do," and she would burst into sobs of utterly sincere (though brief) contrition. She had often suspected that punishment might even come as a relief; when it did come, not from her parents, this hypothesis turned out to be false. There didn't seem to be any way to get what you deserved without atrocity, except in porn.

Desiree herself never did remember this, but the night of her arrest, when she'd been thrust into the back of a police car and had wormed her way more or less upright, she'd informed her arresting officers brightly, "My father says if you can't pay your debts you don't have to."

The cops had laughed. "You believe that?" one of them had asked her.

The cops, pulling out onto Beach Drive, had turned on their siren. "Woop woop," the younger one said contentedly.

"Oh, *no*," Des had moaned. Though it wasn't clear if that was her answer.

The women were walking in a ragged line strung out along the edge of Lee Highway in the honeyed golden heat of an early Monday evening: Ray Ray in front, Toya hobbling quickly behind her in an ankle-length skirt and that same awful cardigan, then Des, Caretta, Zita and Douceline further back. Fang had said to invite everybody

to her concert—the band was now called Defective Delinquents—
which was why Toya was there. With a big bruised knot at the back
of her skull, which they could all see under her sparse blonde hair.
She said she'd fainted. Lucinda was driving and would meet them
at the club.

Des was dissatisfied. Her chunk heels were wearing down
unevenly, and she couldn't read signs across the street. (She'd been
sure that "EVEN YOU CAN EAT A BURRITO" was a trick of
her glasses, but no, that turned out to be a real ad. Apparently once
you crossed the D.C. line people's expectations were more realistic.)
She was also unpleasantly aware of her teeth. Every part of her had
gone unchecked in prison, and was now asserting itself.

She had made things worse by masturbating in the shower, so
now she felt slack and everything seemed pointless. It hadn't even
been too satisfying, since she knew too much now about the criminal
justice system to roll with her typical prison-guard fantasies. She
kept getting caught up in fixing plot holes.

She wished she'd waited until after she'd seen Lucinda. But it
was hard to wait when you felt like you had to wait for everything.

Then, too, she had been convinced that if she didn't masturbate
she would find a way to drink that night. In retrospect that didn't
seem like a logical thought, but it had been overwhelming at the
time, as tangled yet as rigid as an ironwork toy. And she had been
right, apparently: Drinking now felt like it would be as pointless as
anything else. Anything except, in the moments when she was able to
notice them, the golden sky, the tired white lights on the storefronts,
the evening cries of insects.

At the club they met up with Lucinda and piled their bags into
her trunk. Then they lined up to be patted down. Toya flinched a lot
and the other women judged her for it.

Fang and the rest of Defective Delinquents were already

backstage when the women were let in and given their entry bands. Des tugged at the blue band around her wrist, like a hospital bracelet. She liked how it looked with her elbow-length sleeves—she had elegant wrists that looked better when they were chained.

Inside the club the crowd was small, which annoyed Fang but came as a relief to Des. It turned out to be Industry Night, so Lucinda knew several of the people there, all the cooks and bartenders buying shots for each other on their night off. Des barely had a chance to talk to her before she got into an intense conversation about burrata with a fellow cook.

"Do I have to actually plunge my hands into boiling water?" the other guy asked. "Or can you kind of... pat it down into the water with your fingertips?"

Lucinda replied, with the strict professional ethic Des remembered only too well, "You have to learn to give a fuck about what you're putting out there. It's punishing work. If you don't honor your own labor nobody else will—it's not like you can take pride in your paycheck."

Des, who had nothing to contribute on the subjects of either cheesemaking or taking pride in one's work, tagged along behind Ray Ray. Standing by the stage they at last found Ty'heaven, the one and only.

Desiree actually opened her eyes wider at the sight of her. She lacked the words for how Ty'heaven looked; a Yale education had left her only with, "Holy shit, Ray Ray. She is bangin'."

Ray Ray couldn't stop smiling—a little, sneaky smile, the irrepressible grin of a child who's about to tell you the awesome mischief she just pulled. She was shy and even nervous, edging up toward Ty'heaven, waving a hand to get her attention, as Ty just watched, coolly.

She looked young and untouched. Smooth rich brown skin, long lashes over big brown eyes, that interrogatory kiss of a mouth that Des recognized from the pictures by Ray Ray's bed. She was sapling-slender but her breasts were full and her ass was, you couldn't help noticing, sublime. A perfect high arch. She was wearing an orange and blue shirt in an African-style block print with a deep V-neck, over black leggings. Des reflected that she had never been properly grateful for stretch fabrics.

Ty'heaven bossed Ray Ray like a champion. Ray Ray's brow was furrowed, her head lowered, a small careful smile on her lips, and she did everything Ty'heaven said. She was standing around in her baggy jeans and dress shirt holding Ty'heaven's little golden scaly handbag like it was a live animal.

The Industry Night people danced less than the crowd at the Crystal Stair; they flirted less, and the flirting was less goal-oriented. People mostly hung around the bar trading work stories. Ty sent Ray Ray to go and get her a Coke, and Des drifted after her, hoping to satisfy her curiosity.

Under cover of the opening band, Des asked, "So what is the deal with you and her?"

"Oh, I shot her," Ray Ray said, trying to catch the bartender's attention. "That's how I caught a charge. Her too—when the police came they got me for shooting her and her for beating on me."

"I," Des said, "don't really know how to assess that. I'm going to choose not to ask you who did what first."

"I used to have a real bad temper when people would hit me," Ray Ray said.

"How did she end up serving so much time?"

"She had a couple warrants out. Conspiracy, all that shit. Ah, fuck, I don't know. Now I gotta do anything she says. If I'm like, 'Oh, I don't know,' she be all, 'You shot me!' and it's like that settles it."

"That seems fairly forgiving, under the circumstances."

"Yeah but like... I wasn't even meaning to shoot her! It was just one of those things where you just waving a gun around and, like, roaring. And then she was screaming all, 'You shot me, you fucking shot me!' I hate when you both be going ham on each other but then I'm the one who crosses a line so I got to be the one to blame for all of it."

And that, Des had to admit, she could relate to.

When Ty'heaven finished her Coke, she said she was going outside for a cigarette. Ray Ray, frowning, said, "I thought you said you was quitting."

And Ty'heaven, barely moving her perfect, serene features: "Are you telling *me* what to do?"

Ray Ray said, "Aw, shit."

She followed Ty out the door.

Ty'heaven had a way of smoking where she'd purse her lips and release the cigarette with a little kiss after each puff. Ray Ray watched her hands, her long ruby-tipped fingernails, watched the smoke curling in the summer night. She listened to Ty smoking, *kiss, kiss* on the cigarette, and her heart pounded. It was the sound she had imagined in her cell. She couldn't make herself look at Ty's face, at those lips. She couldn't make herself test if this was real.

Ty tossed the cigarette butt to the ground and crushed it under one golden high heel. "I got to go to the bathroom," she said.

Ray Ray grunted in acknowledgment.

Ty'heaven laughed. "And you got to come with me," she said, and Ray Ray felt very stupid, as a wild grin danced across her face.

There were girls at the sinks, washing their hands and fussing with their hair, but Ty and Ray Ray pushed past them and bundled themselves into one stall. Ty'heaven grabbed Ray Ray's ass through her jeans. Pressed herself against Ray Ray and murmured, "How you been doing, girl?"

Ray Ray was eager to tell her all about it. "I'm doing good, I'm making my move," she said. "I'm on the come up at my job." She slipped her leg between Ty'heaven's thighs.

Ty'heaven laughed. "Nigga, it ain't no 'come up' at the National Park Service!" she said. "You on parole, you cut grass! You think you *making that money* riding on the back of a lawnmower?"

Ray Ray wanted to hit her, but then Ty squeezed her thighs together and moaned, rocking on Ray Ray's leg, and she couldn't think straight. *This how you fucked me up before*, she thought ruefully, but she started rocking her body against Ty's, and her voice wasn't as angry as she'd wanted it to be when she said, "Bitch, we in a public place. You can't think of nothing better to do with your mouth than put my business in the street?"

And with that, Ty'heaven laughed again, lifted up off Ray Ray's leg and settled herself down onto the toilet seat with a daintiness that tinted the whole scene with elegance. She classed the place up, lending the toilet stall her own grace, so its stains and smells somehow made her even more regal. She grabbed Ray Ray by the hips, stuck her hands in the back pockets of Ray Ray's jeans and pulled her in so Ray Ray had to brace her hands against the stall's tiled back wall.

"This ain't a public place," she said, with her mouth against the seam of Ray Ray's jeans. "This our place now. We have all the time we need."

Ray Ray moaned, and scrabbled with her fingertips at the graffiti-laced tiles. This was what Ty'heaven had always been able to do for her: make a place in the world. And also, Ty's other relationship skill, unbuttoning her jeans without using her hands.

Ray Ray pushed her jeans down to her knees and braced her hands again, more firmly.

"I ain't need but five minutes," she said humbly.

Ty'heaven was sucking her through her underpants. She took her mouth away long enough to say, "I need more than that from you, nigga, so don't you fail me."

Ray Ray writhed on her, sobbed, one hand on the tiled wall and one clutching the brown flesh where Ty's shirt had slipped down from her bare shoulder. She rode Ty and when she'd come she moaned, "I always been a triflin', bum ass nigga and I'm sorry, I'm sorry, I need you."

And Ty'heaven, reaching up to pull Ray Ray's bracing hand down and setting it against her cheek, said, "Nah, Ranae. You all right."

Then as Ray Ray shook with gratitude and sorrow and yearning, Ty'heaven laughed one more time and said, "Now get on your knees and get my feet up on your shoulders before my P.O. call me. That's the last thing I need, trying to talk to my P.O. while you neck deep in my pussy."

Ray Ray glanced over her shoulder to make sure that the stall door was closed. Her knees hit the floor.

Ray Ray came swaggering out of the ladies' room, leaving Ty to touch up her lipstick, as Defective Delinquents took the stage. They'd added a Casio keyboard, and they talked between songs now. After the first few numbers, Fang, in a heated and quavering voice, dedicated a song to the stolen owl.

"Hey Ray Ray," Caretta called. "You sure you ain't push that owl into somebody's locker?"

Ray Ray gave this suggestion the one-fingered consideration it deserved. And muttered to Desiree, "*She* the one told me to eat the fucking thing."

"Whatever happened with that whole thing? Did they hire that other woman back on?" Des asked.

Ray Ray looked at her for a long moment. A bass guitar churned, angry and restless, under the clear nostalgic Casio piano chords. The music made a strange feeling lift behind Des's ribcage, a paradoxical mix of memory and urgency. Like reflecting on something she'd survived only to see it turn its face toward her, open its mouth, and show its plentiful teeth. The bass rose up over the piano and Des had never felt a flashback coming on but she thought this might be what it would sound like.

"I didn't do shit," Ray Ray said. She looked Des straight in the eye.

The bass and the piano crashed down the scale together.

Ray Ray said, "I didn't tell anybody what had happened. So no, they didn't hire nobody back on. I got away with it."

"That's understandable," Des said quietly.

"Fuck *understandable*. I am not losing my fucking job. I am not going back to prison." She took a deep breath. "If you tell Miss Imani I will fuck your shit up. This my chance, not just for me but for me and Ty."

Des shrugged, and winced in sympathy. "You know I don't talk," she said.

"Yeah." And then Ray Ray did look away, and she couldn't meet Des's eyes.

"Let me just say," Des said, "people always act like it's funny that I don't talk more in group, like I should be more trusting with Miss Imani. But you don't trust her either. Not with this."

Ray Ray didn't say anything. Des realized she had not asked herself, before her last comment, what would be the most humble thing to do.

Up on the stage, the Casio keyboard was playing a rippling harpsichord coda, tinny and lost, a gone-away sound.

"What are these songs even about?" Des asked. Doing the favor of changing the subject.

Ray Ray gave a quick laugh, forced out like she'd been hit in the stomach. "I think this joint about how if you date dudes who look like your father, you like a girl in a horror movie who don't kill the killer."

In this new band Fang did a lot of howling about romance. Apparently she was a heterosexual with a tormented romantic history, none of which Des would have guessed.

Fang introduced one song with, "This is about being the other woman."

There was a frosty American silence—an uneasiness as the crowd's scales tipped—and then Caretta whooped.

Fang burst out laughing.

"You're not supposed to fuckin' like it!" she said, shaking her long black hair behind the microphone. "What makes you think these are songs you're supposed to cheer for?"

After the set they were standing around talking, and Caretta was complaining about how she hadn't done anything wrong, even though silently she felt certain that somehow she had.

They were arguing about the lyrics to one of the songs: Ty'heaven thought it was, "All I want is a sip to see."

"All we are is a symphony," Toya said.

Des, confidently: "It's, 'Everybody is a chimpanzee.'"

"I just don't know why she got to be insulting people if she's one of us," Caretta said.

Des suggested, "Maybe that's the only way you can insult people with humility."

Lucinda was still talking to hospitality-industry people, and didn't seem interested in joining up with the others. Des had tried to figure out how to include her; she'd already asked about her kid, her kid's health, his first words, and his diet. She'd even resorted to asking about his length at birth. Des literally didn't know how long an inch was, so she had no idea if she should be concerned when Lucinda answered; she decided to go with, "Oh, how precious!" And then she had run out of questions.

As they were walking back toward the bus stop Ray Ray and Toya were out in front again, talking. Des tried to catch up but on her uneven heels she kept stumbling. She shook her head and tried to grin through it: the realization that she no longer had much in common with Lucinda, and belonged more with the women from prison.

They were far enough out in Virginia that they could see stars, and it was late enough in the summer that the sky was dark. Idly, wondering if she was being dislikable, she pointed out Orion and the Big Dipper. With her bad eyes they were wiggly, like lights seen through shot glasses.

Near the metro Toya bent down quickly to the pavement and picked something up. "Oh, I wish I'd found this before the show!" she exclaimed. She began messing with it; and then applied it in raw straight strokes to her lips.

"Is that a lipstick you found on the *street?*" Caretta asked. It was. Des felt intensely embarrassed. The Love's Labors women all side-eyed her.

When they were on the second of three buses and it was just the women from the halfway house, Des asked, "So what did you and Toya end up talking about?"

Ray Ray nodded and then shook her head.

"We call her the Little Shorn Lamb," Des said. "Because of her hair."

"Uh-huh. We mostly talked about the weather, I think. It hasn't been one of those big storms yet—that kind of thing. She a little bit," and Ray Ray tapped her forehead.

Des laughed a little, in recognition of this obvious truth. And then stopped laughing, as Ray Ray said, "But different from you. With that girl it was like she didn't know how things are supposed to be—how people 'posed to talk to each other. Like if I say a thing, she don't know what's supposed to come next. You know and don't give a fuck."

"I'm not sure that's true!" Des said.

"See, even now, you know I'm talking shit about you, not her. She would think maybe she was the one who got curried."

Ray Ray paused, gave one of her low head-shaking laughs, and said, "I asked her 'bout that bump on her head, and she said she liked it."

"Liked it as... fashion?"

"She said it made her feel," and Ray Ray drew her hands apart, like she was making an invisible cat's-cradle, "separate from her emotions. She didn't have to feel them as close to her anymore. I ain't know what to do with that, to be honest with you."

When they got back home Des went up to the room she shared with Ray Ray and took out her phone to set her alarm. She had three new voicemails. One was a housecleaning client asking, in a strangely nervous voice, if she'd found a dog biscuit in his pocket when she laundered his pants. ("It's important.") One was Lucinda, from only an hour ago: "Hey," sounding tired, "I forgot, I'd been meaning to invite you to a workshop I'm doing at Chains and Roses on shibari. Rope work. I don't know if you remember, but you said you were interested in doing me a favor, if one came up, and I need a volunteer for this. Let me know. It'll be August 28th. Okay, bye—uh, good to see you tonight."

"Amends isn't a 'favor,'" Des muttered. On the other hand, she wasn't sure when she'd next get an opportunity to make amends through kink.

The last voicemail was from Trash. He also sounded unusually tired and stressed. "Hi darling. Sorry to call you, but Helen King has passed on."

He paused, and she could hear him take a deep breath. Into the pause she asked nobody in particular, "Who is this person? Is this a person I knew?"

"The funeral is this Saturday and I would really, *really* appreciate it if you would come. I'm trying to get a hold of everybody I know, since—for reasons that don't need excavating—it's possible there won't be many people there. Please do come if you can. Don't say no."

Chapter 11
Wig-Wam Bam

Helen "Helly" King, it transpired, was not somebody Des had met or married in a blackout, but rather a champion figure skater. She'd won U.S. Nationals twice and been the third American lady at the Nagano Olympics. During the skating boom of the late 1990s and early 2000s she'd twice led the Americans to victory at the Perdue Chicken Breast Cold War Challenge, and she placed seventh in the Odor Eaters Legends and Losers Rematch. She'd toured the Russian Federation as the Nanny Goat in Gazprom Zoo on Ice, and been milked by Evgeni Plushenko. ("The milking scene was surprisingly respectful," the *Wall Street Journal*'s teenaged Russia correspondent wrote.) She had also appeared, as part of a probation agreement, in Walt Disney's Choices on Ice: A Special Presentation on Drug Abuse, and she was featured on "Hard Copy" (just rumors) and "Inside Edition" (full confession for the cameras). She had been found dead in a motel in beachfront Delaware, reportedly as the result of an overdose of more or less everything. She had not left a tip for the cleaning staff.

The funeral was being held at Mary, Mother of the Guilty Church in Cabin John, Maryland, near the rink where Helly had gotten her start. Des got there early, hoping to catch Trash before the funeral. She had something she needed to ask him. She found him hiding behind a dumpster in the alley beside the church, smoking.

"You smoke?" she asked, and he jumped.

"Oh hello! I thought you were my family," he said. And, lighting another cigarette off the burning stub of the first one, he said, "I quit."

He looked at her like he knew what she was thinking, but all she said was, "I'm sorry for all this."

"Thank you," he said formally. "We—I really looked up to her. I know that's a strange thing to say, but she had so much honesty in her. I mean when she wasn't stealing my checkbook. She never had anything but praise for her competitors, and she never pled innocent. And she had an *amazing* Ina Bauer."

He sighed. "Helly and I used to sneak smoke breaks together when we did skating shows," he said. "You have to find some way to keep your weight down. Some people apparently try *self-control* but we always preferred smoking."

"Really? You're thin."

"I'm a hippo in skater pounds. Back when I was still in juniors my coach would make me do public weigh-ins. Like something from a *documentary*. And if I was over my goal weight, which was always, he wouldn't say anything right then. But as soon as I made one little mistake it would be," and he dropped his voice an octave, "'This is why we do not eat burrito.'"

A man in a sweatsuit came hurrying down through the alley, but stopped when he saw Trash. "Brother," he said, "can I buy a smoke?"

"You can't *buy* one," he laughed. "That's so degenerate! That's the modern world, where people try to make you *buy* a smoke."

He handed over the pack, almost entirely full.

"Aw, I can't take all these——"

"No, you'll be doing me a favor. I've quit."

"Oh, good for you, man. Take it easy."

"You too." And as the man headed out onto the street, Trash said, "I've missed that. It's the best part of smoking—how people ask you for things you're happy to give."

"I wanted to catch you out here so I could ask you, before other people got here: What is your actual name? It can't really be Trash—can it?"

He laughed so hard that he started to cough. "Oh no! Oh, thank you, I needed that. Oh, you poor thing, to be wondering if my family really did that to me! No, no, my real name is embarrassing in a totally different way. My *dark secret*: I am 'Tiger Joseph Melty.'"

"'Tiger.'"

"You can imagine, I go by T.J. Oh—there's my brother. Quick!"

Trash threw the cigarette butt behind the dumpster, popped a breath mint into his mouth, and swiftly sprayed himself with cologne.

"Oh," he said, in disappointment. "I'd meant to put that out on my arm or something, like a kind of memorial for her. She would have laughed at that. Well, we always remember things too late."

And then, grinning angrily and fighting sudden tears, bracing himself: "Yea, though I walk through the Valley of the Shadow of the Dolls, I shall fear no evil."

They went down the alley to meet his family.

Trash's brother turned out to be a priest in a cassock. He was taller than Trash, with the same curly hair; his features were similar but arranged with much more competence, in a dashing symmetry. He had an old-fashioned male beauty: adult, worldly, with an exotic privacy. There was a man with him, or lurking near him, who couldn't have been more dissimilar. This was a longhair with unnecessarily prominent cheekbones, in a khaki t-shirt, black jeans, and a dark jacket a size too big for him.

"My brother, Father P.J.," Trash said, waving a hand. "And a… person?"

"This is Frank," Father P.J. said. "We were in seminary together. Back hall bros!"

"Back hall bros," Frank admitted, with a fond, dubious laugh.

"He's staying with me at the rectory while he… for a little while."

"While I get my shit together," Frank said.

"Ah-ha. And this is Desiree," Trash said, "my friend."

"*Really*," Father P.J. said, and the brothers exchanged significant glances: assessing on the priest's side, pleading on Trash's side.

Desiree pondered the circumstances that would make someone *hope* his brother was dating her.

"Who else is coming, do you know?" Trash asked. They fell into conversation about which of Trash's siblings were expected— one sister and two more brothers, but this would still leave plenty of surplus family who might show up afterward.

"I'm so grateful you came," Trash said to Father P.J., as the bells began to ring and they started up the long flight of steps into the dark cool church.

His brother hesitated and then said, "Can I ask if you were eating a breath mint just now?"

"I can't take Communion anyway," Trash said, with a slightly nettled grin. "You know that."

"I'm not gonna ask anything I know you don't want to answer," his brother said, "but how's your prayer life, T.J.?"

"I—is this necessary? I'm sorry, it's just—for what it's worth, I think my skating is a form of prayer."

"Oh, you know better than that," his brother said, with a smile.

Trash looked away, heading for one of the frontmost of the many empty pews.

"Bad prayer is still good prayer," Father P.J. said, "but bad skating is just negative G.O.E."

And at that, Trash did turn and smile at him, head tilted in surprise. As Father P.J. went to confer with another priest near the altar, Trash turned to Des and whispered, "That was so sweet of him. I didn't think he knew what Grade of Execution even is!"

Trash looked around and found two people sitting by themselves in the second row of pews, near the center of the church. He went over to talk to them while Des and Frank lurked and looked around and didn't speak to each other. Eventually Trash turned and waved them over. There were very few people in the church.

Trash knelt and crossed himself, and slid into a pew two rows behind the couple. Des followed him, wondering how much of what he did she was supposed to do, and Frank slipped in after her. Trash pulled the kneeler down and went easily onto his knees. Des thought she remembered that Jews weren't supposed to kneel—not for prayer, anyway. Off-label uses of the knees were fine as long as you were Reform.

A short bearded man approached the little pulpit and adjusted the microphone. Trash looked around and scowled. "Lizzie and Toya told me they'd be here," he said.

"I guess Little Bo Peep is still asleep," Des said.

"Well Lizzie's definitely hungover, I got like four sympathy texts from her after dawn, but that's no excuse. 'I'm sorry your *fiend dried*,' she says."

The bearded man at the microphone cleared his throat. Just as he was saying, "Welcome, friends," Lizzie Pearl tumbled into their pew.

"I'm sorry I'm late!" she hissed across the ex-seminarian. Lizzie was wearing black lipstick, vampiric eyeshadow, lace-up black stiletto heels, and all of her jewelry at once. She was draped in a startlingly short and decollete thing, black and tattered and complex; it was shapeless but showed flashes of breast, hip, and shoulder when she moved, a sort of whorish sack. She had rhinestone-crusted sunglasses hooked onto the front of her sex-shroud but at least she wasn't wearing them in church.

The organ moaned into life and everyone stood, the Catholics first and then the rest in ragged disorder. During the singing Des looked around, to figure out who was who and what she had to do. Aside from her clump and the couple ahead of them, there was a knot toward the upper middle of the church of about six people who were middle-aged and cunningly dressed. The women had big outdated hair, lush expensive ESPN Classic hair. One of the men wore a black blouse with a ruffle, open almost to his navel.

The couple in front turned to look at Des and she caught her breath. A man and a woman. Short, stolid. The woman's short red hair lay on her head in flat curls; the man was bald except for gray tufts in and around his ears. They were not thin, but their ill-fitting funeral clothes made them look fatter than they were. They wore expressions of profound disapproval of everything around them, and especially of their own unfathomable misery. These must be the parents.

They were supposed to stand now and proclaim their sinfulness. Trash lowered his eyes and beat his knuckles gently against his breast, like he was knocking at a door he didn't want opened.

The atmosphere was affecting her, and her mind was wandering as she looked around the church. She stopped trying to figure out what to do; her gaze became less social, less moral. The ceilings were high and arched, and all around the upper level of the church there were nooks and niches where statues stood in their observation posts.

Her eyes were too bad for her to make out their faces. In at least five places throughout the church there were black ironwork ranks of dark red votive candles with low flames flickering. In one side chapel there was a huge statue of what Des thought might be a woman, white marble rushing, about to fall on her knees, one arm held out to grip or invite you and the other flung back. Behind the woman everything was a blurry splash of blue and gold.

The windows of the church were stained-glass, so you couldn't see outside. Enclosure, observation from above, the statues in their tiers, prescribed movements and restricted speech and the bearded man at the pulpit reading from the Bible about being chastised and blessed, punished and hopeful—it all rushed together and Des thought, suddenly, *This is a house of correction.*

It was so beautiful. The smell of incense and snuffed matches hung in the air; Trash's light voice beside her said everything they were supposed to say. The huge open space around them seemed to be a place for the exhausted couple to drop down and rest. They were not crying.

It had reminded her of prison, but not because it felt like prison. *Obviously,* she thought, *because you can walk out whenever you want.*

But as the priest began his homily she realized that that wasn't why. It wasn't the unlocked doors that made this place feel different from the place it uncannily resembled; it was the tenderness, of which the beauty formed the greatest part. There was in all this order no contempt.

The priest who did the homily wasn't the same as the priest who had said most of the Mass so far. He was older, broad-shouldered; age had melted the flesh on his face into strange uneven wattles and lumps. His nose stood out and his eyes were big, in deep hollows under bushy gray eyebrows. He limped over to the pulpit.

"Hiya," he rasped. "Wanted to use that thing," pointing a crooked, knuckly finger at the other side of the altar, where marble stairs led up to a grand balcony, "but I can't haul this old horse up those stairs. You can see I got a limp. Had some surgery. But like many of you, I gotta work hurt.

"I didn't know Helen King," he said, nodding hard at her parents, who in their grief and humiliation nodded back. "Don't think she was what you call a good Catholic girl. But I gotta tell you, and I hope, parents, that this consoles you, 'cause it's true, there's no such thing as a good Catholic girl. Only place you find a good Catholic girl is in a triple-X movie."

The other priest on the altar coughed, once and sharply.

"Except for the Blessed Mother," the old priest conceded. "But what it is to be a priest, what it means, is that when they call you, you say yes. You go and do the funeral or whatever it is that people need." And, plucking at his lilac robes to illustrate, he said, "You do what the uniform tells you to do."

He nodded, messed with his papers and held them further from his face. "I got a story here to tell. I asked some people, tell me what you know about this young lady, this poor child, and one of them told me a story about how she also said yes when they called her name. This was in the mid-'90s, guy who told me this thought maybe '95 or '96, in Boston at a big skating championship. Hannah—excuse me, Helen King, she's in the back getting her costume on when she sees this cop. Big Boston cop. Probably a good Catholic kid. All decked out, he got the billy club," and the priest grabbed his own hip, "he got the gun. He comes up to her and says, 'Miss?', and she, bless her soul, she gets up and turns around and puts her hands on the wall."

Trash chuckled—a little confused, but playing along—and the priest laughed too. "Thought he was gonna cuff her right there and book her for narcotics," the priest said. "But he was there to sing the national anthem! Boston PD sent a little pack of choirboys in blue. She was gonna go nice and quiet, and give up on her dream of skating in the championship, make his day a little easier. And all he was coming over for was to tell her to go out there and stand for the 'Star-Spangled Banner.'"

The priest looked out across the empty pews. "That's a story she never told her mom and dad, I think," he said, "although I guess I'm telling it now. It's a better story than you think, Mama. Your kid did good."

Helly's mother's head was bowed, there in the front row. Her husband sat stiffly beside her.

"'Chastised but a little,'" the priest said. "We think that's a bad thing. We think God sends our bad things to chastise us and cleanse us—we think Purgatory is full of bad things. Fire, cancer, rats, what's bad… raccoons are bad. Unjust wages! But what chastises us is the good things in life. Love—if you've ever loved so much it hurts, or if you've ever been loved by somebody, maybe your mother, so much that it hurts you to think about it—that's the fires of Purgatory. In this life and the next."

He took a deep breath, up there on the altar—so deep it made him hack and cough. "Okay," he said, "okay. We don't know where your kid is now. It's not popular to say this, but we don't know. We can trust God, but we can't trust ourselves. And I think maybe your poor child, you maybe couldn't always trust her to go where she should go."

Helly's parents were crying, stiff and silent. They made no movement to wipe their cheeks. It was as if they hoped ignoring the tears would dry them.

The priest said, "All we know is that wherever she is, God is just and good; whatever happens to her is His fire of love. If it's peace, if it's punishment. If it's something worse than punishment."

Trash took a quick shamed breath and nodded his head once, sharply. He tried to look up at the priest but he had to look down at his hands instead.

"But I pray," the priest said, "and we can all pray together, that God's good attention is chastising your little girl now, and cleaning her up. And when you see her again, Mama, she'll be beautiful."

He coughed. "Arright. Let's stand for our common profession of faith."

At that moment Des smelled something familiar and heard the uneven clapping of broken soles against the carpet of the church aisle. And then the Little Shorn Lamb was leaning right against her ear and panting, hot and pungent, "I'm sorry I'm late!"

Des twitched away and wrinkled her brow. "It's fine," she whispered, and then stood up quickly as she realized that everybody else was standing. In such a thin crowd it was obvious who wasn't paying attention.

Six people from the pews went up to receive Communion, mostly Trash's siblings. Helly's parents were the first ones; her mother was crying. Trash, kneeling next to Des, put his face in his clasped hands and took deep breaths. She wondered if she should pat his shoulder or if that would startle him. It seemed too much like something someone in a movie would do. She was just about to try it anyway when he lifted his head and looked up toward the altar, red-faced and sniffling, with a strenuous smile on his lips and utter trust in his eyes.

After the funeral there would be "a small gathering of remembrance" in the church basement. Des trailed down there. A few more people had come—various of Trash's extra siblings, and a muscular, chipper bearded man whom Trash introduced as Javier, without further explanation. A television on a wheeled cart was showing Helly King's career highlights, and there was a coffee urn, styrofoam cups, and donut holes. Everything except the donut holes had emerged from a door labeled, FR. RAFAEL MURILLO MEMORIAL SOCIAL JUSTICE CLOSET.

On the television Helly King, dressed in layers of spangly lace and ropes of whirling fake pearls, was skating to the Bangles' "Hazy Shade of Winter." Des noticed that the man in the ruffled black blouse was carrying a dog in a grocery bag.

Lizzie bent over to pick up a donut hole and kicked her heel up behind her. Father P.J. swallowed hard as he stared at her, all black and golden. "Now that's a memento mori," he commented covertly.

"Yeah, she has that effect on people," Trash laughed.

"I'm sorry I was late," Toya said again.

"Oh, it's all right," he said. "Things happen."

"Yes."

She looked at him urgently. Neither of them knew what she wanted to say.

"Do you—would you like to see the ladies' room?" he asked.

"No."

The funeralgoers were separating out into small knots. Trash tried to circulate among them and draw them together, but the closest he got was convincing some of the disparate attendees to watch the television side by side. Helly was skating now to Katchatourian's "Masquerade Waltz" as Terry Gannon said in voiceover, "The embattled skater's coach released a statement today that said King has never failed, I quote, 'any official drug test by the International Olympic Committee.'" On the screen she had lilting arms, perfect reedlike extension of the free leg, and no clean jumping passes. She finished her program and shrugged, grinned ruefully, blew the audience a kiss.

"It's good to see my family," Father P.J. said to his friend Frank.

"I miss the seminary, you know. Our life there was a rhythm—work and prayer. Now I can't tell if I'm praying all the time, or practically never. It's all pretty chaotic."

"Nothing at seminary felt like work to me," Frank said. "I wonder if that's why I fucked it up so much. I like working, believe it or not. But seminary felt like I was helping people—giving something of myself to them—and I started to feel like I didn't have anything to give. Like a scam artist."

"You've always seemed so empathetic."

Frank laughed. "Seemed, yeah."

"Well—but if you want to be it and you seem like it, doesn't that mean that you are it? Desire and performance, I'm not sure what else there is to an action."

Lizzie, chewing on one leg of her sunglasses, inspected Toya's head. "It looks like a Monet back there," she said, touching the base of her own skull.

"Oh, thank you!"

"Are you okay?"

"I think so. I don't want to act entitled to... being not in pain."

"It's good of you to come to this. I hope you don't need a ride back someplace after the ice show, but if you do, I'm calling an Uber."

"Do they track where you go? I can't leave any record that I was here."

Lizzie hung her sunglasses back in her cleavage and gave Toya a long, skeptical look. She wasn't sure if she should praise Toya for trying to make a joke.

On the television Helly was performing in Stars on Ice, skating to the Sweet's "Wig-Wam Bam" in an ill-conceived pseudo-Indian costume with sparkling blue fringe. She mimed shooting a bow and, as Trash hid his face in embarrassment, put up her hand and mouthed, "How."

"Okay, I'll ask," Lizzie said. "Why can't you leave a record that you were here?"

Toya's concussion had given her all kinds of new sensations: memory loss, headaches, exhaustion, inability to concentrate; a sound in her ears like someone banging on a piano. Waves of pain at the base of her spine when she stood up. She'd even had the entirely welcome experience of losing her sense of smell. But the aftereffect that surprised her the most was the freedom from responsibility. She told herself that she was too tired and she ached too much to remember why she shouldn't say things.

"The leader forbidded me from leaving the house," she said. She made her eyes big, and looked down—and then glanced back up at Lizzie to see what would happen next.

"Forbade," Lizzie said. But then: "The leader? Like, your dom? He should let you go to funerals, you know. I don't mean to judge your sex life, but even Trash's clown guy let him honor the dead. Some things are bigger than your vagina."

"Not many," Toya said mournfully.

"Tell me what the leader is," Lizzie said. And then, with a face like a penny dropping: "How did you hurt your head?"

"Max Lord is a rational and empathetic man," Toya said eagerly. She knew how to answer this question, because it was on their website. "He runs a nonprofit to teach underparented females how to attain personal and professional success. I don't know why he said I couldn't come here, but maybe it's because he doesn't think I've learned the etiquette for funerals? He taught me to speak clearly and sit correctly and shake hands."

Lizzie looked at her for a long unspeaking moment.

"Did he teach you how to wash yourself," she said. "Desiree takes a class on Work and Hygiene, if you're into classes. She can give you some pointers."

"Oh—I—no," Toya said, looking down. Her chalky face turned a mottled red. "I'm not allowed to wash myself regularly."

Lizzie's eloquent expression intensified.

"I don't really understand *why*," Toya said. "He says that it's a challenge—that he trusts me, he sees my potential to overcome obstacles, such as personal smell. But Trina just says it's punishment."

"I want to stop asking questions right now," Lizzie said, "but a funeral is no time for bullshit. How did you hurt your head?"

"I fainted during punishment. In the Training Parlor."

"Oh, fuck me," Lizzie moaned. "I was so *sure* that when I left Indiana I'd never have to have the domestic violence talk again! And yet this is like the third time this year. Okay, Trash is grieving right now, so you're stuck with me and Desiree. Oh, and that priest, maybe. Come with me."

At that moment Trash and his brother were engaging in what Father P.J. thought was lighthearted banter. "In the words of Dietrich Bonhoeffer," the priest said as he refilled his coffee, "'Only the obedient believe.'"

Trash couldn't look him in the eye. He didn't know the word "floored," which was too bad, because in that moment he would have appreciated the spatial metaphor. He was abject before his brother, and even though he didn't think it was his place to contradict a priest, he said, "But—I have to have hope. Don't I?"

His brother realized that he was being unnecessary, and said with intentional gentleness, "No, that's true. Maybe that's how you're obedient."

Trash laughed in relief. "It's a much more fun kind of obedience than the kind you do," he said.

Father P.J. wasn't sure if he was being made fun of—as an older brother he was incapable of seeing the degree to which Trash was in awe of him. He was about to work out what he intended as a tactful, probing question, when Lizzie came up to them with Toya trailing behind her.

"Hate to interrupt," she said, "but can I borrow you? The priest one, not you."

And when Father P.J. in some bewilderment followed her into a corner of the basement room, under a print of Our Lady of Mount Carmel consoling the souls in Purgatory, Lizzie said, "Okay, Pope Guy, do your thing. This chick is being abused."

Toya squeaked in protest. "I don't think that's an appropriate label!" she said.

"Yeah no, she's living with people who don't let her see her friends without permission and punish her, in ways that I don't even know about and *really* don't want to imagine, to the point that she faints. Not in a sexy way, which I'd totally understand, I've never fainted from being whipped but probably that's a thing that can happen, but it sounds like Toya's thing is more like a cult. Oh, and they don't let her shower. Okay, I'm going to get Desiree, you guys talk. Ask her how she hurt her head."

"'Cult' is a totally unfair word! Is Crossfit a cult? Is—you work for the Republican Party, right? Is the *Republican Party* a cult?"

Ticking off the questions on her fingers, Lizzie answered, "Yes; not really; and sure, apparently. Byeee!"

Des at that point was trying to console the King parents, under a print of the Virgin Mary punching a devil in the face.

"What I always ask myself," Helly King's mother said, "is, 'When was she beyond all natural help?' When could we still have done more?"

And then, in an intense and clotted voice, "Do you think it was her name? Do you think it created expectations? Should we have named her after Heaven instead of—Hell?"

"I don't think Heavenly King is a good name for a girl," her stolid husband said.

"I just feel that we must have done something wrong."

Des wanted to say that parents weren't always to blame, but she wasn't sure if it would aid her credibility to start off, "Speaking as a drug addict myself...". She was relieved when Lizzie clacked up to her, charged with purpose.

"Des. We've got a situation."

And, turning to the parents, she said, "I am so sorry for your loss." She had the gift of making her voice autumn-rich, suffused with honest sorrow, her breasts swelling softly with shared grief.

Then she took Des's arm—making her jump, which she was grateful Lizzie didn't notice—and pulled Des over to Father P.J. and Toya.

The conversation in the Purgatory corner was not going as Lizzie had hoped.

"But I don't *want* human dignity!" Toya was saying. "Dignity separates us. Dignity is a barrier to intimacy. We must strip ourselves of dignity so that we may be known and disciplined."

"Desiree," Lizzie said, "help me out here."

"I agree with her," Des said. "I didn't know she knew that stuff."

"You see? And she went to Yale!" Toya crowed.

"What the fuck, Des? Excuse my language, Mr. Priest, but she's talking about a cult that doesn't let her take *baths*."

"Whoa, wait, back up," Des said. "Baths are important. Especially for anger management."

"Dignity has to be earned," Toya said primly. "If you insist on dignity or respect before you've earned it, you show that you still have a child's mind. Respect is like underwear: The leader will give it to you when you're ready for it, and not before."

Des said slowly, "Huh, I disagree with basically all of that— respect doesn't have to be earned, you owe everybody respect and gratitude no matter what they're doing to you. And the underwear thing is weird and unsettling."

"I do respect people who do things to me," Toya said.

"Okay, that's admirable," Des said. "I don't do the whole dignity thing myself, so I feel you on that."

Lizzie, at the end of her tether, full-on growled. "Rrrrrrrrrhhhhh! Desiree, stop fucking around and *ask her how she hurt her head.*"

Obediently Des asked, "How did you hurt your head?"

And then, as she realized what the answer might be: "Wait, a cult, like—a cult?"

"It's not a cult!" Toya said. "The leader tells us all the time that it's not a cult."

And she tried to imitate Max Lord—making her voice spooky, holding her hand up high with the fingers splayed, Toya doing Max Lord doing Bela Lugosi: "'Ooh, look deep into my eyes, do as I say!' The leader tells us himself that he would be terrible at building a cult. Because of his limp."

"Up until today," Des said, "you've never talked about a leader. I know you do a self-help group. But this 'leader' stuff is new."

"Good point!" Lizzie chipped in fiercely.

"Does it feel good?" Des asked. "To be able to talk about it now?"

For the first time since she started arguing with the priest, Toya paused. She felt thrown off. She had been eager and even gleeful, enjoying the totally unexpected feeling of self-approval—a priest had just the right balance of authority and discredit to make him easy to oppose but satisfying to defeat. Since she had started talking about Max Lord as the leader she had felt free, and she had rolled around in the pleasure of freedom without attending to the unfreedom that surrounded it.

"How did you hurt your head?" Father P.J. asked.

"I fainted," Toya said, returning to confidence. "That's all. People faint."

"That sounds frightening," he said—he had taken a class on empathy. "I hope you had someone with you, who could care for you."

"There was someone there," she said slowly. She remembered very little from that afternoon, but she knew this part because the woman who'd seen her faint had teased her about it.

"Did that person help you?" the priest asked.

"Well... yes," she said. Somewhere in the uneasy part of her mind she recognized that she had decided to lie.

At that moment Trash came over to them. "Is everything all right?" he asked. "We're going to clean up here and then go over to the ice rink for the Memorial Spectacular."

"Everything is fine," Toya said, with such conviction that Trash boggled at her a little.

Across the room on the TV Helly King was finishing her Nagano short program—a ferocious whirling spin with her hands pressed to her cheeks and her elbows out. She stopped herself, toppled onto the ice, and lay prone in the applause. She'd just fallen on her combination jump, placed seventh with no hope of pulling up into the medals. She rolled onto her back and lay there, her chest heaving, laughing.

Cut to an interviewer asking, "Many people have said that if you applied yourself, with some discipline, you could be the best in the world. Do you want that?"

Sincere, in a light blue sweater, her bleached-blonde hair pushed back with a pink headband: "I want to be everybody's favorite."

"Everything is fine," Toya said again, less certainly. "Let's—uh, let's memorialize."

Chapter 12
Memorial Spectacular

In the locker room at the Cabin John Ice Rink, Trash was trying to figure out how to get into his costume. The news of Helly's death had caught him off-guard. He'd been grateful that the Halloween stores were already open; he had picked up a Sexy Piñata costume, driven to his parents' house to use the sewing machine, and transformed it into a tribute to Cyndi Lauper.

"I wish they'd do Halloween costumes that were, like, *Tasteful Piñata*," he muttered, untucking a tattered pink ribbon from his armpit. "Modest Zombie. Demure Donald Trump. Oh well, it's better than the year everybody went as sexy Gitmo prisoners."

He checked his makeup—it didn't quite give the air of elegiac masculinity he'd been hoping for—and sat down on the bench to put his skates on.

Javier came into the changing room without warning.

"Oh hello," Trash said. "Are they starting? Did you give them the CD with 'Time After Time'?"

"Yeah, you're good. I didn't know people still owned CD players?"

"Skating rinks do."

"Huh. There are so many hidden worlds."

Trash smiled up at him and yanked the tongue of his skate to open it up. "Thank you for dealing with the music. Should I call you 'sir' here? I should. Thank you, sir."

"Glad to know you've decided that for me," Javier said, grinning. "They just did the order of skaters—you're second—and the announcement about how the concession-stand proceeds will go to paying the funeral expenses. I bought a hot dog," and he held it up in its tinfoil wrapper.

Then, awkwardly, he came toward Trash and got down on his knees. Trash tilted his head quizzically. Javier set down the hot dog. He picked up Trash's left foot, tenderly and even reverently, and started lacing up his skate.

"*Oh,*" Trash said. "You don't have to do that."

"I don't *have* to do anything," Javier said.

Trash was suddenly aware of how alone they were in that chilly, enclosed space. Javier's warmth radiated toward him. He had never been taller than Javier before; he wasn't sure how to look at him if he couldn't do the usual longing upward gaze he gave everybody.

Javier glanced up at him and smiled, oddly tentative. Trash put out a hand to stop him and then caught himself. Half admiring the pose, half superstitiously unwilling to stop his dom even with a touch, he let his hand stay there with the fingers stretched, an inch or two from Javier's face.

Javier, misunderstanding him, smiled wider and pressed Trash's palm to his stubbled cheek. Then he returned to his task.

"You," Trash said, and cleared his throat. "You need to be lacing it tighter, if you're going to do this. Yank on the laces like you want to hurt me."

"I can do that, if that's what you want," he said.

"It's literally what I need you to do so I can skate," Trash said, scooting forward on the bench and leaning back on his hands so Javier could get a better grip. "I'm sorry to be practical, but if my feet move around too much in there I could really get hurt. I hope that isn't what you want because I have very bad insurance."

Javier nodded and applied himself, and worked hard for about a minute on his knees. He lost his grip on the skate lace and cursed, shaking his hand. Trash watched him silently, almost pityingly. It was a new look for him: He had always looked at Javier with gratitude, with the attentiveness of someone being instructed, with willingness to obey and suffer and improve, but never with this wonder.

"I wish I knew why you're doing this," Trash said at last. "I guess I don't understand you very well. I wish I did."

At that, Javier glanced up at him and laughed softly. His fingers were starting to show shallow red welts from the laces. "Maybe I'm teaching you a lesson," he said. "It's not my job to explain these things to you. It's your job to suffer whatever I choose to do to you."

"But only to me personally," Trash clarified. "Let me wrap the laces, please, sir."

"Of course. Is this good? And yes, I heard you, we've been over this, the voting thing was a mistake on my part."

"I don't mean to be critical."

Javier picked up his other foot and began to tighten the laces from the toe.

Trash watched him in silence. When Javier was almost done he said abruptly, "Sometimes, and I know I'm stepping out of my place here but *so are you*, I think you say that things are a lesson for me when you don't know yourself why you're doing them. That's good, thank you, please let me wrap the other one now."

Javier yielded and sat back on his heels while Trash took over. He grinned and said, "So now I gotta know why I do things? Be grateful I'm doing the things. Don't ask for reasons."

"Oh, this conversation is getting theological," Trash said. "I don't know if I can handle theology at a funeral."

He rubbed his face, suddenly exhausted and miserable, smearing his makeup.

"It must have been hard for you," Javier said carefully, "growing up Catholic. With a brother who's a priest and the whole bit."

"Oh no, my brother—you saw his friend who came with him," Trash said. "He's always befriending people who are... sort of obviously sinful. Of course everyone's sinful. But he's always been very kind to me. I love the Church—I guess you have to."

"Okay, T.J." Javier laid a hand on his knee.

"Oh, you can call me Trash here, sir," he said. "'T.J.' is just for work and my family. Or you can call me anything you like, of course."

"You should probably go out there," Javier said gently. "They're clapping so it sounds like the first lady must have finished. Get your game face on."

Trash dropped his head into his hands for a moment. Then swiftly he looked up, gave a huge rueful grin, grabbed Javier's forearm and pulled himself upright with unexpected flowing grace. And thumped bowlegged out of the locker room on his skate guards.

Javier picked up his hot dog but didn't bite into it. He was watching the doorway where Trash had been.

In the stands around the skating rink, Toya sat rubbing her temples; she was surprised when Des offered her a couple Tylenol. Toya thanked her and sat, chewing the non-chewable tablets. She couldn't taste them, so that was something to be grateful for.

Prisoners of Upper Northwest

Chapter 13
Rope Work

Desiree was late for check-in at Chains and Roses, and still in her uniform. She'd told herself she'd be fine according to the bus schedule on the Metro website, and she wanted to get this oven really clean—nothing was as satisfying as hidden cleanness. Then her first bus had come and gone early and her second bus was the 70, which ran at random based on the complex interactions of police activity, construction, parades, and assholes, and as she waited in helpless fury for it to arrive she remembered her Community Supervision Officer saying that when people are late it's because they want to be.

"Or they have kids," she had argued, "or they don't have money. I mean Metro is a joke."

"Let me rephrase," her CSO had said. "When *you* are late, it's because you want to be."

This had not even been scolding; it had been the explanation for why, if Des was late to her aftercare appointments, she would be violated back to prison.

Des tried to work off her anger by hitting the plastic-enclosed box that held the bus's totally fictional schedule. At the sound of her fist against the box a little old black lady in a hat turned to her and said, severely, "You scared me."

"I'm *sorry*," Des said. Hearing the whine in her voice just made her angrier. It's the worst feeling: to feel as though you're being unfairly judged, but know you're being judged fairly.

So now she was standing, sweating and smelling wet and bleachy, in an orange and teal outfit with polka dots and at least three ruffles, including one along the headband, holding out her passport to what seemed to be a bondage cat.

"I love your outfit!" the cat said, checking her name against a list. "Subs this year are so creative with their humiliation costumes. At the breakfast buffet I saw a devil playing the flute with his bottom!"

"Thanks," Des said. She wondered how you got to be a bondage cat if you couldn't say "ass." "Look, I'm not actually registered for the con, I'm just the model for the shibari workshop."

"Oh, so you're not on the list. Hold on." The cat was a light-skinned black woman in her early twenties, in elaborate makeup, cat ears and clawed gloves, and a collar. As the cat shuffled through a new set of lists and papers Des admired, or tried to admire, the leather straps displaying two rows of pink plastic feline nipples.

"I forgot this part of kink," Des said, trying to make conversation. "All the paperwork."

"Your security is our priority," the cat said.

At last Des got her name checked off and got her con badge, and headed up to the second floor, where the workshops were being held. She took a moment on the escalator to look around the hotel lobby.

C'n'R had changed while she'd been away. There was an aggressively childlike air to it now: a cartoonish flavor, a lot of thirtysomething women in baby-doll getups and unidentifiables in colorful animal costumes. It was cheerful, in its way, but it felt a lot less gay than the convention Des remembered. Or it felt less like what she considered to be gay: less louche and throwbacky and survivalist.

There were diapers, which didn't seem to be about humiliation or helplessness—those were desires she could understand—but about a carefree toddlerhood, being taken care of. The whole animal scene hadn't been much of an element the last time she'd attended, but now it seemed like half the congoers were dressed as either fascist bondage dogs or helpful polka-dotted children's-television dogs. Des looked right at home but felt completely foreign.

On the second floor Des hesitated, then headed for the bathroom. She had resolved to try something, which she was supposed to have done before now but she kept forgetting about it. She was going to take a suggestion.

The door to the ladies' room had an "All-Gender Restroom" sticker on it, for the benefit of the S&M convention. Inside, a man was putting in contacts and nipple rings while gossiping on his cell phone: "Let me just say," the nipple-rings man was telling his confidante, "he told me he was an otter but I saw him at the marmoset brunch and he looked very much at home."

Des slipped into one of the stalls, locked the door behind her, and stood there wondering what to do.

Hello, she thought experimentally; and then grimaced. Too much melodrama, doing it that way: Oh, *I'm trying to find God*, aren't I interesting? She told herself she was supposed to be seeking help, doing as she'd been told. Whether Anyone was listening wasn't the point. Maybe this was just absurd self-abasement, but hey, she'd never find a more appropriate setting for it than the toilets of an S&M con.

Why the bathroom, she wondered. AA people were obsessed

with praying in bathrooms. Was it because of the associations with self-exposure?

This one had green walls, a deep beachglass green rather than an institutional green. There were no scratches and no graffiti. The toilet seat was uncracked and pristine.

You have got to stop dawdling, she told herself. *Okay. Higher Power, please help me. Make me have whatever humility I need to deal with Lucinda and make my amends to her. I know I will fuck it up on my own so you've gotta come through for me here, Pal. Do a sister a solid.*

Please.

After that she couldn't think of anything else to say, and anyway she was now really late. She shrugged and unlocked the stall.

"Well, darling, one is a member of the weasel family and one is a *monkey*," the nipple-rings man was telling his friend. "They're completely different personality types."

Des let the door swing shut. She tried to tell herself she'd done what she could to get ready.

"*There* you are," Lucinda said when she found the room for the shibari workshop. And then, getting a good look at Des's uniform, "Jesus. You look like Minnie Mouse's DT's."

Des laughed—she hadn't laughed like that in a long time. Surprised by how badly she still wanted Lucinda, even now when there was nothing between them but the lingering desire for obligation.

"I know you didn't remember to bring the consent form or the health checklist, so I printed them out for you," Lucinda said, holding up a sheaf of paper. She was standing at the front of the room, next to a table with a pile of multicolored rope on it and an array of carabiners and other outdoorsy metal things. There were a few eager types already seated throughout the room; the perky ones were being welcoming at the awkward ones.

"Oh right. Uh, sorry, you know how it is."

"I know how you are, yes."

For a moment Des thought of her Community Supervision Officer telling her she wasn't an abstraction; she wasn't a criminal type, she was a person with a unique identity. *Yeah*, Des thought, *which has always been my problem.*

She signed the consent form without reading it, which she knew would irritate Lucinda; she didn't have to look up from the form to see that familiar thinning of the lips. She tried her paperwork joke again.

As she scanned the health checklist—are you asthmatic, are you pregnant, are you *sure*—she was grinning a little. Not sure why. Possibly she'd been understood and humiliated by so many strangers in the past four years that it was thrilling to be humiliated by somebody who knew her, and tried to respect her anyway.

"Maybe some people have a kink for bureaucracy," she said, as she signed the bottom of the checklist.

Lucinda took a deep breath. "Maybe some people *don't* have a kink for consent violations," she said.

"Wouldn't know! Is this where we're setting up? Should I take my clothes off?"

"Before we do this," Lucinda said, "I need you to know that this is important to me."

Des felt her face heat and redden with what she wished were anger. *I am not an asshole*, she thought, unconvincingly. Her voice was low when she said, "I do know. I'm sorry."

"You don't have to apologize. Look, parts of this are going to be very difficult for you, so just vocalize—talk your way through whatever you're feeling."

That sounds like the difficult part, Des thought, but what she said was, "That should be entertaining for your audience."

"The one thing I'll tell you in advance is that you won't be upside down for too long. But if you start to feel short of breath or lightheaded at any point, say so *immediately*. That's a command, if you're still taking commands from me. We can have a safe word if you want—"

"Nope."

Lucinda sighed. "I hope you don't think that's impressive to me."

"You're *married*, I'm not supposed to be impressing you."

There was an uncomfortable silence. The couple in the front row didn't know where to look.

"You can get undressed now," Lucinda said. And then, with a soft furtive cackle, "You can leave the headband on."

Des grinned. But when she put her hands up behind her back to the row of buttons on her uniform, suddenly she couldn't lift her head. Her hands and face felt hot and swollen and her chest felt tight. It had been a long time since she had undressed in front of other people consensually.

There wasn't anything to be done about it. The room was almost full now, and she had to hurry so they could start. She shook herself, turned away from the audience, and unbuttoned. Reminding herself that nobody could tell that her heart was pounding, and anyway it didn't matter.

She slid the Minnie Mouse dress down, holding it off the floor since it was her work uniform and she felt it deserved some respect, and stepped out of it. Kicked her shoes off, rolled down her stockings, and unhooked her bra. She rolled her shoulders. Even pulling her underpants down made her back ache more. *There was a day when you would have done this for me*, she thought at Lucinda's placid audience-directed smile.

She could tell that she was hunching and trying to cover herself, and she didn't like it. Miss Imani always suggested that when they were having trouble with "re-entry," when their bad memories got in the way of their current obligations, they could try to "be present to the moment." Focus on what was happening right now and let the small sensory details crowd out the past. Des felt the pebbly hotel carpeting yield under her bare feet. She focused on the unnatural whiteness of the light in the room, and the way the light and the heat came from different directions. None of this helped her to be present in the moment where she was naked in front of sixty-some strangers and her ex.

Lucinda started talking. Welcoming everybody. Introducing Des as "my model," with no name; Des stood up straight and smiled at them, opened up her body language and wondered if it would help to pretend she was at a job interview. Lucinda rhapsodized on the history and traditions of the art of Japanese rope bondage. Knots symbolized public shame, "so we'll be using them here." The symmetry of the rope patterns represented harmony, she suggested, peace with the universe and peace within oneself. Asymmetrical patterns represented an internal conflict you hoped to resolve as your body became one with the beauty of the ropeworker's art.

Des wondered if she should have shaved her bush.

"The rope itself is rich in symbolism," Lucinda said brightly. "The colors have meaning—purple is a traditional choice—and the material is a poetic reference to the hemp ropes used to—uh—"

Des perked up. What was bad enough to embarrass somebody at a BDSM con?

Lucinda glanced at Des but didn't meet her eyes. "To restrain prisoners during arrest and transport," she finished.

Des rolled her eyes.

"This rope is made of jute," Lucinda went on quickly, "but the

Japanese term doesn't distinguish between jute and hemp."

Des elaborately scratched her ass.

"I've asked my model to vocalize what she feels," Lucinda noted, "even though in general you want to achieve an internal silence. Serenity through acceptance of discomfort, even pain. I think by the end of this workshop you will agree with me that silence is the best expression of the spirit of shibari."

Against her will Des was moved by this part—she had never admitted to Lucinda how much she responded to the spiritual side of S&M. For the first time she wondered if her attempts to be casual and cool, her mockery of Lucinda's strenuous sincerity, had been a part of the wreckage of their relationship.

She resolved to do exactly as she'd been instructed: to express everything she felt, no matter how humiliating. This was, she felt sure, the humblest approach.

"Let's begin," Lucinda said.

Des lifted her hands and crossed her wrists at her breastbone, offering. Her body twisted at the waist; she dutifully commented, "I realize I'm turning away from you guys, the audience. I'd rather turn my face and I guess also my breasts and wrists this way," gesturing with her crossed wrists toward Lucinda, "but I hope you all appreciate that I'm still turning my pelvis toward you. Enjoy that. If you're so inclined."

Lucinda said, with intense patience, "I actually need you to put your hands behind your back. I'll guide you what you need to do."

Des obeyed slowly. "I don't like this," she said. "My heart is pounding again, actually. This specific position is too much like— things I don't think I want to talk about—*ugh*, fine, this actually is too much like prison, so points for historical accuracy. *Honesty*, I hope you're happy."

Lucinda came around to look her in the face. "Desiree," she

said gently, "I'm sorry I said that. We don't have to do this if you don't want to."

"Oh for fuck's sake," Des said. "I am already naked. I am *trying* to do what you told me. I signed your form, do your thing. Don't make me keep saying yes to it."

Lucinda, her eyes narrowing and her head tilting to one side in annoyance, went back to stand behind her again. Des felt the ends of the rope flick her hips sharply, and then felt it brushed along her wrists; it fell along the cleft of her buttocks like a tail, and then Lucinda secured her hands behind her back.

Lucinda narrated as she dressed Des in a kind of barnyard shapewear, a rope corset that pushed her sagging breasts up.

"Can I see?" Des asked. She was intensely aware of Lucinda behind her.

"No. Sit on the table and lean forward."

Des wriggled onto the table and did as she was told. The corset came off quickly—Des was impressed at the grace with which the ropes flickered away, like an X-rated version of the "Sorcerer's Apprentice" sequence from *Fantasia*. Lucinda came around in front of her and spread her knees wide, then restrained her so she was bent painfully forward. Des could see the audience: their eager interest. They were intent on Lucinda's descriptions of what she was doing to Des, and what she was planning to do. Des wanted to be intent too—the only way she ever liked consent discussions was when they could be understood as threats, *here's what I'm going to do to you*. But she kept thinking about what the crowd knew about her, and how mulish she'd acted with Lucinda, whether she'd been justified and whether it mattered.

As she squirmed, which didn't do much to relieve either the physical or emotional discomfort, Lucinda was telling the audience about safety technique. Cream you could use to salve rope burns.

How to check to make sure your partner had good circulation, which she demonstrated on Des's wrists, crossed high up behind her back. Medical issues, safety shears, all the stuff on the consent form Des hadn't read. "I recommend the book *Shibari for Klutzes*. It's available in the merch hall."

"This part is boring," Des chipped in.

"How do you feel?"

"My mind is wandering. My shoulders and back ache a lot but I am thinking mostly about a fantasy where I'm in a prison where the behavioral therapist spanks you, which has nothing to do with either my actual prison experience or the sex act I'm performing right now."

Lucinda let her up, and started to truss her up again, the rope making geometric shapes across her body like the lead partitions of a stained-glass window.

She moved slowly, so that everyone in the audience could see how she was making the patterns, which gave Des time to elaborate.

"I bet they really do this, you know," Des said, "the spanking, in some horrible hidden treatment center somewhere off a highway in Montana, except there it's abusive and makes people kill themselves, whereas in my fantasy it makes you a better person. This therapist is very classily-dressed, I didn't know I had a thing for maroon pencil skirts and cream-colored blouses, although I definitely did know I have a thing for '80s hair. Let's call this place the Correctional Care Center, how creepy is *that*. They're making us eat bowls of nutritional mush laced with estrogen to make us compliant and sexually-needy, which I don't think is how estrogen works, maybe I should go with oxytocin? They're going to put me in the guards' break room tonight to have some fun with me once the mush kicks in. Obviously I am treated worse than anybody else because I am the star of my miserable sex world. I wonder if you're regretting having me do this. *Ouch*, okay, that hurts a *lot*, I'm gonna take that as a yes."

Lucinda did something so that Des was lifted off the ground, and she took deep breaths and hung by her arms. Sinking into the pain and getting to know it.

"When I asked you to express what you feel," Lucinda said, just a little tightly, "I meant what you feel physically."

"Okay, I get it, but it's sort of depressing that I'm coiled around with all these ropes," and she wriggled, to accommodate herself to their reality, and the rough edges twisting against her raw places made her hiss and gasp, "and even though you really are hurting me pretty effectively, all I'm thinking about is my weird sex fantasies, and old resentments and things from my group therapy, and what's that Depeche Mode song about how he prays too much. I feel like that's a problem with our culture. I wonder if there can even be a truly masochistic fantasy, since you have complete control and you're the star. The center of your own attention. Does anybody fantasize about being overlooked? I mean, sexually."

"Talk," Lucinda said to the audience, raising Des's torso and extending her legs with graceful movements, "is a social action. The social world is a moral world. Even when we're alone we so often check our phones, we talk to ourselves and create an audience, an imaginary social sphere where all the townspeople are us. I understand," and this was gentler and more directed toward Des, "that you're trying to do what you're supposed to do. It's surprising, to be honest."

"Prison has changed me."

Lucinda twined her arms with Des's as she reached around to pull Des's ankles up in back. They flowed in and around each other like a dance, controlled completely by one partner. Even Lucinda's explanations took on a subtle rhythm, her words moving with the cadence of Des's limbs. Des tried to look down or away, tried not to catch Lucinda's eye, for reasons she didn't care to investigate. But she could feel her body loosening, her skin taking on more importance wherever Lucinda touched her.

Lucinda said, "Shibari is a refuge from the moral world. A flight into silence and the sublime. It provokes an essential inner oneness with the hidden self."

Des, not dancing: "So why the consent forms, then, is what I always wonder."

But then, ruefully: "Remember when we used to hurt me instead of fighting and making up? When you were giving pain you knew me inside out. And now it does hurt, you're doing a great job! But it isn't the old thing, the thing I used to feel or anyway think I was really close to feeling—pure, white fire—contact."

Lucinda went back to talking about how ropes worked. Des would have shrugged, if she'd been able to. She felt that it showed trust and vulnerability to try to have a relationship conversation under such challenging circumstances.

She felt something happening at her ankles. The rope slithered down her legs and across one thigh, and then her legs lifted and she was swinging and hanging batlike.

"Okay, this is neat though," she conceded. "*Swoop*. Soothing. You guys should try this one."

Lucinda, talking about safety and trauma and the difficulties of being upside down, adjusted the ropes so that Des's left ankle slid down to rest beside her knee. Des laughed.

"The Hanged Man," she said. "See? I pay attention to your things. It means, what, personal change?"

Lucinda, with a small gratified smile Des could hear but couldn't see, said, "This is a position inspired by the tarot. It's reductive to assign one meaning to a card," which was for Des, "but the Hanged Man is associated with patience and endurance. Learning to change your point of view."

"Blood is rushing to my head a little. In a good way. I might talk less now." There was a smattering of applause.

Des shut her eyes and swayed.

Transparent, tangled luminous threads drifting through red-tinged blackness. Small comic-book explosion clouds when she squeezed her eyelids tight. Her heart pounding. The generic, clean hotel room disappeared: the room designed for people the designers might meet socially.

In the darkness of her pulse she heard an echo of a woman coughing, choking and unable to breathe, her own voice begging, she could feel the officers' conviction and their fear that felt like anger, and she could feel how all of the prisoners were lying completely still, face down on the floor, in agony, except one who was in terror.

A different place too much like this place. No natural light or natural heat. The temperature controlled from outside, like her strained body. She wondered where her flesh was swelling against the rope and how long the swelling would last.

Pull yourself together, she told herself. In her drug offenders' aftercare program they'd told her that recovery was just a matter of paying attention. This was obviously true. There were so many bad afternoons when she'd come to and looked around her apartment and some of the objects in it would seem to glow and throb. The black screen of her laptop; the not-entirely-empty handle of Evan Williams. ("It's better than you think," she'd say. "The thinking man's poor man's Jack.") The never-unpacked box of books standing next to the empty bookshelf. There were times when she thought that if she could pull herself together enough to touch and interact with one of these throbbing objects, then her unnamable emotions would flow out into the object and away from her. Or, to put it more directly, there were times when she wished that she smoked.

She heard the climate control kick in above her head, and felt a blast of air-conditioning raising pinpricks on her inner thighs. Someone had set the temperature to which she was now having to surrender. Des wondered why she resented that faceless person so much, when she loved surrendering to the humid heat outside.

D.C.: the fetid, mammalian heat of August, or the shallow golden heat of October that barely lasted a half-second after the sun sank behind the low skyline. Rain-washed light, and the scent of rain. The tidal shriek of insects at night, and the wind lifting and rushing off-schedule, driven by a whim that wouldn't spare her and yet was still so welcome. In the exercise yard even the wind had been wrong, tamed and muzzled by the high wire-topped walls, powerless and stripped of weather's scent. It had been four years since she'd smelled that first acrid autumn wind twisting through the heavy heat. She still had no guarantee she'd ever smell it again. Every day she remembered something she hadn't even thought to miss.

Physical circumstances could all be adjusted to, even in prison. The smell and the look of it, the constant damaged light—the dull red light that came on when the hard white lights flicked off. The sounds of the locks and the other awful sounds from places she couldn't see. She had adjusted. What you couldn't ever adjust to was the people. You always knew that you had no idea what they would do next.

The C.O.s had a thing they called "safari," where they'd strip-search everyone and herd them into the chow hall, then toss the cells. They probably didn't have a choice; this was probably something they had to do, assigned and scheduled. And although the prisoners would always say, "Yeah, but they don't got to do it the way they do," that also was probably not true from the perspective of the C.O.s, trained and formed within an embattled community to which they owed a duty of loyalty.

Their two catchphrases were "inmate-friendly," which meant "disloyal"; and "voluntary compliance," which was what they told you they were trained to achieve. "Our goal is not to force you," they would shout. "We help you decide, for your own reasons, to comply."

They had been telling everyone in the chow hall, "Let us facilitate your decision to lie face-down," which was what they said whenever there was chaos. Everybody was obeying, except the woman having an asthma attack. Des had been trying to explain, to the floor, that Lyla's inhaler was back in her cell; she was still trying to explain this when Lyla died.

She had played a desperate game of You Should Be Grateful against herself when they let the women back into their cells, around three hours later: You should be grateful that you only heard her die, and didn't see it, because they wouldn't let you look up.

On safari they would always take things away. It wasn't just knocking all your shit over and throwing it around. Whatever they'd knocked off your bed became "trash," and inmates from another part of the prison would have to come in and sweep it up into trash bags. You would have to do it to them later. Trying not to look at what you were sweeping. There would always be something missing that your family had bought for you or that you had worked for several weeks to buy. It was to teach you not to be angry. "Learn some acceptance," one woman officer had said, as she was letting them back into their cells to clean up the disorder.

In one of her prison AA meetings, another woman on her tier broke through Des's judgments and boredom by saying, sharply, "Admit you're powerless."

Des had always wanted to admit that, right up until the moment someone told her to.

While they were waiting through safari the guards would ask questions. "You like how this place smells?" was a favorite. Mostly a taunt; sometimes, without warning, a gesture of wry camaraderie. *We're all in this together.*

Then they'd ask the lady who saw snakes how her snakes were doing, and they weren't all in that together at all.

(At least one of the snakes had turned out to be real. Much to the distress of one specific C.O. with one extremely gratifying phobia. Desiree grinned. She'd have to find some excuse to jam that story into her group counseling; there wasn't anywhere else she could tell it where people would laugh.)

In the dark all of this could be accepted.

Lucinda's husky tutorial voice, like Veronica Lake explaining the fire safety regulations, reached her from far off. She was enclosed. It was an unsettling sensation: in pain, displayed, but unhumiliated and untouched.

Silent, deep red, in contact with herself. Her head felt heavy and hot. It ached in a pleasant way, an absurd longing throb, as if her head had become a groin. She felt deformed and ridiculous; and in the dark, all of this could be accepted.

She entered an experience of suspense and longing—or it took hold of her, like clouds coming up quick over the sun. All her public daylight was blotted out.

Hanging there, she touched a depth inside herself. And thought of Toya.

She felt a flash of irritation, which was the first social, moral sensation she'd had in at least ten minutes.

And then she turned her deep red consideration on Toya. She discovered that she was worried about Toya: another public emotion. This one made her feel guilty, which, to her surprise, felt a little better than being irritated.

Lucinda was moving and turning her. She submitted to this without thought. Not wondering if she was on display or, more punishingly, exposed. In fact Lucinda moved her in ways that concealed her genitals and revealed her in soft curves, a private maze, a secret garden. She looked gentler than she was. Gentler, sweeter, old-fashioned in a charming Victorian pornography way, something that used to hurt people but had now been rusted and chipped and worn smooth. She was also drooling.

Lucinda lifted her by the hair—explaining how to do this without yanking it out; Des's head felt heavy and pressured but didn't really hurt in any moral sense of the word—and laid her out on the table to start untrussing her.

Slowly her consciousness took on edges. She experienced ordinary sensations: itching and tingling, the feeling of blood shifting its flow. She lay with her eyes closed and tried not to return to the social world. But all she was left with was the conviction, *You have to do something to help Toya.*

"You see how easy she is now," Lucinda said—and then, catching herself, "how at ease."

Desiree, who under most circumstances would have had a comment to make here, just moaned.

Lucinda had to tell her to get up and get dressed. She opened her eyes. Lifted a lagging hand to wipe her mouth and sat up on the edge of the table. Lucinda put a bottle of water in her hand, and she guzzled, letting it splash across her neck and chest. The audience was looking at her dubiously; she didn't feel like she was supposed to bow, but when she stood and bent forward slightly at the waist, some of them clapped. She shook her head and turned away from them—from their attentive, diligent hedonism—and got back into her uniform.

As the workshop was breaking up she stretched, sighed, drank more of the water, inspected the marks on her wrists and forearms. The room still felt woozy and unreal. The attendees smiled at

Lucinda in embarrassment as they left, looking like they wanted to apologize for having been there, but they didn't look at Des at all.

Lucinda came up beside her and said, "Well, that didn't go entirely as I had hoped, but I recognize that you were trying."

"Oh shit," Des said, "I'm sorry. Once I got upside-down I sort of forgot to talk about everything I was thinking and feeling."

Lucinda looked at her for a long, resigned moment. Then said, "That part was fine. Don't worry about it. I'd like you to meet someone—Midori, my wife."

"Oh, like the drink!" Des said. Trying to give a compliment. This time they both looked at her.

Midori was short and plump, and wearing a sleeping toddler on her back in a complexly-wrapped and knotted shawl. It had a pattern in pinks and purples which turned out, when Des said it was lovely, to be the stages of cell division.

Making me meet your wife is really shitty aftercare, she thought. Then scolded herself: It wasn't Lucinda's fault if Des couldn't remember her high-school biology.

"Thank you for helping Luce with this," Midori said. "Have you ever done rope work before?"

"Not that I remember," which Des had learned was usually a safer answer than "no."

"To me it's not about pleasure and pain," Midori said. Des noticed that she was beautiful in a noir-film, glamour-girl way, her lush, rippling black hair threaded with silver. She had done her makeup and even curled her eyelashes. "I appreciate her rope work on the level of craft. You see, I have a fetish for competence."

Lucinda grinned. Des felt herself growing hot across the face, all the way down to the ruffly scoop-neck of her stained uniform.

"Well," she said, "you and I would never have worked out, then."

"I don't think it was a sex act," Lucinda said, husky and a little edgy.

"I'm sorry?"

"When you were talking all the time. You said you were performing a sex act."

Both Lucinda and Des looked at Midori, and tried not to look like they were looking at her.

"I didn't mean to misidentify your workshop," Des said wearily. "It seemed like a sexual...ish act. At the time. Maybe just in my head."

"Rope work is a spiritual practice for me."

Des, giving her left shoulder a hard massage, said only, "I Can't Believe It's Not Bondage."

Back down through the convention. Des spotted a vampire chatting with an adult infant, and grinned as she wondered if she'd really stumbled into a convention for addiction metaphors.

Then there was a sign for "Erotic Decompression and Vacuum Sealing," and Des boggled. *Vacuum sealing?* Out loud she muttered, "What ever happened to good old-fashioned electroshock? I mean, where's the emotional connection?"

An electronic display had replaced the old black signboard with white lettering where they used to announce the events. She scrutinized it but didn't recognize any of the handles or workshops. "Conjugate Me!: Latin for Kinksters"; "The Physical and Mental Health Benefits of Fisting"; "Healing the Planet Through Your Service Submission." Where was the talk on keeping your cats from clawing up your dungeon furniture? The workshop where you matched your submission or dominance style to the clans in *Vampire: The Masquerade?* (Des was a Malkavian.)

Or the spirituality panel, that was always a trip. One year

there'd been a guy so prodigiously pierced that his face looked like Silly Putty, who had entered a twelve-step group for codependency but left when he realized that his boyfriend really had been his Higher Power all along. The next year it had been three plump pagans having an indecipherable argument about chaos gods—and one whip-thin, greasy-haired, brooding Russian Orthodox convert dressed all in black with a Burger King crown on her head, who explained, in between bites of a cheeseburger, that God had called her to prophesy and proclaim the Gospel by dressing and acting like Jughead Jones. Where had Jug the Revelator gone?

Where, Des wondered with a pang, was the Spanking Orchestra?

The Spanking Orchestra had been one of the highlights of the con for her. It happened at the end of the second day, when everyone was keyed-up (and Des was a little coked-up). You lined up on stage and became part of a long percussion instrument, with a note assigned to each cheek, and when you were struck you yelled your note. The audience shouted out which tunes they wanted—usually simple stuff like "Twinkle, Twinkle Little Star," but Des remembered one especially ambitious bandleader who'd tried to paddle them into singing "Für Elise."

Des had the musical ability of brutalist architecture, but nobody cared. You lined up and bent over and when they hit you you yelled as best you could. Everyone laughed at you; the first time they'd laughed she'd been frustrated and chagrined but after a while she started to appreciate the punishment of her pride as much as that of her backside. She remembered gasping and sobbing her way through a rendition of "Flight of the Bumblebee" that sounded like a pack of shtetl cats celebrating Purim, only to have the bandleader segue into "Clair de Lune" without giving them a reprieve. Afterward everybody would be red-faced and panting and giggling, exhilarated by their own stupidity, by their inevitable failures of harmony.

Higher on camaraderie than on endorphins. And then they'd have a disinfecting party under a disco ball.

This year the only evening entertainment was a seminar, "This Bridge Called My Ass: Intersectionality and the Politics of Kink."

There were snack tables set up, and she snagged a croissant and a bagel. They had basically the same taste and texture. Once again Desiree realized the wisdom of her father's maxim: Never eat bagels with the goyim. There is an "us" in life and a "them," and the them put wrong things in their bagels. You think it's fine, cinnamon-raisin bagels are quite pleasant, and then the next thing you know it's jalapenos and blueberries.

Feeling overstuffed with dough, she stepped outside. The late August sun was still high, which surprised her; in the ropes she'd lost track of time. She turned her face up to the kiss of natural heat, lingering and painful. It soothed her and made the rope burns ache more.

She got home in time for group counseling. She did her breathalyzer test and sat down carefully at one end of the fainting couch, leaning forward, stretching and trying to get relief for her lower back. They were talking about work again; Zita had been told off for taking too many steps between the stockroom and the cash register. "They told me, 'Waste of movement is one of the Seven Wastes,'" she said in bewilderment. "But didn't nobody know what the other six wastes was!"

Douceline had been working as an actress, demonstrating unprofessional practices for cosmetology students. She was angry because her supervisor had said her work ethic was exceptional.

"Why would he say that? Does he think I *need* all this coddling? Does he think I need extra attention because of my offender status? It's like he expected me to be lazy—have people been telling him that I'm lazy?"

The others tried to help her. Des gave herself some time to just watch the play of the late sunlight across Douceline's blue-black skin, her high cheekbones and narrowed eyes. That small Betty Boop mouth, always in a moue, how sexy it always was when women let you know they still weren't satisfied. *God, you have the kind of taste that gets you in trouble*, she thought.

Learn better desires. In one of those prison AA meetings, one of the women on her tier had said, "Everything I wanted made my life worse. So I'm trying to want different things."

An older inmate said, with complacent grandmotherly wisdom: "And that's making your life better."

But the other woman had answered, "No. It's making my life unbearable, actually. —Is everything we say here confidential?"

In the present day, Fang had made a Twitter for the missing owl.

"You need a, like a hashtag," Zita said. "Hashtag, FindTheOwl."

"Hashtag, GiveAHoot," Miss Imani suggested, and everyone ooh'd.

"I thought you didn't like owls?" Des asked. "You told me owls were little bitches."

Fang glowered. "I don't have to *like* an owl to want some justice in this world."

"It was their owl," Ray Ray pointed out. "You gotta be loyal."

"Desiree," Miss Imani said. She usually didn't call on people; Des wasn't sure if always being the exception was a good sign or a bad one.

"So, I actually have a question," Des said. "Not about work."

For a moment she looked around the circle. Zita, who thought Michael Jackson was oldies music. Caretta, who last week had asked if it was true you couldn't get pregnant if your man had spent his "strongest sperm" in his wife. Douceline, who cavity-searched her compliments. Fang, the stealth heterosexual and vultures' surly friend. Imani Rollins, whose good advice didn't seem like it was calibrated for scabrous fuck-ups like yourself. And Ray Ray, who was Ray Ray. She wasn't sure why she should "share" with them, or how she expected them to help.

They had done their share of sharing. Maybe that was reason enough.

"So okay," she said, "what if you have a friend who's gotten involved with, let's say a group. And it's not a good group, and you want to get her out of it."

"Aw, shit," Ray Ray said. "What did you do? It ain't them wolfmens, is it? Do you need me to talk to them? I come up with that one werewolf, he my play sister's baby brother."

Des protested, "It's really not me! She's a friend or, not a friend, but someone I spend time with occasionally."

"Ooh," said Caretta, who thought she'd scented sexual scandal.

"And it's not a gang. It's more like a self-help group. Except that they don't help people, or they're not helping her. They're hurting her. Destroying her, I don't know, we're supposed to care about self-esteem, right? Destroying that."

Miss Imani nodded. "There are a lot of these groups now, especially with social media. Young women reinforce one another's urges toward anorexia, bulimia. People form communities based on their desire to self-harm."

Des, carefully: "Bracketing the question of whether harm is the worst thing you can do to yourself—this specific group sounds like bad news. Do any of you guys have experience helping people break free from something like that?"

Zita said, "At my high school we had a prayer group that went bad. A bunch of girls went away for kidnapping and torture because of that."

"Jesus," Des said.

Miss Imani asked, "Is this person a minor?"

"Not legally speaking, no."

"And you believe that your assessment of her situation is the most important thing we could be discussing now, rather than something in your own rehabilitation."

Des reared back a little. "Hey, you asked me to talk! You asked for my assessment of situations. This is it."

Douceline said, "I wonder what your defensiveness might mean about your relationship to your own opinions."

"You're shi—you're kidding me with this." *In every action you take*—

"You can swear here," Miss Imani reminded her.

"Great! Can I get some fucking advice, then? It's a cult! They don't let her take baths! She fell and hit her head!"

"Maybe the baths is a health thing," Zita suggested. She generally believed that old people didn't always grasp health and beauty, because they didn't use the internet.

"We have rules for our lives here," Douceline pointed out. "This is a group she chose for herself, right?"

Desiree, sitting in the parlor of the halfway house where she was required to stay as a condition of her release, tried to remember what was so bad about Toya's group and came up blank. And then, triumphantly: "She has to get permission to see her friends!"

"So do we," Douceline noted.

"That sounds like a therapy thing," Caretta said.

Ray Ray was chuckling to herself. Des had the angry, abasing feeling that she was living down to expectations.

"There is something not right going on with her," she said.

"Okay," Miss Imani said, "but what are we here to focus on today? Is it your friend, or is it you?"

"She put on lipstick she found on the ground," Des said: her closing statement.

"Did you see your ex?" Ray Ray asked. She was even kinder, and even more humiliating, than Miss Imani had been.

"Yeah, see if I ask you people for help again," Des muttered.

And Ray Ray, placidly: "You will."

Des's mother was equally unhelpful. She meant well, but she was saddened by the idea that her daughter now knew people in cults, and more saddened by the idea that her daughter might think that people were in cults when they weren't. There was, Des had to admit, a certain lack of trust.

Her mother tried to ask whether she was sober without asking if she was sober. "I thought that I should, that it was a responsibility to just check in and see how you're doing lately, with wanting things and... doing things."

When Desiree figured out what she was being asked she almost laughed. "Oh, no, don't worry!" she said. "If I was drinking, man, you'd *know*."

This did not reassure her mother.

The fact that her mother thought she might want to go back to that world—the drowned world, the sickly yellow apartment crusted with bad dreams—made her ask herself if that was what she still wanted. She had wanted it for a long time after it became horrible. Not wanting it had seemed impossible. She'd accepted, at some point in prison, that she would always want to be drunk. That freedom from time, the sticky glass becoming an infinite nutshell, a tomorrowless haven from self, no clocks no windows: a descent from the failure to meet your responsibilities into the wider and deeper failure to have any responsibilities left. A secret self-acceptance nestled deep inside your self-hatred.

The hardest thing to remember, she found, was how much fun it had been. How she had raced to it. Sought it out, hunting for it like the last unicorn searching for the castle of King Haggard—where all the others like her had gone before! How she had treasured up the things people told her she'd said in unremembered hours.

Only some of the things. "When Harold Bloom calls things 'apocalyptic' he just means they've only got two characters": treasured; "You're only dating him because you fetishize his race": gone before she'd finished her morning-after apology. She was surprised and dismayed to see the dice cup of her recovery shake out those particular snake eyes, forgotten until just this minute.

But she'd galloped in the spangled nights, too much perfume under slurring stars, a lit-up carousel in the flood. Sprawled on her unmade bed with her wrists crossed above her head, laughing and begging for addiction to take her body, take her virtue, ravish her in all. And then stop.

She had thought of alcohol and cocaine as bottom-shelf sublimity, reasonably-priced ekstasis for the bacchante on a budget; and she had assumed that they'd demand only as much unconditional surrender as she wanted to give. She had thought she could stop anytime she wanted, because what kind of loser would ever want to stop? She had thought—and at last she recognized this as the characteristic stupidity of the overeducated, the belief that they understand things because they know things—that she had a safe word.

Now she touched the idea of relapse with her mind and found nothing. A numb patch on the flushed skin of her soul. She stroked it and it didn't even itch.

At first you're separated from those you love by your desires. What Bruce Springsteen, at top volume above the pounding of her father on his exercise bike, would call a *bad desire*. (Even if you share the bad desire with the ones you love, it will separate you from them.) But then the bad desire ebbs—defeated, postponed, transformed, you'll never know which one until you die—and it turns out that now you're separated from those you love by belonging. You belong now somewhere else.

Her niece, a thirteen-year-old harpsichordist/cheerleader/robotics prodigy, was complaining about one of their teachers: "She's abusive. We're all signing a petition to have her removed because of it."

"*Abusive*," Des's mother said, appalled. "What happened? Do you know? I suppose the students' privacy needs to be protected, but—"

"She hugs people! Without asking for permission or getting any kind of consent." The niece chewed on the pink ribbon drifting down from her unicorn-horn headband. "That isn't allowed and it isn't okay."

Desiree, appalled but for different reasons, said, "Not to diminish your feelings, but when I went to that school they fired a teacher for straight punching a kid in the face."

"You never told us that happened!" Des's mother said.

Her sister just asked, "Oh, was *that* what happened to Miles? I thought he got fired for smoking pot with students."

Des said, "No, I don't think our school would've fired him for that. He was dealing to the music teachers, so he was contributing to the community. But it was the '90s, people were on a short fuse, I guess. You gotta have that one teacher who takes one for the team even if it means he gets fired. It kept the rest of us in line."

The others didn't want to argue with her so soon after her return. So they created a sort of angular silence around her, a formally-registered dissent, as they all moved around the dining-room table and forked lox or knifed cream cheese onto their bagels.

(Plain, poppyseed which Des avoided, and the rather daring onion.) They sat. Des's cat immediately leapt onto her lap and dug his claws into her thigh. She gasped, then breathed carefully and started to stroke him, as he purred and hurt her.

Des looked at the wallpaper, a harvesty thing, huge nodding furry sunflower heads on vines in faded '70s colors, orange and brown and gold. The blooms were as big as her adult head.

She bowed her head, still petting the cat with one hand, and silently sang through what she remembered of the prayer before meals. *Baruch atah Adonai, Eloheinu melech haolam, la da dee dah dah dah ha-da-dum.* She knew she should ask her sister what it really was, but willingly exposing her ignorance to her sister was an exercise in humility she wasn't yet resigned to.

The half-prayer exposed her own failures—of attentiveness, of filial piety, of solidarity and sincerity—but she was certain there was something in it both human and divine.

More divine than she was ready to face; more human than she was ready to act.

When she lifted her head her family was staring at her.

Toya skipped the first brunch in September. This was held at somebody's house up in Foxhall, in a huge wavy downstairs that melted without border from kitchen to dining room to living room, with wall-sized windows. (The heavy curtains were drawn back but the gauze was left for anonymity.) The crowd was goth-tinged and completely white.

Des arrived with muscles aching, although not from housecleaning this time. One of Ray Ray's coworkers from the National Park Service had come and trained them to identify and clear invasive species. Yanking out hanks of porcelainberry—it was hard not to regret it, the delicate vines and the pearly purple, aqua and turquoise berries. They had hiked uphill to the Catholic church and then rambled down at leisure, rooting out knotweed and plucking potato-chip bags from the pokeberry tangles.

It felt good to be trusted with trash cleanup. Des picked up a crumpled plastic pint bottle of Gordon's vodka and it was only beautiful, seamed and milky—it didn't throb in her attention or her memory.

Now she was standing around wondering where Toya was, while Lizzie complained about her Tinder dates.

"He brought a shuriken and an iguana," she said, tossing her majestic blonde mane. "I took one look at him and was like, 'You're gonna want to choke me, aren't you?'"

This was one of Lizzie's themes: the number of men who believe women want to be choked sexually, even after they have said, for example, "It makes me think of my mother's corpse." One of her dates had asked, "Oh, is that a horror movie?"

"I told him it was my nickname for his dick," she said. She gulped at her cocktail. Des always thought it was sexy when a woman gulped a drink—it was so honest.

"I should change my profile to say, 'Hit me up, sleazebags of Washington! Your daddy issues and my mommy issues can make baby issues!' But I'd probably just get guys with impregnation kinks."

At this point Trash sidled up to them, walking gingerly.

"I see you brought your sideboob," Lizzie said.

"My—oh, you mean Javier," he said. "I won't ask you to be nice, because I believe we should all be true to ourselves. But we are an item again."

"Oh, Trash," she said. "Who's he making you vote for?"

"I won that argument! That's why we're back together. He promised to respect my civil rights. Which wasn't my point at *all*, like I couldn't care less if he searches and seizes me, or makes me blow a sailor, which I feel like is basically the Third Amendment. This election is a lot bigger than just my personal human rights or whatever. But it's still the closest I've come to being with someone who listens to me. It's as nice as you said it would be!"

"I am so proud of you," Lizzie said, as he nodded and beamed. "Not only for standing up for yourself, although I didn't know you could do that so it's like if your *cat* did a trick, I'm pleased but unsettled. Mostly I'm proud that you know what the Third Amendment is."

"I looked it up!" And then he said to Des, "Remember that time Lucinda made you give that guy a blowjob, and I had to give you pointers?"

"I remember that that happened, yes."

"How did it end up going?"

"It was strange."

"Oh, sure. Even if you like dick it's kind of an odd feeling. And not a good taste."

"I'd expected it to be degrading so I was totally down for it, but in the end I think it just felt like work. It made me realize how much I do think about sex as a type of performance. Something I want to do well at. And that's kind of—unnatural, I guess?"

Lizzie, skeptical: "Wanting to be good in bed is the part of this that struck you as unnatural?"

"No, I get it," Trash said. "You're supposed to be giving yourself, like a gift. And not caring if the gift is kind of garbage. It's the thought that counts."

"Then Lucinda got all weird about it because I wasn't a Gold Star lesbian anymore. I didn't get where she was coming from at all. I mean it's a dick. It's life, isn't it? 'Ooh, I'm gay, I'm too good to suck dick.' Why be such a princess about it? It was just like sucking a popsicle, probably. I was pretty wasted so my memories of the whole thing are... pointillist, but it was not about the penis. The guy was totally irrelevant—"

"Always," Lizzie said loyally.

"What I was really sucking on was her authority over me."

Trash peered into the punch bowl. "I wonder if I could ask Javier if I can put some of this ice on my ass."

"You got lucky?" Lizzie asked.

"Very. It's a good thing I work on my feet, since I won't be sitting down for a while if I can help it. It was amazing, it hurt so much—I was crying, I was confused. I was all in a tizzy!"

Des, laughing: "Confused? Is that an emotion we're going for now?"

Trash shifted wincingly from foot to foot. "Oh yes," he said, "I think confusion is underrated, sexually. When I'm completely bewildered by what's being done to me and I just have to trust that the top knows better what I need than I know myself, that's a very consoling feeling."

Lizzie, inevitably: "Even when he thinks what you need is a punch in the eye?"

"No, that was embarrassing for me," Trash said severely. "I didn't like having to admit that that had happened."

Des asked, "Do you think you forgave him—Brandon, I mean, not the clown guy, I'm trying not to have an opinion about Clown Guy—maybe as an attempt to take back some control of the situation? I hear you about how comforting being controlled *can* feel, but—not to get into my personal stuff, but when you're being given impossible and unpredictable orders by somebody who holds you in genuine contempt, that isn't consoling."

Trash frowned. "Oh, that's—maybe I was trying to assert myself by forgiving him. I hope not."

Lizzie nodded. "Like, not to bring my job into it, but the Donald says he hasn't asked forgiveness for *anything*. Even from God, where you're guaranteed to get it! Because he, and this is transparent, it's like the most gold-plated thing about him, he can't let anybody judge him. And forgiveness is kind of inherently judgey."

Trash sighed. "It's very hard to have an adult relationship, where you take responsibility for your actions, and also be *fully* submissive to the other person. I don't think I'm very good at it."

Just then a green-haired woman in a t-shirt showing Hillary Clinton's face on the body of a *Game of Thrones* character strode up to Lizzie, fixed her in the eye and said, "You work for Fox News, don't you?"

Lizzie knocked back her drink. "No, that's Megyn Kelly," she said. "She has short hair. I am a Republican, but if you want to spit on me you have to buy me dinner first."

The green-haired woman asked, "Why are you doing this to our country?"

Lizzie set her plastic cup on their host's marble-topped, curving kitchen island. She looked the other woman straight in the eye and said, "Somebody has to."

Chapter 14
Beauty's Predicament

The problem with rescuing Toya, as it inevitably turned out, was Toya herself.

They were deep into September. The light now was always golden and the heat was shallow. Morning and afternoon alike were lit as if artificially, as if by nostalgia. In the golden light the trees looked exhausted—the leaves wouldn't change until late this year because of the heat, but their green tint had faded and yellowed.

The feud between the werewolves and the vampires was heating up as the weather changed. There were more of the little memorials at the lampposts, Valentine's hearts and artificial flowers in a vase to mark where somebody'd been killed.

The woman who kept a bottle tree in her front yard, a few blocks away from Love's Labors, got a ladder and added a crown of bottles all along the top. Not just green and clear glass beer bottles this time, but deep blue bottles from fancy bottled water. Blue was the spirits' color and it seemed that in this one respect the spirits of the neighborhood would benefit from gentrification.

The nights were cold enough that Miss Imani had to come and fix the bedroom window, finally. Des wound up the venetian blind and tied it off—there was no hook, so she had to tie the cord around the white plastic windowframe. The blind sagged on one end. It smirked at her as on the other end of her cell phone Toya Tannen said, "You live with drug dealers and probably killers of people, and I live with my *family*. Last night Trina and some of the other girls braided our hair!"

"They braided your *hair*," Des said. She'd read on a website about helping people make positive changes that you should never phrase your objections as a question. You should always let your voice turn down at the end, instead of up, and this would make your target feel less interrogated and judged.

"They—I helped," the Little Shorn Lamb said. "I can do a French braid now, and a fishtail. Or—I can do them on other people. And we played Spin the Bottle. I didn't know that was real!"

Desiree said cautiously, "You had to kiss people."

"Yes! And the leader assessed my sexual preference. Like a personality test? I am voracious," she bragged. "Which means that you eat a lot, but also, you're very sexy. He intuited that I have a natural draw toward black men."

Every few days now Des had some conversation of this kind. Apparently Morningstar had been spooked by Toya's disobedient funeralgoing. They'd showered her with attention; they'd even hinted that before the temperature dropped below freezing, she might be allowed to move from the basement up to the second floor. Toya, the world's last honest salesman, shared every detail of her happiness with Des. And Des couldn't even avoid it. Toya always had to borrow somebody else's cell phone, so Des couldn't check the caller ID and let her go to voice mail.

"And *I* said, 'Or black women?' And he said, 'Whoa there,

tiger!' A ha, ha, ha!"

You laugh like somebody in a cult, Des thought sourly, but didn't say. She had been losing this argument with Toya for weeks.

She'd asked everybody for advice. Lizzie had suggested visualization: "When I have to do something that makes me feel awful, like one of those performance reviews where they touch your leg, I imagine that I have antlers growing out of my head. Majestic, powerful prongs. I am strong. I am antlered. Nobody will fuck with me."

Des, though she was dubious, passed this on to Toya. Who called her up angry and crying because now everyone made fun of her for ducking when she went through doorways.

Lucinda had said, "I think sometimes you need to not talk."

Des had argued, "I can't just leave her on her own!"

She couldn't explain why. She just looked at Lucinda's wedding ring and thought, not happily, about how much of your life ends up organized around a conviction that's all that remains of a moment of ecstasy. She had been left with very few convictions other than the criminal kind, and this responsibility to Toya was the most immediate one. Which she was failing at.

"Oh, I told them the thing you and Trash always say, about how we need to be grateful for everything, even punishment," Toya said now. "The leader said that's wise, and you two sound like good friends for me to have."

And then, teasingly, "Do you still think I'm in a cult?"

Desiree muttered, "I don't know what I think."

She had thought that one of the undeniable upsides of sobriety was that she would never again lose an argument with a stupid person. She was starting to realize that was a very stupid thing to think.

Des was trying to explain herself. She wasn't sure why, and she wasn't sure to whom, and she couldn't make out what she was saying, and she was especially confused about why sometimes she had a spiky black tail or a colorful frill around her face. Suddenly on all fours for no reason. Orange and teal rippling out around her head as if her face were the center of a flower. These physical changes weren't helping her credibility.

Waking; then the familiar smell of her pillow (*you should wash this*), the pressure of her eyemask against her eyelids. She scruffed the thing up onto her forehead. "Duck Amuck," she realized.

If she had to be a Looney Tunes character, she would absolutely have picked Pepé le Pew, but she had to admit that Daffy Duck was a better match.

She sat up in bed, swung her legs over the side and prayed. She had her usual morning irony and embarrassment about not knowing how she was supposed to sit (or stand?) when she prayed. She tried sitting with her knees apart and her hands clasped, her head bowed, but she just felt like she was asking a skeptical banker for a loan. She then sat cross-legged on the bed and felt unpleasantly Californian.

It was becoming her usual morning prayer: *Higher Power, please give me the grace or courage or whatever to accept whatever you do to me today.*

And then, as always: *Ugh, I need to look up actual Jewish prayers so I stop saying "whatever." Whatever whatever, yadda yadda—come on, stop being a dick. Please, God or G-d* (which she pronounced, in her head, "Gggggggggd"), *relieve me of the bondage of self.*

With some high irony in that last phrase.

Let me not be an asshole today. Let me remember my own failures and cruelties and like, not forget other people's exactly, because people are scum, but let me look upon others' cruelties as I do upon the cruelties of my friends. Okay, let's go out and face the day. Schlemiel, shlimazl, Hassenpfeffer Incorporated! Amen.

It was more sincere than it sounded.

October was coming in raggedly and without much spectacle. The heat lingered, a shallow daytime heat, doorstep kisses promising little. They got to do group counseling out on the porch.

She tried to tell the others about her dream in group, since sharing dreams was considered an especially vulnerable act. But nobody seemed particularly moved by her admission, "I dreamed that I was a maid, but also a duck."

Ray Ray recounted a conversation she'd overheard on the bus. Two older black women were sitting up in the handicapped seats, talking about the house in their neighborhood with all the women criminals.

"What bothers *me*," one of them had said, and Ray Ray camped it up here, relishing this woman beyond what was reasonable or kind, "is that it be a white girl there."

"Mm-*hmm*. An African-American young lady, it be all kinds of ways she might get caught up in the system. A bad boyfriend. These days they all got these baaaaaaad mens." (Desiree thought this couldn't possibly be word-for-word, but that didn't make her blush any less as she sussed where it was going.) "But if you get a white girl coming out of federal prison, my dear Miss Beu-hilda— that's a *criminal*."

"She's not wrong," Des muttered, not knowing what else she could say.

"We gotta complain 'bout how they dumping *those people* in our neighborhood," Ray Ray finished gleefully.

"Thank you for sharing that, Ranae," Miss Imani said. "I wonder what might be constructive ways for Desiree to prove that she is a responsible member of our community east of the River."

Ray Ray shrugged. "She real good at all that health care shit, or fixing up people problems with they jail fees, all the forms she do. We could like turn her out to the neighbors."

Des felt absurdly gratified by this praise, even though what she actually did with the thousand terrifying forms and bills that the other women handed her was pass them on to Trash. He told her which ones really needed to be paid and which ones would be resolved if she called a certain number and begged. The Yale voice helped, the voice of unbending maiden-aunt WASP certainty: the best use she'd made of her diploma since she'd set it out as a serving platter for her guests' cocaine.

Des had found a lot of websites that claimed to tell you how to free your loved ones from a cult. They didn't seem to offer much middle ground: You could accept the person unconditionally and offer unstinting welcome no matter what whackadoo thing they did or said; or you could kidnap them. The websites all emphasized that you should sincerely express your love and admiration for the person, which wasn't much help to Desiree. There didn't seem to be any advice directed at people who wanted to free their disliked ones from a cult.

Still, she read all these websites, sitting at the dining room table at Love's Labor's Loft with "Strange Bedfellows" playing in the background.

Lizzie, brightly, on affirmative action: "I don't have a problem with college admissions quotas. People get into college for all kinds of dumb reasons. I only got into Indiana University because I told them how I found my mom's body after she hung herself."

And when her co-host couldn't think of anything to say to that and just stared at her, sorrowing and helpless, she added, "Keepin' it real."

"I think," David Lav said, "white people tell themselves that things like that are still meritocratic. The idea is that you demonstrate your merit by explaining how you coped with that kind of hardship."

"Oh, sure," Lizzie nodded, her big empathetic eyes moving easily from him back to the camera, "people act like it's the SATs of hard knocks, but in reality I don't cope. I don't—what are people supposed to do, like go to counseling? I just sleep around. It's a lot easier. When I feel bad I go and find somebody to beat me up. But I'm literal-minded."

David Lav, looking at her instead of at the camera, with a disturbed little grin he couldn't suppress: "You know, the only way you remind me of Trump is that I can't tell when you're trolling."

Lizzie had noticed that she often found herself hitting up the worst guys on Tinder after she'd talked about her mother's death on the air. If she'd mentioned finding the body, she might even plumb the depths of Fetlife. She figured there was probably some third factor which explained both things—*I should start tracking my menstrual cycle*, she thought as she swiped left, standing up on the Red Line on her way to her volunteer job.

When her sideboob video went viral back in 2014, the CNN people said that they liked that she talked about her family, and that she should "feel free" to bring up her background. They used the word "hardscrabble" several times. This had confused Lizzie for a while, until she thought to use her dictionary app and realized they meant she was white trash.

The trick to performing sincerity is that you have to really believe it, on some level—but you can pick which level. Lizzie never faked her thoughts or traumas. What she faked was insouciance. She'd been surprised and a little insulted to find out that she got only a couple hundred extra rape threats after the CNN appearance. On the other hand, the bump to their Patreon account had meant she could finally get her teeth whitened.

"Bullseye," she said under her breath. She'd managed to find a dominant and "heteroflexible" guy who listed his *bylines*. Using Tinder for networking—what is wrong with Washington? There was a seedy desperation there that Lizzie thought might turn out to be appealing.

She was still messaging with him (she'd said he had "a body like a podcast" and he'd called her a brat, which meant he was probably into spanking) as her red high heels clip-clopped out of the Metro and up the crumbling concrete steps to the school, past the sign that read,

FOR THE LOVE OF GOD MONTESSORI

Yes, Montessori—For the love of God!

The other volunteer literacy coordinators wore tennis shoes: toes covered, soles flexible and flat, everything designed for the physical needs of children and their guardians. Lizzie catered to their aesthetic needs instead.

Inside the school Lizzie click-clacked to the teachers' lounge and hid her purse in the microwave. (She'd started taking this precaution after the time Nevaeh had gotten into the teachers' cubbyholes and came back into the classroom wearing Lizzie's last night's underwear draped over her braids.) Then into the classroom, where Yerom made a beeline for her, grabbed Lizzie by the knees and commanded, "Read to me!"

"Okay, but how do we ask for things?"

Yerom, just turned four, grinned up at her and caterwauled, "Pleeeeeeeeeeeeeeeeeease!"

Lizzie sat on the floor, and Yerom raced to fetch the book, then plopped down hard into her lap. Lizzie's left thigh pressed down hard on the point of her right heel and she grinned through it.

Yerom laughed to herself as Lizzie opened the book and began,

"*Machines Do All the Work!*, by Bill Ruttger."

"This book is robot propaganda," Yerom said contentedly, repeating what Lizzie said every time they read it.

As Lizzie read she looked down on Yerom's head. The high curve of her skull, the short-cropped hair and broad high forehead. Lizzie had lived in D.C. long enough to know when a kid was Ethiopian. Something about that felt like success. The child's sweet smell, the heat radiating from her, made Lizzie want to press her nose and mouth against the girl's hair in a full-face kiss. She was pretty sure that was against even the surprisingly human regulations of the Montessori school.

When she finished with the robot propaganda she had to spend a couple minutes sorting out and soothing a sobbing three-year-old. He was pitching a full-on, foot-stamping fit because he'd built a huge wall out of foam bricks, and he couldn't get out from behind it because he wouldn't take the bricks down.

"Honey, how about if I move a couple of these bricks at the top, and then I can lift you out and you can build it back up?"

The boy calmed down long enough to try to figure out if this was an acceptable solution. Lizzie experimentally took one brick down, and he didn't howl. After two more bricks came off the top of his wall, he held up his arms so she could lift him.

Having rescued the prisoner, Lizzie looked around and saw a five-year-old named Jeloni lurking near her. She grinned at him and he came up to her, smiling in eager embarrassment, holding a book.

Back down onto the floor. The child's weight and heat pressed against her breastbone and her stomach. They read to one another, alternating lines and pages. Jeloni sounded out words—he was a kid with a keen sense for others' reactions, shy and alert, and the fact that he was willing to try to pronounce "rhinoceros" in front of her was a sign of deep trust.

This time he'd brought her one of his favorites: a book, published by the Little Sisters of the Passion and Death, about "the nightingale who chose celibacy."

"I feel you, nightingale," Lizzie said, as she said every single time they read this book together; and he giggled and said, "Me too," which he also said every single time.

After this there was a book about trucks baking a cake, and a book about how rain is not so bad really, and then a book of short stories in which animals did improbable things while wearing clothes.

"Have we noticed that all of the stories in this book involve some kind of theft?" Lizzie asked, when they reached the last page. "Why does Harry Hyena have to go to jail just because he stole a plate of spaghetti, when Pa Pig spent the whole last story stealing increasingly-ridiculous vehicles and all he had to do was apologize? Do we think Pa Pig has some relatives on the police force?"

Jeloni giggled and nodded. One of the other volunteers gave Lizzie a sharp look.

Lizzie was trusted less by the other literacy volunteers than by the children—the adults had found out what she did for a living. They were all young white women except for the mixed-race guy who was an organizer for the Industrial Workers of the World. He had long, tangled hair, and called his friends "comrade," and Lizzie liked him even though she suspected him of being a member of the Black Bloc. All the other women were Ms. Something, Ms. Devora or Ms. Anna or Ms. Katie (there were three Ms. Katies: two unhappily straight, one happily lesbian). Lizzie had won the right to be Miss Lizzie by arguing, "Conservatism is my gender identity. Please respect how I identify."

She petted Jeloni's arm and said, in her most teacherly voice, "In a decent society, everyone is punished."

The lesbian Ms. Katie gave her a disapproving, pitying look.

Part of why it was so hard to convince Toya to leave Morningstar was that Des's own, cultless life was not much to brag about. Toya took to asking her, in a bright innocent voice like a hypodermic, how her Work and Hygiene class was going; and Desiree, who had been lectured more than once about how humility required total honesty, told her.

"We had a computer literacy class," she admitted. "The instructor plucked at his Adam's apple the whole time. He wore a velour vest with question marks he'd cut out of construction paper and stuck on with safety pins. He spent a half-hour imitating the noises different modems made, then diagrammed both a computer mouse and an actual mouse to show the similarities, and then he had us re-type articles he'd printed off his social media. Mine was from XOJane, 'I Was Racially Profiled (And I Liked It!)'"

"Remind me how much you pay per class?"

Des, who was idly Googling "where get replacement mop head washington dc," said, "He took off points because I didn't put spaces after the periods in 'D.E.A.' It's been a while since I cracked my AP Style handbook but I'm pretty sure that's just wrong."

By the end of October the holidays were already pressing in on them, a season of bad memories and things left too late. In group they talked about what they had missed in prison. Mostly funerals: Ray Ray's foster mother; Douceline's brother; the teacher Caretta had dated in high school.

The only thing that Des could remember was the time her aunt got a medal from the President. "Yeah, my aunt started a charity to give veterans the animals from repossessed small farms. Pigs for Patriots. So she got an invitation to the White House. I think she met a lot of people, like, George Takei was there."

Imani quirked her eyebrows to show that she understood and was as impressed as professionalism would allow; none of the other women knew what Des was talking about.

"My parents held a big party at their house—they hired caterers and everything. Meanwhile I think I spent that evening helping clean up this absolute *landscape* of shit one of my cellmates had created as, I don't know, a protest or something. Just layers and layers, patterns, swirls, we never did find out if it was all even hers: a diarrhea masterpiece. A diarrhama, if you will."

Again, only Imani laughed. Des had a talent for expressing her traumas in terms all but calculated to repel empathy.

Des and Ray Ray were walking downhill to the Metro, and Des was daydreaming about being a swimmer with the flu. Ray Ray interrupted her imaginary coach's fond scolding to complain about supervised release.

"My fucking P.O. be asking me all these questions," she said. "'What's your goal in life,' and when I be like, 'I'm a get my HVAC license,' he all, 'No, what's your goal in *life*.' Like I should be Mother Teresa or some shit. I got one goal in life and that is to stay the fuck back out of prison! My goal is to get through the day on the outside and not the inside! 'What is your *quest*,' like I'm fucking Harry Potter. Shit."

They were on their way to see Fang's band, Guess the Twist, play somewhere out at the end of the Green Line. Most of the other Love's Labors women couldn't come, but they were meeting Ty'heaven, Caretta, and Trash at the show. There were yellow leaves in the gutters, and walnuts dropped from the trees onto the sidewalk, heavy green balls that made a sharp report when they hit. Ray Ray jumped every time—she'd said she was having a bad feeling. A premonition. Her foster mother would have said, *I feel the wind over my grave. Lord Jesus, come.*

"What do you tell them?" Ray Ray asked. "You always good at that bullshit."

Des didn't know if she should feel complimented or insulted. She shrugged. "I said that my goals were to make amends, to repair the relationships I had damaged, and to walk softly upon the earth."

Ray Ray rocked her head back. "Ooh. 'To walk softly upon the earth.' I'm a use that one, with your permission."

"Sure, it's not mine. I should warn you, though, if you say stuff like that. When I said my goals, my P.O. was like, 'Okay, and what have you done in the past twenty-four hours to achieve these goals?' and I had to be like, 'Well, I cleared the lint screen on the dryer when it wasn't even my turn.'"

A walnut thudded down onto a boxful of books that somebody had left on a front stoop. It rolled across the hardback cover of *Master of the Senate*, then dropped into a crevice between the Johnson biography and a trio of Regency-style drug kingpin romances. (*Caressed by a Corner Boy*, *The Virgin and the Vice Lord*, *She Keistered His Heart*.) A note on the box said, MOVING TO PG, PLEASE TAKE MY BOOKS, so Des squatted down to have a good paw-through.

Under *Master of the Senate* there were more hardbacks: *The Art of the Deal*, *KANYE: King And Now Young Emperor*, *My Rise and Fall*. The *Let's Go* guides to Syria, Yemen, and the U.K.; a 1988 copy of *The Smuggler's Guide* to the European Economic Community; the *Mr. Boston's* bartending guide, with crosstabs; *Robert's Rules of Order*; the Fitzgerald translation of the *Iliad*, with strange bulges that turned out to be various 1998 and 1999 issues of *Jet* and *Soap Opera Digest*. Des flipped through *Mr. Boston's* but ruefully threw it back in.

There was one book that intrigued her: *Beauty's Predicament*. But when she leafed through it—so pristinely unread that its pages held together for a split second before ruffling open—it turned out to be postmodern theology, not porn.

She straightened up—then realized something, and bent down to grab the three *Let's Go* guides and tuck them into her shoulder bag. She figured she could wring a feuilleton out of those. She'd have to borrow a few foreign-policy opinions but she still knew plenty of people who had them to spare.

"You could say your goal is to make amends to Ty'heaven," she suggested, as they started walking again.

"Naw, I told my CSO I ain't see her no more," Ray Ray reminded her. "She like a person, place, or thing. You know how you can't be hanging around the places you was affiliated with."

Just then a bus passed by them and Des spotted something strangely familiar on its side: an ad with a black background, against which a cartoon mouth opened fire-engine lips in an eerie, disembodied laugh. A white sunburst gleamed from the perfect white teeth as a speech bubble said, "I LOVE D.C." DENTAL SPA.

Des was still trying to remember why this ad unsettled her when they reached the Metro.

Distorted, dazzling guitar chords drifted down through the club in angled horizontal planes, as narrow spotlights swept the crowd. Beneath the guitar there was a crunchy, buzzing beat; above it the recorded sounds of barking dogs and, in a horror-movie touch, a tolling church bell.

For once Fang was playing a club with an almost all-black crowd. (Trash was intrigued, delighted, as always. Nothing human was alien to Trash except himself.) There was a guy on a small clear patch of floor, a skinny guy in gray jeans so tight they looked spray-on, doing what Des would've called popping and locking, although it was more like "Beat Your Feet" plus outbursts of mime. He hunched up and made his arms into wings, the hands pointing down—he was a skeletal vulture. Then liquid-limbed, feet dancing and weaving; then kneeling on the floor, worshiping some dude in the circle of friends around him. Pleading, making obeisance, flopping down with his ass in the air and his face on the floor and lifting up one hand, cupped and turned upward, shaking impatiently to make them all applaud. *Maestro! My music!*

Des was reminded of the dances of her youth. Trying to learn to breakdance, spinning on her ass in front of the TV watching "Solid Gold." In fourth grade the girls would make the boys wait until the very end of recess, then run behind the dumpsters and do Da Butt, an outburst of D.C. patriotism which the school had, obviously, banned. In return the boys would writhe on the ground, almost kissing the pavement as their legs worked above their heads, turning the motions of self-abasement into an art of courtship.

Whoever was singing now—not Fang's band—was promoting the Black Israelites. Des hoped these were not the same Black Israelites who stood out on the corner at Gallery Place shouting about how the white man brought homosexuality to Africa. Black Israelites were the only people she'd ever heard use the term "bulldagger" in real life.

The skinny-jeans guy clasped his hands behind his back and proved he was double-jointed. "Ooh," Des said.

"Check this out," Caretta said; and bent the fingers of both hands all the way backwards.

"Yikes," Des said admiringly.

"Yeah, I been able to do that ever since my stepfather slammed my hands in the car door. One of them sliding doors, you know?"

Des had learned that when somebody said that something awful had happened to them, they didn't want you to say, "But you know that was awful, right?" They mostly wanted to be normal, even if it meant their pain was normalized. So she hummed, deep and sincere, like she knew exactly what Caretta meant. Then her phone buzzed against her thigh and she had to go outside and check in with her CSO.

Halfway through the concert Ty'heaven was nowhere to be found. Ray Ray had hunted all through the place, pretending she was dancing. Checking her phone. Finally she'd given up and come over to Des and Trash, where she didn't look at them, just muttered to herself and occasionally banged her fist hard against the bar or her thigh.

Trash tried to console her. He'd had his share of romantic troubles, he said. "In the words of St. Ignatius of Loyola, 'The harder they come, the faster they run.'"

Ray Ray was still fuming when they got home. Pacing around the kitchen looking for the carton of Andy Capp's Hot Fries that Imani kept for emergencies, slamming cabinet doors and flinging around assorted packets of Swiss Miss cocoa, dehydrated soup, "Cajun style" spice mix, edible cake decorations, and Kraft mac & cheese: all the flotsam from countless shipwrecked lives, all the comfort food left behind by people who were in some cases long past comforting. Des watched the pile grow on the kitchen countertop and wondered if she was looking at a dead woman's Funfetti.

She was leafing through *Let's Go: Syria* and composing an email to her cocktail-party friend who worked at the Center for the American Way (né the Center for a Humble Foreign Policy, renamed October 2001). This was a delicate project since, she realized halfway through, she owed this person an amends. Caretta was checking her Twitter.

"They still giving updates from that owl they lost," she said idly. "Ooh, it was a stabbing again up by the 7-11. They think it was Los Vampirez. I don't like all these gangs and killings."

And then, scrolling: "Huh. Ray Ray. Remind me the name of

your—uh, your, I guess girlfriend?"

Ray Ray stopped rooting through the cabinet under the sink and stood up. Turned to look at Caretta.

"Ty'heaven," she said. Her face was very still.

Caretta read out the notification from @ABlackerDC. A woman had died that morning in the P.G. County jail. Cause of death unknown but there were unconfirmed reports that she had begged for medical care and been refused. Cause of arrest currently unknown. If anyone has video of this woman's arrest, please contact. "'Ty'heaven Clark, rest in power,'" Caretta read out.

It seemed as though Ray Ray hadn't moved her face at all and yet her expression had completely changed. She had been holding still to brace herself; now her stillness was masklike, distorting, harrowed. She stood there in front of the sink unsupported. Her arms hung down and they had been hanging loose before she heard the news but now they hung with a heavier uselessness, now it was as if she had been stripped and lopped until nothing was left but that carved and devastated face.

Chapter 15
The Shield of Achilles

Des was on the bus heading to the memorial protest for Ty'heaven, trying to understand the kaddish. The first page she'd found ("Rejewvenation: Prayers your parents should have taught you") said it was for the death of parents, so she'd hunted around looking for prayers that might work for the death of your halfway-house mentor's girlfriend. She'd found a genderfluid kaddish, a "goyishe kaddish" to be recited by Gentiles with Jewish relatives, a kaddish for pets ("Q: May I recite this kaddish for a pet who was not kosher? A: Most pets are not kosher. We do not recommend eating your late pet without consulting your rabbi"), and a kaddish for Communism. These pages referred to the deity as, respectively, gyd; YHWH; G-d; and Jahve, which was also the name of the boy who used to pull her hair in fourth grade. At that point she gave up and figured her Higher Power would get the general idea if she just used the normal prayer.

May His great name grow exalted and sanctified, Amen.

(*Ooh,* she thought, *this is a lot of masculine pronouns for God. Like, a lot. But I don't know how you pronounce "zie" so we'll just have to go with this.)*

In the world that He created as He willed.

Des looked out the window. The bus was passing that Ethiopian-Salvadoran fusion place she suspected of being a drug front; a bedraggled man in a heavy coat was banging on its locked front doors. Next door at Leggings of Tomorrow, three pairs of white plastic legs kept watch on the pavement, ass-first. The question of whether the world as she saw it did have, in spite of all appearances, some relevant relationship to a Higher Power one might want to praise, seemed like a theological argument she had already lost a long time ago.

She was surprised to find that the kaddish was not about the dead person at all. There was no mention of her life's value, and no promise of justice. It was all about how great He was. Des felt, uneasily, like she was sucking up to a C.O. All the praise for His name, when so many people died at the hands of people who reduced them to a number.

Which, she realized, was something the people who made this webpage probably knew.

Blessed is He,

beyond any blessing and song,

praise and consolation that are uttered in the world. Now say:

The whole point of a Higher Power, probably, was that there was something beyond your thoughts and hopes about a Higher Power. Someone beyond your understanding—the twelve-step "God of your understanding" had always rung sort of '70s woo-woo to Des, sort of defensive and self-comforting and not yet sufficiently humiliated.

Was praising that Power a way of honoring Ty'heaven? Maybe it was more adequate than anything else Des was capable of doing.

Amen.

*   *   *

The protest would take place in Malcolm X Park. People were gathering up by the statue of Joan of Arc. Des came into the park from the northwest side, lugging her mop and bucket full of cleaning supplies, with the rest of her work equipment stuffed into an NPR tote bag. The tote was a souvenir from her father's recent radio appearance. (He had argued that presidential turkey "pardons" displayed the ability of the powerful to define justice, and therefore arrogate for themselves the right to be merciful: "What crime did this turkey commit? Shouldn't it be the turkey who pardons the president?") Along its navy blue side a Chinese factory worker had stitched, *NPR: The voice of what's best in the American people.*

Des walked past a few cops standing around arguing: "You can say how mumble rap is 'good' if you want to. What I'm saying is, it ain't even rap." Another cop tried to interrupt, laughing, but the first one just repeated, "It ain't even rap though."

Then ten feet further on, another little group of police asking one another, "If she died in P.G. why they out here? Why they ain't protesting down in Maryland? Get your ass in a Uber!"

The long yellow leaves of the willow oaks drifted down onto the shoulders of their black bulletproof vests.

By that time the halfway-house women had learned a little more about what happened. Ty'heaven had been arrested during a traffic stop for failing to roll her window down all the way, which wasn't a thing Des had known you could go to jail for. She'd been taken to the jail in Upper Marlboro and eyewitnesses said she'd kept insisting that she needed to get her medication. She had been polite with the officers—everyone mentioned this, that she had been polite and said "Sir" and "Ma'am" and "Officer" the whole way through—and she had been coherent in her speech. But after several hours of trying to persuade the guards to give her her medication, she'd had a seizure and lost consciousness. She'd been taken to the hospital within the hour but never came to.

This memorial was not solely or even primarily about Ty'heaven. It was mostly about police shootings all over the country. It quickly degenerated into a Cerberus. There was one guy with a bullhorn who wanted all the people to follow him in chants: What do we want, which for once was a question everybody could answer. But there was also a Howard student with a baritone voice and heavy dreads who was just yelling Ty'heaven's name over and over, and repeating, "She was polite. She was a person." It was about as much as people knew about her.

And in the back an older man was pacing and screaming, "Fuck peace! Y'all just Uncle Toms! Y'all ain't doing nothing! You gotta rise up, you house niggers! Why don't you rise up? Fuck peace, yelling don't do nothing!"

Des looked for Ray Ray in the crowd of a hundred-some people. She found her with most of the other Love's Labors women, standing on the edge of the crowd silently watching the screaming man.

Some of the black men were engaging him, telling him to show respect for the dead, but the Howard girls around them were all just muttering about how they weren't going to have their praxis critiqued by somebody calling them an Uncle Tom. "What does he know?", but you could hear in their voices that they were talking themselves up. What Des's grandmother called "putting the world to rights," when you'd talk until you believed that talking had helped. You had figured out the correct answer, who should do what and how, and when you said it and other people agreed then it seemed like your ideas became a little more real, even though since you weren't the one you were talking about, actually nothing changed.

"I don't completely disagree with him," one old man in a

three-piece suit and hat said. His suit was the color of a White Russian, and his voice was wry.

"He could find a better word than 'house niggers,'" a big young dude chuckled, with a deep line cutting between his brows. His laughing mouth twisted up on one side, just a little. "We have so much richness in our language. 'House nigger,' that's played. What's wrong with 'handkerchief-head'? 'Darkie'? What about 'cotton-picker'? We losing touch with our traditions."

Ray Ray just stood there. She looked like she was crying but she wasn't.

Des stood beside her and tried to keep a look on her face like she was not listening to the sardonic, heartbroken conversations around her. She tried to look like an accessory of Ray Ray's, a soft white handbag. The chanting started up again and she felt like everything she was chanting mattered less because she was the one chanting it; but she chanted anyway, because you have to.

"I don't see how this is doing much," Zita said, and for once she sounded like an old head.

"The struggle is a prayer," Miss Imani said, putting her arm around Ray Ray and giving them all an unhappy grin. "And usually gets the same answer."

Ray Ray checked her phone, and looked puzzled. "What do it mean when somebody send you a deer in a dress?" she asked.

"Sorry?" Des said—and then realized the question probably hadn't been for her, but nobody else was taking it.

"My foster sister," Ray Ray explained. "She just sent me a, like a deer emoji. Look at this."

Des looked at the phone. There it was: a cartoon deer in a dress, holding a pie between its delicate hooves.

"I think it must be a sympathy text," she said. "Like, here, have this pie? 'Have this pie, my *deer*'?"

"Oh," Ray Ray said. She took her phone back and looked at it again. "Yeah, I get it, you can see the, like the kind expression on the deer face. It got kind eyes."

Her tears splashed onto the screen then. She was wiping them off with her sleeve when Toya turned up.

"Hello," she said brightly to everyone. "Is this the funeral protest thing?"

Ray Ray sniffled and wiped her face, and nodded at her. "How do," she said. "Thanks for coming."

"You're welcome! What do I do?"

"Fuck, I don't know. If I knew what to do I'd be doing it."

Ray Ray shook herself and broke through her anger and grief. Her foster mother had always said, "When you feel like you got to throw something, throw a party. And when you feel like you got to break something, break a silence."

So she said, with the tears still in her voice, "L'il Ray Ray—I call this one L'il Ray Ray—she be saying you don't think you in a cult."

"No," Toya said, subdued. "I mean, yes. I mean, yes, I don't think that."

Ray Ray looked at her.

Des said, cautiously, "There's a kind of display up by the statue. I saw it when I was looking for you guys. Maybe we should go and see it."

The display was a large piece of cardboard, hastily assembled, covered with pictures printed off the Internet. These were the black people killed by police or who died in police custody in the past twelve months. The display rose a couple feet above Des's head, so she couldn't see the pictures at the very top. The ones she could see showed a mosaic of the everyday, a tribute to normal life: a man in graduation cap and gown, another one bent over laughing and flashing a peace sign at the camera, another one cradling his baby daughter. A woman hand-feeding a baby opossum, another dressed as Captain America, another pushing a bundled-up child on a swing in the snow. Black people singing in church, a man being baptized in a river, a woman in gardening gloves cutting roses. Bikini and sunglasses on the beach, riding a giant praying mantis in a carousel, crossing eyes and blowing a huge pink sphere of bubble gum. In uniforms from St. Peter Claver Catholic Preparatory Academy, the U.S. Marine Corps, and the Chicago Transit Authority. A hard-used man with missing teeth smiling and squinting into sunshine as he held up a plastic cup of beer; a twelve-year-old boy at the barre practicing his demi-plié. Work and play, care and joy, accomplishment and surrender. Des thought suddenly, *He who makes peace in His heights, may He make peace, upon us and upon all Israel.*

Now say: Amen.

"They told me 'bout this," Ray Ray said, in a roughed-up voice. She pulled a picture out of her pocket and unfolded it tenderly. It wasn't a photo but a drawing, one of the colored-pencil drawings from her bedroom wall. Ty'heaven rode an enormous version of Fang's missing owl: laughing with her head tipped back, in control, one arm folded across her naked breasts and the other deep in the owl's great feathers. Ray Ray used the thumbtacks provided along the edges of the cardboard to press it into place, on the margins of the display. The photos rippled in a sudden wind.

"I wish I could stop this—" She cut herself off, frustrated. Gestured at her face. The tears were still coming. "This shit seem so weak. I seen dudes when they people get killed, they bent over, wailing, holding on each other. Making noise. They honor they people. But I can't—when I—if I think about it, about doing what I'm *'posed* to do to honor her—"

She took a deep breath and turned to Desiree. "You always be talking about humility this and that, and *in every decision you make.*

What I want to know is, is it humble. To call attention. Because I'm just sitting here crying and it's like don't nobody even notice—who she really was."

"I don't know," Des said.

Ray Ray laughed, a sound like a kid dragging her sneaker-toe through gravel. "For all I know if I start up on something she come back and haunt my ass. 'Don't you be playing like you sorry! You shot me!' Her fuckin' ghost be up on me then."

"She's probably over that by now," Des offered.

There was a long pause then. They were a swirl of silence in the heart of the protest. They'd yielded the duties of mourning to those who were confident about it.

Toya turned to Ray Ray. In this charged atmosphere it seemed to her that all the black people were somehow clarified, as if they had access to some higher wisdom. "Can I talk to you?" she asked.

Ray Ray, based on previous experience with Toya, was not sure how literally to take this question. "Sure, probably," she said.

Toya nodded and pulled her aside. Ray Ray wiped her face with the palms of both hands and focused. She wanted to make the most of this distraction.

"What do you," Toya began, and then backed up. "If a person. If there's a thing that somebody tells you to do, and you didn't want to do it but then you think maybe it's the right thing to do, but then when you say you don't want to do it they get very upset, and the way that they're upset makes you afraid to do it or makes you think maybe you shouldn't do it after all—what should you do?"

Ray Ray stared at her and tried to untangle this.

"Girl," she said. "Can you tell me what you talking about? You wanted to do something?"

"No—I didn't want to do it."

"So don't do it."

"But what if it's the right thing to do?"

Ray Ray's face went from shrugging to very wise. She filled with gratitude: In the depths of her grief she had received an opportunity to give back. To help the community—or at least, to help whatever Toya was. She locked her gaze with Toya's and said, with the conviction of someone who had frequently received this counsel and had occasionally even acted on it, "If it's the right thing to do you got to do it. It don't be options when it comes to right and wrong."

"But what if it's *not* the right thing to do?"

Ray Ray dropped her wisdom face with a quickness. "Aw, shit. Make up your mind then."

Toya, shaken, resorted to a childlike voice so that everything she was saying would seem less real: "He was so angry. I've never seen him like that, when I said I didn't want to."

And Ray Ray, turning on a dime for the third time in sixty seconds, said, "Oh. Don't do it. Whatever it is, don't do it and don't talk to him about it no more."

"But he's taught me so many things."

"I bet he has. And now it's *payback* time, far as he concerned. He did something nice for you and now you got to pour him a little sugar. That's some prison-ass shit right there. Hey Des!"

"I don't want to talk to her! I already know what she thinks."

But Ray Ray ignored this. "L'il Ray Ray! You remember that video you told us about, the one they made you watch the first day you was inside?"

Des loped over and assessed the situation. "Sure," she said. "The rape video."

"That shit was jiah funny," Ray Ray reminisced. "All them fake-ass inmates dancing around in they jumpsuits. What was the rhyme they had in that joint?"

Des obediently quoted from memory: "'They'll buy you for a

biscuit, they'll sell you for a smoke. Prison rape: It ain't no joke.'"

(When she'd told that story in group, back when Stephanie the bedridden Bible maven was still at the house, Stephanie had nodded sagely and said, "Y'all laugh, but it's true. It ain't no joke. For you are worth more than many biscuits.")

"The point is," Ray Ray said, "people be doing nice things for you to make you they property. Like if somebody put a Snickers bar on your pillow and you take that joint, you basically saying, 'Come on and rape me!' You took this motherfucker's Snickers bar—you didn't know better—and now he coming 'round for payback."

"That seems like such a cynical view of the world," Toya said, not too confidently. "That may be how it works in prison, but—"

Just then the cops came up behind the crowd and said into their own bullhorns, "Attention, attention. We have received word that there is some violent and unproductive things being said on Facebook and on Twitter. We have no choice but to ask that this assembly disassemble."

And, when everybody muttered and milled around but nobody actually went away, and people started to lift up their phones, the same cop said, "Y'all, this 'bout to get real. I need you to know. If you on probation or parole I kindly advise you to get the hell out of here."

Des glanced at Ray Ray. Ray Ray looked scared; but then pulled herself together and said, with a high angry hilarity like she was welcoming it, "Let it happen."

Des looked then at Imani. Ray Ray might've had the moral authority in this situation, but she was aware that Miss Imani had all the other kinds. Imani took a deep breath and opened her mouth.

But before she could say anything, the protester with the bullhorn announced, "Uh, all right, fam, we are marching to the White House!"

And so nothing did happen. The bullhorn guy came down from his makeshift platform and spoke with the cops, off to one side. The man who had been yelling about Uncle Toms melted back against the crowd, who muttered a little at him, "Not so big now," but didn't turn on him. And the protest rally agreed to turn into a protest march, so they could all save face and also get the hell out of there.

"To the White House!" the bullhorn kid yelled again.

The crowd fell into line. People threw out a few experimental chants before one of them stuck: "We're fed up! We can't take no more!"

Chanting this, they headed down out of the park. Des was partly worrying about the cops, but mostly thinking of the look on Ray Ray's face. *Let it happen.*

They marched down the steps and spilled out onto Sixteenth Street. At the end of that first block they almost lost track of Toya. Des had to go back and fetch her; she was stopped in front of an ad in a bus shelter. The fuchsia ad said, "A WOMAN'S PLACE: A chic, modern abortion experience."

When Toya saw Des she jumped a little, and then giggled and pointed to the ad and said, "I was just wondering what this word means."

"Chic, like tasteful, classy. Oh, see, it says here at the bottom, 'An abortion as classy as you are.' We're going to lose the others if we don't hurry."

"Oh, I'm sorry!" And they joined the tail end of the march and pushed through it back to Ray Ray.

All around them, again and again, Ray Ray yelling with the rest of them at the top of her lungs: "We're feeeeed up! We can't take no more!"

But Imani Rollins looked away from the residents of Love's Labors Loft and with a skull's smile said, to nobody in particular, "Yes we can, and we'll have to."

Chapter 16
Misrepresentations

Just over a week later, "Strange Bedfellows" taped its November 8 morning show with election predictions.

"Easy like Saturday night," Lizzie said. "A big win for Hillary and an early night for all of us."

"You don't sound too sorry to see your side lose," David Lav noted.

"Well, I am a masochist! ...Ooh, I wasn't expecting to wave that around on camera. Today's the day we *all* let it all hang out." That bit was cut in post-production.

After the show David mused, as Lizzie was fishing her microphone out of her cleavage, "I thought masochism was part of Trump's appeal? I've only seen a few seconds of Milo on YouTube but he was very, 'Punish me, Daddy!' It confirmed my belief that conservatism is abnormal and disturbing."

Lizzie laughed. "Sure, everyone wants an authoritarian, this shouldn't be news. But only a person with hair dye and hit counts where his brain should be would pick Trump for that. You've seen

Secretary, right?—no, probably not, it's hashtag problematic, but there is no way Trump could play the James Spader role in that. Oooggghh, I think I just reverse-ovulated at the thought. My egg leapt back *up*."

"You can't be seriously arguing that the problem with Trump is that he's not sexy."

"No, the horrifying unsexiness is the result of his lack of character." She shrugged. "You should watch *Secretary*. I need to find a guy like Spader—he feels really guilty, I think that's a sign of good character."

"I feel really guilty," David Lav offered.

"Oh sure," Lizzie said, "but about different things." She congratulated him on his candidate's coming victory and peaced out.

Trash's polling place was a former church, turned into a hospitality-industry charter school after its congregation moved to P.G. County. The polls were run by black women, beaming and laughing with a Sunday warmth and welcome the place hadn't seen since its AME days. They gave Trash his "I Voted" sticker and he put it on, but then threw it away in embarrassment because it seemed like bragging.

His workplace was in a good mood too, for a while. He had the late shift, so he was there in the packed excitement of early evening, everybody grinning over their phones and laptops. He and Jaquan danced in and out of each other's personal space with the kind of tight footwork that would earn an ice dance team exceptional marks. There was a pulsing, slightly sexual energy in the air; girls and a few guys slipped their digits to Trash or, much more often, Jaquan. This gave Trash a rare chance to boast. "I am exclusive now," he confided in Jaquan during a hot second of calm, handing him a girl's napkin-scrawled number. "My man made me delete my Grindr profile."

Jaquan laughed in his face and said, "And they say romance is dead. I got this chick's digits already, she not picky tonight. We need a new almond syrup from the back."

Then the red started creeping across the map and everybody got a little stiff and overconfident. For once in their lives all the D.C. people pinned their hopes on Northern Virginians.

An hour later nobody was talking as Ohio was called for Trump. Just after that Virginia did go Democrat, but everyone was starting to realize that it wouldn't matter. By midnight they all basically knew what had happened.

Trash and Jaquan looked around at their shocked patrons. Then their gazes met. Trash's implicit question, *Is this going to be as bad as I think?*, met Jaquan's calm hard acceptance that his fears had been confirmed yet again.

"If you want to go home early," Trash said, "I can do all the closing-up." It didn't have much to do with anything, but he felt like he had to *do something*.

All across D.C. it settled in. This city had voted for Marion Barry, had buoyed him up through the crack, which anybody could get into, but also the corruption, the rape (sorry—*alleged* rape), the devastation of the housing projects, the vassalage of the police department, the junketing and graft. Had loved him when he got out of prison and stood in a circle of church ladies to proclaim, "Free at last!" Had loved him, because he claimed to love D.C. when she was prostrate.

In that era the souvenir shops sold, alongside the cherry blossom postcards and the stuffed pandas, t-shirts reading, GREETINGS FROM WASHINGTON, DC! WE MISSED YOU, with a picture of an AK-47, BUT WE'LL KEEP SHOOTING. When D.C.'s lot was nightly gunfire and universal contempt, Marion Barry said he loved her, and so she kept coming back to him. And after all, *Who else would want you?*

Still, Marion Barry was a sharecropper's son, and a genuine civil-rights leader in his unwasted youth. He gave his rapt and friendless city Thanksgiving turkeys and summer jobs, the symbol and foundation of working-class survival. Des would always drunkenly argue, under the misimpression that other people cared, "Before he got into crack he was famous for fiscal—*prudency*. Financiular probity. He's an advocate for ex-offenders!" (It is to her credit that she praised this advocacy before she needed it. Maybe she had greater self-knowledge than anybody realized.) Barry, unlike many, was capable of active denial: the earliest stage of surrender. He served the city before, after, and maybe even during those years when she loved him and lied about her bruises.

The greatest saving grace of the Mayor-for-Life is that he punished his supporters the most. Or maybe his great saving grace is that he got convicted.

So, you know, D.C. could've done worse. People do, now and then.

The day after the election, when Lucinda got in to work some of the front-of-house women were talking at the dishwashers. They weren't quite worrying, they weren't quite commiserating; they weren't *quite* taunting. But what they were saying was, "You know that he'll send you back! It's so terrible, Trump will deport you!"

"I cried all night," one woman said. "I'm so upset, all I've been able to eat all day has been salsa verde Doritos. You'll be sent away now, and we'll have to get all new staff. *Inglés* only, in restaurants from now on."

The dishwashers didn't say anything. There were black front-of-house women, but all the ones who were saying these things were white.

At this same time Des was coming home from a cleaning

assignment. "We wanted to cancel because of the election," her red-eyed employer had said, sniffling, "but we thought people like you would especially need the money now." Des had hoped that might mean more than a ten percent tip but she was disappointed.

The bus was about half full: just Des and a lot of Latinas, silent and weary, in a mix of professional and manual-labor clothes. And then an old, hard-used white man got on. Des could smell the alcohol on him from three rows away, and she looked kindly on him as someone still serving in the boozers' army she'd deserted. He was complaining disjointedly about how he had nothing to eat and no money, and he'd gone and begged at the Five Guys and they'd given him a free cheeseburger but it only had one patty.

"Those Mexicans there," he said, and looked around the bus slyly. When nobody took him up on it he said, in a more conciliatory tone, "Salvadorans."

But then he pulled himself upright and looked around the bus and laughed. "You all wanted Hillary!" he said in triumph. "You all wanted Hillary, but the country doesn't like you. Nobody likes you!"

Nobody said anything. After a little more of this he tired himself out and went to sleep.

In those first few weeks there were all kinds of theories. The *LA Times* said young black men had made a surprising swing toward Trump. This turned out to be because they'd generalized from their sample size of one young black man, Michael Newsome of Tarzana. People said Trump won because of poor white people. Then they said Trump won because of rich white people. But rich white people vote for everybody—nobody's found a way to stop them—so everyone went back to talking about poor white people.

All of that would come later. On election night, in the master bedroom at the Morningstar Center for Personal Restoration (For Women Only), Trina Lawton sat up in bed alone with the covers pulled tight over her knees. Clutching her phone. Watching in horror as the *New York Times* gas-gauge prediction meter slowly swung backward from ninety percent likely Hillary to seventy percent, then sixty, then fifty. The red relentlessly encroaching on the space she had been assured would stay blue. When the meter hit thirty percent likely Hillary, and the reality was starting to sink in, Max Lord came into their bedroom.

He was in a good mood. Enjoying the chaos. Telling her what the Democrats should have done. She just kept staring at her phone. As he climbed into bed with her, careful and jerky because of his bad leg, she twitched away.

"Come on, puzzle piece," he said. "Bramble bush, give me a kiss."

"Haven't you had enough of that from Toya?" she asked. "Why don't you go give *her* some political education? She probably thinks Marxism is discrimination against people named Mark."

"Don't be like that," Max Lord said. "Toya did her little duty, she voted for Hillary like you wanted. I told her to."

"Voted for Hillary. Sucked you like Monica. Did you enjoy stuffing her *ballot box?*"

"Don't be vulgar. Look at the Clintons now. We're a power couple too," Max Lord said, and Trina wanted, once more, to believe him.

Trina Lawton had been valedictorian of a high school whose alumni went on to unsuccessful careers in roofing and car theft, and short but effective careers in suicide. She had escaped her hometown through willpower strong enough that she could even control her menstrual flow. (She had tried to market her method on social media before finding out that other people had already discovered it, and labeled it "anorexia.") The idea for Morningstar had been hers, but only when Max Lord joined her did the group begin to take off. He had financed the house and made her dream come true, and as long as he could be the head of Morningstar he would always defer to her in public.

Things had been good, as far as she could tell, until Toya came. Max had slept with other trainees, but only once or twice—"Just to let them know that they're important," he'd said. He would joke sometimes about "horizontal recruiting," and she decided to find it funny, the same way she'd decided that she liked all his twee little nicknames for her. After all, he never called the other women "honeybee" or "prickly pear."

But with Toya he didn't stop once she'd bitten the hook. Something about the way he fastened onto Toya—something about the way Trina treated Toya, which was just like how she treated the other trainees only moreso—something about the way Toya lost confidence with every confidence-building class—it all suggested something about life at Morningstar. About the world Trina had built for herself, by herself. Not something new, but something slowly being revealed.

She looked at Max, and then back at her phone. The whole gauge was red now. The election was over. There was a sick feeling in her stomach and she saw herself standing on a huge deserted beach at ebb tide, surrounded by sharp broken rocks, feather-scraps on seagull skeletons and the stinking corpses of fish. She saw her man, come to her fresh from Toya's mildewed sleeping bag; she saw the house they had built together, Morningstar, a for-profit educational venture with supervised living. Hands-on instruction. She saw the sales pitch that was her life. She had told herself she cared about these underparented females, but now she knew: Like a real American huckster she had nothing but contempt for the rubes.

She saw her life and drew back from it in horror. But just then Max Lord touched her, drew his fingers along the underside of her arm so that she shuddered.

"You've always been the brains of this operation," he said.

His fingers moved across her breast, toward her nipple. Casual, not grabbing, but making her aware of how he was touching her soft and vulnerable places. It would be stupid to let him do that if he were—

She wasn't stupid. *You've always been the brains of this operation.* She smiled, and leaned in toward him. She didn't decide to ask herself why he had said that—what uncanny instinct had told him he should say it just then. She decided to let him touch her.

By sheer willpower she reversed the tide, so that the cold oily water flowed back and covered up the beach again. She looked at Max Lord's hand squeezing her breast and smiled.

Chapter 17
Now and at the Hour

Every time the wind blew, a shower of maroon leaves cascaded from the oak tree just outside Trash's window. His housemates were downstairs distracting themselves from one week of President-Elect Donald Trump by playing a board game where you competed to be queen bitch of the New York drag clubs, and he was in his attic bedroom on his knees. Looking out the window at the moon and the gutter and the roof where the raccoon sometimes prowled, crossing himself, praying the rosary for the repose of Helly King.

He was counting the Hail Marys on his knuckles, since he didn't know where any of his rosaries were. He'd had one from Confirmation and one from an especially passive-aggressive maternal Christmas gift, and then the one he'd bought when he went to the St. Blaise's Day Thrifty Throats sale at the church around the corner, where they had Gospel Mass but also Zumba. That one had been very cheap pink plastic, with seams on each bead that scraped his fingertips, stapled to a white cardboard backing that read, PRAY THE ROSARY TO RESIST THE ERRORS OF RUSSIA.

And in smaller print: "The 'errors of Russia' are more common than ever before. These enemies of our Catholic faith include:

- a spirit of mistrust and division between employer and employee, parent and child, teacher and student, priest and penitent, government and citizen, God and man;
- abortion, homosexualism, and Devil worship;
- government theft of private property to serve the corporations and the shiftless;
- relativism in fashion;
- the privatization of penance;
- abuse of children and the liturgy."

And then a stamp saying it was manufactured in Rome, NY. Year: 1987.

Trash hadn't necessarily wanted to buy this thing, but the only other things left were First Communion dresses trimmed with kente cloth, and he lacked every single demographic variable needed to carry that off. At any rate, he'd taken it off the backing and promptly lost it; his family was always saying that rosaries were just like mittens.

He thought he heard the raccoon out on the roof, but it was only the clawlike skittering of leaves. Through a crack between the window and the frame he could feel the wet autumnal wind. He wasn't sure why he was doing this.

He had a lot of memories of the nightly family rosary, after the nightly family dinner. The youngest of nine, the eternal catspaw in his siblings' shifting alliances, kneeling at the end of the long family row. Where his parents couldn't keep an eye on him.

He had loved praying the rosary with his family. That was how he always thought about it, as something he had loved. Even after his father had died, when lots of them suddenly had to get jobs and all of his Christmas and birthday presents were just money for skating lessons, when their family dinners were at half attendance and mostly came out of the frozen food aisle, when the nightly rosary took on a certain grim determination, his mother's fierce "Glory be" like a kick against the pricks—even then, he had loved it. It was true that he'd often felt scared and ashamed while they were praying; but these were also some of the happiest and safest memories of a mostly happy and safe childhood.

He had no idea how those things could both be true, but he figured, God was one and three, so math seemed to skip around a little at the edges of human experience.

If he had stood up, he would have seen fog drifting and settling at the low end of the street.

He hadn't been to church since Helly's funeral. And wasn't planning to, although he didn't let himself think about that. He thought, instead, about a link his priest brother had sent him: Apparently Pope Francis had caused a stir by blessing a parrot owned by a male stripper. The parrot had spoken briefly with the pontiff, though the article didn't report what they discussed. The subject line on the email from Father P.J. had read, "thought this would interest you," which was both accurate and embarrassing, like most of what his family said to him.

Trash shook himself and focused on his prayer. The Crowning with Thorns. For Mary to reach a hand through time, and be with Helly in her addiction. The Blessed Mother held out one hand to him, and he took it gratefully; and the other, at his pleading, to Helly, who held it as best she could.

Our Lady's kaleidoscope eyes saw Trash on his knees; Helly, in her many toppling moments; and someone else, whom neither of them knew they were serving. The jeweled discs of the years turned.

Ten years before that night, in a back booth in a cantina in Dayton,

Ohio, in the last week of the long haul for Halloween on Ice 2006, Trash was gazing in awe at Helly King as she picked the cheese filling of a jalapeño popper out of her sweater and ate it. She was reminiscing about her glory days: the night she'd cut lines of coke with her International Skating Union ID, in a West German hotel room after she'd won the 1987 Junior World Championships.

"Partying with the men's *pewter* medalist," she recalled. "Gold was 'a bookworm,'" making the quote marks with her fingers, "which is how we said 'gay' back then. Silver was weird in the face. Bronze didn't speak English and brother, you cannot trust Eastern Bloc condoms. So, pewter for me."

Teenage Trash sucked his Diet Coke—he felt he could trust Helly not to tell his nutritionist about it—and nodded. Eyes wide. Wondering when he could ask his question.

"I remember when we were done I rolled off him and said, 'Six point oh! Six point oh!'" She laughed at her younger self. "And he was so thrilled, until I said, 'A fabulous performance from rising star Helly King!' He got all downcast and upset, and I had to be like, 'Okay, but you liked it, right?' I always try to send the audience home smiling."

And then she said, idly, "My hand's hot."

She held it out to him. "Take the hot hand. Kiss the hot hand, kiddo, it'll make you an Olympic champion."

Trash giggled and didn't touch her.

"Ohhhh," she said. "You're gay?"

He inclined his head and gave a slight apologetic shrug.

"Oh, too bad, good for you," she said. "Is that still really dangerous?"

Trash asked, in confusion, "You mean—physically?"

On the D.C. side of Chevy Chase Toya Tannen was kneeling in the basement of the Morningstar house, under the unshielded light bulb glaring in its cage, and crying until she gagged.

Max Lord stood in front of her. He was wearing shoes—he never stepped barefoot onto the grimy, moist basement floor. He said tenderly, "Toya. You *know* crying is a manipulative behavior."

"I know—"

"At some point you've got to put into practice the lessons in adulting that we've been teaching you here. You can't keep making appointments and canceling appointments and then making them again. You seemed fine with this last week." His Technicolor, syrup-rich voice was patient, maybe just gently amused; Toya had no idea why she was so scared.

Why she had thought, *With his limp he couldn't catch you if you ran.*

"I'm sorry," she said again. And then ventured, "They seemed okay with it at the clinic? They were nice about it."

Max laughed, not quite as patiently. "I'm not sure you're in any condition to make those kinds of judgment," he said. And she had to admit that that was true.

Her non-driver's ID was somewhere in the house, wherever it was usually kept. Her shoes were in the garbage, but that was mostly just to make a point, there were plenty of shoes in the house and someone would give her a pair when it was time for her to have them. Max had borrowed her credit card to arrange the Uber for her appointment and he hadn't given it back. There were all the other women in the house. There were the security cameras, and the electronic locks on the doors and windows.

Her hormones were making her emotional. Her mind wouldn't stop thinking about the street outside, if she could just get outside. If she could just get to a phone. But everybody would laugh at her if she had to come crawling back to them and say, *You were right, I was stupid, it was a cult all along*

Trina would tell them all the things she'd made Toya do, and everybody would laugh. Her life would be over.

Don't be immature. You're in no condition to be making big decisions.

"The fourth Sorrowful Mystery: Carrying the Cross," Trash said. For the holy souls in Purgatory. And especially any souls who might have died in their addictions, in despair if you could pray for people who died in despair. For the relief of their shame—especially if they had once played the Nanny Goat in Gazprom Zoo on Ice.

In Dayton, Ohio, Trash asked Helly the question he'd rehearsed, a question freighted with his hopes: "When did you know you wanted to be a skater?"

She nodded and pulled her sweater up so she could suck woolly cheese from it. "Obbim Cuvvum," she said with her mouth full.

And then, pulling her sweater out of her mouth, repeated: "Robin Cousins. 1977, Skate Canada, I would've been five. The TV commentators said he was skating even though he'd just had surgery on both knees. I don't think I knew what 'surgery' was, but I got it: Skating is something people love so much that they'll go through any pain for it. They love it more than they love themselves—they love it instead of themselves. That's what I wanted."

And then, just as he'd hoped, she asked, "What about you?"

"It was you," he said. And, with reverence, "The Swanson's Frozen Dinners Challenge. I remember when you first got on the ice the whole arena held its breath—it was tense and almost angry, like they weren't sure if they even *wanted* you to do well. And then when you did your layback spin a thrill went through the whole crowd and all that weird tension released."

"Oh man, the Swanson's competition," she said. "I beat Rory Flack Burghardt, that was a travesty. Bullshit reputation judging, she should've been miles ahead of me."

And then, seeing Trash's face, she relented and said, "I did have a nice layback. I had a *correct* layback," signaling for another round of drinks. "Michelle Kwan hasn't got a correct layback."

She laughed at herself then. "Oh, Helen, why such a bitch? Michelle Kwan *also* hasn't got a felony criminal record, probably; so we've all got our ups and downs. The crowd was weird that night—you must've been an infant, good grief—because I'd just been arrested again the week before. DUI. No, wait, that time was the burglary. It's the worst, those months in between arrest and sentencing, you know?"

Trash did not know, but he nodded and made sympathetic noises.

"But it was the same as always, I pled guilty and everybody was like, 'Oh, she's really sorry, she's really going to try this time.' I had to go back to inpatient which was a nightmare, but believe it or not, I have never been sentenced to jail. Not once. Probation probation probation. Sometimes I wonder what is wrong with people."

More drinks came. Trash asked if she had any advice for him. She, on her seventh drink of the night, said, "You're asking *me?* Get it together, Helen, be helpful, you never know who you can help in this life."

And then, having thought about it, said, "Okay: Always dunk fried things in frozen things."

She demonstrated with a hush puppy in her margarita.

Trash, trusting, gazing, dunked his onion ring into her drink as well. He bit into it and tried to figure out what his face should be doing. Asked, "Is it... good?"

"It's good," Helly said with confidence; and Trash believed her.

He'd had to cover the tab, since her card was declined. He'd had to carry her back to her hotel room. He propped her up by the door, got her key card out of her jeans pocket, got the door open.

Got the lights on. She laughed in his face and fell into the room.

Said, "No, let me help you," and swiped her hot hand down across the light switch.

In the Morningstar basement, and across the District from Western Avenue all the way into Anacostia, all the lights went out.

"Shit!" Max Lord said. He hesitated for a second, then said kindly, "Look, I need to take care of things upstairs. You're not the only person in this family, you know."

"I know," Toya said.

Max's hand fumbled over her face in the dark. He slid his palm in a quick caress up and across the side of her head—she gasped a little as he pressed on the strange tender knob her concussion had left behind—and he gently pushed the back of her skull so that her head bowed. Then he took his hand away.

Toya put her hands out to feel across the dirty floor in front of her and just brushed the back of his heel as he turned and groped his way to the stairs. He limped up them, hanging on to the railing. At the top of the stairs he left the door open and she, stunned and numb in the darkness, could hear him asking someone if they'd checked Pepco's website.

"This city is a nightmare," she heard him say. "I'm going to tweet at them. A really savage tweet, that should get their attention."

Her life would be over. Would she miss it?

She stood up.

"The fifth Sorrowful Mystery," Trash said, unfazed by the sudden power outage. "The death of Jesus on the cross." For Helly at the hour of her death, so that she wouldn't be alone. For the Queen of Heaven in her armor to defend Helly, who had rarely sunk so low as to defend herself. For freedom to captives; for someone to be her last resort.

After he'd eased Helly down onto the bed and taken her shoes off, and turned her on her side, Trash headed back to his own hotel room. He had just fallen asleep when his phone buzzed.

It was the first time Helly had called him to make drunken amends. Very far from the last. She had thought about it, she said, and she had more advice for him.

He sat up in the dark and listened. Helly told him, "My last coach told me this at Nagano. He knew everything about me, so he couldn't be disappointed. He said, 'Forget that it's the Olympics. Forget all this hoop-a-la. Your freedom is out there on the ice; all the trouble is in your own head.'"

"Yes," Trash said.

"Kristi Yamaguchi said this thing to me one time. With that voice! California girl, she always sounds like she's got hypoxia even *before* she starts skating. She sounds like if Bubble Yum had a really good work ethic. She said I should let people tell me who I am and what I'm doing. Like when you do a jump in practice, you know? You skate up to your coach and you're like, 'Was that good?'"

"Oh yes, right," Trash said.

"You'll get in trouble if you try to figure it out all by yourself. Let people help you, trust them when they tell you what you're about and how you're doing."

"You're amazing," Trash said.

Helly laughed and said, "You're so young."

And her voice was sadder, and he noticed how eerie it was to be sitting alone in his hotel room, listening to her in the dark. She was only a few doors down but she sounded light-years away.

"You have to stop thinking so highly of people," she said. "How do you ever expect to have a long-term relationship?"

He was still trying to figure out what to say to that when she started snoring.

*   *   *

Toya felt weightless as she walked through the dark. She wasn't thinking or planning; what would be the point? Barefoot up the steps from the basement, barely touching the rickety railing with its peeling paint. Past the hooks where the useless keys hung, from back before Max put in the electronic locks.

Into the dark first floor of the house. Toya slipped into the hallway that led to the back door. Max Lord and Trina and two of the other women were pulling back the heavy harvest-gold curtains in the main classroom. Bumping into things; he snapped at Trina and she told him he was being a child. Toya was breathing through her mouth. She had often noticed that Trina was a bitch, but she had never quite noticed how Trina said to Max the things he always said to everyone else.

Their feet scraped and stumbled. The curtains shifted, with a scratchy, dragging sound, but only a little more light came in; the streetlamps were all dark and the moon was behind clouds. Toya realized that if she went out the back door she would have to climb over the fence, since both paths to the front yard were gated and locked with traditional padlocks. *Why?* she suddenly wondered. For years all those answers had hidden in plain sight.

She had been so stupid.

She had no words for her emotions as she walked from the back hallway to the kitchen. Angry—she was so angry with herself—and grieving for the stupid dream she'd lost. Shame and self-laceration swirling like dirty water. She stepped barefoot on the kitchen floor and noticed that it hadn't been swept and mopped. Somebody wasn't doing her chores.

In her anger and shame she'd forgotten to be afraid. Had forgotten, just for a moment, the baby curling invisibly inside her. Had forgotten that she wasn't alone.

Max Lord stepped into the kitchen and tried again to flick on the light. She stopped dead. He froze by the doorway and said, "Who's there?"

She didn't breathe.

Under the slanting roof of a garret bedroom in Shaw, Trash found himself with nothing more to say than, "…That we may be made worthy of the promises of Christ."

He crossed himself and stood up, clutching at the bed for support. His joints cracked loudly.

He sighed and looked around the darkened, empty bedroom. That had all felt pretty significant while it was happening, but now he wasn't sure what the point had been. He suspected he'd done it just to make himself feel better. A security blanket for the soul.

"Well, you have to do *something*," he reasoned. "In the words of the Little Flower of Lisieux, 'Bad prayer is still good prayer, but bad skating is just negative G.O.E.'"

He wandered downstairs to find out whether the others would let him jump in the game late if he agreed to show them his "Calgary Olympics Battle of the Carmens." It wasn't quite ready: He had his flouncy Katarina Witt down, but the forthright and poignant Debi Thomas was taking him longer. As always it was simpler to be the winner but less drag-appropriate; less sublime.

Chapter 18
If You Want a Friend in Washington

The Morningstar kitchen had windows. Small windows up at the top, so Max's eyes had to adjust, but his pupils widened and as the clouds shifted even a little moonlight made it obvious who was standing there barefoot with her shorn head and her flat, pale face.

"Toya," he said.

I've been so stupid!

Laughing a little: "Toya, Jesus, you scared me. What are you doing up here?"

She couldn't think of anything to say.

"Toya," his voice sharpened. "Go back downstairs. Let the grown-ups handle this, okay? We can't be babysitting you tonight."

Trina called to him from the classroom: "Stop playing patty-cake with your ugly fuckling and find the flashlights."

"That's why she hates me!" Toya said, stunned and grateful. "I thought I was just a bad person! But it's because she knows you like me."

"Toya—"

She walked right past him, into the classroom. He grabbed her arm but she pulled free, barely even noticing him, she was so intent on apologizing to Trina. She stumbled over a chair overturned on the floor and badly bruised her left thigh, but she was used to that kind of thing and it didn't slow her down.

"I'm so sorry," she said to Trina. They were shadowed by the drawn-back curtains and lit by the moon's nacreous, fogbound glow. "I never thought about how hard it must be for you to see a man like Max Lord giving somebody like me the privilege of sleeping with him."

One of the other women said, "Wait, what the fuck, he's sleeping with *her?*"

"Yes," Trina said through gritted teeth, "my partner was consoling himself with Toya's capacious cooch. God, it's like emotional pedophilia. Go *away*, Toya, go back downstairs."

"I'm sorry I'm ugly," Toya said. "Is that why you want me to get rid of the baby? But it would be his baby too!"

And Trina jerked like she'd been hit. Her eyes went wide— Trina never liked to look taken by surprise, she always acted as if she already knew what you were telling her, but now her head snapped around to stare at Max and her face went red, betrayed, exposed. Max Lord looked away from her. She glanced at Toya again, like she wasn't sure what she wanted to do.

Just the sight of Toya's scraped-pale face seemed to make her catch fire.

She lunged at Toya and grabbed her by the face. Roaring, "You got her *pregnant?*" Slammed her backward into a desk, flipped her around and threw her into a different desk.

(One of the other women in the classroom made her eyes wide and laughed at this, crookedly and silently, the way you laugh when you want to convey that something batshit is happening—the way you declare yourself, by fiat, an audience member and not a participant. The other one didn't react at all, and was still just looking at Max. Somewhere underneath the currents of her attention Toya was noticing these things. It hurt to discover that everything in her life had the same answer: an optical illusion where for years you could only see a vase, but suddenly one day you see twenty screaming faces.)

As Toya floundered, trying to catch her breath and untangle herself from the desk and chairs she'd fallen onto, Trina yelled, "You used condoms with me but you got *Toya* pregnant?"

Pain shot through the small of Toya's back. Something was wrong with her face, just under her left eye, where she'd fallen onto the edge of a desk and been unable to catch herself.

"Grasshopper, honeybee, it's okay. It's okay. She already has an appointment to take care of it. It's fine." He had limped over to Trina and was holding her, comforting her. They weren't looking at Toya as she struggled to her feet.

Trina asked, still looking only at Max, "Does *she* know that? She probably thinks it's an appointment to have her feet flossed."

And Toya let go of her last hopes for them. She realized that she'd been making it all up, just like a little kid, prattling on about how if Trina only thought about it the way she had then it would be obvious that she should get to have the baby, and she'd be allowed to move upstairs, and people would be nicer to her because she'd finally done something right, happily ever after amen.

She was on her feet now and backing away through the dark classroom toward the little open area between the staircase and the front door.

"Where's she going?" asked the woman who hadn't laughed when Trina threw Toya.

Toya ran.

The electronic lock on the front door was dependent on the power supply, and useless now. Toya burst barefoot onto the wet lawn. The front gate had a normal lock but she yanked up her cardigan and shoved herself between the bars, gasping as they pressed against her sore breasts. She was sprinting toward Chevy Chase Circle when Max Lord came out of the house.

As the sidewalk rasped against her bare feet, she remembered that he had a car.

It was warm—it had been strangely warm all week—and the fog was starting to burn off as the moon rose above the houses. It was just getting on eleven at night, well past closing time in most of upper Northwest. No lights in the businesses around the traffic circle. Almost no cars. One jogger; Toya flew past him, thinking that something bad might happen, but he had his earbuds in and took no notice of her. She knifed through the traffic circle—so few cars that only one person even bothered to honk. This was smart thinking since the traffic circle would slow Max down if he drove, but her own intelligence was something she never let herself notice.

For the past two hours Douceline had been playing what seemed like random chords on the piano. Chord, chord, pause, first chord again, slightly different second chord.

The power had gone out for about twenty minutes but Douceline had sat there in the dark, with ferocious first-generation immigrant determination, and kept playing. Now that the lights were back on, she had accompaniment: Desiree was watching "Strange Bedfellows," eating a banana for her community-supervision requirements, Googling "how to clean liquefied potatoes wood and tile," and fantasizing about stabbing Douceline in the arm. Ray Ray was sketching Ty'heaven odalisque upon a fluffy white cloud, and complaining about the children's television programming they played in the walk-in clinic where she'd done her last drug test (with its bedsheet banner: WE CANNOT TREAT YOUR PETS). It was the usual prison thing again, where you tried to drown out the noises you hated by making noises the other women hated.

"*Rugrats* is a fucked-up show," Ray Ray declared. "And that's got to be because it come from out the mind of a fucked-up person."

"Miss Imani says," Des countered, "that we can put out into the world what we have not yet received."

Ray Ray sucked her teeth and considered Desiree. "How is it," she said, "that you only talk about what 'Miss Imani says' when you trying to start some shit?"

On the TV Lizzie and David had been arguing about protest. "How much of what we call 'dissent,'" Lizzie had wondered, "is really just mental illness? Real talk, have you ever met a pacifist who wasn't clinically depressed?"

David Lav had retorted, "Wouldn't you be?"

Now they were on to "Rat Park." This was an experiment in which researchers found that caged rats with nothing to do got addicted to morphine, but if you let them play together and gave them "stimulating toys" they kicked their habit quickly and reintegrated into normal rodential life.

"Good for them," Lizzie was saying, "but you can't always be living in a Rat Park! What are they going to do when they get out in the Rat Real World? The Rat *Race*. These rats need to take some personal responsibility."

Chord, second chord, pause. Chord, second chord, third chord. And then Des got it. The chords weren't random. They were a halting, untutored attempt to learn "Adeste Fideles."

This did not make it easier to listen to.

Des's phone buzzed.

It skittered across the creases in the plastic tablecloth. Des picked it up and sighed. A 202 number she didn't recognize; at this hour, probably Community Supervision. At least this time it wasn't four in the morning.

"Desiree Schulman," she said, "I'm at Love's Labors Loft, where I'm supposed to be. I can text you a selfie."

"Is this Des? I'm at the CVS on Connecticut Avenue. I'm borrowing a phone!"

The voice was high-pitched, breathy, and a lot more unprofessional than even the worst of the women's CSOs.

"Who is this?" Des asked.

"Is this Des? *Please*, please come get me!"

In the background she heard a woman saying, loudly and professionally and wearily, "Miss. You got to put on shoes, Miss. Can't come in here without no shoes."

The breathy voice, gasping now, panicky: "Oh my God, I see his car! Is that his car?"

In the background: "All shoes must be worn at all times."

"Please, I'm sorry, come get me! I'll be in the dumpster."

And the call cut off.

Des looked at her phone. "I don't know what *that* was," she said, although she was starting to think that she did. "I think that was Toya."

On the piano, Douceline played, *O come let us a*—and then a loud wrong chord.

Ray Ray just looked at her, like she knew there was more and she was waiting for Des to confess it.

"Do you know a club called something like the Dumpster? Or even a restaurant?" Des asked.

"Now who the fuck gon' name a restaurant 'the Dumpster'?" Ray Ray said.

"I know, but like, I just saw a place literally called For Sale By Court Order. There's a bar called Garbage People."

"That's some white people nonsense," Ray Ray said, with perfect accuracy.

"She sounded really scared, and she said she'd seen somebody's car, and that she would be at the Dumpster. Or in the Dumpster. Which I'm hoping is a club, because honestly, with Toya who can tell?"

"She more likely to be in a actual dumpster than a club," Ray Ray noted, continuing her streak of correct situational assessment.

On the television Lizzie was laughing, but there was something darker in her voice, something saddened and crimson: "These rats can't spend all their lives in their little Washington bubble where everyone understands them. What will they do when they have to go back out into the cold, hard world?"

On the piano, *Sing, choirs of an—bwaungggggg!*

Des was looking something up, though also telling herself she wouldn't do anything about it. "Jesus, 'the CVS on Connecticut Avenue'? There's fifty of them! ...There's literally seven."

"She didn't say nothing about why she was there?"

"Ooh, there's a thing where you can see the peak hours. 'People typically spend fifteen minutes here.' I wonder if it's sad to know that your whole job is making sure nobody ever has to spend more than fifteen minutes with you."

Ray Ray was visibly unimpressed with this little toy feeling.

Des said, "She really sounded scared. She asked me to come get her."

And then, with a wincing angry grin: "I don't think she knows I have a curfew." Tapping her fingernails against her teeth.

Ray Ray looked at her for what felt like a long time. "Why don't you come outside with me and put out the recycling," she said.

Outside, on the back porch, they could see the lights on in all the warm little family homes around them. Yellow oak and willow leaves lay in a wet and slippery mat; Des took the rake from beside the back door and started raking leaves off the steps. The moon hung bright above them in the clearing sky. Ray Ray hadn't dragged the recycling bin outside.

Des, looking down at her work, said she was pretty sure she knew where Toya lived and which CVS was closest; and how to get there by bus, although it would take at least an hour and a half. Their curfew had started at ten.

"Call a Uber," Ray Ray said. And, shaking her head and laughing a little, the black beads on the ends of her cornrows glinting in the white security light on the porch, "Now why the fuck did I sell my gun. I ask myself. Gun should always be the *last* thing you sell. Try to do the 'next right thing' and just end up wishing I could go strapped."

She looked around, then, and for no reason Des could understand she grabbed one of Miss Imani's potted plants off the railing of the back porch. She nodded and tucked it under her arm.

"You don't have to come," Des said, in a low voice. "It could be nothing; I haven't decided myself if I'm going. You can say no."

Ray Ray's laugh was edged with contempt—and something else, relief, joy. Like a Girl Scout she was always prepared. "Bitch, I never say no."

"You take a lot of risks," Des said.

"Yeah, it's called living while black. Are you coming or staying? 'Cause I'm 'bout to leave out."

Des put the rake back.

Ray Ray said, more gently, "All God's children born to die."

They called the Uber to the metro station, not the house, in case someone saw them. As they were walking down the hill Des glanced over at Ray Ray and saw that she was gazing into the distance. A hard little smile curved her lips, and her eyes were narrowed above those easy-living chipmunk cheeks.

It was a look of happiness, the look of someone for whom the world made sense again, someone falling back into an old familiar rhythm. Ray Ray's hips were swinging as she moved fast and easy down the sidewalk, holding the potted plant against her side with both hands. But in her face there was also knowledge of what might be about to happen.

Someone had wheatpasted posters to the bases of the lampposts: YOUR BODY IS A NATIONAL SACRIFICE ZONE. On the pavement the brown oak leaves curled up like outstretched hands.

Toya lay curled in the smallest dumpster outside the CVS and listened to Max Lord and Trina fighting.

"And none of this would ever have happened if you didn't have a wandering dick and a cardigan fetish!"

Max, with a defensiveness that gladdened and surprised Toya (and surprised her by how much it gladdened her), said, "It's not a cardigan fetish! It's a fetish for institutional women's clothing, which happens to include cardigans, along with blouses, knee socks, and smocks."

Something moved underneath Toya. She held completely still and was grateful for the damage the concussion had done to her sense of smell. The garbage warmth rose up around her, as if the dumpster was wrapping her in a soft thick blanket and telling her everything would be okay.

"Maybe," and now Max sounded calmer, rational self-control lying on his voice like an oil slick on an osprey, "none of this would have happened if you occasionally wore a smock."

Something thick and resonant slammed into the side of the

dumpster so hard that Toya jerked and gasped. She pressed sticky hands to her mouth and whimpered in terror.

Trina said, "Did you hear that?"

There was a long moment when nothing happened. And then the top of the dumpster opened.

"Oh, Jesus," Trina said. Toya put up a hand to shield her eyes from the sudden white light—the lights were back on all through Chevy Chase now.

"Don't frighten her," Max said. His voice was autumnal—Toya would have thought of bourbon if she'd ever had any—low and rich, and warm with rot.

She sat up in the trash. The blood on her face was grimy and blackened. She had a Ho-Ho smeared in her hair and there were receipts with foot-long coupon tails clinging to her cardigan: the unwanted reminders that you'd purchased Newports and Nicorette, would you like a discount on dandruff shampoo or pregnancy tests or beer? The coupon tail will drag along behind you forever, your purchasing history from which there's no absolution.

"I wish you'd come home," Max said. "I want you there."

She scrambled and flailed through the garbage as she made her way to the edge of the dumpster so she could peer over it. Cloud-rags were scattered in the sky. Orion was bright overhead, between the black aboveground electrical wires that made the neighborhood so vulnerable to blackouts. It had been four years since she had felt so completely alone.

The thing that Trina was carrying, which had made so much noise against the side of the dumpster, was the souvenir softball bat.

"All you have to do is come back, and learn to take responsibility," Max said. "That's what you've always wanted. Everyone can contribute. You just have to ask us for help."

Desiree would have recognized the voice in Toya's mind then, which said, You don't have to decide now. *You can go back with him; you might have to leave eventually, but you can always do it tomorrow. It was a voice any addict would know.*

As the Uber sped across the river, Des tried to cheer Ray Ray up. "I've never met this dude, 'the leader,'" she said, "but I doubt he's a hard rock or anything. Probably some joke in a fedora."

Ray Ray didn't turn away from the window. "I ain't worried about him. A ramen noodle could mess with that chick's head. He most likely a white motherfucker couldn't ruff off a Twizzler from a two-year-old. He ain't my problem and he ain't really even yours."

That puzzled Des. She'd been running through so many scenarios for what might happen with "the leader" that she had forgotten the thing Ray Ray was really worried about. Then she remembered that they could both go back to prison on the back of this little jaunt.

Her face felt hot—she wasn't sure why dread should feel so much like embarrassment—and her shoulders felt tight. Something bad was happening in her stomach. *You have already survived prison once and anything you can do once you can do twice, she told herself.* Positive thinking. *You quit drinking and using drugs; you did that, and you never thought you would.*

That was true. But it was positive thinking, so it rang false.

Baruch atah Adonai, Eloheinu melech haolam, she attempted—HaShem is the place where, when you have to go there, He has to take you in—but she never could remember how it ended. Not for the first time she thought that she should have tried practicing Judaism *before* she needed it, not during.

She could remember the kaddish, but at this moment, she didn't want to.

As Ray Ray leaned onto the front seat to talk with the driver,

Des tried the old JCC summer-camp chant: *David, melech Yisrael, chai, chai, vekayam.* David the savior of Israel lives and endures! But just like when she was in third grade she could never chant this thing without warping it into the far less triumphalist litany, *Wa-ter-melon, ginger ale; french fry, pizza pie!* (Every problem in your life is a fractal for all the problems in your life.)

With that ringing unhelpfully in her head she tried to trust that there was a Higher Power that could get her through anything. After all, He got the Jews through any—right, that didn't help.

It flashed through her mind, the front cover of that 1989 issue of *Tikkun* she'd rescued from her parents' basement: an abstract swirly painting like Chagall for Best Western, and the headline, "Is G-d Good for the Jews?" Des guessed it depended on what the alternatives were.

What was she relying on to get her through this all right?

Ray Ray, probably. But Ray Ray, at the moment, had sat back down and was staring at the potted plant in her lap with an intensity Des found unsettling. Ray Ray didn't look like a person who was making "getting through this all right" a top priority.

Des watched her with increasing unease. Finally she asked, "What is with that plant?"

"Shh," Ray Ray said, and the furrow between her brows deepened. "I'm concentrating my attention."

Des felt fear billow up inside her, rising toward hysteria. "Is that what we need right now?"

"Shut the fuck up," Ray Ray said, without looking at her. "I can't think about going back inside. If it happen, it happen, but if I think about it, I might jump out into traffic. Miss Imani say when you angry or terrified, concentrate your attention on a plant, so that's what I'm fucking doing. And you should too, because you violating just as much as I am, and you gonna end up in prison on the back of it just like me."

Des stared at Ray Ray, and then stared at the plant. The Uber descended into the curving, empty roads through Rock Creek Park. The trees were almost bare; the creek pulsed low and silent between its jagged banks. The driver had glanced back at them when Ray Ray said "prison," and he was watching them now through the rearview mirror, and frowning.

Des tried to open her mind to the possibility of going back to prison, tried to talk herself through it.

Instead, she grabbed Ray Ray's plant. She jabbed her fingers in the dirt, as Ray Ray yelped and hung on to the little green pot, which was now shaking and scattering soil across the back seat of the Uber. Desiree yanked the plant up by the roots and mangled it, mashing and tearing it in her hands while Ray Ray stared at her in horror. She confronted Ray Ray across the back seat. Struck her palm against the toggle that rolled down the car window. Hurled the plant out into the night.

"Concentrate on *that*," she said.

"I don't like this!" the driver said, anxious, pushing the car to go faster. The women ignored him.

Ray Ray lunged for Des across the car seat. Her fingers dug deep into Des's shoulders.

"Why are we doing this?" Des wailed. "Why are we doing this for *Toya*, who the fuck even is she?"

"What the fuck?" Ray Ray said, shaking Des in fury. "*You* the one got me out here. She *your* friend, she sure the fuck ain't mine!"

"She isn't my friend!" Des said, as they rose up out of the park. "She isn't anybody's friend."

And the force of that struck them. Ray Ray held her still. They looked at each other, but each of them saw someone else instead: the other women they carried with them. Des panted and her breathing seemed too loud in their sudden silence.

"No fighting in the car!" the driver said, in a high fearful voice. "I will stop this car!"

"Yeah, yeah, we good," Ray Ray told him. She subsided against her side of the car seat.

"You may be good!" the driver yelled. "I am not good!"

"You paid, ain't you?" Ray Ray growled.

But Des knew the Yelp economy better than Ray Ray did. She said, placatingly, "We will give you an excellent review. And we'll tell all our friends—or like, we'll tell our stable, hardworking, non-offender friends, to take you and review you too. I have lots of friends who are lawyers and normal things."

The car sped in a grim, resigned silence past big houses whose owners had hung up rainbow flags after the election. Des had cleaned a couple of these places. She recognized the way to her childhood library, before the city got enough money to reopen the one in the neighborhood where she grew up. They were almost there.

"This is your address," the driver said.

Des said, "Can you pull into that parking lot behind the CVS? We're trying to get close to the dumpsters."

The driver sighed. "Of course you are," he said. He made the left turn and the headlights of the Toyota lit up the lot.

"Oh, shit," Des said, as Toya lowered herself from the lip of the dumpster and the three figures in the lot all turned to look at them.

"Time to go," Ray Ray said. She swung the door open and she was out.

Des remembered to thank the driver—possibly because she wanted to make sure he had his cue to leave. She was pretty sure Ray Ray didn't want witnesses. She got out of the car and it backed out of the lot and sped away. They had left the plant pot inside.

All God's children born to die.

"Hiya, Toya," Ray Ray was saying, softly, holding her hands out like you'd do with a cat you found under a torched car.

"Who are these people?" the woman who wasn't Toya asked the man.

"Who are these people?" the man asked Toya, just as angry.

The woman, Des noted, was carrying a softball bat. She'd been trailing it behind her along the ground but now she swung it up over her shoulder. Just casual. Just to make it easier to carry.

"Everything's okay now," Toya said, pleading. Her voice was shaking. Turning first to Ray Ray and Des and then, with real fear, toward Max.

He turned away from her, smiling, and even under the jittery orange-tinted streetlights his eyes burned. He looked at them and both of the Love's Labors women felt that they were suddenly the only living person in the world. They felt as if the truth were known, the jig was up, the one they had been waiting for had opened up his eyes and paid them his complete attention. They felt that they were in the presence of power.

Des, unaccountably, felt so sorry for him.

"Your friend probably called you," he said. "She's having—a difficult night. Sometimes she has these episodes. I'm guessing you know what she can be like."

Toya pleaded mutely for them to tell her: Was he right? Did they know what she could be like?

"I do know that," Ray Ray allowed.

Max Lord relaxed. He turned back to Toya and his voice was just as gentle and kitten-coaxing as Ray Ray's had been. "I hope you realize," he said, "that most people wouldn't be nearly as patient with you as we've been. Most people don't find this kind of thing funny. But we believe in your potential and we value forgiveness."

"We should've kept the Uber," Des realized.

Ray Ray laughed. "We did keep it! When we was still back in Southeast, while you was *thinking* or whatever, I told him to circle the block. Toya, honey, I think you should come home with us for a little bit."

Max Lord said, "Toya, come with us."

He held out his hand to her.

Toya laughed. Not a good laugh—just a little, disbelieving laugh, *are you kidding me with this shit?*—baffled, damaged, angry and sad. She took a step toward Ray Ray and Des. Started to brush the Ho-Ho out of her scruff of hair.

Trina said Max's name, urgently. Desperately wanting him not to fail.

He glanced at her like he might be scared of her and stumbled forward, uneven on his bad leg. Grabbed Toya's arm and spun her.

Ray Ray pulled herself taut and strode forward. She made her shoulders wide and swaggered—*just like a cat fluffing up*, Des thought unhelpfully.

"Naw, son," Ray Ray said, and there was violence and conviction in her voice. Max Lord let Toya go.

Toya staggered a little and had just enough time to tell Ray Ray, "Thank you." Then Trina shouted, "*No!*" and leaped forward. Slammed the softball bat into Ray Ray's elbow so her arm crunched against her side.

Trina lifted the bat again as Ray Ray fell. She turned and swung sideways, aiming with all her strength for Toya's midsection. Des was frozen, watching, as Toya caught the bat by its end, stumbled and hung from it, yipping in pain.

A door at the back of the CVS opened and spilled dim yellow light. A woman stood in the doorway and shouted, "What is going on here?"

Out of the corner of her eye—out of instinct more than sight—

Des spotted the Toyota. She ran toward it and flagged it down as Ray Ray yelled about what the fuck she thought she was running away for. The woman from the CVS yelled that she was calling the police. Max was yelling, hopelessly, "What the fuck, baby? Peach tree, what the fuck?"

Trina jerked the bat from Toya's hands, leaving some of Toya's fingers stiff and bent wrong. Trina threw the bat into the shadow of the dumpster, and fled as it clattered. Max started after her and then, cursing, limped over to retrieve the bat.

Des begged the Uber driver to stay where he was, and without stopping to see if he'd done it she went and grabbed Ray Ray—by the broken arm, which made Ray Ray howl in a way Desiree had never heard before, even in prison. She dropped her, which didn't make things much better. Toya by that time was crouching beside Ray Ray and was the one to boost her to her feet and help her over to the car. They piled inside it, all three into the back seat, while the CVS woman was still wagging her phone at them and threatening to call 911.

"I didn't want none of this!" the driver shouted into the general welter of the back seat. "I don't want no violence, no bleeding, no bare feet!"

"Take us to Sibley Hospital," Des said.

"*Fuck no*," Ray Ray said. She gave the driver the Love's Labors address.

"You need to go to the hospital and I think Toya does too," Des argued.

Ray Ray gritted, "I'm gonna tell Miss Imani what happened and you're gonna shut the fuck up and let me do it. Driverman, go to the address I told you. Fuck a hospital. We can do that anytime."

"I can take you to the hospital but this girl needs to put on shoes," the driver yelled. He swung the wheel with especial aggressiveness as if that would compensate for his loss of control of the situation. All three of the women slid into each other and Ray Ray yowled in pain.

"She's escaping a cult!" Des said. "She doesn't have shoes because they don't wear shoes there!"

Toya burned with shame at what this new person would think of her. But in fact the driver changed his demeanor entirely.

"*Oh*, you are escaping a cult?" he asked. "Congratulations! That is so interesting."

"Oh," Toya said, "thank you?"

"I understand now why these women are so strange. With the plant and everything. They're deprogrammers! Did you meet any famous people?" the driver said. He punched the Love's Labors address into the GPS with perfect docility.

"Uh—I don't think so?"

"Ohhhh of course, you can't say! Did you meet a short man who jumps on furniture? Did you meet, let's say, a black man, who is married to a black woman, and they have very strange children?"

"It was all women," Toya said. And she missed what the driver said next (which was, "Were you forced to marry a homosexual?") because she was trying to understand that she had just said "was."

They were almost at Love's Labors—Ray Ray clutching the door handle with her good hand, panting and grimacing; Toya gamely telling the driver all about the Training Parlor, which he seemed to think was hot—when they heard the gunshots.

"Are you certain there weren't any famous people there?" the driver was asking. "Maybe not real famous, but famous in Washington? Like a senator that they made stand out there in her underwear—are there women senators?"

He considered this, and asked, "Are there lesbian senators?"

Before Toya could attempt to apply her limited civics knowledge to the undergrowth of his imagination, the shots came: those resonant cracks as if God had dropped a stack of plates.

The Uber driver screeched over to the curb. "Please get out now!" he yelped.

"Were those *gunshots?*" Toya said, putting her hands up to her face like Macaulay Culkin doing *The Scream.*

The Uber driver wasn't interested in her any longer. "Get out! Get out! I need to go! I should never have come to Southeast!"

"That's fine," Ray Ray said, swinging her door open with a grunt of pain. "We'll walk."

She hustled out of there and the other two piled after her. The driver pulled away before Toya even closed the door, and wheeled off back toward the bridge with his left rear door swinging open.

"He gon' get pulled over for that," Ray Ray said, with some grim satisfaction.

She looked around. "Where the fuck are we?"

Des, because she wasn't injured, had been able to spend the car ride from Chevy Chase thinking about how bad things would be once they got back to the halfway house, hours after curfew. She'd been gazing, with steadily deepening dread, at the street signs as they passed. That was convenient since it meant she could tell Ray Ray where the fuck they were.

"Oh, okay," Ray Ray said. She looked exhausted in the light of the guttering streetlamp. Drained and slack. "We not far. Actually, we can cut through there"—jerking her chin at a roadside valley full of overgrowth, one of Anacostia's vacant meadows, beautified by neglect—"and come up on it from the back."

She headed over. Des followed, but Toya wouldn't.

"I'm not going in there," she said, in a high breathy voice on the edge of hysteria. "That's like, if I go in there and somebody rapes me, everybody will be like, 'Why did you go in there?'"

Ray Ray didn't slow down. "Y'all can do whatever the fuck you want," she said, "but I'm going home."

Des looked back at Toya and shrugged, with her hands up, like, *What can you do?*

And so they plunged into the low tangle of vines and bushes, surrounded by tall and slender trees. Toya was gasping and stumbling, and laughing a little for no reason she could understand.

It was a good thing that the branches were almost all bare. The leaves cushioned Toya's bare, bruised and bleeding feet, instead of hiding the street light. Still, it was dark and all three of them were hoping Ray Ray knew what she was doing as she led them through the crashing, shuddering wild plants.

They were in the darkest part of the tiny wood when Ray Ray heard it. From a thicket just a few feet deeper: *Hoo-hoohoo-hoo.* And a flutter of gray.

She stopped in her tracks. Des had stopped too, but Toya bumped into her and knocked her into Ray Ray, and there was a lot of furtive cursing and Toya's convulsive giggling before they could sort it out and hold still. Des thought for sure the hooting wouldn't come again. But instead the gray thing in the thicket fluttered, like a distressed thing shivering, and called again, arrhythmic and low: *Hoo-hoohoo-hoo.*

Ray Ray turned to Des. "Do you think," she whispered.

"It's the owl," Des said.

Toya looked at their faces and didn't understand—they were grinning, astonished, in childlike rapture.

"Go in there and catch it," Ray Ray told Des.

"I don't want to scare it—"

Toya, all her life, had tried very hard. "Are we catching owls? I can do it!"

With her broken fingers she leapt ahead of them and plunged into the undergrowth. There was a squawk, which sounded like it was from Toya and not the bird, and a tussle, and then she screamed.

The other two women didn't hesitate. They broke through the screen of bushes and vines and found themselves in a hollowed-out area under the autumn-stripped branches of a weeping willow. Five dudes—a couple early twenties, the others mid- to late teens—were standing in a half-circle with their hands up and their faces blank with surprise and disbelief, and what they were staring at was the gun in Toya's shaking hands.

The guys wore claw-tipped and fur-trimmed gloves. Holding their paws up. Exchanging glances. Caught in weird modern-art poses, bending down to the ground or frozen reaching toward Toya. Everything happening very fast.

The gray and orange owl, tied to a willow branch at the thick point where it met the trunk, lowered its head and made its wings huge, like an enormous moth. Des looked at it, feeling in that moment like she would remember it forever, like she was capturing every detail of this owl with unreal clarity, and she saw that some of its gray feathers were stained pink. She thought, *We've made a serious mistake.*

The werewolves started to talk now, the ones on the tips of the crescent. Saying things that were unnecessary ("She grabbed your gun, cuz!") or weirdly understated ("White girl lunchin'!").

"Shut the fuck up," the werewolf at the center of the crescent said, low and tense. "Ray Ray, what the fuck is going on?"

"Okay," Ray Ray said. "Toya, honey, can you put the gun down?"

"No!" Her voice was ragged and harsh and terrified. "He grabbed me! I'm not gonna let anybody grab me!"

It was like she felt she had to argue for it.

"Donatello," Ray Ray said, "this girl having a real hard night. She don't need no more bullshit."

"Neither do I!" the central werewolf protested. "These fool niggas just shot at a 'migo on the street! I thought we were done with this shit," his aggrieved voice making the sub-werewolves gathered around him mutter and look down, even as the central werewolf didn't take his eyes off Toya and his gun.

"Toya, do you *want* to be holding this gun?" Ray Ray asked. "I know you don't want that."

"I'm not gonna let him touch me!" she snapped.

"Can you give the gun to Ray Ray?" Des asked. And everybody looked at her like, *Why do you need to pipe up?*

"Who the fuck is *this* one?" a werewolf muttered.

But Ray Ray nodded and said, "You have all the power here. You can choose. You can choose how this goes. Do you want it to go bad?"

"No," Toya said miserably. The muzzle of the gun dipped down.

Donatello moved toward her and the gun came back up with a jerk. Toya's hands clenched in panic. The gun went off.

Toya screamed and all the werewolves' guns came up as the lead werewolf fell backward. Des had time to wonder why the trees had changed position and it took her a moment to realize she was on her knees. *I did not think this was how I'd die tonight,* she thought.

Ray Ray didn't raise her voice, but she made it resound through the little clearing: "Everybody stop."

"Oh God," Toya said into the silence, with four guns pointing at her head, "oh God, I killed him! I killed him!"

"Toya," Ray Ray said, and her voice was the only calm thing in that clearing. "Time to make a decision. You can choose. You want to give the gun to me, or to Des, or what do you want to do with it?"

Des was surprised and—later—gratified, that Toya turned to look at her. She stood up awkwardly and said, trying to mimic Ray Ray's tone, "I'd definitely pick Ray Ray if I were you."

Toya nodded. She kept her eyes and the gun trained on the werewolves as she backed toward the two women. She trembled as Ray Ray reached up a hand and took the gun.

Toya stood, bereft. "I killed somebody," she said.

"You did the fuck not," Donatello said. He sat up in the dirt. He was holding his arm just above the elbow.

Ray Ray was thinking fast, stringing a lot of things together. She knew they should get the fuck out of that clearing before the cops came. But she had taken a lot of risks that night already and she was in the mood, she was on a roll, and she saw a way to get a few things done. Not things she herself needed, but things she'd like to do for other people.

She tucked the gun in the back of her jeans. The owl hooted again, that same uneven call, *Hoo-hoohoo-hoo.*

"What the fuck y'all even doing here?" the lead werewolf asked Ray Ray as he got to his feet. Quietly—they were both listening for sirens, for footsteps on the outskirts of their little criminal woods.

"You and me gonna talk," Ray Ray said. She didn't speak loudly, but she didn't have to. Toya was suddenly terrified of her, and didn't know why. Des, for her part, knew exactly why she was suddenly aroused.

Donatello seemed to share both Toya's reaction and Des's. He winced, he checked out the rip in his jacket and the pink streak of seared flesh along his arm, he ducked his head like he didn't know where to look. Nobody said anything. They just waited.

Finally: "Come with me," he said, and motioned for Ray Ray to come out from under the willow tree and further toward the far end of the derelict wood. He padded into the trees, with a lieutenant right behind him. Ray Ray grinned and followed them.

At the furthest edge of the wood, where the streetlights were brighter, Ray Ray settled down in the shadow of an oak and handed the gun back to its rightful, though not legal, owner. She shifted her bad arm, careful and wincing. Pain was coming out all along her skin like sweat.

"What y'all even come out here for?" Donatello asked, with some desperation.

Giggling a little now, shocky, the adrenaline going everywhere, like her blood was rushing into her and out of her all at once. "I come for the owl," she said.

Donatello stared at her.

"This shit is about a *owl?*" he said, almost in a wail, like his world was tilting out from under him. "Y'all three females out here for a feather-ass bird? This is like *Harry Potter* meets *Charlie's Angels.*"

"The thing is," Ray Ray said, "you looking at serious time here. You got that thing out of a federal park, and federal park is federal *prison.*"

"How you even know it's your owl?" Donatello asked. "You all 'I'm here for *the* owl.' It ain't no the owl. This just *an* owl. You like a police scanner, 'Suspect is a male black owl,' then you hem up all the owls for six blocks. Think we all look the same. You a owl racist, is what it is."

Ray Ray glowered. "You think I can't recognize one great horned owl from another one? Also she is a lady owl. A fe-mowl."

Donatello, now very unsure of his footing, said, "That can't be what they call it. It can't be you 'posed to call it a femowl. I read on my phone about how you feed it and shit, and they didn't say nothing about no femowl."

Ray Ray pressed her advantage. "And you painted that poor

animal! You cuffed a *owl*, what the fuck, young, and then you dyed it pink. You already looking at Unauthorized Use of a Federal Animal. Now you got Defacement of Public Birds. I know you can do time, but can you do time for a *bird?*"

"You wellin'," Donatello said, uncertainly. Ray Ray just looked at him.

"This shit is fucked up," his werewolf lieutenant said. "I'm real-life sick of this owl. Give her the damn bird and let's make a move."

"Make a move where?" Donatello asked in exasperation. "You just tried to shoot up a 'migo in the street. It ain't nothing out there but eses and police. You the one fucked up. I'm a keep my owl."

Ray Ray was about to start arguing with him when she put her bad hand down by mistake, trying to steady herself on the grass, and gasped in pain. She felt like the ground was falling out from under her. She had time to think, *I'm gonna fall* and time to think, *I can't stop it* and time to think, *Aw fuck, my face is hitting the dirt.*

And then she was sitting propped up in her play cousin's lap, Donatello who they always made fun of for his ninja-turtle name, he'd shed his wolf jacket and taken off his shirt and he was wrapping her arm in it. Dumb-ass-atello. *Where the other turtles at now? I ain't hitting you, mo, I'm just checking your shell!*

Looking up past the bare shoulder of his bullet-seared arm she could see the stars. One bright star, falling—she was just about to make a wish when she figured out that it was a police chopper.

"Leave this crazy bitch and let's go!" the sub-werewolf was saying as Donatello hunted around on the ground with his long wiry fingers, found a suitable stick, and splinted Ray Ray's arm.

"*Weak,*" Ray Ray said. The two dudes under the oak tree each thought she was talking about them, but she meant herself.

"Aw, Ray Ray, don't be like that," Donatello said. Unsure when or how things had turned around on him. Feeling like by bandaging her arm up he'd incurred some kind of debt, which seemed backwards. Like having done this one thing for her he now would have to do more.

"Hey," Donatello said, partly trying to be kind and partly trying to get back on the moral high ground, "how you been? How you doing with the whole thing with your girlfriend?"

And, turning to his lieutenant, he explained, "She the one who the P.G. Jail killed her wife."

The sub-werewolf rocked back a little, screwed up his face in sorrow and respect. Ray Ray sat up. Gathered up the authority of her grief. "I don't know how I been doing," she admitted. "And I don't want to talk about it. But I want to do something for you. I can solve your vampire problem."

"And how's that?" Donatello asked. Skeptically; but not as skeptically as he would have a few minutes ago.

"What it's been is that they hit you so you hit them," she said. "Right? Back and forth. And whenever you think shit is quieted down, somebody fucks it up."

"And?" the head werewolf laughed. "You gonna change niggas so they don't fuck things up no more?"

"Look at your arm," she said, almost kindly.

He was having none of her gentleness. "You look at your arm! You done fucked up your arm, cuz, so why you lecturing at me?"

"Yeah, I think it's broken," she said. "But like. You can say to them, 'My man shot at you, then you winged me. So we even.' You can offer them some justice and peace of mind, and a truce."

"But they did not wing me. I do not get shot by amigos."

"You like it better if they knew how you *did* get shot?" Ray Ray laughed a little at the idea.

"Fuck, cuz, you wouldn't do me like that! I ain't going to those motherfuckers telling them I can't protect myself. You doing too much."

Ray Ray was still sitting between his legs, still leaning back against his broad left shoulder so she could look across at his face. It was a weird position to argue in, being held by him, and it made her want to fuss and fight to get him to take her seriously. But in her mind she heard, against her will, Des's voice saying, *In every decision you make you must ask: What is the most humble thing to do?*

And so she said, "I been doing this all wrong. Look, I'm a be honest with you. I don't snitch and I don't fuck up my family, and you know that, so you know this all just empty threats and bullshit. I wouldn't drop a dime on you to the police or Los Vampirez or the National Park Service. But when you out here do you ever think about how *I* feel if you end up twenty years old in a wheelchair? You got a closet full of t-shirts with all your dead friends. I know, 'cause I have the same ones. What do you do when you start to like a nigga, do you go down and put in your t-shirt order on standby?"

"Oh, do you know a place that would—"

"I want you to go to these 'migos and offer a truce because you fucking up the neighborhood and you gotta take a stand, be a man and do the right thing. I want you to give me the owl because my friend is its keeper and she can care for it a lot better than your ass been doing. I'll go with you to Los Vampirez if I'm not back locked up, which I guess I should tell you I probably will be."

Donatello started out, "Anyway what if I was to go to them," but as soon as he said this he felt like he was making a mistake, like in shooting down this idea he had somehow given it more weight and reality. He soldiered on: "And then they start up with us again? You want me to call the police? Last time they solved a crime, it was 'Bitch set me up'! '911, what's your emergency?',", and he imitated the voice of every woman who'd ever turned him down, "'Oh, this is D-Money? Didn't I tell you to lose this number?'"

"'D-Money,'" Ray Ray giggled.

"I need to be able to protect my people."

"'D-Money.'"

"You can also say, 'Deezus,'" the lieutenant werewolf put in helpfully.

"I can, but I won't," Ray Ray said. But then, sighing: "If I go and talk to Los Vampirez, will you honor a truce?"

"The fuck, you think I'm not honorable? My word is bond."

She smiled. "Good, so we agreed."

Donatello stared down at her. *What the fuck I just agree to?* he thought. But he couldn't figure out how to get out of it.

He helped her up. Tried sucking on his wound to see if that made it hurt less; it didn't really, although it changed how it hurt.

In the clearing under the willow, while the negotiations were going on, everybody else suddenly had nothing to do. Toya abruptly moaned and stumbled backward, and Des, realizing what was going on, caught her and told her to put her head between her knees and take deep breaths.

"I know how to *breathe*," Toya snapped—and then she swayed woozily in Des's arms. And did as she'd been told. She began to sob, almost silent, into her shaking hands.

Des, kneeling beside Toya, looked up at all the werewolves. They were trying to look like they had very important things to check on their phones. One of them crouched down with his furry hands hanging between his also-furry knees. Another one sat down with his back against the willow trunk, stripped off his gloves and lit a joint.

She could see the butt of the pistol poking out of his waistband.

He caught her looking and laughed. Patted it. Grinned at her— sexy, threatening.

"'Man's best friend," he said.

She smiled back: the careful, neutral, eternal smile of the woman who doesn't want to pick up what a man is putting down. Then that Gioconda smile quirked up on one end as she considered the werewolf's twist on the old line.

If you want a friend in Washington, get a gun.

On the ground beside her, Toya sobbed out, "I am so *stupid*."

"You're not stupid," Des said. Which might be true, she figured. Being in a cult probably made it hard to display whatever intelligence you possessed.

"Yes I am," Toya said, banging her fists on her knees. "You went to Yale! Don't pretend you don't think I'm stupid."

Desiree said, with complete sincerity, "You are significantly smarter than some of the mollusks I went to college with. I've actually read," and this was true, too, "that intelligent people are more vulnerable to scams and cults."

Toya lifted her head. "Really?"

Des didn't say that this information should make people question the value of intelligence. She just nodded and said she'd send Toya the links. Let Cracked.com handle the girl's self-esteem for a little while.

Toya smiled tentatively, and Des patted her shoulder. Tried not to wonder if she was patting a shoulder wrong; tried not to feel like an idiot.

Five minutes later, while Toya with intense concentration was picking glass and rocks out of her feet, Ray Ray strolled out of the underbrush. She had her arm in a splint, wrapped in a sling made from a t-shirt. Donatello trotted reluctantly behind her, with no t-shirt on under his werewolf leather jacket, looking like he'd eaten someone who'd gone rancid. She walked over to the owl and waited while Donatello untied it—the huge bird clicked her beak, and flapped so violently that it almost yanked him off his feet—and then tied the leash around Ray Ray's waist. The owl jerked around some more, but eventually resigned herself, with just a few last little shakes of her great head, and settled down on the shoulder of Ray Ray's good arm.

Des noted with interest that the part of the leash holding the owl's leg was made of what looked like Ace bandages cut into strips, which were tied to a dog leash and secured with duct tape. The homemade equivalent of fuzzy handcuffs, she figured.

Little more was said. Ray Ray went to hug Donatello but he just shook his head and patted the owl—who snapped at him—and told both of them that they were vicious. Ray Ray and the owl led the other two women through the back end of the woodlet and she had been right: They were only a block away from home. The moon rode high and the midnight street gleamed. At Love's Labors Loft the porch light was on.

They skulked all around the house but didn't see any sign of the cops, so they let themselves in the back. Miss Imani was waiting for them in the kitchen, under the little egg-shaped security camera. Its light was still red—nobody had turned it back on after the power outage. Miss Imani was drinking a cup of tea; when they came in, she set the teacup down on the stovetop, and Des didn't like its decisive clack.

"I know what you gotta do," Ray Ray said. "I just want to say—because you always telling us here to give thanks—I just opened truce negotiations between the Werewolves and Los Vampirez. In exchange for me not telling the FBI them wolfmens stole a federal owl. Also, this girl needs a hospital, and probably like therapy or something, 'cause we just broke her out of a cult."

Miss Imani took this in. She searched Ray Ray's calm face—looking for the lie, for the hustle.

Ray Ray said, "If I ain't lived here I never would've cared about doing none of that, so thank you. But I got to say. Before whatever happens next. You always telling us we need a balance of work and pleasure, and all the shit that happened tonight was hard fucking work."

And she grinned. That tilt-a-whirl grin, that open bar, that glinting grin that would steal your heart and then your credit cards. And she said, "I can't remember when I ever had this much fun."

Miss Imani said, very quietly, "When I choose to, I can use the clock on the microwave to determine whether my guests have broken curfew."

Des and Ray Ray and Toya all looked over at the microwave. In broken red slashes the clock was blinking 12:00. Just like the security camera, in all the confusion over the missing women nobody had reset it.

"Must be noon," Imani Rollins said.

Chapter 19
The Soul Searchers

On the afternoon of Saturday, November 19—four days after Toya fled Morningstar, when everything at the halfway house was still confusion and figuring out what to tell the authorities—Lizzie Pearl and David Lav were prepping for their show. She was leaning forward with her hair in an elaborate array of clips, powdering her cleavage. He was watching her and straightening his tie, which was the only thing he had to do before they went on the air so he did it several times.

She was saying, "Yeah, that one lady at CNN got in touch—you remember how one person liked us?—and when I said I wouldn't be available in the future she was like, 'Oh, but why?' People never have to pay for anything in this town. Hashtag, ThisTown."

He tried buttoning his jacket. "Do you know when you're leaving?" he asked, carefully casual.

She blotted herself elaborately with a coffee filter. "Yep, January 1st I have a flight out of Reagan at nine a.m. Back to Dynamo, Indiana, or whatever's left of it. Gotta figure out what to do with my bedpost bow tie collection, let me know if you want one. I can teach you how to tie it."

He unbuttoned his jacket. He was glaring at her as he said, "I still don't understand what you'll do there. Is this one of those new off-coast reporting jobs?"

"I don't think those are real," she said. "I might be an anchorwoman? Do they have television there? A lot has happened back home while I wasn't paying attention.... Don't worry—you're always so sweet to me—I have plenty in my savings account. Like seven hundred bucks, which makes me a millionaire in Indiana dollars. And if things get crunchy there's one way I can always get work."

"Lizzie."

"What?" she laughed. "Waitressing, obviously! Well, but also stripping, if they don't have normal restaurants anymore."

And then, ruefully slapping her legs, "Gotta do more squats if I want to get these thighs back up on the pole."

David Lav thought of himself as a feminist, who respected women's choices even when the women were Lizzie. So he was surprised at how angry he sounded when he said, "Can I ask why?"

She cocked her head to one side. She had to think about it, while she moved her boobs around to powder all the angles. Finally she just shrugged and said, "Somebody has to."

And then, when he couldn't come up with anything to say to that, she added, "I owe them."

"You owe them for what exactly?"

Lizzie laughed. In the pearls-and-gloves, D.A.R.-P.T.A.-G.O.P. voice of the '80s sitcom mother nobody ever had, she declared, "People don't have to do things for you before you owe them! That's entitlement mentality, that you only owe people who do things for you."

She unclipped her hair and shook her head so her hair cascaded around her face. David Lav pulled the knot of his tie down—suddenly it was right up against his Adam's apple.

"I hope you know you can't save them, or help them, or whatever it is you think you're going to do," he said. The artificial blush on his cheeks seemed to have spread across his nose and over to his ears.

"I'm them," she said. "Or—I'm not them, I'm sure they won't think so, but I've really never been you."

Then, with a saddened grin, she said, "I was so proud of myself when I got out of there. Well, I should've known it's a mistake to do things that you're proud of."

And so at the end of their show—an unusually strained show, with a lot of awkward pauses and unrelated interjections—Lizzie announced, "Here's the part where I should take personal responsibility and tell you guys that Trump is my fault, but I still don't know why any of this is even happening, so instead I'll just say that I failed here somehow. And there have to be consequences in life, even if you don't know why. So at the end of the year I'm going home. If you're in southern Indiana and you don't have a girlfriend," and she mouthed "call me" as she waggled her pinky and thumb by her face in the traditional, anachronistic sign.

"But only if you're pro-life," she added. "I don't want some dude blowing up my phone all mad that he has to pay child support."

And with that she gave a decisive wink and shimmy to the camera, and handed it over to David Lav, who looked like he was strangling, to close them out.

When she strode off the set she was smiling in a way David had never seen on her. Relief and joy and gratitude—confidence and freedom—the closest thing he could think of was his one friend who'd kicked heroin. "The amazing thing," that friend had said, "is that on one level it's all the same shit. Like, I did a lot of awful, humiliating shit because of my addiction, and now I have to do humiliating shit because of my recovery. And before when I was—I don't want to talk about—like, I can talk about some stuff, but a lot of it, I'm just not there yet, okay—but like, when I was shooting up, or whatever, and the blood was spattering around, I'd think, 'Yeah, you deserve it, this is your place in life.' And I still totally feel like that, I still think that same thing when I have to do hard shit in my recovery. But it *feels*—you can't imagine, it feels so good. There's seriously no better feeling in the world than doing humiliating shit and just accepting it, because it's part of the process. Fucking peaceful."

David caught up to her and said, "Lizzie. I have to ask, before you go—I mean—will you marry me?"

She turned and there was so much tenderness and pity on her face. She looked at him with empathy—but without what he was asking for, which was solidarity.

"Should I get down on one knee? I know it's traditional, you'd probably prefer that—"

"Oh, you're so sweet," she said sorrowfully. "But I think you know that I can't. I have other things I have to do. It's great to see that you have a self-destructive streak, though! I never would have guessed."

"Please don't leave," he said.

"Back home," she said gently, "we used to have a thing, when people just randomly disappeared from a party, we'd say that they 'Lazarus'd.' So like, 'Hey Lizzie, where'd you go last night? You were passed out on the porch and then when we came back out you'd Lazarus'd.' I've been at this party for a while and it's been great, for real, but now I gotta Lazarus."

She looked at him. "Should I kiss you?" she asked. "In movies I think this is where the girl kisses the guy on the cheek. It always seemed cruel to me, but I think it's what you're supposed to do."

"Please do," he said; and she did. She was glad to do her duty and satisfied when it was done. He wondered why, when he had accepted this humiliation, he felt no peace at all.

At that moment, on the porch of Love's Labors Loft, Trash was telling Toya, "You need to hold the light saber in your mouth. Can you do that? Because we're going to be putting hooves on your hands."

Toya gave a fierce "uh-huh" and grabbed the handle of the glowing pink plastic weapon with her teeth. She took her hands away experimentally and it tilted wildly and almost fell.

This was happening because Toya's therapist said that she had an absolute right to tell anybody anything, and Toya took it to heart. Most people wouldn't stick around to listen to her, but Trash had over a decade of service-industry experience. So he submitted to lists of which foods were the same size as her fetus (the Taco Bell Cravings app even sent you a fifty-cent coupon when your baby reached the size of a chimichanga), what she could currently smell, what she'd been forced to put in her vagina (*"A rubber duck?"* "Yes, with the head sticking out—I had to squeeze it to make it quack—"), and what she missed about Morningstar. He commiserated and got indignant on her behalf much more satisfyingly than her therapist. She said that she missed taking orders, and he nodded intensely, although he was caught at a loss when she explained, "It made me feel so important!"

So she'd been telling him all the ways she had tried to shut down Morningstar. At first she'd wanted to call the cops on Trina, at least, if not Max. Des had explained, guiltily and obliquely, that pressing an assault charge against them would probably expose the fact that she and Ray Ray had violated their release conditions. But she was so oblique that Toya hadn't understood at all, and Ray Ray'd had to make the same point with unabashed bluntness: "If you go after them, me and her gonna get locked back up. My CSO is not gonna care that we was helping you."

Then Toya had tried, at Des's urging, to tell her story to the local press. The problem was that neither Toya herself nor anyone she knew projected an air of respectability, credibility, or basic coherence. To put it another way, being in a cult is very hard to explain. Two interns from Seven on Your Side nodded and smiled and didn't take notes; the *City Paper* promised to investigate, but bumped the story in favor of a political hit piece on mushroom-hunting Russians in the Blair Witch woods.

Lizzie Pearl had made her sole venture into reporting, dedicating a full show to Morningstar. She'd prepared to argue David into it: She'd made a list of points including, "This place being a cult is the one thing I successfully analyzed in my entire 'career.'" But she had just informed David that she was leaving Washington for good, and one aspect of the American political landscape she hadn't analyzed correctly was his emotions. He was in no condition to argue with her about anything. So she interviewed Toya, made up to look even paler and with her spiky little curls stiffening upward as she sweated under the hot lights. The women of Love's Labors made up a full twenty percent of the viewership.

Then Toya protested outside Morningstar. She and whichever of the Love's Labors women she could persuade to join her would march up and down along the sidewalk holding signs that said, NEIGHBORS—WHY DON'T THE WOMEN HERE EVER SAY HI TO YOU? and (Des's fairly indolent effort) LOL THIS PLACE IS SO CREEPY. They chanted, "Hey Max Lord, you're not an adult! You're the skanky leader of a skanky cult!"

This was how Toya learned that six women had left the group right after Toya's escape. She was gleeful and gratified by this news until she found out that they'd left because they couldn't believe their leader had shown the poor taste to use Toya and not one of them for his sexual release.

"If it helps," Trash offered, "my dom says people don't always know why they do what they do. And that seems true, from my experience. Anyway, you did help them, or you did things that ended up helping them."

At one point Caretta in her enthusiasm started shaking the bars of the gate, and the Morningstar people called the police. Both Des and Toya were tongue-tied and terrified in the face of the cops, but Ray Ray chatted with them for a bit and loudly instructed everybody to respect the law. Des started chanting, "We respect boundaries!" and so they all chanted that, pointedly, while the cops watched and chuckled, and the curtains on the first-floor Morningstar windows twitched.

That had been good, Toya explained. She was following Trash around while he swept his workplace. She didn't help—his manager had said she wasn't allowed to—but because she was a trauma survivor, the manager let her crawl around after him while he scraped filth off the floors on his hands and knees. He was giving her the same compassionate attention he gave the customers when she said, "But the thing I really want—my unmet need—is closure."

"Oh," Trash said, in the same tone of voice he used with the lady who always tried to pay with coupons from the Clinton administration. He didn't want her to be disappointed after all she'd been through. "I don't know if I believe in closure. I think Catholics don't? Or maybe it's just that my family holds grudges. They still talk about stuff the British did in like 1900."

"Oh—what do you do instead?"

"Well, I think what you're supposed to do is pray. But what I actually do is drag shows."

Which is how Trash ended up choreographing a skit to be performed at the Dragsgiving Brunch at Nellie's on the Sunday after Thanksgiving. Toya would portray the Little Lamb, of course, who valiantly defeated the Two-Headed Dragon played by Trash and Javier strapped together with an array of bondage gear. Upon defeat the dragon transformed into Lucinda's aging therapy chihuachschund and Fifi la Flamme, La Poodle Plus Belle des Ballets Trockadero de West Texas. The skit ended with the Love's Labors women bursting onstage dressed in white, brandishing green feather dusters and singing "Lean on Me."

"Why do we got to have feather dusters?" Caretta groused.

"It's drag," Trash said, "feathery things are traditional. Hope is the thing with feathers, darling."

"It's not for dusting," Des pointed out. "Just sort of wave it around like you're threatening somebody."

"Why are they singing 'Lean on Me'?" Toya wondered. "I don't see how it's relevant."

Ray Ray said, "Yeah, but we all know it already. I ain't got time to be learning no new song."

"You can have 'Lean on Me,' or you can have just the chorus of 'Stop! In the Name of Love,'" Des said. "And most of 'Beat It,' but not in order. Those are the songs we all know."

This cathartic drama would also be a protest, or, as Lucinda put it, "nonconsensual immersive theater." Trash and Javier would be draped in a beauty-queen sash saying MORNINGSTAR CULT, and Trash would hold a large Christmas-tree star that they'd painted blood-red.

"All right, everyone," Trash said regally. "We are aiming for an atmosphere of flamboyance, and yet poignance. *Flamboignance.* Remember your fingertips. Remember that the energy flows from the core of the body all the way outward. Do not forget the edges of the body."

Des's Thanksgiving began early, with emergency cleaning jobs at two different apartments. She recited the kaddish silently on the bus to her first assignment. Already the kaddish was becoming familiar to her; like home, she could lose herself in it, she could fail to notice what she was praying until suddenly it would catch her attention and she would realize that she knew these words and belonged to them:

> *Blessed, praised, honored, exalted, extolled, glorified, adored, and lauded*
> *be the name of the Holy Blessed One,*
> *beyond all earthly words and songs of blessing, praise, and comfort.*

She noted with some satisfaction that when her lips were moving in prayer, nobody tried to sit next to her.

The first clients refused to pay her, after she'd already cleaned their oven, because it still wouldn't turn on. She tried to explain the difference between cleaning and fixing, with examples from her own program of recovery, to no avail. The second client spent an hour alternating between tearful screaming at her and tearful screaming into the phone. At last, while Des was on all fours scraping giblets off of faux-Arabic painted floor tiles, her client realized, "Oh—is this the suicide hotline? I'm so sorry, I thought this was the Butterball hotline!"

And then, giving Des an embarrassed laugh, "Must've hit my speed dial. There's some of the gizzard still in the grout there— you'll need to really get in and scrub."

Des forced herself to smile. Tried to muster up some humble solidarity, after all who hasn't screamed at a service professional who's on all fours amid your filth, we all have our foibles. But when she was scrubbing the bathroom she noticed her client's toothbrush and had to take several long, slow, deep and mindful breaths. She had ideas for that toothbrush and they were just, but they weren't nice.

Instead she lowered her head and focused on the bathroom floor. The uneven white tiles seemed to harbor enough pubic hair to knit a merkin.

It was Des's settled belief that submission was, at its heart, a discipline of the attention. More than once she had suddenly become aware, as if against her will, of the beauty of a shoe she was being made to lick. In encountering the cracks and dirt of its surface, the roughest and least appealing parts of its reality, she learned to love it. Now she tried to apply the same obedient attention to this woman's bathroom tile.

And to her surprise, it worked. First she saw the haunting beauty of the black kinks of pubic hair caught against the cloud-white tiles. Then the peace and power as she swept and scrubbed until the tiles glowed like the winter sun. Order was a gift she was being allowed to give to this place; and the littleness, the embarrassing physicality and humbleness of the place was good for her as well. She bagged up the trash and scrubbed the wastebasket. Even the trash looked strange now, like trash in a movie, somehow clarified and heightened as she attended to it. The crisp or very slightly ragged edges of the bleach wipes surprised her, their fuzzy gray or flat yellow stains delighted her. The hard uneven tiles left welts on her knees and she grinned at them, these girlish red fingerpaint-streaks of pain. Her back ached and even the ache felt somehow strange to her and new, as if she were being introduced to it and coming to know its best qualities.

When she came out of the bathroom she was smiling. She looked kindly upon her distraught client, with a vast gentle patience in which there was no condescension. She listened and did as she was told, and her complete acceptance of the client embarrassed the woman and made her laugh awkwardly and tip Des twenty-five percent.

From work she headed to her family's Thanksgiving. She would have liked to drop her vacuum and cleaning supplies back at Love's Labors, but she didn't have time; so this year she was bringing the consequences of her criminal record instead of, for example, marshmallow sweet potatoes. She let the conversation swirl around her and longed, unexpectedly and involuntarily, to be back at the halfway house. She imagined explaining to her family, "It's really more of a halfway *home*." But instead she just smiled and listened and passed the tsimmes or the kugel.

Her parents drove her back there afterward. Her father couldn't come in—men weren't allowed, since they were over-emotional and caused drama. But Des's mother came up the porch, past the fake hibiscus, into which somebody had flung part of her weave for no reason Des could understand. Up to the front door, where Des brushed her fingers against the mezuzah she'd made out of an airplane-sized Hennessy bottle from the vacant lot next door, decorated with owl feathers.

She stashed her cleaning supplies in the coat closet, next to the table where *The Homegoers* lay. She watched with some sorrow as her mother read Diamond Dawkins's (LLL class of '11) mission statement: "The goal of this place is to make sure people miss you when you die." Her mother looked dismayed, and Des felt a Mobius-strip emotion made of shame and pride: shame at how much pride she took in her new life; pride that she loved her mother enough to feel shame.

After her mother went back to the car Des dropped in on the tail end of her housemates' Thanksgiving. The women were sharing family stories, always an intermittently harrowing event.

Caretta was telling them how her mother had peed all over the living room rug the day she left Caretta's father. She had cut holes in the pockets of all his pants, so that he'd always be losing things and never know why; she had forked a full can of tuna fish down the slats of the radiator; she had hummed to herself as she squeezed a tube of toothpaste into his DVD player.

The Love's Labors women howled with laughter. "We should get your mom in here to teach, like, assertiveness classes," Fang said.

"Oh, you can't," Caretta said casually. "I don't know where she live now. She used to make me wear flip-flops, even in winter, so she'd always have something to beat me with."

Desiree thought about her fury that morning, how badly she'd wanted to stick her client's toothbrush where the Lemon Pledge don't shine. She reflected that the answer to, *What is the most humble response?*, rarely if ever involved forking tuna fish into a radiator.

After dinner she sat on her bed working over her review of Jabez Pruitt's *Custodian of Souls*. Des typed, *At first, when Pruitt would go to Cambridge cocktail parties, he was embarrassed to say what he was doing with his time. But he found that reactions weren't what he had expected. While some people were confused and embarrassed by his situation—"I could see them examining me," he writes, "and I wondered if they were trying to figure out if I smelled"—many others treated him like a guru with some deep spiritual insight one can only gain through hard and humbling work.*

When one of the cocktail-party class picks up a mop and bucket in order to find himself, it's as if these tools become newly fascinating. Pruitt quotes friends and relatives saying what the blurbs on his book jacket say: Through his creativity and dedication he has learned humility, and gained a deeper empathy for the working class. He chose this path, and so it is an expression of his personal character; the mop and bucket are sanitized by his choice. (His fellow janitors, endlessly patient, never ask why Pruitt is taking a job that could've gone to a hardworking Salvadoran instead.)

When someone volunteers for poverty and service, he shows genuine respect for those who were never allowed to choose otherwise. Pruitt's coworkers respond to his obvious belief that the work they do is honorable and important. They too (at least in his telling) seem to feel that a Harvard grad's presence in the bucket brigade lends a certain glamour to their lives: the glow of dignity acknowledged.

But what Pruitt cannot choose, and doesn't seem to understand or honor, is precisely his coworkers' lack of choices. Constraint, too, has its dignity. There is a sublimity, found nowhere else in life, in the acceptance of what we would not have chosen but cannot change. Is there a way to volunteer for nonconsensual suffering? I've found drug addiction extremely useful in this regard, but I hesitate to recommend it.

Des checked her word count. Looked over that last paragraph, realized it sounded kind of rapey, and replaced "nonconsensual" with "unchosen" in the hopes that that might help. (Later, her editor would cut the entire paragraph.)

She spent a few minutes crafting an exquisitely catty byline, which would identify her solely by her cleaning credentials. Should she list her Yelp rating? Maybe even give her prison record? Really rub it in Pruitt's face that she knew what he was talking about—that he was an Ivy League writer who happened to spend a year touring toilets, while she was the real deal, a worker and not a thinker-about-workers.

But then she deleted all that and wrote, *Des Schulman, Contributing Editor, is a writer and housecleaner in Washington, DC. She is a certified detergents professional.*

Nellie's was decked out for the Dragsgiving Brunch with strings of orange Mardi Gras beads and pumpkins wearing tiaras. The servers were topless and the mimosas bottomless. One television was showing the Redskins playing the Dallas Cowboys, while the other showed a general's son kneeling in the snow in reparation for the

Dakota Access Pipeline. Someone had left a *New York Times* scattered over one table; the top headline read, "In a Whiter D.C., Fears that Trump Will Attract the Wrong Whites."

Des set the chihuachshund's carrier on the table, and a server asked her to put it on the floor. She was in charge of the dog because Lucinda was working a Sunday double shift. She tried to be admiring of Luce's work ethic and grateful to be trusted with this responsibility, but in general, she really hated that dog. It had done a much better job of obeying and pleasing Lucinda than she had, which was humiliating given that it pooped on the carpet at least twice as often as she did, and yapped almost as loudly. It was yapping right that minute, and she could only hope that it wasn't also pooping.

Over the barking of the affronted little service animal, Trash and Javier were having an intense discussion, which Trash refused to call an argument, about why Javier had forbidden him from talking to Brandon.

"Of course I'll do as you tell me," Trash said, "but at least let me know if it's jealousy of me or judgment of him. If you're jealous then I'm very grateful. I've never had anyone be possessive of me before except my family. And possibly God, if you can be possessive but also weirdly unreliable and withholding. But if this is about your judgments of Brandon then in my personal opinion that's about him, not me, and shouldn't be relevant to what you ask and expect of me."

Javier looked at him in bafflement. "How is judging him for how he treated you not about you?"

"It shows integrity on his part, you know, that he's here to look after his poodle even though he knows we all think he's my evil ex."

Brandon meanwhile was sitting by himself, petting his poodle and grinning tightly. Trying to look above it all. He hadn't expected anybody to be nice to him and he was taking a certain satisfaction in being proven right.

"If we're not judging people today, it seems strange that you're dressed up as that cult lady," Javier said.

Trash, suddenly dismayed, touched the blonde wig he was wearing. He'd given himself Joan Crawford eyebrows and dressed in a women's softball uniform to complete the impression. "Oh—do you think—that's a good point," he said. "It's sort of shaming. I could just dress normally, then you and I might be more like the concept of a cult. The act of... culting. Cultery?"

"This is actually a *drag* brunch," Javier noted. "It might be more respectful if at least one person in our show is a man dressed as a woman."

"Oh, that's true too," Trash said. "Well—in the words of St. Monica, 'The show must go on'.... I should start buckling us together." He ran his hands through his wig in housewifely confusion, then nestled against Javier and started wrapping them both in one corset.

"It just bothers me in what it says about you," Javier said, wriggling and stretching to try to make room. "If you'll forgive *him*, what are you going to do to *me?*"

Ray Ray, in an arm brace and a sling and a white three-piece suit from the display window of The Last Shall Be First Secondhand, came up to them and asked, "Y'all know where Toya at? Ain't no point in getting dressed up if she not coming."

But Lizzie, who had been going around the room filching Mardi Gras beads to give as going-away presents to her Montessori kids, said, "Looking fabulous isn't pointless; it's a service to the community. It's the only proven remedy for depression."

They were still waiting ten minutes later. Des had already talked to the M.C. to tell him that they'd need to start late.

Caretta was complaining about Toya: "She don't know how to talk to people," which Des thought was a bit rich coming from the resident bamma. "I be making breakfast and she come up all, 'Oh… *bacon.*' Like what do you say to that?"

Ray Ray laughed and got in on it: "'Did you forget something?'" she mimicked Toya's breathy, innocent voice. "No, bitch, I always walk all the way to the Metro, then come all the way the fuck back and run up the stairs! She gappy, is what it is. She don't connect things up in her curly little head."

Des was trying to figure out how to stick up for the Little Lamb when Ray Ray added, "She worse than L'il Ray Ray, how she smile—have you all noticed this?—she smile at black men on the street, and then act scared when they smile back. Like she don't know things lead to other things. Consequences, I been in enough programs to learn that shit."

"She understood the consequences for us pretty clearly," Des said slowly. "She didn't have to do anything for us, but she did."

And that settled Ray Ray down, and the other Love's Labors women. They remembered the morning after Toya'd fled Morningstar, when Ray Ray and Des had sat with her, all three of them on one side of the dining room table, and Ray Ray had said, "You got a right to call whoever you want to call. But if you go after them, me and her gonna get locked back up. My CSO is not gonna care that we was helping you."

"I just want *justice,*" Toya had said, almost in tears. Fumbling for a tissue with her splinted fingers.

Ray Ray had said, this time more sincerely, "You got a right to it. I can't tell you what to do."

She couldn't help but add, "I can tell you what I *hope* you fuckin' do. But that's just my life, not yours."

Now in Nellie's she stood quietly and considered how Toya had given up her right to justice. Ray Ray and Ty'heaven had never had the option. Just thinking about the difference made her want to curse, want to hurt somebody—anybody who could feel the pain; she was starting to understand why girls cut themselves. But she didn't know if things were harder for her or for Toya. Harder never to be allowed to choose, or harder to have to sign your name to the paper where you waived your rights.

At that moment Toya was on the 90 bus, just a few blocks away from Nellie's. She had been taking notes for her job applications, using all the semi-honest resume skills Des and Douceline had taught her: Being beaten with a softball bat became *Managed complex interpersonal dynamics involving heavy physical labor.* Practicing for a drag show was *Found innovative solutions to setbacks* and *Worked well with a diverse and bizarre team.* Pregnancy was *Monitored development of new personnel.*

She stared out the window. For some reason she never worried or felt stupid when she was staring out a window; for this reason she tried to minimize it, since it distracted her from self-improvement. She let the city slide past her.

The bus lurched to a stop and a woman sitting toward the front, whom Toya had noticed without realizing she had noticed, stood up to get off. Toya jerked upright in her seat and gasped out loud. Her hand flew to her belly. She stared at Trina Lawton.

Trina had cut her hair, but it was still blonde—Toya didn't know why she wished Trina would have dyed it. She didn't want Trina to want to look the same. Trina was dressed in high-waisted white pants and a loose blue shirt, cute and casual. She had a bookbag slung over her shoulder that said, *REFUSE RESIST RECYCLE.* She looked like a normal person, with a normal-sized vagina.

Toya's terror pulsed into anger—a rage so huge it seemed to rise up over her head and choke her. Her teeth clenched and her chest felt tight, like she couldn't figure out how to breathe, which honestly anybody should be able to do. And then the rage washed out of her and she was cold with fear again, cold and horrified and sick.

The bus moved forward. Toya's hand went to the cord and rang for the next stop. She stood up and almost fell down the stairwell, plunged through the opening doors and onto the sidewalk. People hurrying past turned to look at her. She pressed her hand against her stomach and felt her throat burning. She had thought the morning sickness was over but she barely made it to a trash can before she was heaving, hanging onto its edge, vomiting in public, screwing her eyes shut and trying to disappear inside herself. Sunbursts against her eyelids, green and gold. *Jean Grey died*—

Something was pressing into her stomach. She pulled away from the trash can and opened her eyes. Felt around cautiously in the pockets of her cardigan and found the cardboard hooves she was supposed to wear as she defeated the Two-Headed Dragon.

She put the hooves on her hands. Pulled herself upright and looked around. Trina was gone. She turned toward Nellie's but she couldn't move. She looked dumb—she knew she did, with the hooves and that same Morningstar cardigan which was the only warm thing she owned, and they were probably talking about her there, talking about how she was late and annoying and how was she even going to open the door with these hooves on her hands?

She was walking toward Nellie's even though she knew the people there were laughing at her. Why do you always walk into it? she asked herself in desperation. *Why do you let people do this to you? Normal people don't let this happen to them!*

Dully, her head hanging, she lifted her hoof and knocked on the door of the bar.

Zita opened it.

"*There* you are!" she said. "Y'all, she here! Tell the M.C. we gonna start in a minute. Toya," taking her arm and propelling her toward the stage, "you gotta get your butt in that lamb outfit real fast, we late."

"There she is," Fang said, and pointed; and all of them echoed her, waving Toya over, calling to her. She laughed in shock and relief all at once as she obeyed their summons.

"Okay," Trash said, taking her hooves in his hands, "these are a little bent but we can make it work. Turn around so I can tie your tail on, please?"

The M.C. announced, in a hammy, oily cartoon voice, a voice like a thin black mustache, "Heads up, hos!" The lights blinked on and off. Several already-tipsy queens tapped forks on champagne glasses.

"We have a special performance," the M.C. said, "to begin the extravaganza. A group number dedicated to," reading off a napkin Trash had handed him forty minutes and a couple mimosas ago, "Hello Kitty—no, it says 'Hell King,' that's a little edgy, folks—Hell King, what looks like 'The Heaven Clark,' and survivors of abusive cats. Cults! Sorry, excuse me, folks, survivors of cults."

"Ty'heaven Clark," Ray Ray said loudly. The M.C. nodded at her distractedly and pressed a button on his switchboard. "Danse Macabre" began to play.

Toya, in fuzzy ears and a tail, waved her hooves and danced as the Dragon chased clunkily after her. She clenched her light saber so tightly in her teeth that her jaw ached. "Danse Macabre" was succeeded by "Bustin' Loose" and then "I Will Survive," all stitched together by Trash. ("This music montage is very Tonya Harding," he'd said, "or, let's say, Robin Cousins.") The crowd cheered and clapped as she wagged her light saber at the Dragon and the Dragon retreated. They booed when the Dragon chased her.

She pushed with her hooves and Trash and Javier fell over, Javier remembering to fall the way Trash had taught him, so that the meatiest part of his ass and thigh would absorb the shock. From the side of the stage, Douceline and Caretta released the dogs. Toya held the light saber between her forehooves as the dogs raced between her ankles. Carefully she stepped over to the prone Dragon and set one hind hoof on Trash's chest.

The disco lady wailed in triumph, and Toya tipped back her head and howled.

The women of Love's Labors Loft rushed onto the stage, feather dusters held high, and began to sing.

After the lights had gone down, and Trash and Javier had crawled in tandem off the stage amid cheerful booing and a shower of beads and napkins from the audience, the performers gathered at two big tables, congratulating one another as a way of congratulating themselves. Des briskly swept the stage, then joined Lizzie in unbuckling the Dragon's corset. Trash, through a complex sequence of lowering and shyly raising his eyes, tried to convey the message to Brandon, *I can't talk to you because I've found someone who won't let me do self-destructive things without his permission, but I don't want you to feel badly about yourself. Also I am not flirting with you.*

This attempt at Morse eyelashes was unintelligible to Brandon and worrying to Javier.

"Excuse me," a drag queen said, "are you Lizzie Pearl?"

Lizzie turned and saw the skinny black queen in a blonde wig, and her big eyes went bigger. "*Lauryn Order?*" she cried.

"You recognize me? I based my persona on you! I'm a Republican drag queen!"

"Aren't we all," Lizzie said. "I really liked your Scandaleezza—

with the piano, very classy. I saw it on YouTube."

"We're a marginalized group, you know." And, leaning in toward Lizzie, with one confiding red-taloned hand draped over Lizzie's bare arm: "Sometimes I feel more at home as a black drag queen among Republicans than as a black Republican among drag queens."

"Yes," Lizzie said, "home can be a very alienating place. Here, let's take a selfie."

"Let me do my wiggle, girl! Oh, let me do your wiggle."

"Do you want everyone?" Lizzie said. "Let's get everyone."

And so she handed her phone off to a man who Des could swear had been the nipple-rings marmoset-watcher from Chains and Roses. He waved for them to get closer to each other as they all crowded in a line, the Love's Labors women ranged on either side of Lizzie and Lauryn, Trash and Javier on one end and Brandon, holding Fifi, on the other.

Des stood between Javier and Caretta and considered her community. Trash and his Clown Guy, still as close as when they'd been corseted together; Caretta, who'd almost gotten arrested just to stick it to the people who'd hurt Toya; Fang, waving at her band (current name: the Aunts of Mercy); Toya, waving at anybody. There in the middle Lizzie flashed her goodbye grin at the camera as Lauryn Order winked and shimmied, and glitter from Lizzie's hair fell and drifted into Lauryn's décolletage. Then Zita and Douceline, like matching portraits of naive and cynical youth; and Ranae "Ray Ray" Goins, her mentor.

The horrible chihuachshund, quiet now and resting at Douceline's feet gnawing a light saber. The evil ex, who had done the bare minimum to support Trash, which was more than a lot of people would have done.

Her eyes went back to Toya, and when the nipple-rings guy

took the photo she was looking away from him, down the line at the awkward, beaming Lamb. Ray Ray was looking in that direction too; their eyes met. Ray Ray shook her head and smiled, and in that crooked grin Des could see the sorrow as well as the vindication. They looked at each other and then looked back at Toya. Toya waved with such intense sincerity that her hoof flew off and arced above them, over the crowd. They all tipped their heads up to watch, and they all laughed, but not at Toya.

And as the hoof plopped down in somebody's bottomless bellini, the District gave Des back the world she thought she'd lost forever, her piece of the broken diamond city from west of the Park to east of the River, not quite free but home at last. Good night, D.C., none of us deserve you.

ACKNOWLEDGMENTS

This book needed its own little city of readers and editors: dissatisfied, sharp-eyed, beloved. I owe great debts to Leticia Ochoa Adams, Helen Andrews, Tristyn Bloom, Christine Emba, Matthew Hahn, Richard "Conway" Jackson, Oksana Kirichenko, Kate Havard Rozansky, Nicola Wilson, and all the Rooks writers, especially Kathleen Torrey.

Gabriel Blanchard read multiple drafts and offered incisive comments on each. Hannah Katznelson and Melinda Selmys gave pages of the kind of insightful responses which are every author's dream. Ben Faroe at Clickworks Press also provided extremely helpful comments on what I'd hoped would be the final draft. Any remaining banality or wrongheadedness will testify that I didn't listen to them enough.

I hope it goes without saying that many things people do in this book are bad ideas. Please consult a Doctor of the Church before performing any sex acts, not least those involving stinging nettles.

I am very grateful to my parents for their support, and to my confessors for their gentleness.

Eve Tushnet is a writer in Washington, DC. She grew up by the old Walter Reed site, and now lives near the ghost of the barrel from Barrel House Liquors. She is the author of *Amends: A Novel* and the far more well-meaning *Gay and Catholic*. She also edited the anthology *Christ's Body, Christ's Wounds*. Hobbies include sin, confession, and ecstasy. This book was published without the imprimatur.